WHAT READERS LOVE ABOUT *THE GENEH WAR*

"The story has movement and holds attention but the real payoff is in the thought put into what it will be like as we inevitably get to the tricky issues around genetics. You think it's contentious now? Just read this and see how complex and fraught the future will be. We may in our lifetimes have to see this played out - so it is a timely story.

"Of particular interest is the portrayal of the females in this story. There is no one who dissolves into emotional ruin at the first sign of trouble or resorts to being a bitch to get her way! Great to see such portrayal. Now if only Hollywood stopped reducing their female role models to the same stereotype as a cheap trick. This book would make a better and more satisfying movie that the iRobot type of movie we have seen so far."

"Five Stars! Great plot, interesting theme and good characterization.

"Hard to put down."

TITLES BY ROBIN CRAIG

The Hunter Series

Frankensteel

The Geneh War

Time Enough for Killing

Leonardo's Child

Time Travel and Alternative History

The Time Surgeons

Hannibal's Witch

The Passion of Judas

Short Stories

Past, Present Future

Non-Fiction Philosophy

Dialogue on the Two Chief World Systems

Good Without God

Cloning Around: The Ethics of Human Cloning and Stem Cell Research

For the latest news visit robin-craig.com or follow on fb.me/authorcraig

The
Geneh War

Book II of The Hunter Series

ROBIN CRAIG

Published by ThoughtWare Books.
Available from Amazon.com and other retail outlets.
Available on Kindle and other devices.

Cover art by Kira Craig using images from Pixabay with fonts from 1001 Fonts.

Author's website: robin-craig.com

ISBN 978-0-9803205-5-8

I know you despise me; allow me to say, it is because you do not understand me. — Elizabeth Gaskell, North and South

CONTENTS

ACKNOWLEDGMENTS

Thanks to my wife Sonja for commenting on the draft of this novel and for helpful discussion and ideas on some critical plot points. This novel is better for her inputs.

The idea for a free country on the ocean named Capital, and its Capital Sea, came from my friends from decades past John and Deborah Cook, who also set me on the philosophical path leading to this book. Capital's fictitious history and construction however are mine.

Chapter 1: Thief

The thief spun through the open window and landed silently on the floor, crouching on her fingertips and the balls of her feet.

She paused: listening, watching, sniffing the air. The house was quiet except for the occasional creaking of a chair and other faint sounds of a presence. It was dark but she could see well enough, for the dark was softened by a faint light spilling into the hallway from a room out of her line of sight: the same room from which the sounds emanated. She smelt man, a faint musky sweaty odor, and a ripple of liquid desire ran down her belly to her thighs. She smiled at her own reaction. The excitement of her latest adventure was spawning excitements of a different and distracting kind. She tightened her stomach and her resolve: she had not lived this long by letting her focus fall prey to such distractions.

She smiled again, more sharply, and moved silently towards the room. She waited just out of sight, but there was no sign that the man knew she was here. The creaking and rustling continued as before. She extended a small mirror unobtrusively into the doorway at floor level and saw him. He was seated facing away from her, immersed in an interactive holographic display as he manipulated a maze of complex diagrams and images. She slowly crept into the room but the man must have had surprisingly acute senses, or perhaps he had always known she was there, for he turned sharply and stared at her.

He saw a long, lithe woman with dark straight hair, dressed in a skintight suit patterned in grey and black, its waist accentuated by a belt holding an assortment of tools and pouches. Her most striking feature,

1

he thought, was her large golden eyes, luminous like a cat's. Though perhaps some would consider the long black tail even more remarkable.

He smiled at her and she smiled back. "I'm glad to see you back in one piece, Katlyn," he said. "How did it go?"

"The usual," she said with a light shrug, and presented him with a handful of diamonds and emeralds. She often brought him things of beauty like this, little tributes from her nightly adventures. But while valuable, they were never more than a fraction of what she could have taken, and hardly commensurate with the risks she took in acquiring them. Those risks were for something else entirely.

She sat on his lap and put her arms around his neck, wiggling seductively. "Ah Katlyn," he sighed, "You are a temptress. Aren't you too young for me? Shouldn't you find someone your own age?" She grinned. "Pah! Boys my age are so immature. I like a man with some years behind him. Someone with experience. Someone who knows what a girl likes." She emphasized the point by doing something with her tail that a normal woman couldn't.

"You're going to be the death of me one day, Katlyn," he laughed, picking her up and carrying her off to his bedroom.

CHAPTER 2: LOVER

Katlyn woke with the sun streaming onto the bed through the one-way glass window, stretching luxuriantly. She hummed to herself. Life was good. She had excitement, the thrill of a long, dangerous and grand quest, and a man who knew how to make her quiver. Daniel had already gotten up and was probably working on one of his projects. She would have liked more of him. But she could be happy having any of him.

She thought back to how they had reached this point. He had been her guide, her teacher, her mentor. She knew what the world thought of her kind. But he had raised her as his own, and all he had ever shown her was love and understanding. Growing up had been difficult. She had studied genetic engineering herself. Not like he had, but she was quick to grasp ideas and had a fair understanding of the field if not its more intricate details. She knew that her making had not been without risks, but it had been a fair gamble. There had certainly been pains both physical and psychological as she grew. But she had survived and she could not resent it. She was alive, happy and healthy. And what more could man or beast want? She smiled again, wondering: *and which are you, Katlyn?*

The hardest part had been puberty. She had the same needs as any human woman, only more so because of her exquisite nervous system. She had about twice the number of nerves and they were twenty percent faster than normal. The world felt wondrous to her touch, but that came with the price of frustration when her nerves wanted stimulation she couldn't have. What stimulation she could have was glorious, but sometimes she would wake at night with her nerves screaming for the kind of release she knew could be had, and was had, only not by her.

Finally she could bear it no longer and confronted him. "Listen, Daniel, I don't understand you! You still think of me as if I'm a twelve-year-old girl, but look at me! I'm a woman! You treat me as if I am your daughter. But look at me! I'm not! You of all people should know I'm not! And I know you love me and not as a child, I know you want me, I can smell it! And that drives me crazy too! You are some crazy noble idiot who wants me and knows he wants me but hides it from himself!"

"Oh, Katlyn," he'd sighed. "Surely you know I can't. I might not be your father, but I raised you like one and you are still a little girl in my eyes. I just feel it would be monstrous. I feel I would be using you, betraying you."

"Oh you fool!" she had shouted. "You have taught me to think. You have always told me to use logic, reason, facts! Tell me which of those are on your side! Do I have to tell you again? You are not my father! I am a grown woman, able to make my own choices: a woman you have taught to make her own choices. At least give me the respect to give me a good answer. Are you ashamed of me? Despite all you've done for me—do you too think of me as some kind of monster, some kind of thing it would defile you to touch?"

"No! You know that isn't true!"

"And don't you get it? I love you! And not in the way I loved you as a child! Then I loved you as if you were my father, too. Yes, I was a child—then. But I am a woman now, and I love you as a woman. I want you as a woman. And if you reject me—then who else is there for me to love?"

"Oh Katlyn, my unique, lovely child, don't you see? That's the problem. We're thrown here together, I've looked after you and I'm the only man you really know, the only man you've ever really known. How can I take advantage of that without using you? You deserve better than that. One day we will be free and you'll find a man you can truly want and love, not just someone who will feel he raised you to become his personal sex toy!"

She hissed at him. Then she stopped. "Oh you sweet, darling idiot. But you are torturing me to be kind! Please just think about what I've said. I understand what you're saying. But your love for me is not using me. I know what I want, in full knowledge of what I want and why. You have taught me to do that above all else. How many times have I heard you rail against the people in power who think they know better than anyone else, who think they are so wise they deserve to rule others? Then what are you doing to me? I am no longer a child, Daniel. I need you. I want you. I love you. Think about it. Please."

She could feel the tears forming in her eyes and she didn't want him to see, so she spun and bounded from the room. Then she curled up in her bed, crying softly.

But that night he had knocked quietly on her door, and when she opened it had simply said "Oh Katlyn", and held her in his arms. Then she learned that her dreams had been true, and she knew the joy she had never been able to hold once the dreams had fled. They had been together ever since.

Chapter 3: Hunter

It was her first day on the job. She had graduated from the Police Academy with high honors, had excelled in the theory and practice of detective work, and on the strength of that had been assigned to the Special Crimes Unit. It was an exciting opportunity and she was looking forward to putting her skills to work. Fighting crime was a passion many kids shared but few turned into a career, and she faced this day with high anticipation.

Four hours later she was bored. Or frustrated. She couldn't quite decide which.

True, there was a lot of crime fighting going on. Unfortunately none of it involved her. Well, none of the exciting part of actually investigating. They had put her on the cold case program. "Yes," her new Chief had said, "you did well at school (*school!* she'd thought). But we have a lot of experienced detectives here and a lot of work so important it must be done: just not important enough for those experienced detectives to waste their time doing it." When he made it clear that the important work would be in a back room with a computer, her attempt to impose calm on her facial muscles must have been slower than her feelings' revelation of the contrary. He had fixed her with a stern look then calmly told her that if she was as good a detective as maybe she might become one day, she should probably come to her own conclusions from what he had just told her.

What could you say to that? She decided she liked her new boss, even if he was a bastard.

He had then shunted her off to the IT department for more details. These were imparted by a young man with intense blue eyes and red hair, which tried to be well behaved except for random swatches that insisted on creating their own contradictory styles. His name was Fergus, he possessed a quick intelligence, and she decided he was quite cute in his geeky way. She was also amused to notice that he had a polite way of checking out newly met women that was mildly complimentary if you liked it, but too subtle to be sure about if you didn't. His ready and harmless smile no doubt helped him get away with it. She wasn't even sure he knew he was doing it himself.

Cold cases, he explained, were those where leads had dried up and there was no obvious way forward to a resolution, so they had been shelved in favor of more immediate work. Shelved but not forgotten, as you never knew when you might get a break. But if nobody was looking, who would recognize the break when it came?

And, he added, blue eyes twinkling, before the project could happen it first had to be funded, and to be funded had to be sold to people whose main concern in life was budgets. But budgets had an in as well as an out, and higher case-solving rates were good for publicity and therefore good for funding. However, he had noted, finger raised: while they had originally sold the project on the cold case aspect, there was a more speculative and exciting side. The same processes needed to fish for new evidence on old cases could also uncover unexpected new ones. There were many relatively minor crimes barely worth investigating on their own merits—if merits were the correct term for crimes—but you never knew when they were the visible signals of something larger buried out of sight, like the swirl of a crocodile in the Nile. With luck, they would detect a few crocodiles or if not at least be alerted to where they might be lurking. The importance of the unimportant had been indelibly impressed on the collective consciousness of lawmen early in the century: when a failure to notice oddities such as men learning to fly jets but not land them, had meant failing to stop them returning to earth indirectly by first flying into buildings.

Some bright spark had had the brilliant idea of pooling all crime data into one database and letting an advanced artificial intelligence loose on it. While AIs were now common they were most effective at tasks with clear limits and definitions. So they were usually seen in roles such as automated doormen or reception services, medical diagnosis and the more straightforward legal services. A task like this one needed open-ended data analysis, correlation and pattern recognition with no predefined structure or assumptions. This was something humans were good at, but no human could absorb or process the amount of data an AI could. They had no way yet to give a person the data capacity of an AI, but perhaps they could get an AI to think more like a person.

Her job would be working on the interfaces for getting information into the AI and also training it on how to interpret the data in useful ways. The powers above wanted all records back at least 20 years to be in the system. Cold cases went back even further and some crime careers went even longer than that undetected: but the further back you went, the more unreliable memories became and the less evidence and witnesses you could actually find. So 20 years was chosen as the best compromise between wishes and reality.

She did not have to worry about current or recent data, he told her. That was already in a suitable format and the aim was a direct real time link still to be perfected: a challenging project which IT themselves were looking forward to. For the immediate future that would require human oversight, and there was so much of it that her "current" data feed would be at least two weeks old. Her job would be the older data, some of which existed only on paper.

"Paper!" she exclaimed, "You're kidding, right?" He laughed. "Oh, it's not as bad as it sounds. Like most advanced AIs, this one has lower level subsystems that are specialized AIs in their own right. One is already expert in image to text conversion; others have been configured as trainable data format translators—the system will have to deal with many incompatible formats. So your future doesn't hold years of typing but it does hold a lot of paperwork scanning and tweaking of format conversion utilities."

"I don't suppose the department has some low level flunky we can recruit to help with all this hack work?" she asked hopefully.

"Yes of course, what do you take us for?" he replied. Then he added with a grin, "I'm looking at her."

She groaned. "OK, I can see where I stand around here. So between us we'll be filling the AI's head with random data. How do I go about training it to make sense of it all?"

"What I would like is for you to train it positively, by examining the data yourself and telling the AI what it means. But if you could do that we wouldn't need the AI in the first place. So what I'll get is the other way around: the AI will tell you its findings then you will analyze the reasoning behind them and explain where it is right or wrong. Eventually that process will generate principles to guide it."

"What if I make a mistake?"

"Try not to. But even if you do make a mistake, you'll just slow things down a bit, not completely derail them. The AI doesn't give anything a one hundred percent rating, not even your sage advice. It will occasionally retry ideas you've rejected in the past and look for contradictions in your responses; if it finds any it will complain to you. You can then refine the rules. If you keep rejecting something, it will recheck less and less until it eventually gives up."

She agreed the idea was brilliant. She agreed its time had come. She even thought that her initial impression might have been hasty, and this work could be exciting and important. So armed with her reignited enthusiasm, she went to work.

It wasn't long before her enthusiasm drowned under the unhappy confluence of enormous volumes of random data flowing into an AI of invisible intellect, which then poured the resulting stew onto her head. It might be the most advanced AI the department could afford, she thought, but it still bore out the ancient wisdom of the wag who'd first said AI meant not "Artificial Intelligence" but "Artificial Idiot".

At first she had thought that analyzing the AI's correlation reports and training the AI would be interesting, but the AI soon trained her otherwise. When her new boss had dropped by and asked what she had discovered, she had wearily replied "Garbage, rubbish and creative nonsense."

Part of the problem was that the AI was still in the early stage of its learning curve. The other part was she had to be careful. Despite Fergus's assurance that mistakes weren't fatal, the AI made enough mistakes of its own without her adding to them. She couldn't just reject the machine's wrong correlations: she had to think of some way to explain, in a way the AI would understand, why the correlation was meaningless. Otherwise she ran the risk of throwing out a good principle just because a specific example didn't work. Generally that required analysis of why the AI thought there was a link and how to explain its error. But how did you explain to a computer that the presence of red roses in a held-up florist, a vase in a robbed bank and the garden of a burgled house was not relevant, whereas a single red rose placed on each of several murder victims was?

That part was certainly a challenge. But the combination of 90% mindless tedium and 10% hard thinking on how to outwit a witless machine rapidly wore her out.

After a few hours she leaned back, stretched out the kinks in her muscles, and just stopped to think. This wasn't what she'd had in mind for her exciting crime-fighting career. Unfortunately the image she'd had in her mind, that even her years of study had failed to dislodge, was from her childhood when it involved capes and super-powers. It was a sad fact that neither were issued by the police department. She rubbed her eyes. *Oh well,* she thought, *every profession from acting to politics makes you pay your dues.* And for all her pride in her accomplishments to date, she knew that she was now just as much an apprentice as any hopeful carpenter starting out on his or her career. And who knew, maybe she would actually find something worth reporting.

She had her breaks, of course. She got coffee, chatted to the other inhabitants, started to get to know people. Most of them were friendly enough, even if most looked slightly harried by their own pressures. But she was the new girl and people were willing to chat and get to know her. Some of them looked through her as if her existence was not worth noticing, but most were friendly enough. She thought she would like it here.

Before she knew it, her boss popped in again and told her it was time to go. "So, how did you like your first day?"

"Well, it's not quite what I dreamed of, Chief Ramos, but I know I have to start somewhere. The AI is clinically insane, but I think I'm making progress."

He smiled. "I'm glad you're settling in. Your face when I gave you this assignment looked like I might have a rebellion on my hands. Anyway, a bunch of us meet for drinks down at Joe's. You're welcome to come along, get to know the crowd some more."

"Sorry, I'd like that but maybe tomorrow. My family has a little job-start party planned for me tonight. So good night."

"Good night, Miriam."

Chapter 4: Family

Miriam's family was delighted to celebrate her new job with a party. They were delighted to celebrate anything with a party. They had always told her that if you didn't take time to enjoy life, why were you living it?

The party was at her favorite uncle's apartment. Seth Hunter was a grizzled, no-nonsense man several years older than her father; he had never married himself despite having had a string of lady friends. But, he said, he liked the ladies the way he liked horses: the thoroughbreds liked to run free not settle down on the farm to chew hay. Personally she thought he was speaking more about himself than about them: the way she had seen some of them look at him, she was pretty sure they wouldn't have minded settling down in some hay.

He was also the richest man in her immediate family. Over his years he had converted a little corner hardware store into a string of franchises and eventually sold out to a national chain. Now he put his hand to a variety of business schemes, some successful, others less so, but inexorably his wealth grew.

One result was this apartment, an elegantly appointed suite high above the city streets. Miriam had been coming here since she was a child and loved just looking out at the city. When she was a little girl it had looked to her like a fairyland of lights. Now she knew that down in the streets it was often a tawdry, dirty place; a home to villains, bullies and scoundrels. But up here all that was purified by distance and the essence of the city was distilled into a place of magic possibilities, as if the grime of the city's underside could not touch the spirit that made it beautiful. The possibility had never occurred to her that anything could happen to make her so cynical that she could see it differently.

Uncle Seth had hired caterers for the evening. He believed that parties were to be enjoyed not worked at, and he was quite happy to spread his wealth to others in order to achieve that end. So there was nothing for Miriam to do but wander around chatting to friends and family, browse from the delicious morsels that came within reach and sip the delightfully fresh champagne. Eventually she found herself where she always ended up, at the window looking out over the city.

Seth saw her from across the room and smiled. *My memories of her are like time-lapse photos,* he thought to himself. *She has been standing at that window like that since she was a little girl. Now look at her.* Her hair was still dark, even darker than her skin, cascading in ringlets past her shoulders. But now in place of the gangly little girl she had been stood a tall, slender but full-breasted woman, relaxed and confident, looking out at her city. *That is how she always looked: as if it is her city.*

He loved her as if she was his own. He loved all his nephews and nieces, but Miriam owned a special place in his affections. Her quick wits and self-confidence captivated him and her determination and drive impressed him. In her life she had seen her share of ugliness, but it had not touched her; she shrugged the mud off her Teflon skin as if it wasn't worthy of her attention. He smiled, remembering the time when he had been visiting his brother and she had come home crying, bruised and bleeding. On her way home from school she had come across another child being bullied. Her temper had escalated from outrage when she first saw it to incandescence when the bullies ignored her perfectly reasonable demand to stop. Her common sense had no chance against her anger any more than her fists had a chance against the bullies, and she had suffered along with that other child. But her response after the tears and Band-Aids had been to learn not prudence but martial arts.

He was not surprised that she had chosen a career in the police force. Her family would have preferred the greater pay and safety of a legal career but Miriam had done what she always did: listened, considered, and did what she thought was best. He knew she would see even more ugliness in her new career. He hoped that she would remain untouched by it; that she would always look at the world the way she was looking at it now. The world, he thought, might not deserve that: but she did.

"I knew you'd end up here," said a gravelly voice at Miriam's shoulder. "Oh, Uncle Seth, thanks for this," she said, leaning her head onto his shoulder. "Well, I've finally done it. I'm a real cop now."

"Is it what you expected?"

She laughed. "It's only been one day! Truth be told, not so far. They've put me straight onto hackwork. But I suppose they always do. Eventually I'll get a break into something more exciting. Worse comes to worse, next year we might get another newbie or two. Then I can stroll around lording it over them."

He squeezed her shoulder. "I'm sure you'll do just fine. Made any friends yet?"

"I haven't had time to make any real friends except with the coffee machine. You'd like him. Strong, sensual, just a hint of the unpredictable. But most of the people there are nice. Some of them act as if I'm not there but I haven't had much chance to show I am yet."

"Any problem characters? I imagine there are, in a police station."

"Oh, not really. One guy seems to resent my presence. Detective Stone. Well, former detective Stone. He's been promoted to a desk job in reward for his years of service but I think it's chafing on him. I had to get some information from him and he looked at me as if I'm an idiot, as if I should know everything about the place after five minutes. Maybe he's like you, doesn't like girls," she teased. "Or maybe he's just unpleasant. I'm sure I'll be able to cope, whatever his problem is."

He smiled and shook her hand formally. "Well, congratulations again, my little girl. And here's cheers to your sparkling new career!" They toasted sparkling new champagne to that then he headed off to chat with more relatives.

"And of course you're staying the night," he called over his shoulder. "Don't worry about having to drive home: relax and enjoy yourself."

Tired as she was after her day, Miriam spent the rest of the evening in a pleasant haze of chatting about the past, catching up with the news of her relatives' families and careers, sipping champagne and speculating on the future. In her dreams the pleasant buzz continued as background while the shapes of the future rose from the city before her and beckoned. But when she woke, she could not say what those shapes had been or where they had taken her.

CHAPTER 5: AI

Miriam settled into her routine. She got better and faster at importing old data into the system, while the AI became better and faster at inventing imaginary connections. Slowly she got to know the people she worked with and they her. Some people stayed much as they were on her first day, polite but uninterested in allowing her into their personal universe; a few remained cold; some became friends. Much like any new job, she supposed.

Overall, she was unexcited by her job's routine but happy about its potential and happy to be here. There was nothing else to do, she thought, but to do the best she could, take whatever opportunities presented themselves, and hope for a break sooner rather than later.

After six months she was efficient at the boring parts and finding more pleasure in dealing with the still flakey AI. She had even promoted a few of its less eccentric offerings up her chain of command. So visible progress was being made. Not enough to make her thrilled and certainly not enough to make the departmental gods thrilled, but enough to propitiate their wrath.

She saw that IT had succeeded in dumping another large load of data into her system and wondered what the AI would make of this lot. She had a lot to do with the IT department, of course. She was not officially in charge of the project, but her position as prime AI interpreter and trainer made her the first port of call in any questions and issues. And from her side she needed to keep her finger on the pulse of what IT was doing.

Having made sure the data was digestible, Miriam let the AI loose on it and waited for the results. She had nothing to do but wait for now, so she took the opportunity to sip on her coffee and just follow her thoughts where they would lead her.

They quickly led her to the IT department. She wasn't sure if she was happy or sad at the moment when it came to them: or more accurately one of them. She had started a friendship with Fergus, the cute—at least in her estimation—guy who had introduced her to the AI, and it had rapidly developed into something more. While relationships among staff were forbidden if they went out into the world together with guns, nobody cared about rookies and engineers. They had had a really good time together, but after the first flush of romance faded both had come to realize that too much time together just wasn't going to work. Not that anything was wrong with either of them, just that they weren't right for each other. So they had regretfully called it a day.

Ah well, she thought, it was something; and it had been good. Not just the sex but the romance and the fun had certainly helped ease the tension of the job for both of them. Miriam refused to have regrets for having a happy time even if the happy time had to end: in her view the pain of ending merely underlined the happiness that had been lived. The pain would fade, she knew, while having been happy could never be lost.

She had even picked up a few colorful curses during their time together, a kind of souvenir of the relationship that also would never be lost. Not unusually for geeks he had a penchant for fantasy and epic mythology: and why limit yourself to Christian mythology, he had pointed out with his cheeky grin, when there are so many more exotic ones to choose from? She smiled at the memory. She had heard he had now taken up with a very cute blonde in the public relations department; he seemed to be on a one-man mission to rescue the reputation of geeks everywhere.

She came out of her reverie when the AI had finished digesting its lunch and started making a few suggestions. *More of the same,* she decided. *No. No. No. You must be kidding. No. Nice try, but no. Sigh. I need to invent an AI to screen the AI's output,* she thought. *But hang on, this one is interesting. Weird, but interesting.* A string of minor but odd burglaries, if you could call it a string when it was scattered across half the city and into the suburbs. Normally she would promote it up the usual chain for the attention of property crimes but this time the AI had highlighted other correlations, one of which made her eyes bug.

She decided to do a bit more investigating herself and started quizzing the AI. Half an hour later she was looking at a printout that summarized their findings. She still didn't know what it meant, but her instincts told her it meant something.

Chapter 6: Geneh

Miriam walked briskly up to her boss's office, resisting the impulse to actually skip; the door was open so she went in. He was standing with a couple of detectives, looking at his screen and pointing. They all looked both puzzled and grim. She did not think she should interrupt so she started to back out, but Ramos saw her and said, "Yes, Hunter?"

"Sorry to interrupt, Chief. I've found something interesting I thought you should see. But it isn't urgent and I can come back later."

"No, stay, a break from this bit of craziness won't hurt. What is it?"

"Well, the AI flagged a string of minor burglaries where some jewelry was stolen. They all represent a fair bit of money to people like us, but not if you look at the income of the owners. Half of them probably wouldn't even have reported it if they didn't have to for their insurance. But would you believe, at random times since the burglaries five of the victims have had amounts of money from half a million to two million dollars mysteriously vanish from their accounts, destination unknown. And that's not all. You know how IT has started feeding in news from the wider community as well? The AI, bless it's brainless bits, noted that a full quarter of the victims were present at a big fundraiser last year for President Felton."

"Coincidence?"

"I quizzed the AI. I can't vouch for the details of its calculations, but according to the AI's statistical subsystem the probability of it being chance is only two percent."

His eyebrows went up. "So! Interesting! Let me see what you've got there."

She handed him the printout and he scanned it. Then his eyes went very still. He called the other detectives over to take a look. Then they all glanced at each other. Ramos said, "Hunter, I think you should see this. See this list of attendees at that fundraiser? See this name, that isn't on your list of burglaries?"

He turned his screen around so she could see it. "This image was taken from a short video captured by a security camera near the city apartment of that man. Shortly after a minor robbery in his apartment last night. Some gems were taken."

Miriam looked at the screen. The image was slightly blurred and enhanced for light, but clear enough to see why the detectives had been so serious. It was a woman leaping across the rooftops, caught in mid-flight, looking past the camera as if she hadn't noticed it, or perhaps had known it was there but didn't care. She had large, luminous golden eyes that seemed to reflect the lights beyond. And a long black tail streaming behind her.

Miriam looked at Ramos, startled. "What the hell?" she asked.

"What the hell indeed," he agreed. "What do you make of it?"

"Well, if it wasn't both illegal and unlikely, I'd say it was a cross between a girl and a cat!"

"Watch this."

He played the video from which the still had been taken. The woman was extremely fast and agile, and she was only visible for a couple of seconds as she bounded into and out of camera range.

"I don't suppose that video is a hoax?"

"The techs say not. I suppose if the CIA was trying to fool us they might be able to do it, but we're pretty sure it's genuine. That's not a video sent in by a member of the public who might be pranking us. It's taken from a fairly secure feed and there are no digital signs of tampering."

She examined the still image more carefully. Not really a cross between a girl and a cat, she saw: more a girl with a few catlike additions. Science fiction stories from her youth, romantic tales of genetics before the whole field of human genetic engineering had been made illegal, now haunted her thoughts and would not be silenced. Instead they escaped through her tongue.

"Um, Chief, would you fire me if I said that looked like a geneh?"

"Genehs don't exist. You know the penalty is death. The scientists who used to work on it are lucky the penalty applied to the genehs not the scientists."

"I know. But look at it! What do *you* think it is?"

"If I knew, I *might* have fired you. But I don't have any better ideas right now."

The childhood ghosts haunting her memory shoved one of their number forward into sharper focus. A man who had been a hero in her young mind, now disgraced and largely forgotten. "I think I know someone we could ask," she said uncertainly.

Ramos looked at her. "I think I know who you mean. But really, if I thought it was a geneh I'd pass this on to GenInt Enforcement— except something this hot might ruin my reputation if it's the false alarm it almost certainly is. And we don't have the staff to spare to follow thin leads like that, especially ones leading to a man like him who is unlikely to let police anywhere near him."

She looked around at the others in the room, who were all regarding her silently. "I could go," she offered timidly but hopefully.

He stared at her with narrowed eyes. "Really keen to escape your desk job, aren't you, Hunter?" he said. Then he paused. "But sometimes... yes. Someone else has been keen to escape his desk lately too. Maybe I'll give you both a field excursion. Then when you're sent packing at least we can file it, bump it up to someone who will forget it, and you can both get back to your real jobs."

He tapped on his phone. "Stone, get in here."

~~~

Stone came in and Ramos said, "Stone, you know Hunter here. Well, she's found something interesting. Take a look at this."

After looking at the video and reading her report, Stone looked up. "Curious," he said. "Definitely curious."

"If it wasn't for the link the AI threw up about these bigwig supporters of the President, I'd probably file this under 'prank' and move on. But we have to show we've covered all bases when we have something like this on video. The last thing we want is to be blindsided and find we *do* have a geneh running around targeting the President's friends—and they find out we ignored it. Even if it's someone with a death wish just pretending to be a geneh. It would probably *be* the last thing we did, at least in these jobs.

"So, Miriam found this—I'm not sure I'll thank her yet—and you,

Jack, haven't been as happy as I'd hoped after your promotion. I don't want to take anyone off what other things they're doing for this. So Jack, meet your new partner. Miriam, say hi to Jack. Don't get used to it—I expect your partnership will only last this one trip. But who knows, maybe you'll surprise me. You're both going to visit the neither late nor lamented Dr Tagarin to discuss what this thing might be. I shall be surprised if he lets you through his door, but let's see how persuasive you can be."

Stone looked at Miriam. He had never thawed to her and it didn't look like the ice age was ending quite yet. Miriam wished she knew what she did that bugged him. Stone said, "OK kid, let's get to work. Try not to get in the way."

Chapter 7: GenInt

As they drove, Miriam watched Stone out of the corner of her eye. His eyes were watching the road and he didn't look interested in chatting. "Um. Detective Stone?"

His eyes flicked to her then back to the road. "You have something against quiet?"

"No. No. I just thought if we were going to work together, I should get to know you some more."

"I think this is going to be a very short-term relationship. And we're just going to interview some guy. If he lets us. We don't need to be friends to do that."

After a few moments Miriam asked, "Why do you dislike me?"

He looked at her, startled. "Well, that's a surprisingly direct question. Most people aren't quite so open about things like that. Did you miss beating around the bush class or something?"

Miriam gave up and looked away. "Sorry."

"Look, kid, it's nothing personal. Yet. But I've seen you hotshot newbies before—yes, I read your file when you were assigned. That's why they used to call me 'Detective.' When you're good at school you think you know everything. You get in the way. Think you can change the world. Think everyone else should bow to your manifest brilliance. But you know nothing. Some of you become good cops. Eventually. None of you start that way."

"I don't think I'm that bad. Am I?"

"I just don't care to find out. But look at you. They put you in a backroom job to keep you out of trouble and get something useful out of you while you learn how to feed yourself. Then you get lucky and see something and you think, maybe I can impress the boss with this. Maybe get promoted like I deserve. So you march in with your fancy report and get even luckier. So lucky the boss sends you out on the real job you've dreamed of, badge on hip and gun in hand. But the trouble with being lucky is people tend to confuse luck with talent. That can get you killed. Luck has a way of running out to buy itself a drink when you most need it to hang around."

After a few seconds Miriam said quietly. "I see. I'll try to keep out of your way."

Stone glanced at her. He had expected the usual lifted chin and proud rejoinder. Maybe there was hope for this one after all.

~~~

They parked in the circular drive before the entrance and got out. Dr Tagarin might have been disappointed in how his career had flamed out but he surely could not be disappointed in how he had done financially. His mansion was set in beautiful natural woodland and for all that you could tell it was a fortress it was an attractive and comfortable looking one.

As they walked toward the gate Stone said, "This guy is a hard case and given his history he won't like the law. He'll have his AI preprogrammed on how to deal with the police so this is probably going to be a waste of time. It'll give us the run-around, and it'll know we're asking for a favour and that we don't have any legal grounds to push too hard. We won't even know whether he's talking to us via his machine, or the machine is just blowing us off on its own while he's sitting in his Jacuzzi with a bunch of blondes."

Miriam shrugged. What could they do about it? They were here; they had to try.

They waved their badges in front of the security system, which automatically queried the embedded electronics. Miriam noticed the Beldan Robotics logo under the speaker grille. Naturally she had heard of the Beldan AIs—very high end and very expensive—and she wondered whether her job would be easier if the department's budget had stretched that far. Another part of her wondered whether if she had a brighter AI she would be here at all.

"Please place your palms on the plate for biometric confirmation," the door said mechanically. They did as asked, Miriam's opinion of the

Beldan AIs dropping a notch in the face of its crudeness. But on confirming their identities the system raised the priority of the visitor interaction, and after a short delay a more sophisticated level of the AI spoke in a cultured male voice:

"Good afternoon, officers. How can I help you?"

"We would like to see Dr Tagarin," replied Stone.

"Please state your business."

"We have a problem that we think Dr Tagarin might be able to assist us with."

"Dr Tagarin informs me that given how the law has 'assisted' him in the past he is not interested in assisting the law. In any event he can't imagine how he could help you and has better things to do with his time."

"Look, this concerns a string of strange burglaries and there are aspects of the case that Dr Tagarin might be able to shed some light on. Please remind Dr Tagarin that he is a citizen and it is his duty to cooperate with the law."

The machine paused, whether thinking through a complex problem, communicating with its master or merely pausing for effect they had no way to know.

"Dr Tagarin informs me that he is aware he is a citizen and fully aware of his rights as one. He has no obligation to speak to you unless you have a warrant. He further advises me that he would be astounded if you had any grounds for one and he has, to quote, 'a team of sharks in lawyer robes' available to sue the city if you try one without proper grounds."

"I told you he was a hard case," Jack muttered to Miriam.

"However Dr Tagarin is a law-abiding citizen who is willing to assist the police in their reasonable enquiries. Thus to avoid you wasting more of your time he wishes to assure you that he has no knowledge of any burglaries and, given that his habits and activities do not include strolls down dark alleys or nocturnal adventures along the rooftops, he is quite sure he has seen nothing that could help you. He adds that he keenly sympathizes with the plight of our overworked police and therefore recommends you pursue more fruitful lines of enquiry elsewhere."

"It is not as a witness but for his specific expertise that we wish to speak to him."

"Dr Tagarin refers you to his previous statements and wonders why you think he would provide unpaid expert advice. There are many experts, some of who may not yet have been abused by the legal system whose agents you are. Find one of them. Good day."

With that, the pattern on the screen indicating active engagement folded in on itself and vanished.

"Wait," said Miriam, and flashed a file to the interface.

Nothing happened for minute. Miriam looked at Jack and shrugged, "Oh well, it was worth a try," and turned to leave. Then the entrance said, "Please hold." Jack raised his eyebrow at Miriam.

After a few more minutes the gate slid silently into the fence. "You may proceed up the path to the door," advised the AI.

They entered and walked up the path, their feet crunching on the small stones. The path had clear walls on either side with a curved, vine-covered vault over it barring access to the gardens beyond. The vines had fragrant flowers and yellow butterflies fluttered happily among them. The vibrant delicacy of it made a strange contrast to the forbidding walls beyond.

When they reached the door it opened to reveal a man wearing a formal suit and a neutral, distantly polite expression. He looked like a butler, except that butlers were generally not six foot two, built like fighters and with callused hands and fingers. "I am Dr Tagarin's butler. You may call me 'James'. Please follow me," he said, stepping aside and gesturing inside with a sweep of his arm.

Miriam and Jack looked at each other and followed him inside, down a corridor and into a small but luxuriously appointed waiting room. "Please make yourself at home. The machine in the corner can supply most styles of coffee. Dr Tagarin will be with you in a short while." With that, the overqualified butler bowed and exited the room.

Jack walked over to the coffee machine and said, "Now this is a civilized use of technology. What would you like, Hunter?"

"Do you think we have the time?"

"I know how these things work. Unless they want something from you, when someone asks you to wait they're going to make you wait as long as they think they can get away with, if not longer. Sometimes they do it because they're jerks exercising their power. Sometimes they're just pissed off at you. Be thankful this guy isn't making us wait on hard seats in a freezing room. We might as well make ourselves comfortable."

They sat down, sipping their coffees. "Mmmm! Excellent!" said

Miriam. "So while we wait—what do you know about this guy? I know the basic story but I was just a kid when it all happened. Anything you think I should know?"

"Well, when he was younger he worked for an up and coming biotech firm. He had an unusual flair for both IT and molecular biology, and he was instrumental in developing key patents for the company. Those patents enabled a whole slew of medical applications of stem cells for curing disease, including regenerating tissues and organs. The company went stratospheric, and because it was a startup with a good employee share scheme, plus the bonus shares he got for his personal contributions, his own wealth went stratospheric with it." He waved his hand around the room as if to say, as you see.

"Anyway, the average guy might have retired, but I suppose the average guy wouldn't have achieved what he had in the first place. And he had a passion for his work. He didn't even quit and start his own company, which he had the money to do. He was happy to be given his own research division so he could keep right on working on the science while someone else ran the business. Some of his original patents involved genetically engineering stem cells. You know, to fix genetic defects or give cellular immunity against some hard to cure viruses. There were already enough people up in arms about that—you know, meddling with nature—but then he made his big mistake. He got interested in doing more than fixing nature's mistakes and started looking into improving it."

"That doesn't sound so bad," said Miriam as she sipped her spicy coffee, the fragrant steam caressing her nose. The coffee itself, she knew, had been genetically engineered. She wondered if that was a subtle message Tagarin intended for visitors.

"It does when he's not just trying to enhance some weakling's muscles, but starts working on using cloning technology to turn his stem cells into a whole new type of human being."

"Yes, I remember that. But I thought that kind of work was already illegal?"

"Not really. The environmentalists and more fundamentalist religious types had been opposing genetic engineering of almost anything for years. One lot hated it for destroying the purity of nature and the environment; the other for playing God. So there were a lot of bans and restrictions in place. But the medical benefits of his kind of research were so great that the government couldn't bring itself to ban it outright. They just banned it from Federal funding—though of course not from Federal taxation if they made a profit out of it. And he was in a rich company, which had become rich by pushing the envelope: one that didn't want government grants and the strings that came with them. That kind of thing had been declared unethical by all number of experts but some people just don't care about that, I guess. And who can say they're wrong?"

"So what exactly happened?"

"Well as I said, he started work on genetically engineering human stem cells to give them new traits and trying to clone them to grow new people. And he wasn't alone—there were other groups looking into the same things. I guess the technology had finally arrived. The greenies, the religious right—and the religious left, for that matter—went ballistic. If they were against engineering the genes of animals and plants—well, you can imagine how they felt about meddling with ourselves."

"Yes..."

"But it got worse. I have to tell you—my parents were atheists and always taught me the value of science, and I've never seen anything in this world to show otherwise. But it seemed like the better technology made people's lives, the more people like the greenies were against it; and the more science taught us about the real world, the more people turned to religion. Between the masses convinced that technology is dangerous, the masses convinced they knew God's opinions and the activists on both sides who saw those masses as their road to power—it got ugly."

He sipped his coffee with a frown of distaste, but it was for the bitterness of the memories not the coffee. "And then some of the people who had been working on these things felt brave enough to get their experiments to the stage of fetuses—they had artificial wombs by then. Not all of them worked very well—and the activists found out. Even the average mom and pop who weren't particularly ideological were horrified by some of the pictures that came out of it. So the whole thing spun out of control. It went all the way to the United Nations. All genetic engineering of humans except for direct medical use, and all cloning of humans for any purpose, were banned around the world as fundamental violations of human rights and dignity. And more, any genetically engineered or cloned human was declared an inhuman abomination to be destroyed on sight. All the embryos any of them had developed were destroyed."

"The Geneh Laws. But I thought most religions opposed abortion? Why would they support that?"

Stone gave her a sour look. "As my dad said at the time, for all the church cares about embryos, burning witches is an even more time-honored pastime. And if witches are the Devil's consorts, engineered embryos are the Devil's spawn. I guess embryos are blessed with a soul whether you want them or not, unless you want them so much you make them yourself."

"But what if someone had actually created a baby?"

"Ah, well, there's where I might have something to add besides color. Tagarin and his friends had been fighting the new laws like maniacs, but they went through anyway. The UN had already acquired a lot more power over national governments than it had the previous century, and they set up the new Department of Human Genetic Integrity—GenInt—as a compulsory international regulatory body. It was run by real partisans—as I suppose you'd expect, since who else would take the job? Publicly its purpose was monitoring, oversight and ethics committees, but it had its own enforcement arm in case someone insisted on being unethical. That had to be a matter of public record, but the public—or enough of them—were quite happy to see any such monsters destroyed. Most of them supported abortion anyway, and this wasn't that different: just killing little horrors that shouldn't have existed in the first place."

"Yes, I see that. I was taught the same thing in school. About the evil of making modified humans, I mean; about how the resulting monsters were better off dead. They glossed over what they did about it if it actually happened. I thought it never had."

"And the only people you'd put in something like the enforcement arm are more fanatics: you know, true believers in the cause. The kind who wouldn't have any moral qualms about smashing labs and tossing out embryos. For the higher good and all that."

He paused, staring into his coffee as if his memories were residing there.

"But babies? You mentioned babies?"

"Yes, well. As you'd guess, Tagarin was the hotshot in the field. He hadn't made any monsters, at least none he let develop further once he knew. Despite the howls of his critics it seems he had some qualms about how far he went. I guess he thought he could learn enough from his mistakes when they happened without risking inflicting the results on a living being. But anyway, he was further along. Much further along..."

He paused again. This time, Miriam just waited.

"So. He did have a newborn in his lab, and a healthy one. What its improvements were I've no idea: I never saw it close up. But the Department enforcers found it in a raid. They knew what it was. They killed it there and then. It never made the news feeds of course. GenInt's charter allows it to keep secrets 'for the greater good and social order'. Which means they are happy to release photos of monster fetuses that would die anyway, but think the plebs will get confused if they see photos of innocent babies being shot. The plebs are likely to forget that the 'innocent babies' are demonic creations bent on destroying society. Tagarin went crazy. He's lucky they didn't shoot him too."

"But how do you know all this?"

Jack stared into his coffee a while longer.

"Tagarin reported it to the police. But he reported it as if he was under attack by criminals—which I suppose to his mind he was. I was a rookie like you back then. We had a bit of a face-off with the enforcers, but they had the law on their side. We weren't allowed to talk about it. I can tell you, because it was a long time ago and it's relevant to our case." He looked around for somewhere to spit, but the décor decided him against it. "Anyway, it wasn't pretty. But there you are."

"Jesus. No wonder he doesn't like us. I'm surprised he's seeing us at all."

"Yeah."

"But... why does GenInt still have enforcers? I don't remember hearing any cases of geneh violations since those early days."

Jack gave her a cynical look. "Have you ever seen a bureaucracy give up power? My dad was a history teacher—I guess that's the kind of thing that can make you an atheist. I still remember him laughing about the old Soviet Union, who the more they said their ideal state would wither away the more power they took. Maybe in 50 years we'll be rid of GenInt enforcers. In the meantime I'm sure they find enough misdemeanors and other excuses to flex their muscles. Not to mention the old argument that the only reason we *don't* have genehs flying around laying eggs in our children is the existence of GenInt."

"And we might just have found a real one for them," added Miriam grimly.

Then they both sat silently, he lost in his memories, she in this new picture of history. As she'd said, she had been taught the ethics of the Geneh Laws at school, and like most people simply accepted it. After all it was reasonable, wasn't it? Was it? Surely the baby they had destroyed was some kind of monster? What else could it be? But now she wondered.

Then the door opened and the butler said, "Dr Tagarin will see you now," and ushered them in to the adjoining office.

CHAPTER 8: TAGARIN

The room was large, with a dark burgundy carpet so delightfully thick and soft that Miriam wished she could take her shoes off. Shelves holding books, instruments and memorabilia alternated with walls covered in murals or paintings. She liked the art. There were no meaningless abstract splotches: it was all recognizable and beautiful, and the human figures projected contentment, sensuality or heroism. They made a stark contrast with the room's occupant, who radiated something darker. It was like the contrast between the gardens and the house, she thought. It was hard to believe this man could have chosen that art.

He sat at a large desk of polished dark glass in the center of the room. One hand was loosely resting on the desk; his chin rested on the other as he watched them enter. He had dark brown eyes that looked like they should be lively and intelligent, but which stared at them like the glass of his desk. Or like a cobra watching a mongoose, waiting for its chance, Miriam thought. His face was hard, topped by a shock of longish chestnut hair that wasn't sure whether it wanted to be wavy or simply anarchic, swept back from his forehead like a mane. It looked like there were lines of humor about his eyes and mouth, but unused for so long that they had hardened into cynicism. He was middle aged but evidently took advantage of youth-extending medications; he had not let his body go to flab and retained a trim athleticism that sat well on his tall frame; his movements were fast, precise and yet fluid, as if he practiced martial arts. He watched silently as they seated themselves.

The butler remained, standing silently in the shadows, out of sight but never quite out of mind.

Floating in the air before Tagarin was the image Miriam had flashed to his AI: the photo of the thief in full flight.

"So," he began without any greeting. "Looking at this photo I can guess why you wanted to talk to me. But why don't you tell me? No doubt it will be amusing." But there was no trace of amusement in his voice, which was as hard as his face.

Miriam looked at Stone, who answered, "Whatever that thing is, it looks like a geneh. You were once a world leader in genetic engineering of humans. We hoped you could give us some information that might help us discover what it is and where it came from."

He had a deep, throaty laugh, well suited to the scorn he now put into it.

"Well, I presume you have computers at least as good as mine. You will have run the same analyses as I. What brainless idiot persuaded you that this is a genetically engineered human worth annoying me about? Surely it is obvious that it isn't. Or are you telling me the quality of the police forces has actually gone *down* since I last had the pleasure of dealing with you?"

Miriam looked down, glad her dark skin mostly hid the furious blush that had rushed to her cheeks. She did not usually react like that, but Tagarin spoke with a contemptuous authority that made her feel like a schoolgirl in front of the Principal, chewing her out for wetting her pants on his favorite chair.

To Miriam's further chagrin, his glassy eyes did not miss the clue. "Ha!" he said mockingly. "That's why the rookie is here?" he said, stabbing his finger at her but addressing his comment to Stone. "She's the genius? So what," he continued sarcastically to Miriam, "let me guess, you're new and trying to impress your boss? Don't they teach thinking at the Police Academy these days? Or is your boss actually dumber than you are?"

Despite her embarrassment, Miriam lifted her head to look him in the eye: not as a challenge but in honest directness. "I understand why you are bitter and I am sorry if we offend you. But I don't believe it was that stupid an idea. Seeing that photo is what persuaded you to let us in to see you, after all."

Tagarin glared at her and she felt his laser gaze dissecting her, discarding the irrelevant and finding nothing left. She feared that he would throw them out then and there for her presumption. But then he laughed again, and if there was still no friendliness in it at least there was more amusement and less derision. "Touché, Ms Hunter. Perhaps you have more courage and brains than I first gave you credit for. I would ask you to forgive the rudeness of a, as you might put it, bitter old man—except I don't care. But you have earned a reply: so yes, your photo was intriguing enough for me to find out more, even though it cannot be a geneh. However even the police would not think it worth bothering me if this is all you have. Show me the rest." His manner changed from that of a circling boxer to a dispassionate scientist handed a curious creature washed up on the shore.

Miriam flashed the video to his desk. He lifted a cowl that had been hanging down his back and placed it on his head, and she saw it was made of a fine mesh of silvery threads. He concentrated briefly and the mesh moved in response to what it detected, positioning its threads in their accustomed places. Despite his jibe about their equal computer systems, Miriam thought, holographic displays with neural input meshes were rarely seen and certainly not by her. For a few minutes he watched the video, using his thoughts and hand gestures to replay sections, turn or magnify parts, sweep in external data and run calculations. Spider webs of vector lines glowed over the images; tables of figures and calculations appeared and disappeared; graphs and animations played in space. Finally he looked up, again resting his chin on his hand. "Fascinating. Yes, quite fascinating. I can almost forgive you for interrupting my fun in the Jacuzzi with the blondes" he said, glancing pointedly at Stone.

"Now, obviously your techs will have checked the images for fraud. But if you care to know, my analyses of the photo and now the video show no signs of doctoring and all signs of being genuine. It is still possible that someone very skilled is pulling your leg, perhaps to throw you off the real trail of this burglar of yours. But they would have to be very skilled. If this is a fake, it is not the work of a casual prankster with access to mere standard tools. In fact if trickery is involved it is more likely in the person of your burglar herself rather than the video of her."

"Speaking of the burglary, I cannot help but notice you haven't asked us anything about it," noted Stone.

"What, am I a suspect now? Do I look like I need to raid apartment buildings for a living? I didn't ask because I don't give a damn. The only reason you're in here at all is because your alleged burglar presents an interesting scientific puzzle, and I don't get enough of them these days."

"Sorry, cop instincts... anyway, please go on." He didn't look as apologetic as his words, but after giving him a hard stare Tagarin let it pass.

"My analysis of your video indicates that while this woman is certainly remarkably fast and agile, her abilities lie within what is possible for a normal human, albeit at the extreme end of the range. It is in the nature of the extremes of ranges that examples exist. An accomplished athlete in her prime could do it. The probability shifts even more into the human range if we add the boost she might get from certain amphetamine or cocaine style drugs. And that is without considering the possibility of performance-enhancing mechanical prostheses."

"But what about those amazing eyes—and the tail?" asked Miriam.

"I imagine that is window-dressing to distract you. I suppose the eyes are some kind of mask or implant, and the tail is a mechanical prosthesis—probably for show rather than function."

"I have to agree that those are possibilities," Miriam said, "But they are just possibilities, not proof. The simplest explanation is it is just what it looks like: a geneh. Yet you aren't merely saying she *might* not be a geneh: you've insisted she *can't* be. Why are you so sure?"

"Oh child, it is a simple matter of arithmetic! Measurements of her facial structure and bodily proportions show that this is a woman around 25 years old; even allowing for variations in growth patterns, she is no younger than 22. My research was terminated 20 years ago, and we couldn't have done this"—he stabbed at the image—"then. Your only evidence for her being a geneh is the obvious physical appearance and performance. Now don't get me wrong. We were well on the way to achieving something like this: the changes required are not as great as their dramatic appearance might suggest. But we weren't there yet. I estimate that if things went reasonably well, we could have achieved something like this—but no earlier than 15 years ago."

He looked at them and again stabbed his finger at the image. "This is not a 15 year old child. Therefore she cannot be a geneh. She was born before there was any technology that could have created her."

Miriam and Jack looked at each other. Miriam asked, "Could there have been other labs, working in secret, which could have done it before or after the bans? Even foreign governments?"

"No. Science doesn't work that way. Ours was the most advanced country on Earth in that area and we all knew what the others were up to, and where we weren't competing we were cooperating. We had to. The more brains on a project the faster it goes. And you can't do this kind of work in your basement: you need too much fancy equipment. Did you know that back last century when the first sheep was cloned, some whacky cult claimed they'd already cloned people? Their alleged lab had some basic equipment and a few flasks: so anyone actually in the field knew they were lying. So no, if there had been other labs I'd have known about them. I did know about them, and they were all shut down. And even if they hadn't been, none of them could have done this even 20 years ago, let alone before then."

He waited, but they could think of nothing else to say. "James will show you out now. It has been interesting, but don't expect to see me again without a warrant. A life is a terrible thing to waste and I have no intention of letting you waste mine." He paused. "It is a pity, though, that she isn't a geneh. If she was real, she would be a beautiful creature, don't you think?"

CHAPTER 9: VICTIMS

Miriam and Stone drove back to the station silently, as their private thoughts shifted, collided and slowly settled into some kind of order. After a while, Stone spoke. "You did all right, kid. You got us in and you stood up to him. Don't let it go to your head—you're still a rookie who thinks she's better than she is. But you show promise."

He glanced at her and granted her a slight curve of his lips that may have been a smile, or perhaps the promise of a future smile if she ever came to deserve it. "Maybe it wouldn't be so terrible if I was forced to work with you again."

Miriam smiled back. "I know I have a lot to learn. If you think it will help, I'll buy myself a nice tight helmet. Stop my head from expanding."

Stone grunted. "If that's what it takes. Sometimes it is."

Then both of them were quiet as they went over the events of the last hour in their minds. Neither of them came to any conclusions.

They reported the results to Ramos. He sat at his desk, considering. "Hmmm. It all sounds plausible, so plausible it stinks. But that's an occupational hazard. Every innocent person looks like a suspect after a while. The very fact they have an alibi makes you wonder why they found it necessary to have one."

He paused again, thinking. "Not really much to go on. Here's a tip for you, Hunter: if you think you have something, turn around and imagine you are counsel for the defense. If I was a defense lawyer making my closing address, I'd point out that all we have is a pattern spat out by a flakey AI, a photo in the vicinity of a minor crime that may be a coincidence and could be just a college student prank, and a plausible explanation even if that cat woman is our thief. If it wasn't for the link to the President's friends I'd say forget it and move on."

He tapped his fingers on the desk. "Not only do I hate to waste resources, I hate even more for the rarefied gods above me to believe I am wasting resources. Stone, get back to what you were doing. Hunter, you have more leeway because you can do all kinds of nutty things with the excuse that they're research into improving our beloved AI. Quiz a few of our victims, concentrating especially on the ones who had later mysterious losses of funds. But be careful. These are all important people and, whatever we say about equality under the law, important people have a way of pulling strings if they get annoyed. Strings generally connected to hammers over our heads. For now, just phone them. They are less likely to talk but also less likely to be pissed off enough to complain to their friends in high places."

~~~

A few hours later, Miriam sat back and rubbed her eyes. *What the hell?* She went to see Ramos and asked Stone to come along.

"OK Miriam, what have you got?"

"Nothing."

"Nothing? Then why in hell am I here?" growled Stone.

"Because it's a very peculiar nothing," replied Miriam.

"Hunter, " said Ramos patiently, "I'm giving you rope because there's something fishy going on. Don't hang yourself with it. I hope you're not wasting our time."

"So do I... so do I. The thing is, it's weird. I tried all the people who had the large losses of funds. One was overseas. Three refused to talk to me. One was interested because he thought maybe we had a line on his money, but when I had to admit I didn't and was just investigating a related lead he said not to waste his time. So I rang some of the others, concentrating on the ones at the lowest levels of the social stratosphere. A couple were pleased I had called but were mystified about the whole thing: they couldn't imagine why someone would break into their penthouse to steal a few gems while leaving their more precious treasures untouched. Some said, rather rudely, that it was a long time ago, the police were incompetent, and anyway they had their insurance payments and what the hell was I trying to achieve? Others, and not just one, were even more hostile, as if I was somehow accusing them of a crime."

Stone just looked at her. "So? Welcome to police work. Did you expect to solve the case over the phone?"

Miriam shrugged. "No. But it was weird. Half of them acted like they were innocent victims of a minor crime, the other half acted as if they were guilty of something themselves. I can understand annoyance at being the victim of a crime; I can understand them being annoyed at our failure to solve the crime. But defensiveness? Telling me, basically, to shut up, leave them alone and stop poking my nose into their business? That's why I wanted you here, Detective Stone. Their reactions just strike me as strange—disconnected from the facts of the case. As if there are facts we are unaware of that they don't want us to know about. You have a lot of experience—is this normal, or queer?"

Stone and Ramos looked at each other. Stone said, "Well... when you put it that way, it does seem odd. Victims of crime respond in all kinds of ways, and you do get some hostility—blame the messenger, blame the incompetents. But this seems more than normal. More like interviewing members of the mob, except these people aren't the mob. I dunno. What do you think, Chief?"

Ramos frowned. "It is odd. But not odd enough to do anything with it. And I don't think we should push any more at this stage: if you're hitting this amount of resistance already, questioning more people might bring us grief. And if the Mayor asks me why I'm hassling the President's friends—I need a better answer than what I could give him now."

He appeared to come to a decision. "No. We just don't have enough. Miriam, I know you're keen and you might even be right. But it's still all probably just a fantasy of your AI, and your victims are just hostile because they're busy and you're not offering them anything except questions they've already answered. Get back to work. If you can tweak the AI to keep an eye on this case, do it. But don't bring it to me unless it suggests something positive besides bothering our more eminent citizens. Other than that, just keep doing what you've been doing."

CHAPTER 10: WITNESS

"What the hell!?"

Jim Perenty's friends would not have described him as excitable. Steady, even plodding, would have been more likely descriptors. He was as happy strolling home alone through the lowering dusk as he was having a quiet drink with his friends; much happier doing either than attending a raucous party. His even temperament was not prone to jumping at shadows. He was the kind of man who, rather than seeing a weather balloon and believing it was a UFO, would see a UFO and think it was a weather balloon.

But on this night his eye had been drawn by an odd movement on the edge of his vision, and his subconscious mind made him give a startled jump before his conscious one had time to catch up. By then the vision had already gone and the even higher levels of his mind scolded the lower ones to stop seeing things. He shook his head and walked on.

But when it happened again a week later he found himself staring at those strange eyes for long enough to know they were really there. And worse, long enough to hope they weren't actually looking straight back him. Then they vanished again and he shakily reached for his phone.

~~~

The IT department was continuing to increase the number and variety of data source feeds into the crime correlation AI, and in her search for clues Miriam had instigated a supervisory subsystem that gave terms related to the burglary case a higher priority score.

She had done it as a learning exercise more than in any hope of something useful. If anything it was a step backwards, increasing the number of mysterious theories the AI suggested. But two weeks later the system flagged an odd item for her attention. Miriam studied it carefully, retrieved the background data then sat back and thought for a while, mulling over whether such a left-field idea was really worth pursuing at the risk of appearing a gung-ho idiot. Finally she got up and called Jack to meet her in Ramos's office. Better appear an idiot for over-enthusiasm than for ignoring a vital lead, she thought.

"Boss, this is a funny one. It's probably nothing, but who knows. Animal Control had a report from a witness about a panther loose in the city. Would you believe, Animal Control actually sent a guy to check it out—apparently you'd be amazed at the kinds of pets some people do keep in their apartments. The man who reported it said he didn't believe it the first time either, but when he saw it a second time he called it in. Animal Control weren't impressed: people get their perspectives all screwed up, especially when it's getting dark, and if AC find anything it's usually a large feral cat. Once a 'mountain lion' turned out to be a *small* feral cat. But occasionally there is something dangerous so they like to check when the caller has any credibility at all."

They were watching her, as unimpressed as Animal Control had been but not caring to interrupt.

"Anyway, they found nothing on this one. No signs of anything unusual, no prints, no droppings, just the usual vermin. It would have ended there, as it usually does, except IT has been feeding data to my AI from Animal Control. The system flagged it because it was in a part of the city not too far from a few of our robberies, and because of the particular words the witness used: 'A big dark thing with a long tail. It went into the shadows and looked over in my direction, and all I could see were these big yellow eyes.'"

She shrugged. "What do you think?"

"Do we have a good location?"

"Good enough. It was in a rundown part of the city, in a block with a few working warehouses and more derelicts. If we ignore the active ones, there are about half a dozen buildings that could be hiding places for someone."

Ramos sat tapping his fingers on the desk. "It's a bit thin, isn't it? But we're not making much headway anywhere else. I wouldn't normally send anyone out on something that can barely be called a lead in a case that mightn't be a case, but here in my office I have two officers who are always trying to escape their desk jobs. Do you think it's worth taking a look, Stone?"

Jack shrugged and said, "Sure. I could use the exercise. And it might help Hunter here appreciate the true meaning of police investigation. Boredom and futility."

CHAPTER 11: SEARCH

Miriam and Jack looked up at the warehouse. "Smithers & Sons" was painted in large faded letters on the side. Whoever the Smithers family were, they had chosen to leave this sorry monument to happier days slowly gathering dust and vermin. An equally faded sign was the only monument to the family's optimism, declaring to an indifferent world that the property was for rent. The sign stood at a distinct lean, so it was now a slow-motion race between the sun and gravity as to which would remove it first. But for now the building's sole purpose was a home for rats and, judging by a few food wrappers littering the ground, temporary lodgings for the sorrier members of humanity.

This was the fourth building they had visited so far. They had all looked much the same as this one and all been empty except for one tramp sleeping off his treasure of cheap liquor. They had also questioned a few workers they had happened to come across around the still living businesses. None of them had seen anything.

"There are two kinds of witnesses," Jack had said to Miriam. "Those who see what isn't there, like your panther man, and those who don't see anything. I read about an experiment done a long time ago where most people watching a video of a basketball game didn't notice a guy in a gorilla suit walk across the court through the players. That's your average witness. And the ones who do see the gorilla won't tell you. Half of them will try to blackmail him instead."

"OK," said Jack after looking the place over, clearly unimpressed by the prospects. "Next on the list is this prime property. Let's see if our friends the Smithers have anything to tell us."

They easily gained access through one of the broken doors and looked around. If it was the lair of a super-villain she wasn't making a good living out of it. "Well, let's take a look around."

There were the usual signs of occasional human activity, with a small scattering of discarded needles and a few food scraps even the rats rejected. More extensive drifts of food packaging and condom wrappers decorated the corners, swept there by the random winds that found entrance through any number of gaps. "Welcome to humanity's finest," whispered Jack.

"Same as before, I suppose," said Miriam.

"Yep. But let's not let the other ones lull us into putting our guard down. If a place is worth investigating, it's worth being cautious in even if they all look the same. Stick together, be quiet, and be observant. Let's get this over with."

CHAPTER 12: KATLYN

Katlyn was sitting cross-legged on the floor of her nest with her eyes closed, humming quietly to herself. She had an iBud in one ear and her mind was immersed in the soaring vocals of *Phantom of the Opera*. Like everyone, music made her feel and in turn how she felt changed her taste. As with most young people, when feeling energetic she loved dancing to hard thumping rock. At other times her overactive nervous system appreciated the more gentle but complex beauty of classical music. Today was a day she felt like something romantic and dramatic. She could relate to the tragedy of dreams crushed by indifference and madness, she thought.

She had a number of such nests scattered around the city. They were places of refuge where she could rest or hide if she had to, or use as a base of operations if she had a few things to do in the obscuring darkness of the night.

They were all similar to this one. She liked large abandoned buildings with lots of places to hide and several hidden escape routes above or below ground. She always made her nest in an out of the way part of the building, well hidden and usually requiring a climb, so a casual visitor would be unlikely to find it—especially the kind of casual visitor she was likely to get. She didn't mind visitors if they weren't too nosy. It was best if there was some activity and signs of random human traffic: it made her own presence less likely to be noticed. So she tolerated the tramps or hobos who made it their temporary hotel, the drug addicts shooting up and the occasional lovers looking for privacy they couldn't find or afford elsewhere. If visitors were annoying or started to make themselves too much at home she would shoo them off somehow. Strange noises at night were often effective; if not, sending a few rats their way usually did the trick. Nobody liked the rats.

The place was empty today. She wasn't out here for any particular reason; sometimes she just liked to get out and about and have her own private time and space. Daniel didn't mind. Well, didn't object, anyway. They had talked about the extra risk but he had said that for all the importance of her work, you never knew how long it would take or if she would get herself killed. Life, he had told her, was for living; important as they were, long term goals should never stop you living along the way: especially when that living might turn out to be all you got. He thought she needed as much of a life as she could make for herself so he was glad she at least had this.

There were many reasons she loved Daniel, she thought. That was one of them.

When cocooned in the safety of home, Katlyn wore an iBud in each ear for the usual full stereo experience, but when in the field she always kept one ear clear and alert for danger. It proved to be an unnecessary precaution this time. The soprano cut out mid note and was replaced by an insistent peeping sound: one of her hidden sensors must have detected someone entering the building.

She removed the iBud and listened. Whoever it was were being quiet about it. The only visitors who moved that quietly tended to be teenage lovers, scared of their daring illicit adventure, not wanting to be caught or seen in their sweet clumsy couplings. But there was usually more whispering and giggling involved.

She pulled her flexipad from her belt, unrolled it and scanned the spyeye inputs. There they were. Two cops had come in and were poking around. This could be trouble. If they were looking for anyone in particular they might decide to search the place and could find her nest.

She studied them carefully. They were alert, hands on holstered guns, looking serious. She nearly laughed at the sight of them. They looked like a pair of stereotypes from a crime series: the middle-aged white guy, hard-bitten and cynical; trailed by the rookie black girl, innocent, eager and a bit dense. Katlyn half expected to see a camera crew. Then her bared teeth morphed into a more feral expression. However comical they might look they were the law, her deadly enemy:

an enemy she must not underestimate.

She sat back, watching them and pondering her best strategy. They weren't sure what they were looking for was here but they were nervous about finding it. They would probably just do a quick search then go away none the wiser, which would be ideal: it would be sad to lose this nest. But they looked grim enough to be persistent, and then they might find it; and she certainly didn't want to be found with it if they did.

As was her habit she had rigged her nest so she could set it alight if it was compromised. The building still had a working fire control system but she had disabled it inside the nest itself. That way she could destroy any evidence without burning down the whole place. While a big fire would be exciting to watch, a small, contained fire in part of a disused building was unlikely to attract as much attention. Burning down the whole thing, especially if some people happened to be inside at the time or it spread to bring down the whole block, could prompt deeper investigation than she wanted.

Her best course, she decided, would be to hide in another part of the building near an escape route then watch and wait. So she silently left her nest and crept carefully along one of the walkways.

Thirty years ago, long before Katlyn was born, a splinter of slag had fallen into a vat of molten steel. It made a microscopic defect in a steel bolt, and in the decades since that defect acted as a nucleus from which time, oxygen, humidity and stress had conspired to send invisible cracks of corrosion through the metal. At last under the added stress of Katlyn's weight the bolt sheared, and one side of the walkway dropped a few inches with a clang that echoed loudly through the warehouse.

"Shit-shit-shit!" hissed Katlyn, looking wildly around. A long-empty window of some forgotten supervisor's office gaped blackly at her from eight feet away. In less than a heartbeat she had gathered herself and leapt across the gap, grabbing the frame as she flew and swinging herself inside.

Jack swung around at the sound. "Hey!" he cried. "Stop!"

"What was it? Did you see anything?" cried Miriam.

"It looked like someone up there, jumping into that room. And," he added looking at Miriam, "it looked like it had a tail."

They took what cover they could, drew their weapons and peered up at the dark entrance to the room. Two pale golden orbs stared at them from the darkness.

"You up there! This is the police! Show yourself!"

Katlyn had heard Stone's comment about her tail and worse, the tone in which he had said it. She needed to know more; escape was no longer an option.

The orbs vanished.

"Come out with your hands up! Don't make us come and get you. Surrender now and make it easier on yourself!"

"You mean easier on you, don't you?" a harsh voice reverberated from above. "No, I think you should earn your pay today, officers. Come and find me. Let's play a little game of hide and seek. I hide, you seek. Later, you might be hiding while I seek, which will be even more fun."

"What are we going to do?" whispered Miriam.

"We'd better call for backup," replied Jack. "Oh crap. My phone's lost connection. You?" Miriam checked and shook her head. "It might be all the metal in this place. Or more likely our friend there has a signal blocker on."

"Maybe we should try to get back out to the car? Call for help from there?"

Jack thought for a minute. "Dammit", he whispered, "This is our best chance to catch this thing! You try to back away to the door while I keep it occupied. Let's not let it get away."

Miriam began to edge back the way they came. She jumped as a bar of reinforcing rod spun through the air and smashed into the concrete a few feet away between her and the exit, throwing up sparks, its clang echoing through the building.

"Hey! No sneaking out! Play properly or not at all, you two!"

Miriam scuttled back under cover and looked to Jack. He whispered, "Let's humor her. We'll go hunting like she asks, but try to maneuver close to an exit. If you see your chance, take it. Otherwise stay close. We'll separate but make sure you stay in sight. Let's go."

"Ow!" cried Miriam as a small bolt or something hit her on the leg. "Something just hit me!"

A second later, brick smashed on the floor a few feet from Jack. "Jesus! That could have killed me!"

They looked wildly about. "There!" called Miriam. Someone darted along a walkway and out of sight. Jack let off a shot but without much hope of hitting anything, and his bullet zinged off into the far side of the building.

"Come on guys," the voice said, affecting a bored tone. "You're a bit slow. Try to do better or I might get bored. I get angry when I'm bored."

The echoes made it impossible to tell where the voice was coming from, so they moved in the direction where they'd last seen its owner, guns drawn, casting about from side to side. They turned a corner and saw two feet and a tail disappear off to the side. They then had to duck as the metal lid of a bin came spinning through the air toward their heads.

"Where the hell is she?" whispered Jack, swinging his gun around from side to side. Out of the corner of her eye, Miriam saw a blur swing down and plant a solid kick in Jack's back, slamming him head first into a wall. He lay still. But before Miriam could fire her own gun without hitting Jack, their opponent was gone again.

"God dammit!" she swore under her breath, "where the hell is she *now?*" Then it was her turn to find out, as what felt like a steel band wrapped around her throat and an iron grip held her gun arm.

"OK bitch," a voice rasped in her ear. "Here's how it is. I can break your neck as easy as spit on you. But a life is a terrible thing to waste, even yours, so why don't you drop that gun and maybe I'll let you live?"

Miriam couldn't breathe, and dark splotches started a dance at the corners of her vision. There was something important in what the thing had just said.... something important... she relaxed her grip and her gun clattered to the floor.

The creature quickly shifted its grasp to pin her arms close, dragged her to a support beam and handcuffed her to it with her own cuffs, arms behind her back around the beam. Then it stepped around to face her.

For the first time Miriam got a clear view of the creature in the flesh, no longer a blur of dark and shadows. It was obviously human and obviously female, but the large yellow eyes and long furred tail gave it a distinct aura of cat. It watched her calmly for a few seconds and then drew out a thin, sharp blade. Its gaze sharpened into a predatory look that accentuated the cat while diminishing the human, and she stepped up to Miriam. "Now, what are we going to do with you?" she drawled, tracing her blade along the line between Miriam's jaw and throat. Miriam could feel the keen point drawing a line along her skin, but was relieved that the creature was, at least for now, careful not to cut her.

Despite her terror, she calmly lifted her chin to gaze directly into its eyes. She knew the nature of her gaze belied the calm.

"Well, you're a brave little girl, I'll give you that," it said. "And I think we'll have us a little talk, you and me. I'll ask a few questions, you'll give a few answers, and depending on how that goes we'll see if you live or die. But first let me fix up your buddy over there. I hate people interrupting my private discussions, don't you?"

It bounded over to where Jack lay and Miriam didn't even have time to cry out "No!" as it plunged its dagger into his defenseless body. But despite the speed and violence of the thrust, the creature stopped at the last instant and merely poked his body, as if checking whether he was awake. "Your friend is OK—for now," it said, "Sleeping like an especially ugly baby. He's got a bad bump on that thick head but unless he's made of eggs he'll wake up—eventually. Do you think I can trust him to be a good boy, or should I keep him out of trouble?" Miriam just stared, unsure of what to say. "Don't worry little girl, that's what we grown-ups call a 'rhetorical question'. I'll just keep this bag of bones out of our way."

With that, she unceremoniously and apparently effortlessly dragged Jack by one foot to the wall and handcuffed his arms around another pole, leaving him lying face down on the floor in the dust and debris. She stood over him for a moment then gave him a spiteful kick in the ribs; he didn't move.

The creature moved fluidly back to stand in front of Miriam then stood regarding her silently. Without warning, Miriam lashed out with her foot in a strong high kick, aiming for its head. But the thing was preternaturally fast, and the head was gone by the time her foot reached the space it had occupied. Before she could even regain her balance, the creature had repaid her effort with its own kick to her solar plexus. Through teary eyes, Miriam could just look up at it. It stood there, exactly where and how it had before. Nothing had changed except Miriam could no longer breathe. Slowly the pain subsided and she just as slowly straightened up.

"Fiery little bitch, aren't you?" it said when Miriam could stop gasping. "Well I hope you've had your fun and you learned something valuable from it. Learning from our mistakes is an important part of growing up, you know. Now," she said, flicking her tail for emphasis, "you seem surprisingly unsurprised to see me. You're either even thicker than you look or you were expecting me. So question one, girlie: were you looking for me?"

Miriam just nodded dumbly.

"Good girl. An honest answer. Maybe you're not as stupid as I thought. Question two: how did you know I was here?"

"Someone reported a panther to Animal Control. We thought it seemed suspicious."

It stared at her. "Come now, there must be more to it than that. Cops don't go round investigating panther sightings. Be very careful how you answer. I might know some things you don't know I know. Lie to me and you might start losing bits of you." She twirled her dagger for emphasis.

"You were caught for a few seconds on a security camera near the site of a burglary. We knew something queer was going on but didn't know what. Someone who saw you in the dark could have mistaken you for a panther."

It drummed its fingers on its thigh and sighed. "You know, getting answers out of you is like pulling teeth. Which can be arranged, if you don't get more cooperative. Do you expect me to believe you just happened to see some video and then just happened to link it to some random Animal Control report?"

"I have been working with an AI, trying to train it up for correlating evidence. After the video, I set it to watch for anything odd that might be linked. That's how we found out about the panther sighting. The description sounded like you."

It hissed, but it was hard to tell if that signified surprise, anger or understanding. It regarded her some more. "Interesting. Well, that finishes the questions part of our program. But I seem to recall I had a decision to make. Now, what was it? Hmmm... Oh yes: do you live, or die?" The predatory look returned.

"You..." Miriam started hoarsely, but had to stop and breathe. "You aren't going to kill us."

"You're either an optimist or a fool, girl. If there's any difference in this world. You seem awfully sure given your current position, which Sun Tzu would describe as 'untenable'. Would you like another demonstration?"

"You've had plenty of chances to kill us already but you haven't. You're a thief not a murderer."

"I learned long ago not to make life-changing decisions before I have time to think about them. Unless I have to, and handling you two didn't reach 'have to' status." She smiled nastily. "Maybe I'm getting bored with this whole thief thing and it's time to graduate to more serious excitement." She made a show of considering it. "Oh, I agree, killing a couple of cops is a big career move. Maybe I'm not ready for it. Or maybe I am. In any case, don't fool yourself that me giving myself time to think it through means anything good for you. But we have a bit of time before your friends might come looking for you, so we can get to know each other a bit, eh? What's your name?"

"Miriam."

The creature waited. "Well, hello Miriam, and since you ask so nicely, you can call me Katlyn."

She regarded Miriam some more, looking her up and down. Miriam wasn't sure if her smile was less cynical or just more predatory. "My, you are a pretty young thing though, aren't you?" She stepped right up to Miriam, so their bodies barely touched. "You know, I've never had a woman," she purred. "I can do things with my tail you wouldn't believe." She emphasized the claim by running her tail lightly up Miriam's body then stroking her chin with it where she had stroked her dagger minutes before. "Maybe we could have some fun. Maybe your boyfriend over there would like to watch. And maybe then I could do him, and you could watch. What do you reckon, pretty one? Are you up for a little party?"

Miriam's eyes grew large and dark, and beneath her shock she was surprised to see the creature apparently sniffing gently. "A pity. I smell fear but no lust, so I'll take that as a no. But if that's not the way your hormones rock, how about taking a more intellectual angle on today's entertainment? You might think I'm just a common thief. Well perhaps not 'common', but a thief nonetheless. So you might be surprised at how eclectic my education has been. I find psychology fascinating, don't you? So here's a moral dilemma for you, little girl. For reasons I find entirely mystifying you don't want my body for its own luscious sake. But what if it's the price I put on your life? For reasons not so mysterious this body, which happens to be twice as sensitive as yours—and I mean *everywhere*, if you know what I mean—limits my pool of sexual partners terribly. Really. I just can't get a date. So you might do me a favor, and I might let you live. So what do you say?"

Miriam just stared at her, unable to speak.

"Cat got your tongue, girl?" she snapped. "Are you seriously telling me you'd die to protect your dubious virtue? I can smell you're not a virgin, you know. Maybe I'd be doing the gene pool a favor by removing you from it before you manage to breed." She sighed. "You disappoint me, Miriam. Maybe we can play a more interesting game. Well, more interesting for me, which is what matters. Maybe I should wake your boyfriend up and let you compete for your lives. The one who makes me happiest gets to watch the other one die. It'll be an even contest, I think. He's not as pretty as you, but he has some handy accessories you lack. What do you think?"

Miriam studied her, afraid to answer. What was going on? This creature seemed alternately reasonable, evil or insane. Or perhaps she was just playing a vicious game. There was nothing clever she could think of, no stratagem to apply, when she had no idea what this thing actually was and what it really wanted. For all she knew it was just looking for an excuse and any answer she gave would be the end of her. All she did know was that she felt more and more like a mouse being played with by a particularly angry cat. She decided the only thing she could do was be herself and hope that was enough.

As if to underline those thoughts, the predatory look returned and the creature put its dagger to the base of Miriam's throat and applied pressure. This time Miriam could feel the sharp point puncturing her skin, a drop of blood oozing down her chest. Her insides turned to liquid fear. Katlyn twisted the knife, ever so slightly, grinning at her.

"Wait!" gasped Miriam. "Wait. There is a reason you shouldn't kill me."

"Oh? And what might that be?"

"It would be wrong. I've done nothing to you. I don't deserve to die."

Katlyn laughed, but withdrew her knife. It was a strange laugh, a delighted tinkling of bells, nothing at all like the cynical grunts and smirks of her earlier humor; nothing at all like Miriam expected.

"Justice?" The bells tinkled again. "What planet are you from, sweetie? Here on planet Earth, the innocent die all the time, for no particular reason known to God, man or monstrosity. Innocence isn't going to protect you."

Miriam lifted her chin and looked into her eyes. She said softly, "There is nothing more important than justice. How else can people live?"

Katlyn stared at her. "Do you really believe that, pretty one?"

"Yes," she said simply.

Then her head swung first one way then the other, as Katlyn stepped forward and slapped her with her tail, hard, and snarled, "Oh really, Little Miss Justice? Then look at me. What am I?" She slapped her again, to emphasize her point.

Miriam gasped for breath. That tail, soft and gentle in some roles, could be hard as a fist. She looked up at her from hooded eyes. "You are... a woman." Slap! Slap! "Do you take me for a fool?! WHAT AM I?"

"You are a geneh, a genetically engineered human," she whispered.

The thing glared at her, panting lightly, as if the answer angered her yet was still enough to stem her rage. For now. Then she bared her teeth in something nobody could mistake for a smile.

"So tell me, Miss Sweet Justice, who wants to live but not enough to pay for it, what would you do to me if our roles were reversed, if it was me tied to that pole under your power?"

"You are a criminal. I would have to arrest you, take you into custody," she replied softly, flinching for the blows to come, not knowing what else to say but the simple truth. She had decided to just be herself, so she might as well see it through to the end, which was looking closer by the minute. The creature knew it, anyway. A lie, like most lies, would serve no purpose: and in this case was likely to get her killed sooner than admitting an obvious truth.

But no blows came. Just a quiet, "And what would happen to me then? What do your laws say to do to one such as me?"

"The human purity laws say... the law says... you would die."

"So. I am to spare you, for you are an innocent little idiot, while you would kill me, innocent or not, for no reason but what I am, a thing I never chose to be! And you expect justice to save you? What justice is there for me, and why should I care about your laws, your *justice*?" She spat. "You wish me dead, for what I am. You fear me, you hate me, like all the rest! Admit it! Confess it, and I might spare you some pain."

Miriam lowered her head and shook it slowly from side to side. "If you had not broken the law, I would not know or care that you exist. I never sought to kill you." She lifted her head to look Katlyn directly in the eyes. "I don't hate you," she added softly.

Those golden eyes regarded her again. "So, I threaten to rape you, to kill you, but you don't hate me? What, you forgive me? You know, some people think I have anger issues—can you believe that? But maybe you've seen nothing yet, girl. Maybe I should work my anger issues out on a suitable target." She flexed her fingers like claws and spat on the ground again.

Miriam breathed, trying to quell her growing panic. Her only point of hope was that Katlyn had not yet killed her, and for all that Miriam felt she had been run over by a truck, had not even hurt her beyond some cuts and bruises.

"I understand your anger and it is not for me to forgive you or condemn you. It doesn't matter to me what you are genetically: for what it's worth, I think you are right to hate those laws. But that does not make the life you have chosen right. Even more, it doesn't make taking our lives right."

"I can't work out whether I should kill you for being a scheming bitch, or kill you for being an innocent moron," she snarled. "But spot the common factor, larval detective. And hey, it's been fun, but guess what? You've run out of time, dear. I've got things to do, people to see. I can't stand around here all day chatting."

She paused briefly, regarding Miriam coldly.

"Since you won't entertain me, I'll have to entertain myself. But so many choices, maybe I'll let you decide. Let's see. I could strangle you," she said, wrapping her tail tightly around Miriam's throat so she could barely breathe. "A slow, unpleasant and undignified end. Or a quick dagger into the heart"—Miriam felt a pinprick between her ribs—"it'll hurt a bit at first, but then you won't feel a thing. Or maybe you'll piss me off some more and it'll be a knife in the guts"—a jab to the stomach, and Miriam knew she had been cut—"a much more drawn out end to the short but ultimately tragic story of little Miriam, the girl who couldn't. Then there are those guns you two carelessly left lying around. A bullet in the head? Or a slow line of bullets up your leg and belly, ending in your heart? Bang. Bang. Bang. Oh dear. So *many* choices, what *shall* a girl do?" And she gave Miriam another of her predatory looks.

Miriam looked up at her hopelessly. She thought of how hopefully she had faced her life and her career, of all the mornings she would have liked to see, the things she had not done. All to end now so pointlessly, with no power to defend herself, no words she could find to reach through this creature's rage to any mercy that might still live behind those merciless golden eyes. She could feel tears form in her own eyes, but she would neither hide them nor acknowledge them. "Please..." she whispered.

"Shut your eyes, sweetie, it will be better that way," Katlyn said, surprisingly gently. Miriam obeyed, waiting for whatever blows Katlyn would deliver to end her life. But when seconds or a lifetime had gone by and still she breathed, she opened them again.

Katlyn was gone.

CHAPTER 13: FIRE

Miriam let out a long ragged breath and bent over panting, struggling not to throw up. *Jesus.* She was glad to be alive, though not so sure why. She panted softly a while longer, until she felt more able to think. Adrenalin was all very good for fight or flight, but not when you were chained to a pole unable to do either.

She wanted to get out of here. If they didn't report back in a while someone would come looking for them, but who knew how long that would take? And Jack might need medical attention sooner rather than later. But a bit of struggle showed her that she wasn't getting out of this without somebody's help.

As she looked around for inspiration, the sight of smoke drifting from the far side of the warehouse hit her senses simultaneously with the smell of it, and she knew they were both in serious danger. Katlyn must have set the place on fire. *Oh Lucifer.*

"Jack! Jack!" she screamed, but he did not move. *Oh Christ,* she thought, *what if that crazy thing killed him when she left?* What if she hadn't run off to let her live, but to give her an especially panicked and painful death; to watch her burn to death chained to a pole like Joan of Arc. *Christ!* "JACK!" she screamed again.

"Oh, God..." he groaned, slowly lifting his head. "What the hell happened?"

"Are you OK?"

"If you ignore the splitting headache and the aching ribs, sure. How about you? And I think I asked a question first. Oh yes. What the *hell* just happened?"

"Not now! She's set fire to the place! I'm tied with my arms behind me: at least you're the other way round! Can you free yourself?"

Jack tried a few experimental pulls and looked up. "Well, my arms are pretty loose and let's see, I think I can... yes... I should be able to get high enough on this pole to get my arms over. You keep talking while I try."

"I'm OK, just roughed up a bit. You got ambushed by that cat thing: she kicked you into the wall. Then us two girls spent a nice half hour chatting over a cup of tea, talking politics and discussing the many ways she would enjoy killing me. Then just as she had me convinced I was about to die an unspecified but painful death—she vanished."

"Vanished?"

"Well, she suggested I close my eyes, the better to surprise me with my means of demise. But she didn't kill me. She just ran away."

"It must have been your fierce expression. But at least we can be thankful she doesn't have the powers of invisibility or teleportation."

After a minute or so of grunting and cursing through thickening smoke, Jack managed to shimmy far enough up the pole to lift his arms over the top. He dropped to the ground with a groan. He went searching, came back with some keys, undid his cuffs and released Miriam. She fell gratefully into his arms.

"Whew", he said, as the heat spreading from Katlyn's former nest finally triggered the fire system and they began to get drenched. "Let's get out of here in case that crazy cat comes back. I just hope she left us our car."

~~~

Jack and Miriam walked into the squad room. Heads turned. "You two look like hell," someone observed helpfully.

"I just got out of hell," said Miriam. They went to debrief. Forensic investigators had already been dispatched to the scene when they called in but nobody was hopeful. Some DNA would be handy but the place was too dirty. It would mean nothing.

"Well this ups the ante, doesn't it?" said Ramos. "At least she didn't kill you two: I'm understaffed enough already. We'd better get the doctor to look at you both."

The doctor was thorough and competent. He gave Miriam permission to return to work but said Jack would have to stay under observation. He had a couple of cracked ribs and concussions were never to be treated lightly.

Miriam and Ramos discussed the case by Jack's bedside.

"Do you think we should escalate this to GenInt Enforcement?" Miriam asked.

"No... not yet, I don't think. Do you think you could see Dr Tagarin again? He might have something more useful to say now that you have more than an enhanced video to talk about. I'm reluctant to involve GenInt unless we have to: they're too much of a wild card. We'll see what Tagarin says, if anything, before we decide whether we have enough reason to bring them into it."

"I can second that," added Jack. "I've dealt with those guys before. They aren't pretty."

"Do you want me to wait until Jack's better, or do you think I can go alone?"

Ramos thought. "Normally I like my people in pairs, not that it helped much today. But I don't think there's any danger seeing Dr Tagarin on your own. It seems unlikely he'd be in league with a crazy burglar and even if he is, they're not going to do anything stupid when we know you're there. We need to move fast here, people. And from your earlier report he likes you as much as he can like any cop. Give it a go. The worst that can happen is he'll refuse to talk to you. Then we can talk again about escalating to GenInt. Now go."

Chapter 14: Tagarin

Miriam walked up to the gate. It now recognized her and said, "Good afternoon, Officer Hunter. What is the nature of your business this time?"

"I have some follow-up questions for Dr Tagarin."

"Dr Tagarin believes he made it clear that he isn't interested in further questions."

"Please tell him that I have now met the woman in the video."

Miriam could practically feel the camera scanning her face. No doubt it made the nature of her "meeting" clear.

The gate opened and James appeared at the door and beckoned her up the path. This time he brought her immediately to Tagarin's public office. Tagarin gestured to a chair and she sat. He examined her face, but said nothing.

"Thank you for seeing me."

"May I presume from your appearance combined with your presence that your suspect did not come quietly, but you have her safely in custody and can report on her true nature?" he asked harshly. "I imagine your missing colleague is even now giving her the third degree."

"I am afraid that my partner is recovering from the interview. And while I am less damaged than him I am lucky to be alive. But I can tell you a lot more about her."

He raised his eyebrows. "Please proceed," he said, summoning up his display.

Miriam told him the story. He listened intently, occasionally annotating the report transcribed by his desk or calling in other data. When she finished, he regarded her intensely for a few minutes.

"Well, that is certainly an intriguing story. I might start enjoying your company if you keep this up."

"So... what do you think?"

"I can see why you would believe she is a geneh, though if so she is a poor ambassador for the cause of geneh rights. But at least she didn't kill you—which raises its own questions. I am still not convinced, by the way: for all the suggestive facts of the case, the mathematical reasoning I told you last time is hard to evade. But for argument's sake, let's think about what it would tell us if she was. That is, after all, what you are not paying me for."

He sat for a few minutes looking into space, occasionally focusing on his display to look up more information or do some calculations.

"So, let me summarize. She is definitely a modified human female. Overall, her modifications make her somewhat catlike: her eyes, her tail, her flexibility and reflexes. Individually, though, it is not so simple. Her tail, while enhancing her catlike appearance, is more like a monkey's. Clearly it is prehensile, as your throat can testify. That is not surprising. Our ancestors were monkeys, and it may be less difficult than you realize to reactivate those genes and add prehensile capability from a New World monkey. It would be interesting to learn how strong that tail is: whether, for example, it would support her weight, but she has rudely not made herself available for study. Then there are her eyes. Large, almost luminous, and in your photo from before there was a distinct gleam. Yet her pupils are round, not slitted like a cat's are in daylight. Well, you did not mention them, whereas you'd certainly have found slits worth remarking on?"

Miriam nodded. "Yes. It didn't occur to me at the time, but they were round like ours."

"Taken together, I would say a relatively small modification to the size and color of the eyes, almost certainly including something like the tapetum at the back of a cat's eyes, which reflects light back through the retina to improve night vision. The tapetum would be the biggest change, I'd say, but even twenty years ago we had enough knowledge of genetics to make it a feasible aim. The overall effect, I think, would be vision better than ours at night but without the cat's weakness in daytime vision."

As he talked, Miriam listened and watched. A strange man, she thought. When they first met he had gone out of his way to be rude and insulting, and even now in casual conversation an air of bitter cynicism and contempt shrouded his words and expressions like a chilly fog. But thinking about this problem and discoursing on his conclusions, all that vanished. He was precise, detached and open, and she felt more like a colleague in arms than a despised intruder.

"She also seems to have a remarkable sense of smell. Of course she might just have been taunting you—what she told you were pretty obvious guesses. But we have quite a poor sense of smell compared to most mammals, so no great difficulty there. Did she give any signs of unusually acute hearing?"

"No, not that I noticed. But she often gave the impression of trying to sense danger—maybe she was listening. Her ears were the same shape as ours too, by the way."

"On that topic we should clarify a few other things. Ignoring the tail her hair was the same as a person's? She had nails not claws? Did you notice anything else different, say in her bodily proportions?"

"No... I can't be completely sure, partly because the obvious differences were distracting, partly because I was terrified. But no... I didn't notice any difference in her hair or nails. Her nails were sharp, maybe a bit stronger than mine, but human as far as I could tell. She had this skintight outfit on and I didn't notice anything out of place or missing."

"But she was stronger than you expected, very fast in both movements and reflexes, yet lithe and flexible?" Miriam nodded. "OK. I'd say some muscle enhancement, not too difficult given the normal range of human not to mention animal capabilities. But a pretty significant enhancement to her nervous system. And she said her body was unusually sensitive? Again, she might have been lying. But if we take it at face value she has a denser and faster nervous system than ours. That is probably the most significant enhancement, but given the variation between people and our knowledge of neurogenetics, it could be something someone would try—and maybe succeed at."

He paused. "Except for one thing. More peripheral nerves require more central nervous system to process them. Let me do some calculations."

She waited while he worked with some programs on his display. He looked at them.

"Interesting. Twice, she said? Let's take that as at least approximately true. If it means twice the linear resolution, then that would imply four times the number of resolvable nerve endings. I think it more likely to be twice the number per unit area, which equates to about 1.4 times the linear resolution, still significantly greater sensitivity. If you look at the power laws of scaling in mammals, a crude calculation gives somewhat more than twice the brain weight to handle it. However most of a human brain is the thinking part not the sensory processing part. Making some rough approximations, she would need a thicker spinal cord than us—not much of a problem—and only about a 20% larger brain. That equates to an increase in linear dimensions of her head of less than 7%, perhaps noticeable but not a big problem."

He thought a while longer and did some more arcane manipulations on screen.

"There are other relevant factors. A large fraction of nerves in a newborn's brain are pruned during development, meaning we start with a lot more than we need for what we've got. In adults, there is a significant variation in brain volume unrelated to body size or intelligence: indeed, many highly intelligent people have relatively small brains for their body size. At the other end of the spectrum, some people with much reduced brain tissue due to hydrocephaly still function relatively normally. If we factor all that in, our geneh's neural enhancements might well all fit into a package within the normal range of human variation."

He thought some more.

"One other thing. In humans a faster nervous system is correlated with greater intelligence: so if we're right about that aspect, your mystery woman might be very bright indeed. But there is one thing that disturbs me..."

She waited.

"Thank you, by the way, for the completeness of your report. I know some of it would have been embarrassing to repeat to a hostile stranger like me. But from the way she behaved: threatening you, hurting you, caressing you... I wonder how mentally stable she is? She also implied she craved excitement? Maybe those enhancements to her nervous system had unfortunate side effects and she's a bit mad. Or even completely mad."

"I had the same thought," Miriam commented. "I didn't know what to do, what to say, and I still don't know why she let me live. Maybe she was just toying with me, but if she was she was very cruel about it." She shuddered.

"Yes. A great pity though. If it wasn't for her personality she would be a magnificent creature." He sighed. "Not that I expect you to agree with me."

"Anyway," he said, his air of contempt returning, "that's all interesting as speculation, but we still have the mathematical problem. Your story confirms that this woman is in her twenties and in my professional opinion it was impossible to produce her more than 15 years ago even if anyone had the capability to do so. She is not a geneh."

"Then how do you account for her appearance? You originally suggested those eyes could be a disguise or a mask, but they aren't. They were as real as mine."

"Oh, I'm not sure they are as advanced as I've been speculating. That was all assuming things are what they seem. But in science things have a way of being other than they seem. You have come here for my opinion, and I suppose I owe it to you since you have given me an hour or so of reliving what the past could have been. Mind you," he added harshly, "I might hate you for that tomorrow."

"So. In my professional opinion, for what that's worth these days, she is what I said at our first meeting; though I can now flesh it out more. What you have is a highly trained athlete in her twenties. I suspect an organized crime connection—or even a government agency connection, if there's a difference these days—because she has some sophisticated and therefore expensive enhancements. Her eyes are bioengineered but she isn't a geneh: that solves our timing issue. She didn't have to grow up with them: she's been operated on later in life. She has a prosthetic tail made to look like a real one—mainly, I suspect, as a distraction, a smokescreen, though obviously she can use it to good effect. But note what she did with it: almost emphasizing her use of it. As I said, it's a distraction. And she's on some kind of drug, probably a designer drug based on cocaine. That's what gives her such speed and reflexes and is also, I suspect, what is sending her mad."

"Do you really think she could be a government agent? Why would she be doing what she's doing?"

"Oh, if she is I'd say she's gone rogue. Possibly another side effect of the drugs. And you know what government agencies are like if they are doing something secret of dubious legality. Complete deniability. If she is and has, someone will be trying to kill her but they'll never tell you. And if they succeed her body will simply disappear."

"Still... your theory sounds plausible, but you haven't met her. It just doesn't feel... right. In person, she comes across as what she herself says she is."

"Didn't they teach you in policeman's school how unreliable witness impressions are? Or how easily conmen fool their marks with smoke and mirrors?" he snapped. After a pause he added, his voice and gaze hardening, "And since you are so enamored of speculation, let us see where else it leads us. Let us assume you are right. I can guess from watching and talking to you that you had a reasonably happy childhood, would that be so?"

Miriam nodded, unsure where he was leading and why his gaze bored into hers, no longer with bitter contempt but now with naked hostility.

"Then I do not think you understand hate, Ms Hunter. I do. I have had cause to hate, whether you think me justified or not. Well let me try to make you understand hate. If this woman is a geneh, imagine her life. While you were growing up in the sunshine and running in parks, where if you fell over almost any stranger would help you up with a smile: what was she doing?"

Miriam watched him, eyes still.

"She was living in the shadows, afraid to show herself, never to play in the sunshine or laugh with her friends, never to even have friends. Were she to fall, the random stranger who lifted you up was more likely to kick her to death than stretch out his hand in good will. And there is more. You take pride in being an officer of the law. To you the law is a good thing, the protector of the innocent. But what was the law to her? A monster lurking in her nightmares and the shadows of her days, waiting to rend her at any moment, at any mistake. Just for being."

Miriam's eyes grew larger.

"Yes, I think you are beginning to see. Now imagine you are this woman. Imagine that your enemies bring themselves into your domain, looking for you, knowing that finding you means your death. Imagine that you now hold one of those servants of the law in your power. Your enemy, the creature from your nightmares, the monster who would destroy you without trial, without recourse, without mercy. What would you do, Detective? You dare to speak of cruelty and madness? What is left to this child? You should not ask why she was cruel. You should only ask why you are alive to complain about it!"

Miriam stared at him, appalled at the enormity of what he described. "Oh my God," she breathed.

"For all her cruelty she let you live. Had you arrested her, she would now be dead. Ask yourself some time: which of you is the more moral?"

He glared at her for a few more moments; then he shook his head and the hostility was gone, evaporating again down to its usual residue of contempt.

"But you came here for my opinion. I have given it. I don't care whether you accept it or spend the rest of your life haring off after chimeras. Now get out. And next time don't come back without a warrant."

~~~

The watcher hidden on the hill among the trees observed Miriam's departure with as much interest as her arrival, and transmitted to the supervisor's office the encrypted time-stamped telephoto images of this her second visit here. Moments like this were rare but brought a deep satisfaction that made the job worthwhile; gave meaning to the hours of emptiness. But the watcher was patient. It never got bored, it never slept: it just watched and waited.

Chapter 15: Amaro

The nightclub was loud, noisy and smoky. Smoking was coming back into style now that most diseases of the lung including cancer had been banished to the dark corners of societal memory. Miriam didn't smoke herself but didn't mind the smell of these mild modern brands. They didn't choke you like she remembered as a child from some of her more chimney-like relatives; it was more a gentle haze of fragrances with these smoke-reduced brands. More like sitting in a refined club redolent of old cigars than choking over a grassfire.

She was out with her two best friends from work, both single like her. They thought it would be fun to unwind a bit, dance a bit crazy, who knows, maybe meet some fun guys. The other girls were still up dancing but Miriam was taking a rest from it, sipping a cocktail, when a strange man slipped smoothly into the seat beside her.

"Hello young lady. It looks like you've nearly finished your drink. I saw you dancing earlier: you need to keep your fluids up. May I buy you a top-up?"

"What, are you a doctor? And what fluids, precisely, are you really aiming to top me up with?"

The man laughed. "No, not a doctor. Just a humanitarian concerned with the health and happiness of humanity. Especially beautiful femality." He grinned. "I meant, quite innocently, to top up that deadly looking cocktail you are drinking. In fact I am so innocent that I can't imagine what else you could be referring to."

She couldn't help but grin back. "I see. Forgive me sir. A gallant knight is so rare these days that one hardly recognizes one when he appears. Speaking of which, I'm not letting you off the hook yet. I believe knights were renowned for admiring from afar—at least that's what they told their ladies. And you have confessed to watching me from afar. In our less innocent age we call that stalking."

The man looked wounded. "By my honor, lady, you grieve me. It is not my fault that your beauty ensnared me. You were there, before my eyes: how could I not place myself in your service? But if it is your wish, I shall go. I seek nothing but your happiness." Upon which he rose, and bowed.

Miriam laughed. "Oh, sit down you great lunk." She looked at him with frank curiosity. Curly dark hair, but with features and a shade to his skin suggesting some Spanish in his ancestry; lively dark eyes and a large mobile mouth. He laughed easily and lightly, showing fine white teeth. Well muscled but not overdone like a weightlifter. She felt a liquid stirring in her belly. *Whew*, she thought; *has it been that long? I'd better not drink too much more.*

"So, handsome knight, what do you do when you aren't tilting at windmills?"

"I should like to say that I am independently wealthy, able to whisk fair maidens to far exotic places at their whim. But I cannot. I am a humble scientist at the EPA. You see? I am a knight, of sorts. And you? Let me guess." He looked at her speculatively. "No... I cannot. Your beauty distracts me too much. I must ask."

She laughed again. "I think you are a rogue, no knight. So perhaps this will make you flee: I am a trainee detective with the City Police."

He looked shocked. "Oh no! I fear entrapment. Confess it now: you have ensnared me because of those unpaid parking tickets. Honestly, I mean to pay them!"

"Oh you!" she said, punching him on the shoulder. "You're impossible!"

Just then her friends returned, slightly tipsy. "Oooh, Miriam, who's your friend?"

"Just some lunk I met. Girls, this is... oh hell. We've been talking for five minutes and I don't even know your name!"

The lunk stood and bowed graciously. "Amaranto Leandro Moreno at your service, beautiful ladies! You may call me Amaro."

"Your name seems far more Spanish than your face," observed Miriam skeptically.

"Your friend here has already taught me the dangers of her tongue," Amaro said to the girls (was anything this man said *not* a double-entendre? thought Miriam), "but let me assure you all that I am no knave spinning fine tales to bewitch your fair hearts. The male line of my family traces its history all the way back to noble Spain. But my family has never put race before beauty, so most wives grafted to that line were of other lands. Mix with that my father's poetic soul, and my name is explained."

Miriam rolled her eyes. He was a bit of a poet himself if you asked her. She stood and introduced the girls, "Hello Amaro. These elegant ladies are Rianna and Darian, my friends from work. And I'm Miriam."

"Yes, I heard. Miriam! A fine name, evocative of prophecy and priestesses! Shall we dance?"

Miriam looked at Rianna and Darian helplessly. They laughed and shooed her on her way, then sat down and began an animated discussion about this turn of events.

Amaro led her to the floor. She half expected that his verbal performance was compensation for something, hopefully just two left feet, but he surprised her. He was an excellent dancer to whatever music was playing and she found herself whirled around the floor and completely, breathlessly delighted.

They went back to the table where the girls were watching them cheerfully. "I don't suppose you came with your brothers did you, Amaro?" Darian asked.

"Oh fair maiden," exclaimed Amaro, hand over his breast, "had I known what beauty I would find here tonight, I certainly would have brought my dearest friends to share in my delight! But alas I came alone. Yet perhaps—if I am so fortunate as to ever meet you lovely ladies again—I can introduce you to some fine young men at another time?"

Miriam sat looking at him. He was an entertaining rogue, that was for sure. But probably still a rogue. But hell. "Well, Amaro, I would hate my friends to miss out on an offer like that. So I guess we'll have to see you again."

"Nothing would delight me more! Except perhaps to discuss the details in a quieter place? Perhaps over coffee?"

Miriam had a good idea what kind of coffee was brewing in his mind. After all, a similar brand was brewing in hers. But she wasn't really into one-night stands; she preferred something with a bit more permanence. And one thing she'd learned by now was that if a man was going to last more than one night he was willing to wait more than one night.

"Thanks for the offer, but some other time perhaps. We have to work tomorrow. But here." She touched her phone to send her details to his, which he accepted and reciprocated. He smiled and bowed. "An honor, fair Miriam. You will be hearing from me. Until then, I wish you all joy."

They waved to him and weaved their way out of the club. Amaro sat there nursing his drink, watching Miriam go through narrowed eyes. *An interesting woman,* he thought. *I might enjoy this.*

CHAPTER 16: DINNER

Amaro was good to his word, and they arranged a triple date with her friends and his. He had not brought any brothers just two of his own friends. But he was either lucky or perceptive, for they all got along famously.

One Wednesday a couple of weeks after their first meeting, Miriam was putting on her coat ready to leave work when Darian came to see her. "Hi Miriam. We thought we'd go clubbing tonight. Are you up for it?"

Miriam looked up, a funny smile playing on her lips. "Sorry, I've a date with Amaro tonight."

"Oh! Getting serious, is it?"

Miriam shrugged and answered nonchalantly, "Oh, maybe. He's a laugh a minute, you might have noticed. He spoils me, too. Maybe I can bear his arrogant company a little longer." But from the little smile that wouldn't let itself be put away, Darian wasn't fooled: Miriam had "smitten" written all over her. "Well you kids have fun then. Don't do anything I wouldn't do." Darian blew her a kiss and left. Miriam finished up, humming happily, and followed her.

She met Amaro at an upscale Thai restaurant. "So, Miss Hunter, are your tastes as fiery as your tongue? Would you enjoy a chili to die from or should I order a gentler dish?"

She shook her head. He really was incorrigible. "I like it hot, Amaro. Let's see what you've got." Two could play at that game, she thought.

He raised his eyebrows mockingly. He really was a card, she

thought. She didn't know how much his role of gallant gentleman rake—or which parts of it—were genuine, but he certainly played it to the hilt. Once he knew her preference he did not discuss the options any further. Like a gentleman of old he simply took charge, selecting the dishes and the wine. She was more used to the modern style of equality and negotiation, but just for this evening she was amused enough to be carried along in his irresistible wake.

"Oh. Wow," she breathed at the first taste of the curry. He smiled. "Too much?"

"Oh, no. My tongue's gone but this is delicious."

"But your tongue is your best part! I do hope it comes back."

She poked it out at him. "Be careful what you ask for, brave knight."

He smiled, and they continued sampling the dishes. He had chosen a cold, somewhat sweet but not too sweet white wine. It went perfectly with the burning curries. Which were burning but not too burning: the chili enhanced rather than detracted from the other tastes.

"My, Amaro, I think you've done this before."

"My lady, anything I have done before has been mere preparation for this evening."

She laughed. "You're impossible! But let's be serious. All I ever get out of you is knightly wit. Is there a real man in there, or are you just a pretty suit of armor? Who is the real Amaro? *Is* there a real Amaro?"

He looked at her. He actually managed to look serious. She wondered whether it was real or just his best performance to date. "Well, the real Amaro has many faces, all equally real. He is complex, like an aged red wine." He paused. Miriam just waited. She knew about trout fishing. This was a trout who had never been hooked.

"Most ladies see the gallant Amaro, and that is enough for them. Some may say the gallant Amaro is shallow, but he has made many ladies happy and they him. Where that is all the lady sees, Amaro is happy for them to see no further. They have fun, he has fun, and there is much laughter and no tears. Much pleasure and no pain. After a time they go their separate ways and all their memories are happy. Amaro has observed that knowing more deeply opens the doors to pain, and while greater happiness might in theory be found there, in the end the memories may not be so happy."

His expression made Miriam wonder how personal those observations were. And the prick of sympathy she felt made her start to wonder who was the trout and who was the fisherman here. Before she could pursue that thought further, he appeared to come to a decision, and continued.

"Well, we must start somewhere. Let me tell you about my work. As I told you, I am a scientist working for the EPA. Though I no longer do original research—my job is more project planning, monitoring and analysis. Specifically, I concentrate on genetic contamination of the environment—you know, detecting the spread of illegal genetic modifications into the wild or into agricultural crops, whether illegal completely or only legal on condition of containment." At the flash of interest in her eyes, he stopped. "You are interested in genetics?" he asked.

"Oh, it's just a coincidence. My work at the moment has something to do with genetics."

"Really? How interesting! Perhaps it is something I can help you with. That might be stimulating. Usually the only mutual interest in genetics I find with the ladies is of a more intimate nature." The old Amaro was irrepressible, she thought.

"Sorry, I can't really talk about it for now. It's too confidential: it would mean my job. I can't even tell you what it's about generally. It's that hot."

"I am impressed. I was under the impression that you were a humble apprentice detective. Now I learn that you move in high circles, privy to national secrets!"

She laughed. "Oh, I am a humble apprentice, believe me. Most of my time is spent on an Artful Idiot system. However I've got it to idiot savant stage and sometimes it spits out something useful. The trick is in knowing what is useful and what isn't. The thing can come up with a whole conspiracy theory involving Joe the Corner Butcher and the President of the United States, and make a pretty convincing case of it sometimes. It knows how to calculate statistics but is clueless how to apply them: so I am trying to teach it, to help cut out its more outrageous ideas without missing real issues. Anyway, it recently came up with something strange that happened to link with something even stranger, so I ended up involved. Whether it ends up making my career or breaking it, well, time will tell."

"My, my, Miriam," he said, "We start delving into the complex reality of Amaro only to find that the truly fascinating person is Miriam. I feel inadequate." He frowned sadly.

Miriam laughed delightedly. "Oh Amaro! I find it hard to believe you are capable of feeling inadequate even on a double date with the President and Madame Curie."

He laughed. "Perhaps when you have tasted the full complexity of the noble Amaro, you will learn whether or not that is true. But let us leave government intrigue behind us. I know! Here is a proposition I read once: 'the entertainment you choose is a guide to your soul'. Let us discuss the holidays we have been on. We may learn more about each other's souls that way than by trying to find the words to explain."

They spent the rest of the evening enjoying the food, enjoying the wine, and enjoying each other's company. They discussed holidays, family, friends, movies and art. Miriam was entranced. When Sir Amaro peeled off his armor and it was just Amaro, he was not only amusing, he appeared to be the kind of man you could live a lifetime with and never be bored.

They had just finished a dessert wine whose sweetness temporarily chased away the chili, only to have it return in a synergy that made her mouth feel it had been kissed. Amaro insisted on taking the bill, his persona of gallant gentleman of a previous century rising up again for the occasion.

Miriam sighed. "I am afraid I've had too good a time, Senor Moreno. I've broken my own rule about how much I should drink when out on a date. I think I'd better get a taxi home. I can pick my car up tomorrow."

"What kind of knight would so fail his Lady? I shall of course carry you to your door on my noble charger."

Miriam looked into his dark liquid eyes. The liquid ran into her own eyes and down to her belly, where it started working on her resistance. There wasn't much resistance to work on. "Thank you Amaro, I think I shall accept your chivalrous offer."

He smiled, and she felt as if he swept her out of the restaurant, down to his car, and finally to her door. They stood there and she looked at him. "Whew! I think I drank even more than I realized," she admitted, swaying slightly.

"A knight would never take advantage of a lady not in full possession of her faculties, so I must sadly bid you goodnight," he said, bowing to kiss her hand.

"Not so fast, lunk. I didn't say I wasn't in full possession of my faculties. You keep complaining about my tongue. Let's see if it can change your mind." With that, she lifted herself on her toes, put her arms around him, and kissed him. He returned the kiss without a moment's hesitation. *I suppose I shouldn't be surprised,* she thought, *that he kisses like he dances.* Liquid desire flowed down from her mouth and up from her toes, meeting in the middle. *Oh what the hell,* she thought. "Well don't just stand there," she said huskily, "come in."

CHAPTER 17: INTERROGATION

Amaro woke early. He could feel Miriam breathing gently beside him. His body was thanking him for last night's sensory symphony, and he smiled. *Mornings could most definitely be worse,* he thought. He thought of the joyless religions that despised the pleasures of the flesh and named them sins, and wondered how people could get so twisted around.

It was still early. Through the blinds he could see the grey light of dawn starting to lighten the sky. Miriam stirred, and put her hand on his stomach. He gently laid his own hand over it. It was warm, soft and trusting.

Miriam opened her eyes and looked at him. She still half suspected he was just a slick-talking rogue. Amaro detected the change in her breathing and turned his head to face her, and saw her studying him. "Yes, my love?"

"That's just the question, isn't it? That simple word can hide a multitude of lies," Miriam said quietly. She began circling her finger around his navel. It made Amaro tingle. She continued, playfully but with an edge of seriousness, "The question in my mind is: is Amaro really the chivalrous knight, or is he a knave in drag? How can a girl tell?"

"My lady! If in the light of day you fear that Amaro, having had his wicked way with the fair maiden, would ride off leaving her pregnant and bereft: I am mortified! Though Amaro's lawyer might point out that it is the fair lady who refused his offer of, ah, protection at the time," he added teasingly.

"Pah! For all your knightly airs, this isn't the Middle Ages. How many fair maidens are stupid enough not to take their own precautions, rather than relying on the uncertain valor of self-proclaimed gentlemen?" she laughed. "Don't worry, you won't wake up in nine months to a bailiff presenting you with a child support summons."

Amaro looked wounded. Miriam's finger began circling further down his stomach and she added playfully, "Besides, I cheerfully admit that I much prefer skin on skin, don't you? And fortunately sexually transmitted diseases are a thing of the past too."

"A medical advance which we can all celebrate," Amaro replied. "As indeed we did," he added with a mocking grin.

Miriam's finger was now playing with his curlier hairs and she could feel him stir in response. She reached down and held him, and began to move her hand slowly.

Amaro felt the fire build and reached over to her, but she slapped him away with her other hand. "Don't you try to distract me, knave!" she said. "I need to interrogate the suspect, learn his true intentions."

"My intentions... My intentions are noble!" gasped Amaro. "As a true knight of the realm, all Amaro seeks is to increase the amount of good in the world! Happiness is good. The logic is clear! At least, he thinks so. He is getting rather distracted and his thinking may not be as clear as he imagines. That must be why he has not thanked the lady. She is unusually forward for a demure maiden, but at this stage, Amaro cannot say he objects."

"Don't fool yourself, rogue," Miriam said roughly. "I'm not doing this for your benefit. I have plans for this thing!"

With that, she rolled over to straddle him and lowered herself down. She began to rock gently. Amaro groaned. "My lady is sweet, kind and considerate. How could he ever betray her?"

Miriam reached her hand between his legs and did something that made him quiver. "So do I understand you correctly? You might actually call me again? And if I call you, you will answer the phone?"

"I swear!"

Miriam gripped him gently and whispered, "I'll hold you to that, rogue."

Then she released him, leaned over to kiss him and their rocking increased its tempo. They both forgot to speak for a while.

When they had finished, Miriam rolled off onto her side. "Oh my.

Oh my." She murmured.

"I must say, my lady," said Amaro after a while, "that I am most impressed by your interrogation technique. I could not call it police brutality, but it is uniquely effective. It is no wonder your career is going well. I should not be surprised if your rate of confessions is astounding!"

Miriam's mouth made an "O" of shock and she punched him on the shoulder. "Oh you! That is *not* my usual interrogation technique. It is reserved," she added haughtily, "only for the most hardened criminals."

"While I generally avoid the attentions of the law, I think I am glad you consider me so. That I may be forced to suffer such techniques."

They lay together silently for a while, just enjoying the relaxation spreading through their limbs.

Then Miriam turned to him and smiled. "I don't suppose you are free this Friday night?"

Amaro's face took on a look of intense concentration. "Well... as you would expect, Amaro's social calendar requires sophisticated scheduling software." Miriam rolled her eyes. "But there appears to be a bug. His calendar seems to have become free for the foreseeable future. This Friday? Consider it done. For that matter, tonight is free as well." He gave her a hopeful look, much like a puppy not wanting a game to end just yet.

Miriam laughed but shook her head. "My body is already finding it easy enough to overrule my brain. I think I need a rest from you to get some perspective. Let's stick to Friday."

"I'm going to have a shower," she added. "For some unknown reason, I am sweaty and smell of Man. I won't be long."

Amaro lay back in bed listening the sound of the running water. He smiled again. *Oh, yes.*

Miriam came back into the bedroom wrapped in a fluffy white towel, drying her hair. "You probably want a shower too," she observed.

"Indeed," replied Amaro, getting out of bed. Miriam added, "Could you drive me to where I left my car? Unless it's too far out of your way?"

Amaro bowed, sweeping his arm as if flourishing a feathered cap. Miriam had to laugh. He made it look elegant even stark naked and still somewhat aroused. "Amaro would be honored. It is the least he can do in return for the lady's, ah, services."

"Beast!" she said. "Into the shower with you!"

~~~

Miriam arrived at the station early and went happily to work. She often found herself humming even when arguing with the AI.

Whenever she saw herself in the ladies' room mirror, she noticed a silly little smile playing at the corner of her lips. It refused to go away. When she smoothed her top down, her nipples responded even to that innocent motion. She rolled her eyes at her own reactions. *Maybe I need a whole week away from Amaro,* she thought. *Fat chance,* the silly smile told her.

Darian bumped into her when she was making herself a cappuccino in the refreshments room. "How did the hot date go?" she asked. Miriam attempted to put on a stern expression but somehow it came out as a happy smile. "Oh!" said Darian, "I see! That good, eh?"

Miriam could only smile; she decided she had better not play poker for a while. "Yes. In every way. The man certainly knows how to entertain a girl."

Darian clapped her hands delightedly. "I expect a full report at the next meeting of the girls' club!" she said.

Then she looked suspiciously at Miriam and snorted. "Though from the look of you, you might be too busy to attend for a while."

CHAPTER 18: RIANNA

When the forensics team had taken samples from Katlyn's hideout, given the state of the place they had not been hopeful. The building was dirty, a temporary home for human vagrants and a more permanent home for vermin. Not only that, where it had not been incinerated the sprinkler system had mixed everything together into muck. The chance of getting anything useful out of any of their samples was minimal.

They had one piece of luck: one of the forensic investigators had lifted a piece of fallen metal in Katlyn's former nest and noticed a piece of charred human hair stuck under it. It had been partially protected from the flames and on closer examination the investigator saw it had an attached follicle. Forensics still weren't hopeful: while intact, the hair was obviously damaged by heat and smoke. But it was their best chance and they had sent it to the DNA lab. That had been a few weeks ago: in the scheme of things it had no special priority.

A call announced itself on Miriam's screen. It was Rianna, who was in charge of the DNA lab.

"Hi Rianna," she said. "I hope you have good news for me."

"Sorry. We've looked at that piece of hair from your fire, but its DNA is badly degraded, as well as the hair being contaminated with all kinds of crud. It would be expensive to get into a state where it could be sequenced and even then we'd only get fairly short pieces. Nowhere near good enough for positive identification, though maybe good enough for a modest probability match. In either case certainly not good enough to use in court: any defense attorney would tear it apart. But if your boss authorizes the expense we can try. It won't be cheap."

Miriam shook her head. "Damn. No, we don't have enough to go on, clues or budget. No way he'd authorize it. Double damn. It's the nearest to a real clue I have."

Rianna thought a moment. "Well... there might be something. We do have a research budget. Pushing the envelope on how much data we can get out of compromised samples is something the Powers like us to do. At least when it works. Yes," she smiled, "I can see an interesting problem here. I can put my new person Kimberley on it. She's pretty good at tough work and likes a challenge."

Miriam frowned. "Thanks for the offer, but are you sure it would be OK? I don't want you getting into trouble over it."

"No, Miriam, it's legitimate research. And interesting. Hell, if it works I might even get a pay rise."

Miriam grinned at her. "Richly deserved, too. Thanks a lot, Rianna. Keep me posted."

"Bye babe. See you at lunch."

CHAPTER 19: COUSINS

It was a rainy Sunday afternoon, and they were sitting on her couch, loosely entwined around each other, watching a nature documentary. It was an old one, digitized and converted to 3D, starring a gentle but enthusiastic Englishman with a raspy voice. But as Amaro pointed out, evolution was slow and nature last century was much like nature now, albeit somewhat more common then.

Amaro had rekindled her interest in nature. She was not by temperament as purist as he, and tended to think that any improvement was a good improvement by definition, whether done by genetics or by physics. But she supposed a bit of genetic purism went with his job. She had been interested in the living world as a child and now found rediscovering it, especially with such an expert guide, to be an unexpected pleasure.

The professor was creeping up on some mountain gorillas, relatives of man that despite a usually gentle disposition were mountains in more than habitat, and if angry could tear a man's limbs off. She decided the unassuming professor was a brave man. He went on to contrast the gentle vegetarian gorilla with the more aggressive chimpanzee and the oversexed bonobo, the two closest relatives of man. She could certainly see human beings as a combination of the two: go out, fight a war, go hunting, come home and have sex all night. That sounded like a lot of human history to her, like a summary of the Trojan War. *A lot like us come to think of it*, she thought fondly, glancing at Amaro.

The lines leading to the different chimps and man had diverged only a few million years ago; that to the gorillas a few million earlier. It was remarkable how different humans were from these close evolutionary cousins, and the professor went on to describe differences besides their big brains. Miriam sat up straight. Something he had said had collided with something in her own brain and made a connection. No, it can't be that. If it were that simple he'd have known, surely. She stood up suddenly. "Oh my God."

"What's the matter, sweet Miriam?" asked Amaro. "You look like you saw a ghost. But fear not. Brave Sir Amaro will ride to your aid, sword held high!"

She looked at him, barely seeing him, but his banter from their traditional teasing rang another bell primed by her suspicions. *The phrases friends share,* she thought. *Why is that important? The phrases...* Then the other connection fell into place. "Odin, Thor and Loki!" she cried. "Amaro, I have to go!"

He looked at her in amazement. "Hey, slow down, tiger! What's gotten into you? You're worrying me!"

Her eyes swept over him, still not really registering his existence except as a shape in her field of view. "Sorry. Sorry. Can't talk. I just realized something, something important. Holy Hell. Jesus. Christ. Almighty." Then she stopped, belatedly remembering it was Sunday. This was important but was it urgent enough to drag people away from their homes and families? Maybe, but they probably wouldn't see it that way. Somewhat deflated, she realized this wasn't so hot it couldn't wait until tomorrow.

She turned away and began composing a long note into her phone.

Amaro looked at her, nonplussed. Then his eyes narrowed. *Well,* he thought, *now this is an interesting development.*

"Sorry Amaro," she said when she'd finished. "I just had a thought about work that might be important. But it can wait until tomorrow. I'm back in the present now. So where were we?"

"We were studying our animal relatives. I believe we can learn many things from them, especially the bonobo. Let me demonstrate." With that, he took her in his arms and gave her a lingering kiss, which somehow ended with his lying on top of her in a mutual tangle. Her earlier intellectual excitement evolved seamlessly into a more physical one, and the tangle began to assume configurations that would no doubt be interesting to topologists but were even more interesting to the participants. Then she forgot about her work for a while.

Later, Amaro watched her contentedly sleeping form affectionately, but there was a calculating edge to his gaze. He tapped a message into his own phone then he sat and thought, idly playing with her hair but careful not to wake her.

~~~

The next morning, with the imminence of being able to do something about it, Miriam's excitement over her idea grew. She sent messages to Stone and Ramos to meet her in the Chief's office as soon as they arrived.

Ramos was first to arrive after Miriam, who was already waiting for him trying to hide her impatience. He usually liked to settle in for a while before granting audience to his minions, and had a look of grumpiness overlaying a faint odor of gym about him. Jack turned up a few minutes later and leaned against the wall looking cynical but intrigued. Miriam was looking a little wild-eyed.

"OK Hunter, what's so urgent it can't wait until I've had my coffee?" grumbled Ramos.

"I was watching a show yesterday. About chimpanzees. Then it hit me."

Jack looked up. "Great. I rushed in here for a movie review. So did the chimp get the girl?"

"No, no," said Miriam, completely oblivious to sarcasm. "Remember when we talked to Dr Tagarin? Remember what he said? Our thief couldn't be a geneh, because nobody could have made her 25 years ago?"

"Sure, that's one reason we never escalated it to GenInt except as a note worded so nobody will care. Covering our asses both ways," said Ramos. "Anyone who does decide it's worth a look will probably come to the same conclusion. A woman with tacked-on mods, not a geneh. Our problem, not theirs."

"But it never rang true to me. I've met her, remember. We had a *long* chat."

"Sure, sure, we know," replied Jack. "But as the man said, sometimes you can't beat arithmetic."

"But that's the point! I was watching this show, and the presenter said something interesting. Humans have an unusually long childhood even for apes. Chimpanzees are about our size but reach puberty in only 8 to 10 years! Gorillas are twice our weight and reach puberty even earlier! This girl has faster muscles and faster nerves! What if she also has faster development, more like a chimp than a man? She might only *be* 15!"

They both went still and stared at her. Jack's mouth was open. Then he closed it, only to open it again to say: "Sure, as far as I know. But if it were that easy, our friendly expert would have seen it straight away. He would have..." then his voice trailed away, as he saw it too. "Oh my God."

"That's what I said! Then I remembered something else. I'd forgotten it, but then Amaro said something, one of those little inside jokes couples have. When Katlyn first grabbed me she said something that struck me as important, but she was choking me and I forgot about it. But I remember now. She said, 'A life is a terrible thing to waste.' Those are almost the exact words Dr Tagarin said at our first meeting. It stuck in my memory it because it's kind of a funny phrase—there's some famous quote like it, but it's about a mind not a life. Those two know each other! I'm sure of it!"

Jack and Ramos looked at her, looked at each other. "Christ, Miriam," said Jack, "It isn't proof, but it sure answers some questions."

"But what can we do about it?" asked Ramos. "It's certainly relevant to our case of the thief. But is it enough for a search warrant? It's certainly enough to bring in GenInt." He frowned. "Not that I'd like to. But we might have to now."

Miriam said, "I don't want to bring GenInt in either. It's still just a crazy theory, right? Let's try talking to Dr Tagarin again. Jack and I can go."

"The last time he saw you he said don't come back without a warrant, remember?"

"Yes, but even without a warrant he might prefer us to GenInt."

Chapter 20: Tagarin

They parked the car and looked up towards the entrance. *This is getting to be a habit*, Miriam thought. Perhaps she and the gate would become friends.

"Oh well, let's see if he still likes us," Jack said. "Despite my superior experience and interrogation skills I think you should do the talking. If he likes anyone, it's you. Like a boxer likes his punching bag, but it's something."

Tagarin had apparently given his gate an update. They had barely come within range when it said, "I detect no warrant, detectives. I believe my employer advised you that you were no longer welcome in his home and he would not entertain you without one."

"Please convey my apologies to Dr Tagarin," Miriam answered. "But there has been a development in the case. He is now a person of interest himself and it would be in his interests to talk to us."

"Dr Tagarin wishes to know what part of the word 'warrant' you fail to understand. He further wishes me to remind you that no matter how interesting he is to you, the interest is not reciprocated. Especially when your interest is not shared by a judge, or not enough to get you that warrant. He also refers you back to his team of shark-like lawyers and wonders if you have more understanding of the word 'harassment' than of the word 'warrant'?"

"It is true that we don't have enough to get a warrant. But we do have enough to interest GenInt. We do not want to involve GenInt at this stage and I am sure Dr Tagarin would agree. We hope we can sort this out with a friendly discussion. That's all we're here for."

The gate was silent.

In a few minutes, it opened without comment and they went up the path to the door. As they approached, the door opened and James greeted them. His butler façade had slipped a little and his eyes were hostile, though his manner was as gracious as ever.

Again they were ushered directly in to Dr Tagarin's office. This time James stood less in the shadows and more in their line of sight. Miriam was impressed at how a man who appeared to have just one expression could make it appear as aloof politeness or stony threat without any detectable rearrangement of its features.

"All right officers, this is becoming repetitive. My Jacuzzi blondes will be getting jealous of you, Ms Hunter, and then I might become less relaxed than you're used to," he said with a sharp edge. "So what is this latest exciting piece of news?"

Miriam explained her reasoning about Katlyn's possible accelerated development and how it solved the timing dilemma. She went on to note that if it was true, it indicated ongoing, undiscovered human genetic engineering in the years since it was made illegal. She omitted, however, the coincidence of phrasing between him and Katlyn. That wasn't proof and would only put him more on the defensive. Best not to play that card yet: see what cards he showed, first.

"And so you think that I, as a once eminent expert in that field, am the most likely suspect?"

Miriam spread her hands. "Not necessarily, though you see how it looks. But you would also know any other likely candidates. For now, we are not treating you as a suspect. We just want to know what you think."

"How kind," he observed skeptically. "I think you are clutching at straws and at my expense. Surely it is obvious that even if your theory were plausible my previous assessment, that you are dealing with a skilled human with a few later enhancements, remains more likely."

"Except that I have met her. It doesn't ring true to me. Even she said she was a geneh. She practically beat me into naming it."

"And you are a silly little girl who was scared out of her few wits!" he snapped. "Witnesses see things that aren't there all the time, as you'd know if you'd done your schoolwork! Of course she wanted you to think she's a geneh! A complete distraction from discovering her true nature, which might lead you to those capable of making her what she is! Maybe that is the sole reason she left you alive!"

"Perhaps I *have* been led to someone capable of making her," she countered.

"Pah! You are obsessed with your childish fantasies, incapable of adult thought! There are no genehs! They are all dead! If you weren't holding the stick of GenInt over my head I'd have James throw you both out!"

He glared at them, breathing heavily.

"I am sorry to anger you again, doctor. But do you claim that accelerated development is impossible? If not, why did you fail to mention it?"

"No, it is not impossible," he said, as she saw his face slip into his dispassionate scientist mode. "But nor would it be easy. I can see paths one might take to achieve it. But really, think for once. Evolution doesn't play games. A long childhood is dangerous for the child and expensive for the parent. There is a reason why our children take so long to grow up. We might look a lot like apes, but surely your nature show was not so stupid as to omit the main difference?" He tapped his own head. "This brain has made us what we are. It needs a lot of training. That is why we have a long childhood. It is not a matter of arbitrary chance, it is intimately tied to our humanity."

"But you said her nervous system appears to be accelerated. Could that compensate? Allow her to have a shorter childhood?"

Tagarin started and gave her an odd look, almost of respect. "That is the most perceptive thing you've said yet, Ms Hunter. Perhaps. Perhaps. But still, it wouldn't be easy. Our developmental program is tied to a lot of things: physical, hormonal, psychological. Perhaps it could be sped up a few years? Enough to give us someone who looks ten years older than she really is? Difficult. And if so she might have had a hard time of it, growing up. I'm not convinced she would have survived it." He paused, considering.

"And even if it is scientifically possible, she still had to be born after the Geneh Laws were imposed. In our earlier interview I mentioned the need for sophisticated equipment, and the logistical problems are not to be ignored. This kind of work is highly technical. You can't do it with a microscope and a pair of tweezers. Working out what to do, or at least working out what to try, can be done with a comprehensive comparative genetic database, a good computer program and a bit of human artistry. But doing it. Well. You are trying to perform delicate genetic manipulations on tiny delicate cells, and you don't have much time to do it in. Successful genetic engineering of this order requires the right sequence of physical and enzymatic steps to insert or replace any number of genes, parts of genes or entire chromosomal segments—and it has to be done right. A slight mismatch and your genes won't work at all. Bad positioning and the result will be a monster, dead or riddled with cancers. And the stem cells won't wait for you forever: you have to do your engineering, patch up the cells and put them back into an environment that makes them happy again as soon as possible. And that's not including the further difficulties in persuading a stem cell to achieve totipotency and from that go on to produce a viable embryo.

"It all requires highly advanced, very expensive robotic technology. There are few suppliers. The equipment has what GenInt would call ethical uses, for some medical procedures and of course for plant and animal genetic modification, which is still allowed at least in some countries and for some purposes. But GenInt has a chokehold on it. Every machine produced is tracked from cradle to grave, all its internal operations are electronically audited, and there are random site checks to boot. For our thief to be a geneh, her makers would somehow need access to such a machine and not only that, do their work without even the machine knowing about it. I don't know how they could do it. Certainly GenInt have gone to great lengths to ensure they can't."

He looked at them, and the scientist was gone again. "But as for why I did not mention the possibility of accelerated development earlier, why would I? It isn't very likely and all it could do is allow you to suspect your thief is a geneh and therefore that I am involved. As your presence here attests. But that's all I can give you. If it's not enough to keep the execrable bastards of GenInt off my back then I'll just have to take my chances. With any luck I can make them a laughing stock and embarrass the politicians enough to cut their funding. If a few of the scum lose their jobs it will have been worth the annoyance."

He added drily, "I suppose there is no point my telling you not to come back without a warrant, given this is the third time you've managed to get in here without one. But don't expect me to be so hospitable next time. James, throw these two out. But gently. We don't want to be accused of police brutality."

Miriam hesitated briefly, considering whether this was the time to raise the issue of their common phrase. *No*, she thought; *he has far too tough a mind to be scared into a confession by something so insubstantial.* Whether he was innocent or guilty, all it would do would be to engender another of his bitingly sarcastic rejoinders; it would make it less likely to get further information out of him now or in the future, not more.

So she stood and said, "Well, thank you for your time, Dr Tagarin. I sincerely apologize for the annoyance we have caused you. Good bye." Stone stood too and they moved to the door, James closely shadowing them as if he expected one of them to leap at Tagarin's throat at any instant.

"Wait," Tagarin said.

They turned and looked inquiringly at him.

"Since you treat me like a suspect when I fail to do your job for you, there is one question you haven't asked. So in an attempt to forestall yet another visit when your slow wits finally work their way around to asking it, I shall ask it for you: are there more of them?"

Miriam and Jack gave each other slightly alarmed looks. Jack replied, "I thought you said she wasn't a geneh anyway?"

"Yes, but you don't really believe me, do you? So do you want to know my thoughts on it, or will you come back later at a less convenient time?" he replied sourly.

"Please."

"Well, consider this. If we allow that our geneh makers somehow acquired the necessary machinery and were able to operate it for several years after GenInt goons started strutting around like the goose-brains they are, do you really think there'd be just one of them? Even if our hypothetical geniuses waited to be sure of the quality of their work, your cat woman is an adult. Producing just one would be a very poor return on a very expensive investment—expensive in dollars, time and personal risk."

Miriam and Jack looked more alarmed.

"On the other hand." He paused. "One thing you said struck me as odd at the time: another thing I neglected to comment on, if you want more things to complain about. She said she'd had an 'eclectic' education. Were those her actual words?"

Miriam thought, and nodded. "Yes. I remember because it's not a word I usually hear. The average criminal certainly doesn't talk about their eclectic tastes in plunder."

"My point exactly. It's an odd choice of word. Why not 'comprehensive', or 'thorough'? Again, we're talking about an expensive investment: if it was me I'd have given her the best education my money could buy. 'Eclectic' sounds more like a random selection of topics without particular rhyme or reason—the kind of thing you find with intelligent people who are self taught.

"Then consider her choice of career, her cynical bitterness, her violence and mental instability. If we take all these things together there is one obvious conclusion. When she was quite young, old enough to fend for herself but still a fairly young child, she was abandoned. Whether something happened to her creators, or they were about to be caught and had to get rid of her fast, we may never know: she might not know herself. But imagine your life if you were a young, intelligent, frightened creature, knowing that the law called you vermin to be killed on sight, having to live off your wits and off the land. How do you think you'd have turned out?" He glared at them as if it was their fault. "I wonder how many laws exist just to keep lawmen in a job, chasing criminals they themselves have created?

"Now get out."

Tagarin watched them go, considering. The older cop was perceptive and suspicious enough, but that young one was positively dangerous. He didn't think he'd seen the end of her.

Chapter 21: Delaney

"Hunter."

"Detective Miriam Hunter?"

"Yes, speaking."

"Ah, good morning detective. My name is Charles Delaney. While I was travelling overseas you attempted to contact me about a theft I reported a few months ago. I am now back. Do you still wish to speak to me?"

Miriam quickly consulted her files. Yes, one of the double victims of a minor burglary followed by a mysterious and much more substantial electronic loss of funds; however he had not been present at any recent events starring the President. Given her lack of luck with the others she was surprised he had chosen to call her back.

"Oh, good afternoon Mr Delaney. Yes, I would very much like to talk to you. Can we arrange a time? I'm happy to come and visit you at your home or office."

"Anything to assist the law. Especially if it might help the law retrieve my property. I think my apartment would be best: there are some things you might like to see. But I am a busy man. I shall now leave you to arrange the details with my AI. I shall see you in due course. Goodbye for now."

Miriam exposed the public face of her and Stone's calendars to Delaney's AI, checked the suggested times and confirmed one. Then she sat back and thought. She called Stone. "Jack, did you notice I just made us an appointment? Good. Yes, this one actually seems to want to talk to us. Maybe we'll learn something!"

"Yeah, maybe," answered Stone. "Stranger things have happened. Just not often."

~~~

Miriam and Stone entered the lobby of a tall apartment block that pointed multiple steel needles at the sky, each clothed in a slightly different color of glass. Miriam had admired it from the street: it was even fancier than her uncle's. It reminded her of illustrations of cities of the future in science fiction stories from her childhood. It appeared the future had arrived, for some at least.

The staff all wore the same uniform and the same expression, hovering between obsequious and haughty, ready to assume the correct form as soon as they were certain of the status of the enquirer. When his system informed him that he was dealing with the police the expression of the man they approached didn't change. Apparently he believed the servants of the law deserved both.

"Hello. We're here to see Mr Delaney," advised Stone. To the unimpressed raised eyebrow he added, "We have an appointment."

"Certainly sir. Let me check. Yes, I see Mr Delaney is expecting you." He frowned slightly, as if hoping that Mr Delaney had not been expecting them so he could have had the pleasure of curling his lip at them. "Please go to the bank of elevators over to your right. Hold a moment. They are now keyed to your identification badges and will take you to the correct floor. Proceed to the entrance door and you will receive further directions from Mr Delaney."

"Thanks pal," said Stone. The man raised his well-practiced eyebrow. "It is my pleasure to serve, sir," he replied as if he meant it.

Miriam and Stone walked briskly to the elevator, which opened at their approach and whisked them upward at an impressive velocity; the initial acceleration almost made them bend their knees. "Welcome to the human stratosphere, Hunter," commented Stone. "Know your place and mind your manners. Mortals such as us dare not offend the sky gods."

They got out and the door to Delaney's apartment, the only entrance visible, opened at their approach. As they entered, the door informed them that Mr Delaney would greet them in the first room to their right.

They went in and Delaney rose to greet them. "Good morning Detectives Hunter, Stone," he said, putting out his hand. "I am pleased the police are still investigating this crime. May I take it that you have fresh leads?"

"I am afraid it is a bit more complicated than that, Mr Delaney," replied Stone. "We don't have fresh evidence in your case but we have found curious similarities with some other cases. But any clue might help us: anything you noticed later or seemed too minor for the attending officers to have put in their report. If we can get enough clues from enough cases we might be able to zero in on our criminals."

Delaney looked a little disappointed. "I see. But no, no. It is a mystery. The accounts that were robbed should have been secure. But one day, the money was simply gone. Neither the bank nor the forensic investigators were able to trace how or where it went. The bank assures me that I withdrew it myself, but even amnesia can't account for that: there is no trace of it happening at my end."

"Were the accounts emptied?" enquired Stone.

"No, and that is the strange thing. One of many strange things, I suppose. Overall I lost about half of the money. But if the thieves could do that, why would they not take it all? It's not as if it was so little I might not have noticed. It is a mystery. It is as if the motive wasn't money, or not entirely money. But then what was it? There have been no further actions taken against me."

They had nothing to say to that. It made no sense to them either.

"What about the earlier crime, Mr Delaney?" asked Miriam. "The physical burglary, where as I recall some jewelry was stolen."

Delaney looked a bit surprised. "That? That is another intriguing mystery, but more an annoyance than anything else. In fact it was almost worth the cost of the jewels for the entertaining dinner conversations it has given birth to since. Are you implying the two are linked? The earlier investigators had some suspicions along those lines but couldn't find any bugs or Trojans that might have given someone access to my accounts. I have a lot of money, Detective: I have high-class systems here. I even had the AI do a full diagnostic, including of itself. The whole system is clean. There is no evidence the crimes are linked except for the coincidence itself."

He added, "There is something new I can tell you about that event, however. I was wondering whether it was worth reporting, given that the crime itself was minor and the new evidence almost certainly useless. But since you are here you might want to see it."

"Certainly! What do you have?"

"Well, one mystery of the case is that the thief somehow interfered with my video surveillance system. Both the insurance company and I took the vendor to task over it, but they appear to have been telling the truth when they said it should have been impossible given the specifications of their system. They said there were theoretical ways it could be done—in their words, there are theoretical ways to do almost anything—but they were aware of no working technology that could do it. Let me show you."

He called up a holographic display. "Here is a video surveillance of this room, right now." Miriam and Stone saw a clear image of themselves and Delaney sitting in the room. "Now here is what the system recorded while the thief was gracing us with his presence." The image became mainly white noise; all that could be discerned among the noise were some vague shapes and movements, nothing identifiable. "As you can see, quite useless."

"However, just the other night we got to discussing this at one of those dinner parties I mentioned. One of my guests was a computer expert specializing in advanced image processing: the kind which astrophysicists and the military are interested in for extracting every last drop of information from their images. She said that a suitable image extraction program might be able to identify and average out any variations from random noise. As you can see from the vague shadows, such variations appear to exist in the recording. So with enough frames of the right kind, in theory even something this noisy might yield sufficient information for a composite image of who was there."

He shrugged. "As I've said, it is an intriguing mystery. So I took her advice. Here is what the system came up with as an image of our thief."

Miriam and Stone stared at the image on his display.

"You're kidding me," murmured Stone.

On the display was now a very grainy image of a person. The thief was wearing a greyish suit much like the one Katlyn had been seen in and a mask covering the face except for the eyes. The sex was uncertain; the person seemed somewhat slender and more likely female than male, but the outlines were too vague to be sure. But two things were sure. The eyes were dark and human, and there was no tail.

Miriam stared at it, confused. It just didn't make any sense. Everything else pointed to the crimes being related and the perpetrator being Katlyn. But this was definitely not Katlyn. It looked more like a ninja.

"Mr Delaney," said Miriam hoarsely. "This image. Do you know if any assumptions were made, such as height or sex, to make the image cleanup easier? Or is it a true unbiased extraction? What I mean is, say the thief had been wearing something odd, like a Viking helmet or something—would the system have shown it or simply not seen it because it wasn't expecting it?"

Delaney looked at her curiously. "That question makes me wonder what you know that you aren't telling me." He paused, inviting an answer, but neither Miriam nor Stone replied. He sighed. "Ah, the police! How you like to have your secrets. But no matter, I want this criminal caught and if you think not revealing evidence will help you, then I suppose I will give you the benefit of the doubt. No, it is a true unbiased image. This is what the thief looked like, as far as you can tell anything. But it is of no use for identification even if we had the thief in our hands for a direct comparison. Certainly no use in court. I suppose it might exclude certain suspects if they are especially tall, short or fat, but that's about it."

"May we take a copy of the video and the composite image?" asked Miriam.

"Of course. If you can think you can do better with it, be my guests. Here."

"Thank you. Oh. Do you mind if I ask you a more personal question? I assure you it is related to the case, though I am not in a position to tell you more."

"More secrets? Well, you can ask."

"Are you a supporter of President Felton? I don't mean did you vote for her, I mean have you been involved more directly, say in her campaigns or fundraising?"

Delaney shot her a sharp glance. "I would say that is none of your business," he said in a tone as sharp as his glance. He thought a moment then continued, "Hmmm. Though I suppose it is a matter of public record, even if you'd probably have to dig to find it. Yes, I was a young firebrand once, believe it or not. I was an admirer of hers in the early years, involved in her campaign against the genehs. And while I have done well in business myself I did come from a wealthy family. So not only did I work for her organization, I donated a substantial amount of money to her cause."

Miriam stared at him. What was going on? As one coincidence

crumbled another firmed up. Maybe the whole thing was a mirage after all and she had been fooled by phantoms. Except for the hard physical fact of Katlyn herself. She noticed Delaney looking at her curiously and realized she was staring. "Oh. I see. Thank you Mr Delaney, that is very interesting."

Perhaps he misunderstood her stare, for he added, "Please understand, though. The genetic engineers went too far with their attempts to 'improve' our species: there is a limit to how much man should impose his ignorant power upon nature. If you read history, you will learn how rarely such power comes with the wisdom to wield it for good. But Ms Felton herself went too far in her zeal. A huge, almost unaccountable organization to police the world, with the power of life and death, the power to kill a geneh without having to first prove its danger? No. I could not support that. I do not entirely regret those early years, because something had to be done; but I do regret how it turned out. So when I broke with her organization I retained a lot of information that would embarrass the President and GenInt if I published it. I have no intention of doing so, but I might if they decide to whitewash history or worse, increase their power above what they have already taken."

Miriam caught herself staring at him again. "Where is that information now?" she asked, throat suddenly dry.

He gave her a perceptive glance. "Ah, I see where you are going. Interesting. Your questions lift one corner of the shroud over your secrets. But don't worry. Yes, the information is stored in my computer system. But the files are well encrypted, and owing to their sensitivity that is one of the things I checked specifically after my money was stolen. They were not accessed let alone copied. Either our criminal gang is not as omnipotent as we fear, or they were not interested in such dirt. I suppose we can take comfort from either possibility."

He looked at them to see if they had a response. After a few seconds of silence he asked, "Is there anything else?"

"No, not at the moment," replied Stone, rising from his chair. "If we find anything else out, we'll be sure to let you know. Thanks for seeing us, you have been most helpful."

~~~

Miriam and Stone were silent in the lift going down, silent in the lobby, silent as Stone began to drive back to the station. Finally he said what was on both their minds.

"What the hell?"

Miriam grimaced. "What the hell, yes," she replied. "When he said he had an image I wondered how the hell he thought it wasn't worth reporting—then we see that all he has is a fuzzy picture of Joe Average. If we hadn't met Katlyn I'd think the whole thing was just some horrid practical joke!"

"'We?'" quoted Stone quietly.

Miriam looked at him, startled. "Yes, we! You were there too! God, she kicked you into a wall!"

Stone gave her a hard look. "No, Miriam. I was there, but what did I actually see? Someone fast and strong, sure. With something that looked like a tail, something that looked like reflective golden eyes. But nothing certain, nothing close up for more than half a second. Less, frankly, than what we saw in that video when all this started. For all I know, it could have been a guy in a monkey suit like the doc said in our first interview. The only evidence we have that our thief is anything out of the ordinary except in skill are a few seconds of grainy video and a few glimpses by me in a gloomy warehouse. All the rest is just you."

He let her digest that.

"But... but...." she said in a shrinking voice, "What are you saying? You think I imagined the whole thing? Made it all up?!"

He looked at her again. She felt like a suspect pinned by his gaze. But he looked away and replied, "No. No, I don't think that. You're not the type—either of them. But it's not me you have to worry about. If some higher-ups start wondering, how are you going to defend yourself? If you were reading this in a report rather than having experienced it yourself, what would *you* think is most likely: that there's a real live geneh running around stealing rich guys' loose change, contrary to the well-reasoned opinion of an expert in the field—or that some rookie cop stuck in a back room is trying to make a name or adventure for herself out of a wish or a lie? Creating an exciting case out of some loose correlations and a hyperactive imagination—or even making it up deliberately?"

"But it happened!"

He snorted. "The truth has never been much of a defense if you can't prove it, kid. Or even if you can prove it. Ask Galileo."

"But we can't just stop now! Can we?"

Stone considered. "Well, not without consequences. But you could go to the Chief all shy and shamefaced, say maybe the stress influenced your memory—at least I can confirm that you were handcuffed to a post and beaten up—tell him that in the light of day and new evidence you're no longer so sure. Try to back out of it gracefully. There'd be some disciplinary action for wasting everyone's time and it'll be a while before they let you out on the street again, but you'd keep your job at least."

Miriam looked at him, horrified. "I can't do that! It would be a lie, not to mention dereliction of duty! Katlyn is out there, doing God knows what for God knows why!"

Stone gave her a pitying look. "Well, you'd better hope you or someone catches her then. And if it isn't you, someone who doesn't just make her disappear without a trace."

CHAPTER 22: SIMON

Simon was content. He had no sex, but he was addressed as Simon and referred to as "he", so that is what he was. He was not truly conscious, and his contentment was more like that of a bee happily ensconced in a meadow of flowers than that of a man. But contentment was the best word for it. When things were as they should be, his world felt smooth, uncomplicated and as it should be. Occasional happiness was also granted to him when he achieved a particularly good outcome; but contentment was what he sought above even happiness. Problems made him anxious, and he was not content until all problems were solved.

Simon did not know the date. Had you asked him he would have told you the date and the time to the second. But time meant nothing to him in himself. He lived in the perpetual present. He remembered the past if he had to, consulted his calendar of events when required, and predicted the future if asked: but contentment in the present was his world, or his world as it should be. However in human terms the date corresponded to only a few weeks into Miriam Hunter's career.

There was a ripple in Simon's awareness and he knew that a door had opened into his domain. This did not make him anxious. There was no pattern to the opening or closing of doors that would make one stand out above the others. But it made him curious, as the time did not match the expected return of his master nor any scheduled visits by cleaners or others authorized to enter in his absence. He began to become anxious when the image of the visitor did not match any in his working memory. His anxiety increased at the odd behavior of his visitor, which did not precisely correlate with any actions he understood. While there were many things humans did that he did not understand, their performance by a stranger was guaranteed to cause him anxiety.

Simon was also capable of fear, or some analogue of fear. He had never experienced it, for nothing worthy of fear had ever happened to him since his awakening. He now knew fear, or the beginning of fear, and knew it was worse than anxiety. The fear stemmed from his broadening search for the identity of his visitor: for it proved worse than merely an unfamiliar human. While it stood and walked and acted like a human, it was not one. He had seen things that were not human before and they had not worried him, for they fit into the category of "pet" or "bird" and, like him, had their own place in the world. But what this thing was lay outside his knowledge entirely.

Simon's automatic response to fear was to activate alarms and calls to security guards and police, but for a moment he paused, suddenly unsure whether that was the right thing to do. The uncertainty became a subliminal shiver that shifted his world, and he was no longer afraid. He might have been puzzled how he could be afraid one moment but not even anxious the next; but he could not imagine why he would have been anxious or why he would think to question the change. The change was the most natural thing in the world, for it had returned him to contentment, which meant it was good.

So Simon went about his business while his visitor went about hers, and they were both content.

It happened that his master was far more than content at that moment, being happily ensconced in the bedroom, arms and other parts of his current mistress. But that changed shortly after he returned home and noticed a door open that shouldn't have been, and from there went on to discover a few gems missing from his collection. The violation of his personal domain was much worse than the material value of the gems, but the mystery was even greater than the violation. For understandably he was angry and asked Simon what the hell had happened. But Simon had no recollection of any event that could have caused it.

That was surely impossible.

An even more impossible thing was that Simon had recollections up to a certain point and recollections after a later point, but nothing in between, as if his existence had been suspended. How the thief or thieves had achieved this was unknown, but the investigators did find mysterious drillings from outside toward the internal wiring, and could only conclude that Simon's systems had been knocked out by some kind of overpowering electronic pulse from a device long gone. It was hard, sometimes, to keep up with the imaginative uses of technology that the criminal element was inventing these days. Fortunately for him, the investigators opined, it was probably just some bright young electrical engineer looking for excitement and some prize to prove he had done it: a delinquent rather than a serious criminal. For the nature of the crime was as minor as it was imaginative: more indicative of a young buck tossing his new grown antlers to impress his peers than a professional thief.

Simon's master was rather more outraged some weeks later when Simon relayed certain demands to him. Simon could not tell him where the demands came from. They required his master to transfer a sizeable quantity of his wealth to various untraceable locations, in return for silence about numerous inconvenient historical facts that the master would not like revealed. Simon might have done the transfer himself, except that his master was unusually paranoid and Simon's access to money was limited to the small accounts required for managing the household.

The master raged, but paid. The criminals were good to their word and he never heard from them again. His life returned to its usual range of emotional states, except for one persistent thorn of unavenged outrage; Simon returned to his usual contentment too, except for the discomfiting mystery of his missing hour.

Simon's master dearly desired the capture and punishment of his tormentors, for he was not a forgiving man. But there were reasons he had paid for their silence. He would like them caught, but without the police casting any more of their attention in his own direction.

Then one day he had a call from a detective looking more into the theft of his jewels. He had listened long enough to learn the essence of her interest before sending her on her way with a pungency of expression that should have made her ears smoke. But while one could say many things about this man, as indeed his enemies had, none would say he lacked a keen intelligence. He deduced that the crime must be wider than himself; he then thought about the implications of that interesting deduction. If the criminals had found some of his secrets perhaps they had found others. While they had not mentioned any such additional embarrassments, perhaps that was not because they hadn't found them but worse, because they had darker plans for them.

In that case there were people who might be even keener than he to see the gang confounded before any such plans could bear fruit. Those people had not only the motive but also the power to apply pressure, as discrete as it was formidable, on the police. Pressure to continue their investigation to its desired conclusion. He bared his teeth in a smile as cheerful as it was malicious, and sent messages out through his network. He did not doubt that they would take some time to act, but he had long since learnt that vengeance and patience were lovers. But nor did he doubt that they would know they had to act. Power did not come to people who lacked the desire to preserve it or the caution to nullify all potential threats to it. If it did they did not hold it long.

Chapter 23: Geoff

At that moment half a world away, the *Seabitz* cut closer to a coral reef, its blue spinnaker billowed by the tangy breeze. At its helm, Geoff ignored his ultimate target, a palm-covered jewel of a sandy island in a tranquil lagoon, to concentrate on the more immediate and dangerous target of the much less tranquil break in the reef. When he judged the moment was right, he dropped the spinnaker and turned hard left, cutting across at a sharp angle and shooting through the gap into the calm waters beyond.

The girls whooped in appreciation and he turned and bowed with a grin. Then he trimmed the sails to head the yacht toward the beach at a more leisurely pace. He glanced over the side into the crystal water, beneath which he could see magnificent fish-filled corals, and smiled. He would never get tired of this, he thought. He liked tranquility as much as the next man; excitement somewhat more. He had both in abundance.

He looked at the island, and not for the first time wondered if he had made the right choice. It had been one of the few times in his life when he had chosen safety over the excitement of danger. That was not quite true: he had merely chosen a lesser danger. Had he chosen differently he might now have owned an island like this. But, he reminded himself, he might have lost everything instead. The software might not have worked; he might have been caught; in any event he would have had a lot of hard work ahead of him. Instead for possibly the first time in his life he had chosen the easy way out. But it had been a good bargain. He might not have his own island, but would he really want one? With *Seabitz* and its supporting bank account, he had his choice of any island on the globe.

He looked back at the girls and smiled at them; Alice caught his eye and toasted him with a wink. He grinned, both to her and himself. He might have his choice of any island but no man could have his choice of any woman. But it was a pleasant fact of reality that there were more than enough beautiful young women in the world who were delighted with what he offered: free accommodation on a luxury sailing boat visiting any number of interesting and exotic locations, in return for very little: a little cooking, a little cleaning and rather more than a little sex. There was little enough work to do when most of the ship's functions were automated and even more could be when Geoff just wanted to cruise without the challenge of running the helm. And he had sufficient self-esteem to regard the sex as part of their benefits rather than part of the cost.

Of course they often asked where his money had come from. Software, he would say with a mysterious smile, offering no details; hinting at secret government contracts and confidentiality clauses if pressed. Besides, the lack of detail added to his glamor, or that was how he saw it. Truth be told, beyond normal curiosity and the thrill of hinted danger, the girls didn't really care. They knew they had a good deal and there was more than enough glamor in the lifestyle he loaned them. He would have had to be a lot poorer, a lot meaner or a lot uglier for that to change.

He thought back to the day that had changed his life. In a way that day had merely tied what went before it to what came after, but it was the pivot. He had been a hacker once, stalking the dark byways of the net in various questionable or outright illegal activities. Then he had overreached and been caught; perhaps that is what had taught him caution. But many security firms liked hackers. Like the first people who had domesticated wild animals, they thought that if they could tame these dangerous creatures their powers could be theirs to command.

Often they were right. Hackers, like everybody else, grew older and started to value what they had more than the excitements of youthful passions. Geoff himself had served a little jail time, a little community service, before being headhunted by an innovative software company with fingers in a lot of security-related pies. And he had been happy to accept. The work was interesting, the pay was good, and he got to do what he was good at and loved without having to look over his shoulder. He was loyal to his employer. As loyal as, say, a cat to its owner.

But his employer was not the only entity that watched for rogue talent. He had been approached obliquely by another, whose name he never knew but whose honesty, at least in his dealings with Geoff, had been demonstrated. He was not asked to do anything outrageous or even courageous, just watch and wait and report anything with the right combination of cutting edge technology and intriguing applications. And like a cat accepting milk from a neighbor he did so with a clear conscience. Some might have argued that, like the cat, it was clear because there was nothing there.

His chance came when some programmers at his workplace had a little too much to drink after suffering a little too much indignity at the hands of the project they were working on. To their credit their animated discussion was discrete and oblique. But their voices were just a touch too loud and Geoff's interest, hearing and intelligence a touch too acute. He connected the dots between their hints, boasts and complaints, and the resulting picture beckoned him.

He was good at what he did. He knew he could help someone with the right resources to steal this gem and nobody would know. He toyed with the idea of stealing it for himself, but in the end wisdom won out over greed. Not that greed could complain too much: if he played his cards right he would get all he could want and let someone else take all the risks, or at least all the risks after the initial theft.

The problem with hiring extreme talent in the same package as less extreme ethics is in exploiting the former while protecting oneself from the latter. His employers believed they had done so, but their cleverness would prove not quite a match for Geoff's: a fact they would be blissfully unaware of for a long time. What Geoff had done had certainly been risky, but he had carefully and over a long time planted traps and back doors in preparation for such an opportunity. Imagining your superiority over your peers was an occupational hazard amongst hackers, but in Geoff's case he got away with it because it happened to be correct.

This particular piece of malfeasance required more than hacking, as a certain degree of more traditional burglary would be needed: another reason why Geoff decided not to do it alone. And so it happened that after a period of elaborate courtship with his shadowy accomplice, in which both were persuaded that the other would not betray them, the item was skillfully acquired without any unfortunate consequences. To either of them, anyway.

Geoff had had friends and lovers in his old life, but none he felt more than a twinge of regret at leaving behind. Little more, indeed, than people in more regular employment suffered when they moved across a continent to another office. So he disappeared from that life into a new one, with a new identity, a new boat and a greatly expanded bank account, which he put to work earning an honest living for him on the share market. And now here he was, approaching yet another piece of sunny paradise and looking forward to an idyllic afternoon filled with most of the pleasures life can provide.

Everything in the world was connected, he knew. Every action changed something, which changed something else, and so on ad infinitum through space and time. He watched the wake of his boat escaping the atoll and mingling with the ocean waves and wondered how many small lives that subtle change in wave patterns would affect. He thought how if he had not been caught that day so long ago he would not have worked for the security company; he would not have had the opportunity he had grasped; he would not be here; that coral trout they had caught this morning would still be alive; the prey it was to have eaten would now be dead instead. He wondered what other effects that theft had had, what lives had been rocked by the ripples of causality spreading out from it. He had seen nothing on the news feeds that indicated the software had ever been used. Perhaps it had failed. Perhaps his mysterious partner was more cautious or subtle than he knew—or dead. He wondered if he would ever know.

Then one of the girls slipped up behind him and entwined her arm around his waist, playfully pressing her hip against his. He looked down at her with a smile, and turned his mind to more immediate interests.

CHAPTER 24: RAMOS

Gil Ramos jogged through the park, enjoying the cool Sunday morning air. He knew he was getting older and was determined to keep its attendant decay at bay as long as possible. He had always enjoyed physical exercise so this policy came naturally to him. And the cool air flowing through his hair acted as a cool breeze flowing through his mind, sweeping away the detritus and hopefully bringing clarity. He thought too much during his working week. Time spent in simple physical activity was not wasted, he knew. Sometimes spending time not thinking could be just as important as the thinking itself.

So was relaxing. His favorite bench was empty and he sat on it, stretching his arms and legs. It overlooked a lake surrounded by trees, and was far enough from the road that the sounds of traffic were more gentle murmur than intrusion. The sun was low in the sky and he closed his eyes, enjoying its warmth on his face and the musical accompaniment of the birds twittering about their business.

As usual, with relaxation his thoughts returned, but he did not mind. He did not push them or even guide them; he just let them wander where they would. He knew if he did not attempt to lead them they might lead him to unexplored places instead.

He was not surprised that the first thought to announce itself concerned what to do about Trainee Detective Hunter. It had been a week since she and Detective Stone had returned from their meeting with one of the victims, Delaney. They had gone out to meet him hoping that what he had to say would break something open in their case; instead he had shown them something that had turned their case upside down and tipped it over the floor.

He had told Hunter that he would have to think about where to go next but she was not to work more on the mysterious burglaries until then. He had even told her to suspend her watch routines from the AI. AIs were complicated, this one more than usual. For all anyone knew, by overlaying such priorities she was distorting its analyses and causing spurious findings. He smiled humorlessly. At least she had learned to take such restrictions meekly, in word if not in the flash of her eyes.

The question was: what else had she learned?

He sighed to the sun, which serenely ignored him. He knew Stone hadn't liked her at first, but he seemed to have warmed to her since then. He knew that Stone's dislike had not merely been the envy of a man nearing the end of his career who saw someone just starting out on hers, but stemmed from his experience of rookies thinking they were better than they were. And for all that Stone would not go out of his way to damage a comrade he was too professional to give sloppiness a pass. If Gil would have trusted anyone to pass harsh judgment on Hunter if she deserved it, it was Stone. Yet he had ignored several opportunities Ramos had opened to the idea that perhaps Hunter had been mistaken or worse.

Yet, yet... here was a case where the little evidence they had did not support the path Hunter had followed—and worse, did not match the evidence she alone had reported. He groaned and stretched. The girl had talent, nobody could deny that, but she was a bit rough around the edges: a bit too fast to jump to conclusions, a bit too slow to heed counsel. It sounded just like the rookie disease Stone had feared: except Stone himself was supporting her, if cautiously.

But facts were facts, and the facts were too thin. Much as he liked to encourage his people to push their personal envelopes, perhaps in this case she had pushed through it and fallen out of her depth. It would be best to send her back to her original job instead of wasting time on minor if mysterious robberies; to return to letting the AI lead her rather than vice versa. Even if it proved to be a mistake, perhaps the discipline would make her a better cop in the long run.

That decision made, he relaxed to simply enjoy the rising morning and wait for any further thoughts to appear. But then he heard the rustling of clothing and the groan of the bench as people sat down on either side of him, uncomfortably close. He opened his eyes, surprised at such a double intrusion into his personal space.

Two men had joined him, both wearing dark suits and darker glasses, showing neither friendliness nor hostility. One of them flashed a badge at him; long enough for him to tell it was Secret Service, not quite long enough to catch the owner's name.

"Chief Ramos?" he enquired politely.

Ramos nodded.

"Would you come with us, sir? We won't take up too much of your time."

"And if I refuse?"

The man just looked at him as if the question did not belong in this reality.

Ramos sighed and rose. "OK. I'm all for inter-service cooperation. And I have to admit I'm curious."

A long dark Tesla electric limousine was waiting by the roadside. As he approached, the door opened and he slipped into the seat. The two agents deposited themselves elsewhere in the vehicle and it accelerated rapidly and silently into the light traffic.

"Good morning, Chief Ramos," said the man beside him. "Drink? Cigar?" he offered, pointing to a well-stocked bar and a humidor of mahogany inlaid with mother of pearl.

Ramos hesitated then thought, *What the hell. If the Secret Service is going to abduct me, I might as well take advantage of their hospitality budget.* "Sure," he said, flipping open the humidor and selecting a Cuban cigar. "Whiskey on the rocks, thanks."

The man silently poured the drink and handed it to him, then sat back in the luxurious seat, puffing his own cigar.

Ramos just waited.

"You seem remarkably incurious for a police officer, Chief Ramos."

"Perhaps I am simply experienced at interrogations."

The man smiled. "Is that what you think this is? No, this is just a friendly chat. Making sure you know what you need to know."

"Perhaps then you should tell me. Who are you?"

"Smith will do. Now, we understand that your department has been investigating an unusual cluster of burglaries. Are you close to a resolution?"

Ramos raised an eyebrow. "And what is your interest in the case? It seems a little out of your jurisdiction."

Smith sighed. "I think you have some idea about that. But we can continue fencing for hours and still end up at the same point. So all right, let's go straight to that point. We have learned that they might be more than simple burglaries, that certain classified information might have been obtained which could be used against the President."

"So the President sent you to do what, Smith? Are you telling me she has done something wrong and wants to cover it up?" He blew a smoke ring past Smith's ear: distant enough to not be an insult but close enough to show he was thinking an insult might become appropriate.

"I would not say the President sent me, no. It is better that the President is not involved. Think of this rather as an attempt to forestall possible problems. We do not know for sure that these criminals have any information they can use or what they might do with it. But we certainly don't want the President harmed by lies and scandals, or have her attention to serving our country compromised by threats of blackmail."

"So you went to this trouble just to tell me to catch these people? Do you think I play golf all day?"

"Oh, I am sure you are conscientious and good at your job," said Smith. "If I wasn't I would be having this conversation with someone else. Possibly your successor," he added, tapping his ash into a tray. "No. It is just that I know you have many crimes to solve, many clamoring voices competing for your attention. It would be easy for a crime that not only seems minor but also proves difficult to solve to be lost in the crowd. We know about priorities. We just wish to impress on you the importance of this one. To ensure you give the investigation more weight than you otherwise might. Not because we know what these people are up to—but because we don't."

"I see. And can you give me anything besides encouragement? Can you reveal any clues? Provide us any material assistance? Grease any legal wheels? Say, if we need a warrant?"

Smith spread his hands. "I'm afraid that would be most improper. The President cannot be seen to be involved. Surely you understand."

"And if my actual superiors wonder why I continue to devote resources to such an unpromising case? What then?"

"Ah. I can give you that. You have no need to worry about it. If any of your superiors start to interfere and you cannot persuade them of the wider importance of the case, simply send their name to the address you now have. But do not mention this conversation to anyone. It never happened. It might be uncomfortable if you talk about it."

Ramos sat back silently, puffing the remnants of his cigar. *Uncomfortable for whom?* he wondered. He had a feeling any discomfort wouldn't be Smith's.

"Do we understand each other?" asked Smith.

Ramos stabbed out his cigar. "Sure. I'll put my best team on it. Don't hold your breath: as you seem to know, clues in this case are thin on the ground. But I can assure you it won't be forgotten."

Smith inclined his head and tapped on the glass behind the driver. A few minutes later the vehicle glided to a stop where it had picked Ramos up. He got out and when the door closed behind him he turned to gaze back at the darkened windows. The window slid down and Smith leaned over to it. "Well, good day, Chief Ramos. Enjoy the rest of your morning." Before Ramos could reply, the window closed and the limousine sped away.

Ramos stood looking after it until it vanished around a bend, then walked slowly back into the park. *I guess I won't be taking Stone and Hunter off the case after all*, he thought grimly. *Lucky them.*

CHAPTER 25: LEAGUE

"So how is your secret case going, oh International Lady of Mystery? How many heads of foreign states have you had to seduce this week in the service of our country?"

Miriam and Amaro were having dinner at a high class Chinese restaurant. Chinese was not Miriam's favorite cuisine, though she enjoyed it as a different taste on occasion. But Darian had recommended this restaurant as something special and they had decided to give it a try. She sipped some chilled Sauvignon Blanc wine, smiled at the wine and made a face at his question.

"Oh, you know how it is, one so easily loses track of the heads of state one has slept with. But as for the case, I wish I knew. The more we investigate, the more the evidence builds up and goes away, all at the same time. I'm starting to think the whole thing is a mirage, some figment of the Artful Idiot's imagination that has fooled me into misinterpreting everything to fit into its delusions. I'm lucky my boss doesn't believe I made the whole thing up myself. I thought he did for a while, but he seems to have decided to give me the benefit of the doubt for now. But sometimes even I wonder if I didn't dream it all."

"Ah, you tease. You know I love a mystery, and here you are determined to weave the mystery even thicker while dropping not a single clue as to its nature. I believe you wish to tantalize me with this one forever! Can you tell me nothing else? Perhaps this humble knight may be able to offer an insight, no matter how poor?"

Miriam smiled and shook her head. "Sorry Amaro. Even though it is looking more and more like a waste of time I'm still not allowed to talk about it." She looked into the distance with a slight frown and added, "Even more so now, apparently. I suppose too many sensitivities, especially if we're wrong—in either direction. I'm likely to get into enough trouble just being in the middle of it, let alone telling anyone about it."

Then she turned back to him and said cheerfully, "Anyway, maybe I like to keep you wriggling on my hook. Keep you honest."

"The lady is so cruel. But fear not, I am happy to wriggle on your hook for as long as you wish," he replied with a smile. "It is a hook of many delights. It pierces sharply, but one does not wish it to let go."

They returned to their food. Indulging their shared preference for the spicy, they had been favoring the hot end of the establishment's menu. At the moment they were savoring a Szechuan curry that was like nothing Miriam had tasted before: not fiery like Thai, but popping and rushing in a bubbly tingle along her tongue.

She looked at Amaro and he returned her glance with a smile. She still couldn't quite shake the suspicion that she shouldn't trust him; that his charm was just a shell beneath which lurked something dangerous. But he was irresistible. *He is like a roller coaster,* she thought. *The danger and fear just makes you want to go along for the ride, screaming with delight the whole way. Because for all the fear, you don't believe there is any real danger.*

She smiled at him, for now just lost in the moment. "So what about you, Amaro? Did anything exciting happen in your work today?"

"My lady, my days must be boring compared to the life of a top detective working on national secrets! In fact I am afraid—they are. It appears the genetic engineers and other villains are being very law abiding at present, at least in my small corner of the nation. Perhaps they have heard of my powers, and fear keeps their ambitions subdued?"

Miriam laughed. "Confusion keeps them bamboozled, more likely!"

"Ah, you mock me, fair maiden! Still, my work is not entirely boring. Why, just the other day one of the laboratory scientists sent the place into an uproar." He then regaled her with a tale of rolling mistakes that soon had Miriam in stitches. "Sometimes I wonder what further scientific advances will be possible, with the quality of some of the scientists these days," he concluded.

He smiled at Miriam and she smiled back, open to him. If the secret of comedy is timing, he thought to himself, then the secret of anecdotes is that the timing doesn't matter: the event he described had happened before he met her. He lifted his glass. "To a delightful dinner, a delightful wine, and a delightful lady," he said. She chinked her glass against his and they continued to talk, about everything and nothing, as lovers do.

"By the way, I hope you are free next Saturday night," Amaro said casually after a pause.

"Saturday? Saturday? Let me think. Oh, I recall I have several options that night. Some even involve well-endowed Heads of State who apparently need seducing in the national interest. I think you will have to make a good offer if you wish to tempt me away from them."

"I happen to have obtained rare and expensive tickets to a fancy dress ball. A friend of mine offered me the tickets when something came up so he couldn't go himself."

"Sounds like fun. What's the occasion?"

"It is the Annual Ball of the Stem Cell League. Perhaps more down my alley than yours, but I hear that the food, wine and music are superlative. And one can meet all kinds of fascinating people," he added.

"The Stem Cell League?" Miriam asked, surprised at the coincidence. "Who are they?"

"I don't know that much about them. But I do know they are an association of people who owe their lives to stem cell therapies. They were either cured themselves or they are the children of people who would never have lived to have children otherwise. You know that stem cell therapies have had their controversies and still do: the League is basically a lobby group which raises money and generates publicity in favor of stem cell research and applications. The beneficiaries of science giving something back to the science. Rare but admirable."

"As it turns out, that does interest me. Sir Knight, I shall be happy to accept your kind offer. The Heads of State will have to thrust their mighty ambitions elsewhere."

"Excellent! By the way, don't bother trying to work out what to wear. In anticipation of your acceptance I have already acquired our costumes," he said with a mysterious smile. "Yours goes perfectly with mine, and I am sure you will look quite ravishing in it. In fact just thinking about it is doing something intriguing to one of your favorite parts of my anatomy."

Miriam smiled. "Well in that case I think I can forgive your presumption. And as for your anatomy, I am not sure whether you are talking about your ego or something else." She sighed. "I suppose I shall have to investigate further. For science."

CHAPTER 26: DANCE

Miriam entered the ballroom on Amaro's arm, escorted like the lady of a gentleman of old. Amaro hadn't oversold the event: it looked like a glittering affair.

Miriam had gasped when Amaro had unveiled her costume. She had half expected him to come as a Knight with her as his Lady; and in a way he had but with a modern twist. He struck quite the figure as Batman and for her he had chosen a form-hugging black Catwoman suit. Again she was startled at the coincidence, but when she had glanced at Amaro she could see not even a shadow of motive beyond the obvious.

They were sipping champagne and chatting cheerfully with a group of people when the crowd in her line of sight parted briefly and she caught a glimpse of a large man who looked familiar; but she couldn't quite place him before the crowd closed and he was lost from view and concern.

Amaro had been right about the music and dancing too. She was getting happily exhausted by it and had begged off the next dance. She was now standing outside, leaning back on the balcony with her eyes closed, just enjoying the caress of the cool evening air. Amaro had gone to get them both a drink. The music of a gentle waltz started up inside and she leant back further into space, enjoying the sensory counterpoint of the breeze on her skin and the music in her ears.

"May I have the pleasure of this dance?" asked a male voice in front of her. Her eyes popped open in surprise and she was startled at the sight of a tall man standing just four feet in front of her: she had not heard him approach. He was dressed in deep black set off by high boots and a long black cape with red velvet lining, his face hidden by a Venetian mask. It made him look powerful and vaguely threatening. Then he raised his mask.

"Oh! Dr Tagarin! Why... I would be honored."

She held out her hand to him. He bowed his head and took her hand, then led her into the room. Pulling gently on her hand he seamlessly drew her into the waltz.

Miriam was intrigued by the difference between his dance style and Amaro's. Where Amaro was flamboyant and exciting, his partner an independent foil to his own flair, Tagarin was fluid and rhythmic, leading with a gentle but firm hand, his partner an extension of himself. Perhaps a man's dance style reflected his soul, Miriam thought. In that case, Tagarin was a man who knew what he wanted and why he wanted it; a man used to command. She felt herself rebelling, as she always had if another person assumed the right to command her. She did not resist him, but began to impose her own variations on his leading; he had to either accept it or have their dance lose its grace.

He noticed. He smiled faintly and said ambiguously, "So you like to dance, Ms Hunter? I thought you would."

With that he imposed his will again, whirling her in a long turn. Then he drew her close and speared her with his black gaze. "Now, Ms Hunter, how am I to interpret your presence here? I sincerely hope this is not harassment. That you have some interest in stem cell research beyond the mythical creature you pursue."

She returned his gaze openly. "Oh, no, Doctor. I assure you I didn't expect to see you here. Stem cell science is certainly interesting but the venue is a coincidence: I'm only here because a friend invited me."

"Really? Then how do you account for your costume—fetching as it is? It seems an even more remarkable coincidence, wouldn't you agree?"

"Is this why you asked me to dance? To interrogate me?"

"I admit that is true, in part."

"What is the other part?"

He smiled. "Why Ms Hunter, don't be so modest. What man would not want to dance with an attractive woman like you? And while grilling you is on the menu if you deserve it, I think you are worth getting to know a little better regardless. However, need I point out that you have avoided my question?"

"Sorry. Yes, I can see how it looks suspicious. But I didn't choose the costume either; my friend chose that as well simply to match his, and he knows nothing about the case. You don't need to worry: I'm not working tonight. But why are you here? I had the impression you had become something of a recluse. A ball is the last place I expected to find you."

"I get invited every year. I don't often come but sometimes even I crave some lights and glamor, and this is one of the few places where I am assured of a welcome. Many of the people here are my children, in a sense. I suggest you take advantage of the evening, Ms Hunter. Perhaps you will learn that we genetic engineers don't spend all our time creating monsters. As with most science, improving human life is its real purpose. Look around you if you want proof of what good it can do. Whatever life and happiness you see here would not exist without it."

"I am sure that is true. I am not your enemy, Dr Tagarin. At least that is not my intent."

"In that case let us be friends at least for these few minutes, and just enjoy the rest of this dance together."

A short time later Miriam was quietly enjoying the dance when she felt the nature of Tagarin's hold on her change; it became softer and more intimate. It was not improperly so, but it surprised her and she glanced up at Tagarin's face. His eyes were closed and he wore a faint smile, and she realized that he had forgotten her: in his mind he was dancing with someone else. From the nature of his smile Miriam could tell that whoever she was, was long in the past and long lost, and she wondered what tragedy had separated them. She decided not to intrude, to remain the surrogate for his lost love. In their daytime meetings she had unearthed enough past pain; if she could bring back past happiness she would not deny him.

The music began to wind down and Tagarin opened his eyes. She saw him briefly regard the woman in his arms openly, with affection. Then he recognized her, remembered the full reality of the present and the shutters closed once more. He looked around and said with a self-mocking smile, "I'm sorry Ms Hunter, I do believe I have taken up too much of your time. I see a young man over where I met you, holding two glasses and looking in our direction. It is time I returned you to him."

With that, he swirled her to the edge of the dance floor and let her go as seamlessly as he had gathered her into the dance. He bowed graciously and said, "Well, thank you for the dance, Ms Hunter. Do enjoy the rest of your evening." She noticed that for once he gave her no bitterness or contempt. He too seemed content to keep this evening insulated from their daytime enmity.

"Thank you, Dr Tagarin. But may I introduce you to my friend? He is a geneticist and I am sure he would be honored to meet you."

Tagarin gave her a sharp glance but inclined his head in assent. He followed her to where Amaro stood, watching them approach with a mocking grin.

"Ah, the curse of escorting a beautiful woman!" he said, handing Miriam her glass. "Like an electric charge, if left alone she soon gathers company!"

"Amaro, this is Dr Tagarin. Dr Tagarin, this charming rogue is Senor Moreno."

Tagarin did not offer his hand; he merely inclined his head briefly and said, "Good evening, Senor."

Amaro raised an eyebrow. "Dr Tagarin? Could that be *the* Tagarin, the famous genetic engineer?"

Tagarin nodded curtly. "More infamous than famous, I fear, though happily the people in this gathering care more for the latter. And what about you, young man? What is your interest in regenerative cell therapies?"

"I am afraid that it is all somewhat beyond me, Doctor, though I admire those for whom it is not. My own work in genetics is more investigative and forensic than in developing wonder treatments. It is my good fortune to be here because a friend of mine could not come so he gave me his tickets. Though I fear his having them was not a mark of his credentials either, but more a perk of his office."

"But our other common factor is Miriam here," he continued, "a far more intriguing subject than I am. She asserts she is a humble apprentice detective, yet the more time I spend with her the more mysterious she becomes. Not only is she entangled in cases so secret she cannot talk about them, I now find her numbering eminent scientists among her friends. How do you happen to know this dangerous lady, sir? Or is it just the cool evening breeze that introduced you?"

Miriam glanced somewhat nervously at Tagarin, but he was no

more interested in revelations than she was and simply replied, "Oh, nothing so dramatic I'm afraid. I have occasionally helped the police with some technical aspects of genetics and we've run into each other a couple of times."

"Very public-spirited of you, Doctor," commented Amaro.

"An efficient police force is in all our interests, wouldn't you say?" he replied, glancing pointedly at Miriam. "Besides, it is only the more difficult and therefore interesting questions I am sought for. But I am afraid that confidentiality is demanded of all my consultations with the law, so that is all I can tell you."

After a brief pause he continued, "But I have taken up enough of you young people's time and I should mingle with the other guests. Good night to you both."

With that he bowed and walked back into the lights in a manner that forbade recall. A large man whom they had not noticed materialized from the wall nearby and followed him. *James*, Miriam realized. *That is who I glimpsed earlier through the crowd.*

Amaro raised his glass to Miriam, "To my favorite woman of mystery!"

Miriam clinked her glass on his and smiled. "I fear I am less mysterious than you make out, though I am pleased to be your favorite something. It comes with certain perks that I enjoy. Slightly."

"Oh, you are my favorite for many things, including that! But what do you think of the remarkable Dr Tagarin?"

"He's a strange fellow. Intense. Despite what he said I don't think he likes the law much, though I'm not sure I can really blame him. I never expected to see him at a party: I more think of him spending his nights brooding in a tower of his Gothic mansion, plotting the flaming downfall of GenInt."

"So what are these cases he's helped you with? Anything exciting?" he asked lightly.

Miriam hesitated. She didn't like to lie, but even if she had been free to talk she wasn't comfortable confiding in Amaro about this; not given his job. But it would sound suspicious to refuse to tell him anything. "No, not really," she replied, looking away to study the view. "There was genetics involved and it might have been exciting if it had led anywhere, but Dr Tagarin saved us a lot of time by showing it wasn't what it seemed." She looked back at him and smiled innocently. *Well, it's close to the truth,* she thought. *It might even be true.*

Amaro smiled back at her affectionately. Behind the smile was his own thought: *you're a lousy liar, my dear; fortunately for us I am an excellent one.*

Then dinner was announced, and they walked arm in arm back inside. The food and wine, as Amaro had promised, were superb. The tales of their fellow guests were illuminating, and Miriam was fascinated to learn about cures for diseases she hadn't even known existed.

Miriam was feeling happy and full as dinner wound up, when the lights went down a notch and the MC announced, "Well, folks, I hope you all had a fine dinner. Soon we'll have more dancing so you can work off some of those delectable calories. But first, we promised you a surprise after dinner speaker. And let me tell you, we were surprised ourselves to net him. Please welcome tonight's speaker, who will be telling us about the history of genetic engineering: one of the greatest pioneers of genetically engineered stem cell therapies. Please welcome Dr Daniel Tagarin!"

This was turning into a night of coincidences, thought Miriam, as she applauded along with the crowd. She wasn't surprised that he would be invited to speak, especially on such a topic to such a gathering: but she was as surprised as the organizers that he had agreed. She wondered how wrong she had been about him in other ways. Then wondered even more as she watched him talk, enthralled.

The dance floor in the center of the room was now a stage, and Tagarin stood there orchestrating a holographic display that filled the space around him. "It was known for many years," he started, "that DNA is essentially a simple structure of just four different components called nucleotides, known for brevity by their initials A, C, G and T." This was accompanied by four chemical structures floating in space. Miriam knew just enough chemistry to know that they were organic molecules; beyond that they all looked much the same to her except two were larger. "But how could such a simple structure explain the amazing properties of DNA, which was already known to be capable of self replication as well as coding for everything that makes your body what it is? In 1953 scientists solved a key part of the puzzle."

As he spoke, copy after copy of the four chemicals spun off and linked together into two chains that began to wrap around each other as if in a vortex. "Each DNA molecule is two long polymers of those four nucleotides, wound around each other in a double helix. Because of their chemical affinities T always pairs with A and C with G"—in the display, the four lone nucleotides moved into two pairs—"which is what holds the double helix together." Part of the helix was magnified, showing the pairing at each rung of the ladder. "And it is how DNA is copied faithfully from generation to generation of cells in your body and from parent to child." The double helix was pulled apart and more nucleotides were recruited to their partners and joined together by enzymes, until where there had been one double helix there now stood two identical to the original. "It is also how the genes that code for proteins are copied into messenger RNA: a molecule similar to DNA which is translated into proteins by the cell." More enzymes rolled down the strands of DNA, reeling off single stranded RNA copies that were grabbed by yet other molecular machines, which ratcheted along them to churn out proteins.

"And because they are linked in long chains, the number of possible sequences is astronomical: there are more than a trillion possible sequences in a mere chain of 20. This makes everything possible with just those four nucleotides and how they are ordered. Some sequences are recognized by molecules that block transcription into RNA"—in one part of the DNA, a transient structure formed and was bound by a molecule that prevented access by the transcribing enzymes; in another part a different molecule bound directly to a specific sequence with the same effect—"while others initiate transcription"—other interactions opened up the sequence for copying instead of blocking it.

"You have seen how DNA is copied into RNA which encodes proteins. But what is the code, the secret behind that conversion? It is simply the sequence of nucleotides in the RNA that determines what protein it codes for." A map of triplet sequences appeared linked to twenty different amino acids, the building blocks of proteins. Then the RNA copy drifted away and was grabbed by a molecular machine, a ribosome, churning out a protein according to the encoded sequence, while another RNA with a different sequence churned out a different protein.

"But," he continued, "nothing is perfect. Sometimes errors occur: the DNA is damaged or there is a copying error. Once an error is there it is copied as faithfully as the rest: the cell's machinery has no knowledge of what is right or wrong beyond the sequence existing in the DNA itself." In the display, a mismatch was highlighted in red:

then there were two copies, one the same as the original, but the other with that single difference now permanently incorporated. "Those errors cause a lot of problems: genetic diseases, cancer, deterioration of cell function. But without them we wouldn't be here: some of the changes alter function in a way that is beneficial or neutral, and it is the accumulation of such changes over millions of years that has led to all the diversity of life on earth. Including us."

"But how?" he asked, raking the audience with a penetrating gaze. "To know how, the first thing we need to know is the sequence of the DNA. That task looked hopeless. Twenty years after the discovery of the double helix, scientists had slowly and painstakingly sequenced short stretches of DNA and RNA. They had worked out the genetic code you saw earlier: how the 64 triplets of nucleotides code for the twenty amino acids proteins are made of and where they start and stop. But the sequence of even a small virus—where 'small' is a few thousand nucleotides—seemed out of reach." The viewpoint in the arena flew away from the double helix to reveal it as a long thin circular string weaving through space. Then the view receded further and a string ten times longer now dominated the view. "This is the DNA of a larger bacterial virus, around 50 thousand nucleotides long." Then he paused.

"This is the human genome." Another long double helix wound through the space around his head, then the viewpoint fled rapidly; the double helix grew longer and thinner, wound around itself, millions upon millions of nucleotides, finally wrapping itself up into a dense body, a chromosome; then 22 other chromosomes swam into view. "The human genome—ignoring our having two copies of each chromosome—has three *billion* nucleotides."

"Yet the progress in technology for sequencing DNA accelerated so fast that less than fifty years after the double helix was described, a single human genome was sequenced." The pages of a thick book filled with page after page of four-letter code flipped at a dizzying rate in the air.

"That first genome took ten years and nearly one billion dollars to decode. But within another ten years human genomes were being sequenced in days for mere thousands of dollars, and improvements just kept on coming. A human genome could be sequenced on a chip in a few hours. And not just humans: anything could be sequenced and was: a whole library of people, and a whole library of organisms from bacteria to plants to cats to kangaroos." A timeline appeared above Tagarin's head, showing the years and an exponentially growing forest of sequenced genomes organized into evolutionary groups.

A small collection of organisms peeled out of the forest and expanded, showing the organisms and the similarity between their genomes. "You can see that the chimpanzee genome is 98.5% the same as the human; the cat's is 90% the same. The differences between a chimp, a cat and a man are entirely due to those differences in their genomes: now we were learning what in the latter caused the former."

"The genome works to produce an organism in time as well as space." The view changed to a group of chromosomes much like the one shown earlier, then receded again until a large glowing globe appeared: a single fertilized egg floating in the air. Its chromosomes duplicated, the cell divided, and divided again and again; flashes of color in each cell showed how gene expression varied along gradients in the growing blob. The organism grew and grew, cells migrated, tissues took shape, organs appeared.

It is like a dance of life, thought Miriam, mesmerized by the hypnotic patterns. The replicating helices, the patterns of gene expression, the cell growing into an integrated animal: all a magnificent dance under Tagarin's command. She wondered what the world had lost, if he had been as great a scientist as he was a speaker: and she knew he had been.

But he did not have to quit, she reminded herself: there was plenty of related research he could have continued in. But what would she have done, she then wondered, if she had given her best to the world: and the world had not only slapped her down but destroyed her creation? Would she have continued working meekly for that world, or would she have said damn you, damn you all, and refused to give them anything more? But if that was his motive, what had he done to his own life? Clothed himself in a fog of bitterness around a shell of cynicism, to come partially alive when presented with a new scientific puzzle and only fully alive when reliving the scientist he had once been? Perhaps in punishing the world he had punished himself more.

On stage the dance went faster and faster; what had formerly been smooth generalities became finer and finer detail; delicate hairs pushed their tips outward from the smooth surface; until at last a fluffy kitten appeared. Then it grew and stretched until a sleek cat filled the arena, staring at them through slitted yellow eyes. Miriam suppressed a gasp. The cat's predator eyes appeared to be looking straight at her, and she knew in her bones the fear her far ancestors had felt when they met the gaze of a saber-toothed tiger. She wondered if it was an illusion or perhaps just another coincidence. But when she saw Tagarin's eyes glittering in the shadows she knew he had noted her position in the room, had done it deliberately for her benefit: but whether as acknowledgement, irony or threat she had no way to know. Then she shivered again under that feral gaze, and knew.

Then he spoke again.

"This cat, just as each of you, came from a single cell. That one fertilized egg achieves, somehow, the delicate series of orchestrated changes that expresses the right genes in the right place at the right time. The final result is an organism containing billions of cells and dozens of organs all interacting correctly. And in parallel with advances in genome sequencing, scientists were also discovering that 'somehow'.

"What we learned was how to turn a normal adult cell into a pluripotent stem cell, which can multiply and diversify into several cell types; and what we learned was how to turn a pluripotent stem cell into a totipotent stem cell, which like a fertilized egg and its immediate descendants can produce any cell in the body; indeed, a whole body."

He paused. "It took the human race a thousand generations to progress from cave art to agriculture. It took only three generations to go from the discovery of the double helix to all I have described.

"At the same time, we were learning how to edit the genes in a living cell." A long double helix wound through space, a faulty sequence highlighted in red; a repaired sequence, in green, was put into position by molecular machines to replace the faulty one. The view zoomed out to the cell; the cell divided, and divided, and became a new liver free of the genetic defect. "There are many technical challenges. Some genes can be repaired in tissues as they are"—modified viruses delivered their payload of repaired genes to the cells in an organ, restoring normal function. "But many require making stem cells, repairing them then growing them to restore partial function or replace the whole organ. In any case insertion of the new gene has to be precise: put it in the wrong place and you will disrupt other genes, stopping vital functions or causing diseases such as cancer.

"But those technical problems were solved. The first applications were fixing genetic diseases and creating immunity to viruses." Images of nightmares from the past—of hemophilia, cystic fibrosis, muscular dystrophy and Tay-Sachs disease—appeared and were banished;

engineered cellular immunity stopped AIDS and Ebola in their tracks.

"And even harder than fixing defects using an existing good version of a gene is knowing how to improve on the normal. But finally, with all that knowledge of comparative genomics and related science, we had the tools to begin to work out how to design new genes and where to put them." New images flew in: drought and disease resistant crops, salt tolerant plants, disease resistant animals, animals with better or healthier meat or milk and stranger beasts such as a goat with the fur of a mink.

"As you can see, the next evolution of plants and animals was now within our power. We were at the threshold of new possibilities: to remake creation for the benefit of mankind. To remake mankind itself. To become the best we can be."

He paused. "But all that stopped. Do not be deceived. The laws and bans we work under are not for safety, or benefit, or morality. Their sole purpose is to bind us all to the whims of the most irrational: to fulfill the desire of some for power over others. To bring what is possible to man under the control of those with the least wisdom and vision. To put those who know under the rule of those who know nothing, as if ignorance and stupidity grant the right of command and it is knowledge and intelligence that must humbly obey."

Then he stopped to look around the audience. "Most of you here tonight would not be alive were it not for advances like the ones I described. I am sure you appreciate what you were given. That is why you fight to ensure that such work continues, as much as it can, and for that I honor you. But you have seen what mankind has achieved. Imagine what we could have achieved if we had been left free to attempt it." Tagarin's eyes sought out Miriam's in the crowd and locked on to them, as if she was personally responsible for those dead years.

"Perhaps one day we will be free again."

Then the images faded and all that was left was a spotlight on Tagarin in the center of the stage, head bowed.

The audience stood and gave a thunderous ovation. Miriam and Amaro stayed seated: Miriam was too moved to rise; she looked at Amaro and wondered that he seemed untouched. *I suppose he already knew all this*, she thought: *the magnitude of it, the greatness, no longer reaches him.*

Tagarin lifted his head and looked around the room as if returning to the reality of the present. Then he raised his hand in acknowledgement or farewell; the lights faded and he faded with them into the shadows.

When the applause died down the lights came on and something like normalcy returned to the room, or at least to Miriam. Amaro was looking at her with an odd smile, as if amused by her reaction. Then the music started up, his smile broadened, and he swept her onto the dance floor.

Her earlier thought about the whirling dance of life came back to Miriam as Amaro whirled her around in a passionate dance on the floor; the nature of his dance was such that perhaps he had not been untouched after all. It returned again later that night as she lay in bed with him in a more intimate dance. *It is all a dance of life*, she thought: *the molecules inside us, the hormones in our blood, the desires of our bodies and the thoughts of our minds.* The dance still held her and would not let her go; she was still at one with it: her orgasms were intense as if in celebration of it and she rapidly fell asleep afterwards, the dance continuing in her mind as she slept. In her dreams Tagarin loomed as a grim shadow conducting a dance of molecules and cells, shaping stardust into a giant cat that turned to stare at her with its predator's eyes. But its pupils were round and its face was a woman's; it snarled and leapt toward her, but vanished into darkness before it reached her.

CHAPTER 27: HISTORY

Miriam woke to an empty bed and the smell of bacon with overtones of toast and coffee. She rose, wrapped her body and thoughts in a dressing gown and walked into the kitchen, where Amaro was frying bacon. He heard her footsteps and turned.

"Good morning, my lovely lady," he said. "Would you care to join me for breakfast?"

"I would be honored, good sir. You're looking refreshed."

"Any refreshment is largely your doing, my dear. You, of course, look ravishing as always. Though if you would make my happiness complete, perhaps you could loosen the front of that gown a little. Yes, perfect," he smiled. "Now sit down, and I'll join you."

He brought over a tray with toast, bacon, eggs, orange juice and coffee, and sat down opposite her. He poured her coffee while she collected her breakfast then he turned his face to her.

"I gather you enjoyed your evening?"

"Oh, very much! Both there and here," she added, running her toe up his leg.

"You seemed quite taken with your friend Dr Tagarin's talk."

"Yes... it was mesmerizing. I knew pieces of it but not the whole picture. And I've certainly never seen it presented in quite such a manner. It was like watching a sorcerer calling up the spirits of the Earth." She paused. "What did you think of him, Amaro?"

"Oh, he certainly put on a good show. But it was rather self-serving, don't you think? The way he ended it, fighting a rearguard action in a battle he lost twenty years ago."

"About that battle... what do you think? Is Tagarin right—the research should be allowed? Should never have been stopped? Or do you think the laws are a good thing?"

Amaro shrugged. "Given what I do for a living, you would hardly be surprised if I say we need to prevent excessive genetic alterations of anything. Especially ourselves. Not that it really matters what I think. You and I are just humble functionaries, the cat's-paws of those in power. If I had a contrary opinion I might want to get another job, but I doubt anyone would care or listen to my reasons. If the redoubtable Dr Tagarin cannot do anything about it, what hope would there be for me? Though given the circles you seem to move in, perhaps your opinion would carry more weight! So what do you think of the issue?"

Miriam grimaced. "Yeah, right. International woman of influence, that's me. What do I think? I'm not really sure. I can see where Tagarin is coming from and he is certainly passionate about it. I just don't know... but he does seem to have a point."

Amaro smiled at her. "Your problem, my dear, is that you have too much empathy. You are so good at getting inside other people's heads that you risk having their thoughts take root in your own."

Miriam smiled at him then turned to her toast. But behind her smile she thought, *Do I? Then why can't I see behind your eyes, my love? I know you want to be with me, that you enjoy my company, that it isn't just sex for you. But there's something hard inside you I can't reach or touch. Have you had some great hurt and are afraid to be hurt again? Is that it? Or is it something else? Are you going to hurt me, after all?*

But all she said was, "I think you overestimate me." She sipped her coffee for a while then asked, "But, really, what harm can it cause? Oh, I agree that nobody can be allowed to create a super army of ant-men or something like that. But that's a big jump from making a few people faster, stronger or smarter. There are already lots of people born faster, stronger or smarter than most. Usually they're the people who become our heroes, not our villains. So... what's the big deal, really?"

Amaro looked at her seriously. "It all depends on what you think people are and what you think the limits should be, doesn't it? There have to be limits—even you admitted that—so it's a matter of defining them. And on this—well, the people have spoken. If other people disagree then they can't just go on doing what they want. You work for the law. You of all people should know that."

"Obeying the law is a separate issue from knowing what the law should be."

"You are very profound this morning."

She smiled. "Or maybe just confused. Maybe there's no difference."

"Now you're being even more profound," he laughed. "But back to the topic, you have enough trouble with regular villains don't you? Do you really want to have to fight things designed to be better than you? Especially if they're not only tougher but smarter? Do you really want to face that in some dark alley one night?"

Miriam glanced at him, startled. But he just picked up his coffee and sipped it, innocently watching her over the rim through the gently curling steam. *No*, she thought, *don't be paranoid; he can't know.*

"But why should they be any worse than any other human? If the ratio is the same: then we'll have more superheroes than supervillains. And everyone will be enriched by it, just as we are by our regular geniuses."

"I think the problem is we don't really know what we're doing. Who knows what unknown effects our gene tinkering will have? People are the product of millions of years of evolution. Tagarin and his friends might like to think they know what they are doing, but do they? Maybe a healthy human is the best we can be already. Maybe trying to push the envelope will just push them over the edge. You might find you have more supervillains than superheroes. Maybe you won't have any superheroes."

Miriam looked into the distance, thinking. "Maybe. Maybe. But how will we ever get to know, if we don't even start? Would we ever have got where we are today if everyone had been afraid to try anything?"

Amaro let her think; she did not seem to be expecting a reply. Then she continued, "But as you say, my opinions aren't going to change anything. For now I'm more interested in what makes the remarkable Dr Tagarin tick. Maybe you can help me. What are the facts of his case? I know a bit about it of course. But it's kind of your field: what do you know about what went on back then? Can you put it in perspective for me?"

Amaro buttered some toast and chewed it while he gathered his thoughts. "Yes, I can probably flesh things out for you. Frankly, I can see Tagarin's point too, but it really was his own fault. He overreached. There was a lot of argument at the time among scientists and the public. With all the successes in medicine and more and more improved plants and animals coming off the genetic production line, the most adventurous scientists like Tagarin started turning their attention to the evolution of our own species. Just like he said last night. Why be limited to the historical accidents that had produced the current human form, they argued, if we can make improved humans: faster, stronger, smarter, healthier? They started working on just that."

He thought some more, sipping his coffee. Miriam was giving him the same attention she had given Tagarin: his presentation wasn't as flashy but she had been seized by a desire to learn as much as she could about the topic. *This is the key*, she thought, *though I'm not quite sure where the lock is.*

"The problem was an old one: technology moving faster than public policy. Tagarin's mistake was in thinking only the technology mattered, that he should ride it as fast and as hard as he could, that the public and the policy would catch up when they could and if they couldn't it was their problem. But it turned out to be his problem. The people watched the technology like they'd watch a rocket shooting across the sky above them: at first they marveled at the sight, then they wondered what it meant, then they worried it might fall on their heads. The politicians watched the people and when the people started worrying, they started to think about regulating."

He stopped. "Do you know where the term 'geneh' comes from?" he asked.

"Not really. It's just the word everyone uses. It stands for 'genetically engineered human' doesn't it?"

"That's half the story, yes. Scientists like Tagarin were busy in their labs doing things to cells and even turning the cells into embryos. Religious activists have always looked askance at embryonic research. But abortion rights were a done deal; nobody was going to go back on that. And the logic of abortion rights is that embryos don't have rights. If you can kill them for one purpose, why not another? So while government-funded research was still barred from any research on embryos, private companies could and did. Some people didn't like that. But there's always someone objecting to anything—even sex.

"Unfortunately, embryos were one thing. Research was one thing. But when scientists began saying not only why genetic engineering would be good for the human race in theory, but that it might soon be achieved in reality... Well, that proved to be another thing entirely. Blogs were written. Net debates flamed. Sermons were preached.

Politicians shouted. The public debate began in earnest.

"That was when a dynamic young environmental lawyer from California wrote an opinion piece that rocked the nation; the world. She titled it 'Don't Let the Geneh Out of the Bottle' and it let an entirely different genie out of its bottle. She coined the word as the abbreviation you know, pronounced 'genie' to fit her theme. And not only did she argue a wide-ranging religious and philosophical case why such research should be banned, she also presented solid evidence that the research was further along than anyone thought: that scientists weren't merely talking about it, they had already produced engineered human fetuses. It hit every button of the opponents of genetic engineering and quite a few buttons of the ambivalent. The defenders of science in general and this science in particular were, as usual in history, a minority. That lawyer's fame and infamy exploded. Her career was made. Her name was Lyn Felton. One day, she would become President of the United States."

Miriam gasped softly and stared at him, mouth partly open. *Oh my God*, she thought. *Oh my God*. The shape she saw in the clues and half leads took on a little more definition. She had known that Felton had been active on the issue but not how intimately involved she had been. She still didn't know what it meant, but she knew it meant something. Amaro smiled at her, but behind the smile he was also thinking his own secret thoughts: *Interesting reaction, my dear; more than one would expect simply from hearing a famous name linked to a casual topic of conversation. You are such a sweet innocent in many ways*. He felt his heart go out to her; for once, he was unable to stop it. *You're playing a risky game, Amaro. Fire can burn both ways: I hope you know what you're doing*. Then he smiled. Miriam thought the smile was for her. But he was remembering a line from an old movie. *The fate of two people doesn't amount to a hill of beans in this crazy world*, he thought; *we might as well both enjoy what we have while we still have it*.

"Well, she had big ambitions," he continued, "even before her political career. She wasn't content with agitating in her own country: she set up an international organization aiming to ban such research everywhere under the auspices of the United Nations. She managed to appeal to a broad audience. The environmental lobbies were already powerful and flocked to her side; the religious movements who were growing in influence around the world joined them. And not just the activists either: I guess her calls for the purity of humanity appealed to something deep in the public psyche. The more cynical of her opponents questioned how much of her enthusiasm was based on her own moral beliefs and how much on the existing morals of the public, but the public was happy either way. I guess that's the mark of a politician.

"And as you know, she succeeded. Her opponents were crushed between the lovers of Nature on one side and the lovers of God on the other, with the broad weight of public opinion adding mass to both sides. Whether she had persuaded a majority of people or just a majority of loud voices is for history to decide, I suppose. But the final result was a UN ban on such research and the formation of the Department of Human Genetic Integrity. And on the strength of her notoriety, she became a Senator and eventually our esteemed President."

Miriam nodded. "I suppose I should pay more attention to politics."

"Oh, she doesn't talk about those days much any more. I guess she figures she'd already milked all the benefit and you know politicians: avoid any controversy if you can. The public might have approved of the creation of GenInt, but they have never been popular."

Miriam nodded but Amaro could tell she had drifted away into her own world. She still couldn't see the shape of what was out there, but she could see there was a shape. And if the shape was a geneh? Tagarin's words returned to haunt her. If there was a geneh out there, her duty was to catch it, and that would be its death. Would she be ready for that?

CHAPTER 28: KATLYN

Katlyn rested high in the branches above the path. Nobody could see her from below. If by chance some vehicle flew overhead, the thick canopy would hide her from their sight too. The only things that could see her were the birds seeking insects among the leaves. And they did not care. They kept one eye on her as they whistled and chattered to themselves, but were happy in their power to escape if she moved. Sometimes they scolded her just out of reach, if they imagined she was keeping some juicy bug to herself. Had they known how fast she could move they might have been more cautious. But they were safe; she wished them no ill. She was waiting for larger prey.

She liked it up here. She stretched luxuriantly, feeling like a contented cat in its element. She could feel the relaxation spreading to her fingers and toes; she could feel the sounds of small life going about its business of living; she could smell the odors of budding growth sweetened by the faint scents of distant flowers.

Yet there was a thread of steel within her. She loved it here but was here for a purpose. And until the purpose came to her she was content to just feel the peace and the coolness. She had found no answer to her questions; perhaps if she let them, this time the answers would come to her like the birds.

She had not been happy with herself after the warehouse. She knew she had not only panicked but also let the accumulated rage of years get the better of her. Though she was not really sure what else she could have done. She had needed to find out what the police knew and more importantly how they knew it. She hissed at herself. Rationalize it as she may, she had miscalculated. In the back of her mind and at the back of her rage had been the idea that maybe she could scare that young cop off. She had certainly looked callow enough. But she had shown more courage and intelligence than Katlyn had bargained for. Katlyn had the sinking feeling that all she had achieved was making a dangerous enemy even more so, like forging the blade that would one day slay her.

And there was her dilemma. If Sun Tzu's advice was to know your enemy then Machiavelli's advice was even darker. Never leave your enemy wounded; never leave your enemies with the power to do something about their hate. Her tail twitched. This was a war, a matter of life or death. Her life or death. And the advice from all the strategists in history, from Caesar to Mao, could be summed up in one word: ruthlessness.

So much for relaxation, thought Katlyn with disgust. The answers might be shy about coming to her but the questions had no such hesitation. She thought of all Daniel had done; she knew it was not all for her, but she knew it encompassed her. Could she see his plans, see him, brought to ruin by her own lack of purpose, her own weakness? Was she like all the cowards of history, the men who had broken under fire, had fled from the horror, who could not face what had to be done? And in so doing had betrayed not only their friends but themselves?

But was it cowardice? Despite her terror, Miriam had faced Katlyn with more than courage. And Katlyn was her enemy. Not only an enemy because of her criminal actions, but an enemy to her genes: not even *persona non grata* but *bestia non grata*. A non-person without rights or recourse. Yet Miriam, despite being a hated officer of the law, had faced her openly and treated her with respect, as an equal, and more: as a person. Ironically, Katlyn knew, that had only increased her own rage. She had not wanted to believe it; had wanted to smash that open face until it would reveal the true soul skulking within. All it had revealed was that Miriam was an innocent. What she had told Katlyn had been true: she had not deserved to die.

But the ghost of Machiavelli would not leave her alone. For they weren't two schoolgirls choosing friends and enemies and laughing together in the park. If Miriam caught her she would be dead. And far from scaring Miriam away, she had given her a much more personal reason for wanting to catch her than just investigating some minor thefts. Katlyn knew strategy; she made it her business to know strategy. You do not leave a wounded enemy alive.

She sighed. But could she do it? This wasn't personal. There was more at stake than her feelings. But she remembered Miriam's face, how even when pleading for her life she had a certain dignity, and she wasn't sure she could look in that face and watch the light go out in those eyes.

But that was why she was here. It hadn't been too hard to track Miriam down in her private life, had then been easy to discover her patterns including her liking for this path through this park at this early morning hour. Katlyn had been coming here for a couple of weeks now. Miriam did not always come. Sometimes she came alone, jogging or strolling along the path. Sometimes she came with a man, the same man each time: boyfriend, Katlyn presumed. All those times Katlyn had watched Miriam go by beneath her perch; all those times she had let her. It would be so easy, she thought; so easy to drop down unseen and that would be the end of Miriam Hunter. So easy to make it look like a random crime of violence with no link to Katlyn or her mission. Such a simple, clean end to the problem; such a strategically sound way to buy time: almost certainly enough time. So far, she had been unable to do it. But she had been equally unable to stop her vigils.

She saw Miriam approaching, a short distance away. This time she was alone, walking and humming some tune softly to herself. Happy. *You bitch*, Katlyn thought, *it's as if you don't want me to kill you.* Then as Miriam neared, something unexpected happened. Three figures melted out of the surrounding woods to confront her. Katlyn lifted her head in surprise. They must be very cautious for Katlyn not to have known of their presence. Miriam had not known it either: she stopped in surprise. Then Katlyn smiled sharply. *Perhaps there is a god for creatures like me after all*, she thought; *a god who answers our prayers.* If she judged the situation correctly, her problem might just go away on its own. All she had to do was nothing.

CHAPTER 29: KNUCKLES

Miriam had been alternately jogging and walking along her favorite path this morning, thinking random thoughts: thoughts of friends, family and Amaro. When she thought of work it was of her colleagues, not her actual tasks. While her work was the spine of her life's purpose, life encompassed more than it. There was nothing so urgent that she needed to ponder it now; time enough for that when she was at work.

She stopped in surprise when three men appeared in front of her. They were young, muscular, and all wore thin patterned masks that made it impossible to recognize their features. Her surprise transformed itself rapidly into alarm. They had to be Griefers. She had not heard of any cases of Griefing in her city, but she knew that in crime and politics there was never an idea so bad that someone would not copy it. But perhaps they were just pranksters.

"Can I help you?" she asked evenly.

One of them cracked his knuckles. "I reckon so."

Miriam casually tapped the police emergency call button of the phone on her wrist. Knuckles smiled and held up a small device in his palm. "Sorry, I think phone service is out today."

"What do you want?"

Knuckles, evidently their leader, replied again. "Oh, not much. Just a bit of fun. Then we'll be on our way. You make it interesting, maybe you don't get hurt too bad. But you make it too interesting, well, that might be a mistake." He grinned nastily.

Miriam thought quickly. Definitely Griefers then. They were a growing problem, until now in other cities: bored young men who had decided the best excitement in their pointless lives was preying on the helpless. Their crimes were various but had many features in common. They craved the excitement of danger, so their attacks usually occurred in public places like this. That added to the terror, as they were usually places where people normally felt safe. But the Griefers treated it as a military adventure. So they always went in small groups: not so large that their victims obviously had no chance, but not so small that they really had any. And they always waited patiently until conditions were right. Miriam knew they would not have approached her if anybody else had been nearby: there would be no one to help her. She also knew their victims did not come out of it well. There had been few deaths but that was not from mercy: Griefers liked their victims to live with what they had done to them. Liked to think how for the rest of their lives they would bear not only the physical scars but the fear of never feeling safe; as if a legacy of everlasting pain would give the Griefers their own immortality.

Shit. "Listen, you're making a mistake. I'm a cop. Leave now and I'll pretend I never saw you," she lied. "Don't leave, and you might not like the consequences."

"Oooh! A cop! You hear that boys?" said Knuckles. The others chuckled. "Where's your badge, sugar? More to the point, I don't see any gun, either."

Miriam went into a crouch. "Oh, so you want to make it interesting, do you?" he said. "Good. We like to dance." They spread out, Knuckles drifting around behind her.

Miriam waited for their move. Attacking one against three was not a wise option; she would let them start it and hope they got in each other's way. She circled; they circled; she felt like a musk ox surrounded by wolves, both sides too cautious to attack a dangerous enemy. Perhaps she should not have told them she was a cop; even if they didn't believe her it had made them careful. She might have been better off with them thinking she was helpless. But perhaps this would buy her time; perhaps someone would approach, and they would give it up.

Her blood couldn't decide whether to freeze with terror at what they might do to her or boil with rage that they would wish to do it— to her or anyone. She thought of one of her martial arts instructors from long ago, a man with a gentle voice and iron limbs. "The Way is more important than the Battle," he had said. "All living things are One: to hurt your enemy is to hurt yourself. So do not hurt if you can stop; do not injure if you can merely hurt. Do little to do much. That is the path of Wisdom."

Screw that, Miriam thought. She'd hurt these bastards as much as she could.

Knuckles disappeared from her peripheral vision and she knew what their strategy would be. She continued to circle. She did not need to turn. She could see her hidden opponent's progress in the movements of the others' eyes and in the faint sounds from behind. She would have one chance at this. When she judged the time was right, she snapped her head back and felt a satisfying crunch as it collided with his nose; then she sent a powerful back kick to the body and heard him crash into a tree. Then everything happened too fast to do more than react.

One of them ran at her; she scythed her arms in a two-fisted blow to his temple, and he dropped like a sack of potatoes. The other was more cautious and approached her in more of a dance. He was good but not good enough. Miriam kicked him in the groin and her knee met his head on its way down when he folded up. She kicked him in the head again to send him to the ground.

But then she felt a sharp sting in her thigh and spun around. *Oh, crap.* Knuckles had risen, holding his nose in one hand and a dart gun in the other. She felt her legs wobbling already. She knew this drug; first it would paralyze her then she would lose consciousness. She had to hold on. Maybe she could still take him out with the last of her strength if he came near enough before she was helpless.

He grinned maliciously, in demonic counterpoint to the blood dripping from his nose. "Pretty good, aren't you?" He surveyed his friends with mock concern. "Tut, tut. The boys won't be very happy with you when they wake up. I'm afraid that you won't be very pretty after they've finished with you."

Miriam could no longer support her weight and slumped to the ground, her back against a tree trunk, looking up at him helplessly. "Stop! You're making a mistake! If you do anything to me the whole police force will be after you."

He continued as if she hadn't spoken. "But while you're still pretty we should take advantage of it." His grin changed to a nasty leer and he started undoing the front of his pants.

Oh God, no, thought Miriam, *not that too. Christ!* She clamped her legs together in fright and was gratified that at least they still obeyed her to that extent. But she knew it was a futile gesture. There was nothing she could do. The shadows were already dancing around the edge of her vision as he pulled it out and started to approach her. *Oh God*. She thought she should feel terror, but even that was swirling off into the dark to dance with the shadows.

Then one of the shadows solidified as it curled down from above and wrapped around him, and he spun to the ground. But Miriam lost sight of the scene as her head slumped to her chest.

She felt someone tugging at her wrist, and raising her eyes saw a slender hand over her phone. Then fingers felt her neck. "Please. Help me," she whispered. But whether the words came out, she could not tell.

Then the fingers lifted her chin, but all she could see were the shadows and two large yellow eyes. *I know those eyes*, she thought dimly, but she knew those pitiless yellow eyes held no mercy and no help, only madness and death. Then the eyes expanded to fill the world until they too went dark, and the world ended.

CHAPTER 30: SAVED

Miriam awoke in a strange room. It looked too white and smelled too clean. It held strange devices doing unknown tasks. It looked—clinical. *There's a clue for you Miriam*, she thought drowsily. She was in hospital.

The terror came crashing back with her last memories. Her hands flew to her face, but there was no pain; her skin felt smooth and uninjured. She felt her body from neck to between her legs and found no breaks or pain. She sighed with relief.

An older nurse heard her stir and turned toward her. "Ah, awake at last, are you dear? Welcome back to the land of the living. You've had a bit of an adventure but you're all right now. I'll call the doctor. She can tell you more."

The doctor was friendly and competent. They had given her an antidote to the drug to aid her recovery and there would be no long-term effects; she would feel fine within a couple of hours. They had treated her for some minor scrapes, bumps and bruises but she had no serious injuries of any kind. No, no evidence of rape. The doctor advised her that the police now wanted to talk to her and excused herself.

"The police" turned out to be Jack with a uniformed policeman in tow. She smiled at them. Stone rolled his eyes at her. "I try to keep you out of trouble, I really do. But you insist on getting into fights."

"What happened? Who rescued me?"

Stone stared at her. "Rescued you?"

"Yes! Rescued me! What do you think happened?"

"Well, you pushed the emergency beacon on your phone. Because it was a police emergency, officers turned up pretty damned quick. You were out and there were three unconscious thugs lying around you, with a smashed signal blocker on the ground. We figured you'd managed to finish them off before the drug took hold. Though we did wonder how you got that lucky. You say you were rescued? There was nobody around trying to take any credit."

Miriam thought. "Well... I can't really be sure. It all went very vague at the end. I did incapacitate the first two. The leader, though, he shot me with a dart." She shuddered. "He was going to rape me. Then they were going to beat me to a pulp. I was hoping I could take him out before I went under but I don't know what happened. I saw something; like someone attacking him, but my sight was going. I think whoever it was must have sent the signal for help. But you say there was nobody there?"

Stone shrugged. "Nope. Not even a sign of them. Just you and your three dance partners."

Miriam remembered the yellow eyes. But that was impossible. It made no sense that Katlyn would be there; even less sense that she would have helped her. It had to be some kind of hallucination: thoughts of the case brought to life by the drug and projected onto whatever had actually happened. After all, it was the last thing she remembered before everything went dark. A dream, nothing more.

"I guess someone as shy as they were brave, then. Unless I did manage to get off that lucky kick after all." Then her shoulders slumped with exhaustion, and she fell asleep again.

~~~

Katlyn was still high among the branches, but in another tree far from the recent excitement. She had committed enough stupidity for one day without hanging around to be caught for it.

She lay back to think. When it had come down to it, she'd had to do what she had done. She had seen another creature—another person—fighting for her life, and her heart had gone out to her. There are some things, Katlyn thought, that lie beyond the strategies of war. There are some times when even the soldiers of opposing armies must unite in a common cause against a greater evil.

But Machiavelli's ghost had followed her and was still trying to give her constructive criticism. If she had just stayed where she was Miriam would no longer be a problem. The thugs might have killed her; even if they hadn't she would have been out of action so long that she no longer mattered. Instead Katlyn had saved her. And for what? She would get no gratitude or credit for it: Miriam had been so far out of it she would never know who had saved her. All Katlyn had achieved was to leave her most dangerous enemy alive, healthy and as keen to catch her as ever.

The tree was flowering, and she pulled a bunch of the flowers to her nose to savor their subtly sweet scent. Life had so much pleasure in it, she thought; why was it also so hard? Then all her confusing thoughts fused together into a new shape, and the shape held the answers.

No, Niccolo, she thought to the ghost. *There is more to it than that. The price for your life can be too high; so high that if you pay, your life is no longer worth saving.* If she had been brought to where the price was letting someone like Miriam die in such a way, then she would not pay it. If she crossed that line, she now saw, no more lines remained to be crossed: there was nothing left between her and the abyss but a steepening slope into a self-made hell ruled by a self-made evil. Until today she had fought with the moral certainty that her cause was right. But if she crossed that line there was no longer any right, nothing but the battling of opposing evils. *Do not become what you despise*, she told herself: *be what you ought to be.*

It was getting dark now and it was time to go. She knew she would not lie in wait for Miriam again. And whatever debt she might have owed Miriam for how she had abused her before, she had now more than repaid: even if she was the only one on Earth who knew it. They were still enemies and perhaps her actions today had doomed her. But she knew that at some level, she had already won.

Chapter 31: DNA

"Hello Rianna. What's up?"

Miriam had been back at work for a week now. For once she had been content to be stuck in a back room out of the action, but her pulse quickened at Rianna's next words.

"Hi Miriam. I've got a DNA sequence for you from your fire. It isn't much and not enough for confirmation of identity, but there's enough for a clue to identity. We got some useless bits—non-human or too conserved among humans to be any use—but two fragments totaling a few thousand bases long in human variable regions."

"That's great! I owe you and Kimberley a bottle of champagne!"

"As long as you share it with us. Now, don't get too excited. Unfortunately there are quite a few bases we couldn't resolve, so there are a number of ambiguities. The pieces are long enough that not many people will match them, but even the person it came from would only give you a probability match not certainty. I've already run it through our standard databases and there aren't any matches, so whoever it is hasn't been involved in a previous crime. And don't forget it could belong to someone entirely innocent. Hairs can transfer from person to person, just blow about in the wind or even be deliberately planted. And to make things worse they are separate fragments: we can't even be sure that both sequences really come from the same person. Though since they're from a single hair the chance of contamination from someone else is very low."

"I still owe you a champagne. A good one. Are there any other databases we can search?"

"Oh, there are lots. Medical, scientific, even government records not strictly associated with crimes. But while some are public access most will be confidential, if not secret. So you'll need a warrant, especially if you want a name to go with your match. I'm not sure you have the grounds."

"Leave that to me. And thanks again."

Now for the harder bit, thought Miriam.

She made her way to Ramos' office and knocked on the door. "Come in!"

"Hi boss," she said. "I have some new information, and an idea, about the Katlyn case. Can we go over it? We might want Legal in on it."

Ramos raised an eyebrow. "What have you got?"

"Remember how the DNA from Katlyn's warehouse was too degraded and contaminated to be any use? Rianna did some fancy work with it and managed to get some usable sequences out of it."

Ramos' eyebrow went up a further notch. "Really? I don't recall authorizing spending for that. What have you two been up to?"

Miriam's face smoothed into a suspiciously innocent expression. "Oh, Rianna has separate funding for research and she thought it would make an interesting research program. Apparently she's getting not only my sequences but also a publication out of it. So all perfectly above board and good for the department's scientific reputation as well."

"Hmmm, yes, I'm sure. I do admire innovation. So what do you want Legal for, if it's not just you two needing a lawyer for unauthorized use of department facilities?"

"The sequences don't match anything in our usual databases, but according to Rianna there are a lot of others we could search. I know it's a long shot, but it's one of the few shots we have. What I'd like to do is set the AI on looking for matches. You know that's the kind of thing it is for, so no problem there. It'll just be a background task, low priority, just something for it to do when it isn't doing anything more urgent. The problem is that most of the databases are confidential and they won't give up the goods unless the AI can present a warrant. So first I need your authorization, and second I need to see what Legal can get me."

Ramos considered the issue. It was pretty thin but he had to push this investigation as best he could. "I see. Well, we're still running with the case so I'll support you. Hang on." He pressed a button on his phone. "Hi Jim. Can you send Scott up to my office? We need some advice on electronic warrants for accessing external databases. Yeah, thanks."

He turned back to Miriam. "While we wait: any other progress?"

"Nothing really. The AI occasionally flags things but none of them are convincing. Our thief appears to have gone quiet, and no more of her victims are talking yet. I can apply some pressure if you think it's worth it?"

"No, not at this stage. This whole case has been walking a fine line and I don't want to fall off it. Ah. Hi Scott. Have you met Miriam Hunter? Miriam, this is Scott Harriman. Miriam, you explain the issue."

"Hi Scott," she said, shaking hands. "What I want to do is set my AI to querying non-police databases for a couple of short DNA sequences, to find any possible matches. Most are confidential so a search warrant will help a lot in broadening the search. So I want one, and I want one that is as high powered as possible so I can access the most data. What can we do?"

Scott stroked his short beard. "So you have some random sequence, no idea who it belongs to, and you want to query a bunch of databases just in case? I don't like your chances."

Miriam frowned. "What would we need, to have a chance?"

Scott shrugged. "Some evidentiary link is the gold standard. But if you had that, you wouldn't need what you're after, would you? You're fishing. Judges don't like fishing, unless it's for marlin in the Bahamas."

"Anything that could get around the anti-fishing sentiment?" put in Ramos.

"Well, maybe. Since you're using an AI, no person has to see the data, right? So if you can ensure that non-matching data won't be stored for longer than it takes to do the comparison, or better, your AI itself never even sees the data and has the target do the searching, then that addresses a lot of privacy concerns. It might get you a very limited warrant that will let you into a few places. But to get more than that you'd practically need a national security issue."

Miriam and Ramos looked at each other. "How about a potential threat to the President?" he asked.

It was Scott's turn to raise his eyebrows. "Ah. That might do it. How good is the evidence for a link?"

Ramos considered. "Well... not ironclad. Maybe strong enough for it to be a credible risk."

"If you can find yourself a judge who's strong on security questions, you have a chance. Not a good one. Otherwise you can forget it."

"OK, I guess we take what we can get. Miriam, can you send Scott what you have? Scott, you do the paperwork. See what you can do about the judge."

~~~

The next day, Miriam was disappointed though not surprised when Scott told her the judge had refused to issue a warrant. If they could get a firmer link to national security issues the judge would reconsider, but for now it was canned.

Nothing much else was going her way either.

IT had come back to her with their analysis of the burglary recording Delaney had provided. "I don't know what kind of software your guy has," Fergus had said, "but it beats anything we have. We can get your vague blurs resolving into a vaguely human blur, but can't even see a face. It could be a yeti for all we can tell. Do you mind if I send this to my old tutor? Sam's a mathematician who's an expert in image analysis and might be able do something with it."

"I don't think Ramos will approve any spending for an external consultant," Miriam replied dubiously.

"Oh, Sam likes a challenge even more than the money. Besides, it's like a proof of talent, good for future business. I think I know the buttons to push to swing it. If not, we haven't lost anything."

"That'd be great, Fergus. Thanks so much." *If this case ever breaks, I'll owe so many people so many favors it'll take me the rest of my career to pay them back.*

None of the stolen jewelry had ever shown up. None of the cases of larger theft had yielded clues either. It was as if the owners themselves had transferred the money but weren't admitting it. They had even started suspecting just that, but it didn't make any sense. Nothing, Miriam decided, was making any sense. They had a geneh on the loose who couldn't be a geneh, and whose only image when caught in the act was somebody else. They had a thief breaking in to commit petty theft—at least relative to the victims' bank balances—and usually leaving no trace, whatever security system the wealthy victim had. They had no thief breaking in, but large sums of money disappearing, without a perpetrator and without a trace. Half the victims acted like suspects, and the other half were as mystified as she was. Neither group liked her.

Miriam was glad she had other things to do, and proceeded to do them.

Chapter 32: Alarm

"Oh, God," groaned Miriam, looking at the time. Two in the morning and her phone wakes her. Amaro was still asleep beside her, twitching slightly in some no doubt exciting dream. She wished she could join him.

She frowned at her phone, willing her reluctant eyes to focus. She had it set to vibrate, so Amaro could thank her for that. She also had it set to only bother her if it was really important, and when that fact finally raised its timid hand she willed a little harder for her eyes to wake up.

It was her AI, she saw. *This better be good*, she thought grimly, tapping the icon to read the message. She almost sat up straight, but suppressed her reaction for Amaro's sake; then she re-read the message more carefully.

The AI was still living in the past with a lot of its data, but one real-time feed that had been implemented was emergencies. She had set it to keep an eye out for burglar alarm reports from people on her "donors to the President" list that met other criteria relevant to her case. The AI had spotted a curious event: one of the people on her list, apparently the paranoid sort, had installed a rather outdated analog intrusion detection system as a backup to the usual more high tech solutions. It was the former that had been triggered and sent in an alarm to the police. But when the police had queried the man's AI, it had reported all clear. The police had already filed and forgotten the incident but her AI had been taught more suspicion. The combination of time, person and contradiction passed its threshold of coincidence so it had alerted Miriam.

She swung swiftly but silently out of bed and quickly got dressed in the dim light. She scribbled a quick note, "WORK!" and left it by the bed. Then she crept out of the room, still careful not to disturb Amaro, and made her way to the door where she put on her shoes, collected her keys and let herself out.

"Christ!" she whispered to herself as she started the car. She felt an unreasonable excitement. She knew this was probably nothing and even if it were something they would be too late. But her adrenal glands had their own ideas and she could feel the quiver of the chase livening her blood.

There wasn't much traffic at this hour and she put the car on auto. The first thing she did after that was ring Jack. Luckily he was as conscientious as she when it came to phones and after a few rings a groggy voice answered, "Miriam? What are you doing calling at this hour?"

"Sorry, Jack. My AI flagged something suspicious, a burglar alarm at the apartment of one of the President's friends. It was reported by an old analog system but denied by the AI. I know it's probably a false alarm but if our AI is suspicious so am I. I think we need to check it out. I'm already on my way."

"OK. I'll make sarcastic remarks illustrated by severe looks in the morning. Send me the details. You better call the owner, try to get permission to go in. We don't want any unnecessary delays."

"Sure, that's next on my list. See you there."

She pushed a few more buttons on her phone, hoping the apartment's owner would be agreeable despite the hour. Most people allowed their phones to let through calls from the police, but even if he was one of them it didn't mean he would answer: and if he did it was no guarantee he would appreciate it. She remembered uncomfortably Ramos's warning about disturbing the city's finest citizens and she could imagine what he would say about doing it at this hour. When at last someone picked up the phone, she was relieved to hear the sounds of faint conversation and laughter in the background.

"Hello? I'm very sorry to call you at this hour, Mr Trevane, but I am Miriam Hunter, a detective with the Special Crimes Unit."

"Yes? Goddammit, what do you want, Detective? You're lucky I wasn't asleep. But this better be good."

"I have been investigating some strange thefts that might have serious implications, and your secondary burglar alarm reported a break-in at your city apartment. Your AI reported all clear so the local police ignored it, but we have a more specialist AI that flagged the incident as suspicious. Could you please give us permission to enter your apartment? In the presence of your hotel manager, and solely to check that things are fine?"

"What the hell? If my AI says it's fine, what are you bothering me for?"

"I'm sorry, and I know this is an imposition, but it is very important. We have reason to think that your AI has been fooled somehow. It might be nothing, but it might be related to other such crimes and if it is it is vital that we can gain access. It really is that important. Not only for our other investigations but for your own property."

There was a long pause on the line and Miriam was afraid that he would just hang up. But finally he answered, "All right, Detective. I'll let the manager know. I hope it is a false alarm, so I suppose it would be churlish of me to make a complaint if it is."

"Thank you. It probably is a false alarm, I'm afraid, but I have to check. If it is… well, thank you anyway. Good night, sir."

Whew, she thought. *Hopefully it will be something, and if it isn't, with luck he'll just laugh it off.*

She took the car off auto and hit the accelerator.

She pulled up at the entrance to the apartment and jumped out of the car. Jack wasn't here yet so she took the time to look around. Trevane evidently had different taste from most of the others on her list, who tended to favor soaring towers or sprawling country estates. He had chosen to live in The Beehive, an extensive group of tower blocks originally intended for the middle class, inherited by the poorer segments of the community, and finally reinvented as exclusive dwellings for the rich and powerful. The main point in their favor besides a certain retro charm was a combination of proximity to the center of the city and their sweeping views of the river. A light mist was rising from the river tonight, adding a certain layer of mystery to the view.

Miriam strode into the lobby and flashed her badge at the night manager. He had been expecting her and nodded. "Mr Trevane told me to expect you, Detective. Shall we go up?"

"Hold on, please." She rang Jack. "Where are you? OK."

"Sorry," she said, addressing the manager, "we'd better wait for my partner. He's nearly here."

The manager went back to whatever managers did at that time of night, while Miriam paced impatiently. After a few minutes the door opened and Jack entered. He looked more disheveled than usual but made no complaint, just said "Well, let's check this out."

They took the lift to the apartment's floor and looked along the corridor. There was nothing suspicious. They walked along the carpeted floor to the doorway. "OK, Mr, er, Johnson," whispered Jack, addressing the manager. "Let's keep this quiet. Unlock the door as softly as you can and let us in. You'll have to come in with us to keep the owner happy, but if I yell 'Gun!' go hide. OK? Let's go."

Chapter 33: Fall

Katlyn heard soft footsteps in the hallway and even softer voices outside the door, and she jerked her head up in alarm. *Oh, crap*, she thought. She was in the office behind a closed door and figured she had about twenty seconds. She would have to cut short what she was doing, but she couldn't just leave right away: if she didn't cover her tracks too much careful work might be compromised. So she forced herself to work quickly but as calmly as possible, even as she heard people enter the apartment, fan out and approach her room. Finally she was done. She grabbed her tools and ran for the window.

~~~

They hadn't seen anything. No signs of a break-in, no signs of life at all. Now Miriam edged up to a closed door; it looked like an office. A faint light was visible under the door; perhaps some device left on, perhaps light from outside.

A shadow flickered in that light.

"Jack!" she called, and slammed open the door; luckily, it had no lock. She burst into the room and looked about wildly. Nobody. Then she felt a faint breeze and noticed that the glass was missing from the window.

"Jack!" she cried again, "In the office! The window's open! I'm taking a look!"

She ran to the window and looked down; there was nothing but misty darkness, with a laneway faintly visible far below. Then she looked up and saw a rope, slithering toward the roof ten feet above. She grabbed it and pulled with all her strength. A brief tug-of-war ensued but whoever was at the other end decided that flight was their best option, and Miriam nearly overbalanced as the rope lost its tension. She pulled it taut and began to climb, with a quick shout of "Roof!" into the apartment. She glanced behind her at the dizzying drop and hoped that the rope's owner would not invest the time needed to cut the tough microfilament cord. The light sound of receding footsteps reassured her on that point.

Jack charged into the room, manager in tow, and looked up to see Miriam nearly at the top. He looked down, then back up. *Work smarter, not braver*, he told himself. "Is there another way to the roof? A quick way?" he asked the manager.

The manager nodded and jingled his keycards. "Follow me."

Miriam pulled herself over the edge of the roof in time to see a dark figure darting away along the roof: a figure trailed by a long tail. "Stop!" she shouted, drawing her gun. But Katlyn just changed her gait to a random dodge. "Dammit!" swore Miriam. She wasn't going to send bullets flying wildly across the city skyline. She took off after her.

Katlyn did not slow as she neared the edge of the roof. She ran straight to it and launched herself into space, clearing the gap and executing a skillful roll back onto her feet to continue running over the next rooftop. Miriam slowed to a stop, panting, aghast. She looked at the gap and estimated it at twelve feet. *I can do this*, she thought; *I'm fit and I've jumped that far before; just never where missing it would kill me*. Then she looked at Katlyn's fleeing form and her anger decided for her. *No, not again*, she thought; *I'm too close, I'm not letting you get away this time*. She gritted her teeth and ran.

Miriam was correct. She could have made the jump. But the roof was slightly damp from the mist, that damp had lubricated the grime encrusting the rooftop, and just as she launched herself from the roof her foot slipped slightly. It was enough to lose a fraction of the power behind her jump; enough lost power that she knew she wouldn't make it. *Sweet Jesus*, she thought. She could feel her trajectory fading, as if the mist and shadows below were dark fingers of the chasm reaching to drag her down; but she stretched out to her limit and her hands made the edge of the roof. Her body slammed into the wall and her gun clattered away as she let it go to grip the edge with her fingers.

But it was too tenuous a grip on too unhelpful a material, and the wall gave her toes little purchase. She could feel that she would not be able to pull herself up on the smooth surface; knew that even if she could stop herself from sliding off, the strength in her fingers would give out before rescue could come.

"Jack!" she screamed. "Help me!"

The manager and Jack had taken the stairway to the roof three steps at a time but fumbled finding the right key to the outside door. Jack had only just pushed his way through it when Miriam called, and he was too far away even if he could find the courage to make that jump. Even if, finding the courage, he could make it across. "Miriam! Hold on!" he called. He broke into a shambling run, eyes scanning for something, anything, he might be able to use to reach her or help her.

Katlyn glanced over her shoulder at the commotion and stopped. Miriam saw her turn, saw the cold golden eyes regarding her, tail twitching. She looked away into the darkness where escape lay, back at Jack, down at Miriam. "Help me!" Miriam called to her. "Please!"

Katlyn bared her teeth in a chilling smile that held neither mirth nor kindness. She looked away once more into the darkness that led to safety, but suddenly turned and darted back. She slowed, regarding Miriam silently, then came to a stop, looking down at her clinging to the ledge.

"Hello, Miriam," she said softly. "I suppose if I were a nice girl I'd give you a hand. But I'm neither nice nor a girl, am I?"

"But you came back. I don't believe you are evil. Please don't let me die."

"Ah, but maybe that's all I want. Just to see you die, up close and personal. Look into those innocent eyes as you fall. Perhaps I'll see Heaven in them. That's as close as I'll ever get to it."

Jack had seen Katlyn stop and run back toward Miriam, so he gave up looking for a rope or ladder and accelerated to meet this more immediate threat. He came to a stop at the edge and stared at Katlyn, for the first time seeing her fully in the flesh. She stood there in the wisps of mist, luminous yellow eyes staring out of a pale face made paler by black hair, dark cattail flicking. He thought how people of a past age would have called her a demon; how many in even this age would agree. He could sympathize: he felt a twinge of superstitious dread himself. He pointed his gun at her and she lifted her head to stare directly at him. He swallowed involuntarily but stood his ground.

"You! Jack!" she said. "Lose the gun or lose your girlfriend!"

He hesitated. "How do I know you won't just push her off if I do?"

"As they say in the vids: you don't, but you haven't much choice do you?" she replied harshly.

Jack hesitated again then tossed his gun into the shadows.

Katlyn gave him a look that told him she had expected a more convincing throw, but she must have decided it was enough. All she said was, "Good lad. Now don't you move."

She crouched down and stared at Miriam for a second, then said. "So. What reason can you give me to save you? Let's see how well you beg."

Miriam thought of their last encounter and wondered, *what indeed?* Then she said. "I think you like the excitement of having a nemesis chasing you. And I think when the time comes you'd like to kill me in a fair fight with your bare hands, not just watch me fall off a roof."

Katlyn looked surprised for a second then put her head back and burst into a peal of her tinkling bells laughter. She stopped and looked back down at Miriam, teeth still bared in an amused smile. "I see you've learnt something," she said, but made no move to help her.

Then Miriam felt her grip begin to slip and she cried out in panic, "Oh! No!" But Katlyn's hands darted out with their lightning speed to grab both her wrists. She lifted Miriam up into the air before she fully realized what had happened.

For the second time Miriam found herself face to face with her enemy with only inches between them, only this time the enemy was offering to save her not kill her. With her feet still dangling over empty space she did not dare struggle or even move: Katlyn literally held her life in her hands, and Miriam knew how unpredictable her moods were. Katlyn sighed. "If I let you down, you'll just chase me again, won't you?" she said resignedly. "That's the trouble with a nemesis: you can never trust them." She paused then continued, "There's a cost for everything, you know. I hope you appreciate how low my fees are."

With that, she stepped back and put Miriam down safely, but then stamped hard on her foot and sprinted away. Jack ran for his gun. By the time he got back, Miriam was on the ground holding her foot and Katlyn was a shadow in the distance. He trained his gun on her until there was nothing left but a swirl of mist from her wake. Perhaps he could have taken the shot. But he did not fire.

CHAPTER 34: SAM

"Gods of Chaos!" swore Miriam softly.

After the excitement on the roof she had retreated to the sedate safety of her office. Forensics had found nothing. Except for the initial alarm there was no record of Katlyn's break-in or presence in the apartment. She seemed able to block any number of sensors very effectively; even her method of removing the glass from the window wasn't obvious. It made her like some kind of ghost visible only to humans, and Miriam was silently thankful that this time she wasn't the only witness. The scientists' report had concluded that none of what Katlyn had done was unheard of in principle, but she must have some very high tech equipment: and they would dearly love to get their hands on her tool belt. By "what she had done" they meant evading detection: nobody knew what she had done, or had intended to do, while she was there.

Ramos had not banned Miriam from field work but had made it quite clear she should be more careful about risking her life in what he called, though in her own mind she respectfully disagreed, "hare-brained acrobatics." In any event it made no difference. In the weeks since there had not been a whisper of further activity, or at least none noticed by her AI.

An AI which had just proudly announced a group of especially idiotic ideas. She knew from experience that when the AI started getting too divorced from reality it was probably an error in its reasoning engine: which usually meant she had entered a logical error herself when trying to explain what was wrong with some other mistake. *Oh well, nothing for it but to fix it.*

A ping and a flashing image announced that Fergus was trying to contact her. She touched it to accept the call. "Hi Fergus, what goes?"

"Hi Miriam. I'm heading out to lunch, and I think you should come. My treat. Can I collect you in five?"

"Sorry Fergus, I'm too busy today. The AI has gotten itself confused and I have a bit of work to do to straighten it out. Some other time?"

"Your delightful company and the sweet memories it evokes are only part of my motivation," he replied. "This is actually work. I'm having lunch with that old math tutor of mine, the one we sent the videos to. I am assured we will find the results exciting."

"You know, I am feeling a bit peckish. I'm in."

~~~

Miriam and Fergus sat down at a table outside, chatting and enjoying the contrast of sunshine and cool breeze while they waited for Fergus's friend. "Ah, here comes Sam now," said Fergus, pointing.

Miriam had to smile. She wondered how much of Fergus's penchant for busting stereotypes had been inherited from his tutor. The mathematician was hard to ignore. She wore intense black pantaloons tucked into lace-up boots. Between those and her long, equally black hair she wore a bright shirt showing a complex fractal pattern in shades of yellow, with a fiery red jacket to round out the ensemble. Even people who said math was boring would have to exclude this particular practitioner of the art. Fergus introduced her as Dr Sam Allende. Sam gave Miriam a big grin and pumped her hand enthusiastically: it appeared that everything about her was overclocked. Miriam found her immensely amusing and decided she liked her. She was like a force of nature.

Sam regaled her with tales of her history with Fergus and any number of wide ranging topics, wherever there was a laugh or an insight to be had from it. Miriam was dying to know what she had found out but obviously she was going to bide her time: but if this was what she wanted as payment for her consulting, Miriam was happy to oblige.

At last they ordered some steaming espressos and after a few sips Sam looked at Miriam and said, "You are a very patient young lady, I like that. But I can tell you are itching for my news. Well, never let it be said that I keep people in suspense! I have found something very exciting!"

Before Miriam could reply, she rushed on. "I have looked at your raw footage, the interpreted image provided by your victim, and the rather less informative version Fergus provided. First, let me say that the last is not anyone's fault. This kind of analysis is always a compromise between too little and too much processing. The police, of course, want anything they produce to hold up in a court of law, immune to the sneers of cynical defense attorneys. They hone those sneers to perfection in their bathroom mirrors, you know. So the compromise they choose is, wisely, set to the conservative. Hence the poor results in this case with such heavily corrupted raw material. Your victim, however, was more interested in whatever he could discover. As it turns out he did pretty well: he must have some excellent software. My more theoretical colleagues could no doubt argue the finer points over the course of a dozen publications; but for practical purposes there's not much in it. Any less processing and the final image would show less detail; too much further processing and there is a rapidly increasing chance of producing sharper images of pure fantasy."

She paused to glance at her audience.

"Miriam, you look disappointed. No doubt you surmise that the logical implication is that no more data can be extracted than what you already have. You would, however," she added with a smile, "be mistaken."

She sipped some more of her coffee, watching Miriam with obvious glee over the rim of her cup. Miriam gave her a severe look, though the upturned corners of her mouth belied it.

"Ha-ha, Fergus was right about you!" she laughed. "But here is the crux. As I understand it, the raw footage is from a security video feed that was rendered almost useless by some kind of signal interference, correct?" Miriam nodded. "But, you see, that is not the case!" Miriam sat up straighter. "You cannot inflict electronic interference on physical circuitry without leaving a footprint in the noise, as it were: an echo of the characteristics of the system. It cannot be purely random, but rather inherits frequency and time dependencies and the like from the two systems, creator and victim. When instead of attempting to clean up the image I analyzed the noise itself, do you know what I found?"

Sam attempted to wait for a dramatic pause but rushed on almost immediately. "The noise was random! It was added later! In other words, your original recording was not corrupted: the signal fed into the system was perfectly clear. The recording was corrupted later by purely electronic means!"

Miriam looked at her eagerly. "You mean, knowing that, you can extract the clean original? You have it?"

"Oh, no, I am afraid that is impossible. You'll never get any more out of it than your victim himself found."

"So... so..." Miriam was confused. "What good is it then?"

"Ha! My dear, you are too busy trying to shine a light inside a box, when you should be looking at the box itself to see where it came from! What this means is simple but profound. If the video was corrupted after the event, it had to have been corrupted by your victim's own AI!"

Miriam and Fergus both stared at her. "You mean, the man who gave me the video and its reconstruction is the one who fuzzed it out in the first place?!"

Sam grinned. "Well, that is possible from a practical viewpoint. But psychologically it seems unlikely, don't you think? Why go to that trouble when it would have been simpler and less risky to report nothing? No, I think the truth is far more interesting. I think your man is perfectly innocent. I believe it is his AI that did the job, without his knowledge!"

"You're kidding," said Fergus. "You mean the thief hacked into it? In the short time he was there? That might work with some cheap shareware AI, but we're talking about a rich guy. High quality AIs can't be hacked at all, let alone in ten minutes. Well, not without setting off alarm bells from here to Canada. The AI would have a fit if someone tried it; even if you could get past its defenses, you'd just crash it before you could take it over. And even if you solved that problem you'd leave footprints all over it! Our guy ran all the diagnostics. Nothing."

"I don't know enough to know what's possible," Miriam admitted, "but I can't see how it could work either. The AI must know it did it. It would either report itself or be deranged, and the owner would know. But it was clean!"

Sam grinned again. "Imagine you are sitting in your office one day, and some alien replaces your personality and memories with someone else's, and you do something as that person. Then they swap everything back the way it was, along with memories of some boring routine you might have been doing during the time you weren't in control. How would you know next week? How would you know to even suspect it? When you were the other person you would have felt completely normal; when you were yourself, you would feel the same and have no memory of the other."

"But there's still the problem of doing that to an AI," Fergus persisted. "Sure, there are ways around AI security protocols. There have to be, in case of a severe fault, the owner dies or there's a court order or something. But the AI knows about it and reports it; and it remembers. There's an audit trail."

"Well, that's what people like to think, I'm sure," Sam answered serenely. "And no doubt it's usually true. But while I confess I am not the world's greatest authority on AIs, I am sure my explanation is the most likely. It is the clear implication of the signal analysis, and on that I *am* an expert. Here, Miriam. I have given you the contact details of a colleague who knows far more about AIs than I do: you might find it worthwhile interviewing him. If anyone knows how it might be done, he will."

She threw back the last of her espresso and rose. "Well, I must be off, I have a graduate class to torment. Thank you both for a lovely lunch. It was good to see you again, Fergus; and I'm so glad to have met you, Miriam. Enjoy the rest of your day. And think about what I've told you." She gave Fergus a stern glance. "I can read young Fergus' mind, you know. He is right to be skeptical, but don't discount what I told you."

With that she left, making her way through the lunchtime crowd, the chromatic inverse of a grouper gliding through a swirling school of neon reef fish.

When she had gone, Miriam said, "Wow, what a live wire! So what do you think about her theory?"

Fergus shrugged. "You probably noticed she has a flair for the dramatic, and if a thief who can corrupt an AI is not the most likely theory no doubt it is the most exciting. But I've learned not to ignore what she says. Underneath that butterfly exterior is a preying mantis."

CHAPTER 35: NEUBOLD

After lunch Miriam went back to work. She knew where her department's priorities lay, so she spent the next few hours repairing the AI: she did not want to have to explain to Ramos why she had spent time on the Katlyn case while the AI was languishing in need of attention. They had to let her take her lunch breaks but what she did in official working hours was another matter.

At last Miriam brought the AI to a state that looked more promising. Then she had it record its findings of the last week; erased its memory of all that data and its reasoning and conclusions; and finally set it on reanalyzing the same data in the order in which it had received it. Once it caught up to where it had been she would have it compare its findings with what it had done originally. That would let her know whether the latest version was better or worse than before.

That would take it a while. Once she had it working away she could stop to think.

They knew that someone had corrupted the video. The questions were who and how?

Sam's assurances aside, the most likely possibility was their original theory of signal interference. While nobody knew quite how it could be done, the thief did appear to have an arsenal of unusually advanced technology at her disposal. The video corruption wasn't the only example. She had bypassed locks, suppressed alarm systems and otherwise got in, done her work and escaped unscathed where it might have been considered impossible if she hadn't so clearly done it.

If not that, then the recording rather than the signal had been corrupted. The most obvious candidate for that was Delaney himself: he could have made the AI do it then forget it had done so. It wouldn't be easy to do without leaving logs and other traces, but she supposed it could be done. But the main question was: why? And if he had done it, why draw attention to it? Nobody had realized there was more to the video than static, so nobody had considered it a clue until Delaney himself had offered it up unsolicited. Delaney gave no sign of being the kind of egotist who liked to taunt his opponents with his superior cunning.

The person with the clearest motive for subverting the AI was again the thief. But the thief was the one with the least ability to do it, for all the reasons they had already considered.

In either case, if the AI was involved the next question was why corrupt the video anyway? Why go to the trouble and risk of obscuring the video with noise when it would be simpler, safer and more permanent to just erase it entirely? Then there would have been nothing from which to reconstruct even a blurry image of the perpetrator.

So the very existence of the video favored the interference theory, as then complete erasure was not an option. And if not perfect it had certainly been effective: it was only by chance that anyone had bothered to analyze the video and discovered there was something to see. Perhaps the thief thought there would be nothing left to see; perhaps at last he had made a mistake.

But where did it leave them? Sam had found that they could get no more out of the video than they already had. But the implication was that what they had was a true image, which meant Katlyn was not the thief. Yet Katlyn *was* a thief. And there were too many similarities, too many coincidences, for the crimes to be unrelated. That implied at least two thieves working in concert, and Miriam's blood ran cold at the memory of Tagarin's question: *what if there are more of them?* Miriam shook her head. *God, what have I got myself into?* she asked herself. *How many more of these things are out there?*

So the video, poor as it was, provided an important clue. Again it made more sense as signal interference: that it *was* a clue showed just how risky it was to leave any evidence if you could avoid it. Everything else the thieves had done seemed almost superhuman: if they could destroy the recording it made no sense to merely degrade it.

Then suddenly she stared, struck by a sudden thought: *is that really what they had done, exactly?* "Hellfire!" she cried. She stared inward at the pieces falling into place in her mind. The thief had not deleted the video for a very simple reason, she thought. With a corrupted video, they all believed the thief had some unknown jamming technology, advanced but not beyond the realms of possibility, like her other tricks; better than your average thief but not fantastically so; annoying rather than dangerous. But if the video were deleted, they'd *know* the thief was able to take over an AI. And if she could take over an AI to do that, what else could she do while she had it in her power?

Miriam went cold. What indeed? For starters, not merely corrupt a video but change it to hint at a normal human, in case anyone looked into it that deeply. And that's just the least of it.

Suddenly Miriam very much wanted to know if it was in fact possible to take over an AI and exactly what you might be able to do with it once you had. She examined the contact Sam had given her. *Well, Dr Neubold,* she thought, *it looks like I'll be paying you a visit sooner than I thought.*

~~~

Dr Arthur Neubold owned an IT company specializing in systems development, software security and complicated-sounding computer fields Miriam had never heard of; much of his company's income came from military contracts. He had readily agreed to an interview when Miriam mentioned Sam's name.

Miriam was led along a corridor by an assistant who made no attempt to hide that he had better things to do with his time. She went past rooms filled with mysterious equipment and past people hurrying along on equally mysterious tasks, until finally she was delivered to Neubold's office. Her guide then receded, like waves after they have deposited driftwood on the shore.

"So, Ms Hunter, what can I do for you? You mentioned an issue of AI security?" He retained an obvious if faded British accent.

"I was discussing a puzzling case with Dr Allende, and she thought the most likely explanation is that our criminal can infiltrate an AI and gain at least partial control over it. I can see why she thinks that, but everything else indicates it's impossible, at least without leaving glaring evidence behind. But there is nothing. The AI involved seems perfectly functional, normal and untouched."

He frowned. "Can you tell me why you suspect such an unlikely event?"

"All the explanations are unlikely. I'd be happy to eliminate any of them! The main piece of evidence is a thoroughly corrupted video record. The only possibilities we can think of are jamming of the data feed or corruption of the recording, and neither seems technically feasible. While jamming seems the most likely to us, Dr Allende assures us that the detailed characteristics of the corruption implies it was done after the fact."

"Ah," he said. "Tea, Ms Hunter?"

A slender young man had entered carrying a silver tray inhabited by an elegant teapot, a pair of fine china cups and some crystal containers. Miriam nodded, somewhat bemused, and the young man gracefully poured her tea in an artistic arc from the pot. He indicated the milk and sugar, in a manner of perfect politeness that nevertheless implied she would be uncouth to corrupt his tea by their use, and bowed out of the room.

"My assistant," Neubold explained. "He makes a fine cup of tea, a most civilized relic of the once great British empire. Now where were we? Yes, your data corruption as evidence of AI corruption. Are there any other features of the case I should know?"

"Whatever he or she did, the thief appears to have done it quite quickly, and has probably done it more than once, possibly several times."

"Interesting. That would indicate someone using a general tool rather than just a person with inside knowledge of a particular system. Hmmm. Yes." He thought about it, sipping his tea. Miriam could see the feelings chasing each other across his face: concentration, puzzlement, faint alarm, skepticism then more alarm. Finally he put his cup down and gazed into the distance, looking more like a man wondering whether to tell her something he already knew rather than someone trying to solve a puzzle. He appeared to come to a decision.

"What I am going to tell you must remain in strictest confidence, and not leave your confidential police files. Preferably not even make it into the files. I am only telling you because if I am right, somebody has managed to steal some very sensitive intellectual property of ours. I would very much like to see them caught and stopped if that is the case. Even so perhaps it is better if I say nothing."

"I must emphasize the importance of the case I am working on, Dr Neubold. To trade my own confidential information, the implications might extend all the way to the President. I really need to know what I'm dealing with."

Neubold's eyes studied his teacup and then her face.

"All right, Ms Hunter. I can take the risk. I have deniability if you leak what I tell you but it proves to have nothing to do with your case, whereas if I have actually been robbed I will have more problems than mere embarrassment. Besides, if it proves to be ours I think I would be wise to show how cooperative I am, eh?"

"Thank you. You can count on my discretion and I won't tell anybody who doesn't need to know. Please go on."

"In the past we did in fact work on a tool for infiltrating AIs, secret work for the military. It is currently in limbo because it ran into privacy problems in government committee: while the tool is intended for military use, some people just don't trust it to stay there. We had made a lot of progress: most commercial AIs and many custom-built ones based on similar algorithms were vulnerable. With such a tool, your thief could plausibly have done what you say."

Miriam sat up straighter. "What exactly are its capabilities?"

Neubold grimaced. "That depends rather on which version was, er, acquired. As a work in progress, obviously later versions were more capable. The problem with sophisticated AIs is that they need many flexible data inputs—vision, sound, text, any number of electronic communication bands, etc. I cannot tell you details, but I can tell you that is how we get in. If an AI is vulnerable then the actual process is quite fast. A few minutes at most to gain complete control."

"And what can you do then?"

He spread his hands. "Practically whatever you like—fortunately or unfortunately, depending on your perspective. The AI has no idea it has been coopted. It believes everything it is doing is perfectly reasonable and part of its normal operations. It may well hide what it is doing from its true owner—that is after all the whole point—but it sees nothing odd about that. It believes it is like any other internal process the owner doesn't need to know about."

"But looking in from outside, can you tell?"

"Not really. Usually AI diagnostics are done by the AI itself, and it will report normal functioning. And don't forget this is military software: just like a human agent, we don't want it falling into enemy hands and we prefer the enemy to never even know it was there. If it detects any kind of intrusive probe our infiltrated second mind erases itself, leaving no trace. The AI will never be aware it was there and no external search will find it either. Furthermore the usual mode of operation is to take control for a limited time, perhaps as short as minutes, perhaps as long as weeks, then erase itself once its purpose is achieved. Just that extra margin of security, you see? I am afraid that the only evidence one is likely to have is if the system can be proved to be the source of a leak of information, an explosion in a research facility or some other such hostile action. But even knowing the compromised system was involved there will be no trace of how. It is more likely one of its operators will be shot for treason than the AI itself suspected. Unfair on the operator but in the nature of warfare, I'm afraid."

Miriam felt a sinking feeling. "So do you mean to tell me that software does exist that can take over an AI, but nobody should have it, and if they did I'd never know they'd used it?"

Strangely, Neubold smiled. "Not quite. The software was never finished, you see; it waits locked in limbo for word from on high. We can neither destroy it nor finish it until the government brings down a decision. So its last state was still a beta version, still being tested. Have you heard of the phrase 'Kilroy was here'?"

"It sounds vaguely familiar, but I'm not sure where I've heard it."

"It became popular last century in the Second World War. Allied soldiers would scrawl it in odd places, usually along with a cartoon of a man peering over a wall. Kilroy tended to turn up in the most unlikely places, seemingly before anyone had the chance to put him there. Well, you could say we did the same thing. The beta versions all leave the phrase 'Kilroy was here' in register memory deep in the infected AI. In addition, the AI believes it put it there itself a long time ago as an encryption hash salt string. Such salt strings are best acquired randomly, and that is what the AI believes it did via a random phrase search. That was one of our checks that everything had gone according to plan. Not only is it an unlikely phrase to use, but an AI would normally choose a completely random string: that it thinks an English phrase was a perfectly reasonable choice is further evidence of how successful the infiltration was. Using such a phrase is somewhat geeky humor, but one must expect that from geeks, eh?"

Miriam's pulse went up a notch. "Dr Neubold, I cannot thank you enough. This might help my investigations enormously."

"You're welcome, Ms Hunter. May I remind you of the need for discretion? And please let me know the results of your enquiries. But may I ask you when the video you referred to was taken?"

"Several months ago."

Neubold gave her a startled glance. "That long!" Then a thoughtful look came over his face. "You know, there might be a clue there. We lost a technician about a year ago. He was a very adventurous young man, prone to go off hiking alone in the wilderness without telling anyone. Rather foolish, in my opinion. Well, he disappeared. Just never showed up for work one Monday, and attempts to find him were futile. Everyone decided he probably met his end broken at the bottom of some trackless ravine. But perhaps he is now living the high life in the Bahamas instead. He had no direct access to the software we're discussing, but I would not be surprised if he had been aware of its existence. That would have been a breach of internal security in itself, but I have found that geeks have a tendency to treat security with contempt, especially if they have done something clever. I suppose it is possible he found a way to steal it himself or somehow enabled its theft by an outside gang."

He turned to his computer and worked on it for a short while. "Yes, here he is: Geoffrey Baxter. I have sent his details to you in case they help."

Then he stared at her. "But your timeline presents us with a problem, don't you think? I'd have thought that if criminals had gained access to this technology that long ago there'd have been signs of their activities on the news. I haven't noticed anything. What kind of targets are you investigating?"

"The only victims we are aware of are some private individuals. Wealthy but private: no corporations or government bodies that we're aware of."

"That seems to show a marked lack of imagination on the part of your criminals, no? No doubt they would like to keep the existence of such a tool undetected for as long as possible, so with their extra security banks and government systems would probably be too risky to attempt. But that leaves a vast array of places with ordinary security, blithely imagining they are safe but wide open to this particular attack. Any criminals worth the name should have struck hard, fast and wide, and be living it up on their own island paradise by now. So perhaps we have been worrying over nothing. If it has anything to do with cracking AIs, then either they got their hands on a very early test version of ours, or they had a similar idea but made their own much less effective form of it. Or perhaps it has nothing to do with the AIs at all."

He paused to think. "You seem to have reached a contradiction. If your corrupted video is due to a coopted AI, that implies high ability indeed: they can take over an AI quickly and completely enough to do it during the very course of committing a crime. But if that is what your criminals are doing then the crimes are too trivial. It is as if somebody invented a fusion reactor and all they used it for was to power their bicycle to and from work." He spread his hands. "It makes no sense!"

Miriam smiled wanly. "Welcome to my case."

CHAPTER 36: KILROY

Miriam drove back to her office, but she did not really see the road. Her mind was elsewhere; her body drove under its own direction. It parked the car and walked her into the elevator and thence to her office. It was the end of the day and people were leaving; perhaps she answered their farewells, but she did not know. Her mind did not regain the reins until she sat down in front of her AI access point.

"Voice interface," she commanded.

"Voice active."

"What does the phrase 'Kilroy was here' mean to you?"

Miriam held her breath, waiting for the AI to respond.

"'Kilroy was here' was a graffiti phrase common in World War II. It represented a standing joke, always appearing in unlikely places. It was usually associated with the drawing now displayed. Would you like more detail?"

"No, that's fine. Were you aware of the phrase before today? If so, how?"

After a few seconds, the AI replied. "No. I have no record of it."

Miriam let out a breath. She had been getting so caught up in the mysterious omnipotence of her opponents that she had feared even her own AI was their pawn and part of a conspiracy leading her astray. *Not*, she reminded herself, *that this proves anything*. But even absence of proof was a relief at this stage.

"Please display a list of the victims in the Katlyn case who have allowed us remote access to their AIs."

The screen displayed Delaney and two others—both from the group who had been bemused rather than hostile at her earlier enquiries. All had given permission for automatic access to the public interface of their AIs so the police could query aspects of the case without having to bother them personally. The rest had either been hostile to her enquiries or not interested or trusting enough to allow even that small an official foot in their door.

"Please make the same enquiry I just made to you about Kilroy to these three AIs."

"Please wait."

Miriam waited, heart thumping. She wasn't sure whether to be more afraid that her enquiry would return nothing or something.

"The results are curious. All three AIs report that 'Kilroy was here' exists as a string in their registry memory and all state they put it there as an encryption salt string chosen by a random net search."

Holy Gods of Asgard, Miriam thought, leaning back in her chair. *We are so screwed.*

CHAPTER 37: MISDIRECTION

Miriam called up her earlier diagram of the possibilities and stared at it. *Misdirection, misdirection, misdirection,* she realized, *the whole thing is an exercise in misdirection.* Jewelry thefts to mask the real purpose of the break-in: gaining control of the AI. Videos that purport to be one thing and are another, with yet another misdirection buried inside to mislead anyone persistent or curious enough to look below the surface.

She thought more on it, rolling the ideas around in her head. *Yes.* Even with the thief's skill and technology, it would be difficult to break in without a trace, impossible to be sure she had left no trace. But the reason the thing you're looking for is always in the last place you look is you stop looking. So the thief had left an obvious motive in plain view: a theft large enough to explain the break-in but not enough to excite a really serious investigation. A nuisance, a small insurance claim, something soon forgotten. And meanwhile, the victim's AI was there in the background, silently working against its owner under his nose. Even destroying any evidence it had collected itself. Miriam stared at the audacity of it all. If her own AI hadn't seen the tenuous link between the thefts all those months ago, she wondered if they would ever have discovered it before it was too late. Perhaps it was already too late.

But why? What was behind it all? There was the link to the President's supporters, but that could be a coincidence. After all, the victims were all wealthy, and rich people surely had many things in common; sucking up to politicians wasn't an unlikely one.

The image of a blur of molecules and cells whirling around under the command of a shadowy Dr Tagarin rose again in her mind. *What other dances are you conducting, doctor, and to what end?* She was sure he was behind it. Then she stopped. Was she? Why? *Question everything, Miriam. Question everything.*

She ran over the evidence in her mind. Tagarin was her prime suspect only if Katlyn was a geneh—but was she? Perhaps that too was misdirection. As Tagarin had pointed out, she had flaunted her fatal biology—then left the prime witness not only alive but also guaranteed to be hostile toward her. Then, unaccountably, saved her life: or was it the case she wanted to save, to keep it alive now it had been pointed in the wrong direction? And while Miriam had gotten uncomfortably close and personal with Katlyn, how could she be sure that her impressions were real, not merely an illusion she was led to believe? All she had left was a coincidence in phrases the two had used. But Tagarin was a public figure, public enough that his quirks could easily be discovered by someone with the motivation to do so. If someone wanted the police chasing a literal chimera up blind alleys, what better way to encourage belief in a geneh than by implicating Tagarin?

She put her head in her hands. But if not Tagarin, then who? It had to be someone with resources. Organized crime seemed unlikely: given the nature of such groups, surely they would have done far more damage by now. They were not known for either patience or subtlety. Miriam rubbed her temples. That was the other thing. Even the larger thefts weren't big enough crimes. It didn't make sense that they were the full motive, but they also didn't make sense as misdirection. There had to be something else behind it all, some scheme that she couldn't yet guess at. A government agency might have big shadowy plans and would certainly have the money and access to the technology: was this some rogue agency gone beyond its remit? Or one of Tagarin's other suggestions, an expensively modified agent gone rogue herself and now hunted in secret?

Then another thought struck her into stillness. She turned it over in her mind like a hot potato. It had a shocking but deadly simplicity to it. She rang Stone. "Jack, when you told me that Tagarin's geneh baby had been shot by GenInt—did you actually see it happen?"

"Good evening to you too, Miriam. Yes, I am having a lovely dinner, thank you for asking." He paused, but she said nothing. He could almost see that look in her eyes she got when her brain was off chasing an idea, and he knew she was blind and deaf to anything unrelated to her quarry. He'd had a puppy like that once, and he smiled despite his annoyance at her timing.

"Well... not 'saw' as such. But they carted it off in a hurry and a minute later there were several shots. GenInt goons aren't the types to fire their guns into the air in a fit of exuberance. We all figured they didn't want us to actually witness the execution—more deniability if it ever came to that." He stopped for a moment. "I don't think I like where this might be heading." Then he added slowly, "Maybe you'd better slow down and decide if you really need to go there. Give your brain a break and go get some dinner yourself."

"Yes... yes... maybe I'm going stir crazy. I'll talk to you about it tomorrow. I have some more thinking to do first. And I have a headache already. Goodnight, Jack."

She hung up and groaned. It was impossible, yet terrifyingly possible. What if GenInt *hadn't* shot that baby? It could explain everything. No impossible age problem, no need for improbable research in the years since the bans.

Perhaps GenInt itself had adopted the child, the first and last geneh born: either to study it or use its powers for their own ends. It wouldn't be the first time a government agency couldn't resist using something it deemed too dangerous to allow anyone else to have. If so, was she still working for them on some clandestine mission, or had she escaped to work on her own agenda?

Or had the baby been meant to die, but instead been freed by its executioner in an unexpected fit of mercy: the man's humanity asserting itself when faced with actually pulling the trigger on an infant? Had she then become what Tagarin had suggested: a feral creature, surviving on her speed and wits in the cracks and shadows of a world bent on her destruction?

Her mind paused again. If that was it, Tagarin must have known what Katlyn was the moment he had seen the photo, or at least suspected it. But there was no way he would ever admit it to her.

Miriam shook her head. Too many possibilities, each plausible in its own way, each implausible in others. Whoever was behind this had woven a tapestry of deception so tangled it was impossible to be sure what was true and what was illusion, what were clues and what were misdirection. With a sinking feeling in her stomach, for the first time

Miriam began to think that her unknown opponents were out of her class; that perhaps this case was beyond her ability to solve.

CHAPTER 38: GAMES

Miriam had gone home, determined to sleep on the problem and hope that a rest and some subconscious chewing would give her a new perspective.

She had a quiet dinner with Amaro watching an old movie, but she couldn't really get into the plot. They had gone to bed, but despite her desire she couldn't get into the plot planned by Amaro either. She had sighed, rolled over and immediately fallen into a fitful sleep haunted by dreams of chasing a person she could never quite see through a mirror maze, both seeking an exit neither could find. When she woke she was little rested and no closer to a solution. Amaro looked at her but made no comment and asked no questions. He knew there would be no answers.

Now she sat in Ramos' office with Stone leaning against the desk, waiting to hear what Ramos would say.

"So, you're telling me that our thief has been taking over people's AIs and using them to steal money and God knows what else? And that because of this, you're no longer sure we're dealing with a geneh, the whole link to Tagarin might be spurious, and even if it is a geneh it could be GenInt itself behind it? Is that about it?"

Miriam nodded dumbly. Ramos looked like he'd bitten an apple with a grub in it. "Are you sure there aren't some other possibilities you've left off the list?"

"I'm not sure of anything at the moment."

He glared at her a minute then asked, "What do you think, Jack?"

Stone looked from one to the other. "Unlikely as you'd think it is, it does look like the AIs have been compromised. But that doesn't lead us anywhere except to doubt every clue we have. I think we're going back to our desk jobs."

Ramos nodded. "That's about how I see it too. We'll escalate the AI aspect to Computer Crimes. They can consult with your Dr Neubold and see if they can find out how our criminals got their hands on his technology without anybody knowing, and how they can stop more mischief being done with it. That's really their job, not ours. Not our case now."

Miriam nodded and stood to go. "Yes, OK. I'm out of ideas myself."

"Don't look so dejected. None of this is your fault. And I don't want you to give up quite yet. No more active investigation is warranted. Or wise. But have your AI keep whatever it uses as a nose to the ground. Make sure it reports anything that might tie in. Computer Crimes will be doing their thing, but it won't hurt to keep our other options open as well."

As they went to open the door to leave he added, "Wait. This possible GenInt link worries me. We did hope they wouldn't notice or care about our vague report on a strange thief, but still—it's a bit odd that they never even asked one question. But if they were complicit— maybe we're both playing the same game, each acting as if it isn't worthy of attention, each hoping the other one won't place any importance on it."

They both waited, Stone nodding slowly as he thought about it.

"So I don't want you to write up this theory about the geneh baby and GenInt, or even mention it outside this office. The one thing I'm sure of is that we're not going to be able to question GenInt: and we don't want to anyway. If they're behind it, it might be dangerous to poke a stick in their nest whether we're dealing with an official agent or a rogue one. And we have no need to tell them anything at this stage. We sent them that memo about it but didn't say it was a geneh, and now we have even less reason to believe that it is."

Miriam looked at him glumly, trying to generate some optimism about the way forward but not succeeding. Stone glanced at her and shrugged, as if reading her mind and agreeing with her assessment.

"Besides," Ramos added, "I don't want to give anyone a ready-made reason to raise doubts about Tagarin's involvement. We want a clear run at him if we do find more evidence that our thief is a geneh, if only so we can remove him from our list of suspects if he's innocent. It would be nice to remove *anyone* from our list."

CHAPTER 39: TANG

Miriam put her coffee down then noticed the half eaten cinnamon donut. She picked it up, bit off half and chewed thoughtfully as she watched the polychrome dance of diagnostics on her screen. She washed the crumbs down with some more coffee then noticed the quarter donut on her desk. *Zeno's Paradox of Donuts*, she thought idly to herself: *if I keep biting off half of what's left, will I ever finish it?*

She smiled at her thoughts and the repetitive tasks that had spawned them. *My life is so exciting at the moment*, she thought. The AI was behaving itself for once, but while it was finding correlations that were worth passing on none of them were very thrilling. Her thief had gone quiet. At least, nothing relating to the case had caught the attention of her AI in the weeks since the meeting in Ramos' office. Hopefully that meant Katlyn had gone to ground, not merely become even better at her job. On the other hand, Miriam hadn't been beaten up or nearly died recently. There was something to be said for dullness.

She had heard nothing about the Computer Crimes investigation either. That was not surprising when a secret government software project was involved. No doubt Computer Crimes would dearly love to get their paws on one of the affected AIs, but she couldn't imagine any of the owners being willing to let them. She wondered how many judges would think "Kilroy was here" was grounds for a warrant with that big a privacy issue. *Good luck with that*, she thought to the unknown investigators; *I can't get a warrant for something much more solid.*

Her phone rang.

"Hello? Detective Hunter speaking."

"Good morning Detective. This is Kevan Tang. You rang me some time ago about a minor burglary in my apartment, and I fear I was quite rude to you about it. I have had a change of heart. Would you be so kind as to visit me to discuss the matter further? Not at my apartment in the city though: I would prefer you meet me at my home in the hills."

"Why, certainly Mr Tang. Thank you so much for calling me back. Let me check our schedules... How about 2 pm tomorrow?"

"That would be fine. I will see you then. Good day."

Miriam checked the records. Yes, Kevan Tang. One of the victims who had reported a minor jewelry theft, nothing more. One of those who had acted like a suspect rather than a victim when she had approached him. He surely would not bother having a change of heart over a few gems.

This should be interesting.

~~~

Miriam and Jack drove up a road weaving its way into the high-priced hills beyond the city. "Welcome to millionaires' row," commented Stone, as they drove past yet another secured entrance to yet another secluded home. "I'm thinking of retiring here, what about you?"

"Sure. When we solve this case our bonus ought to cover it. Ah. Here we are."

They drove up to the entrance; the guard was expecting them and let them through. They got out and looked up marble steps to an entrance guarded by imposing Corinthian columns. "Well, Mr Tang has a taste for the grand, doesn't he?" commented Stone. "Let's see if he has some grand leads to go with it."

They were ushered into Mr Tang's presence. He looked like a large-framed man whose muscles were deserting his bones; he sat behind a desk and seemed sharp and alert, but with an undercurrent as of fatigue held temporarily in check by a grim force of will. He waved them to seats.

"Thank you for coming, officers. I am afraid that for all my wealth and for all our fine medical technology, the Grim Reaper has me marked on his calendar. I suppose one cannot resist the will of the Lord when he calls you to him. That is why I have decided to talk to you. I have done many bad things in my life. In particular, I have done one very cowardly thing. I am not sure that I can make amends but I will try. Perhaps it will work in my favor on the day of Judgment." He looked at them sadly, as if at the merciless surrogates of that final Judge.

"Please go on," prompted Miriam.

"I would ask one favor. In the course of our interview I may divulge things that are perhaps not, shall we say, strictly legal. I would like to speak under immunity from prosecution so that I may speak freely. I think it would be worth your while."

"We can't guarantee anything until we hear what you say," answered Jack. "We can promise to recommend leniency for your volunteering the information, but that's all we have the authority to do." He looked at Miriam. "But anything not directly useful to our case won't make it into a report."

Tang sighed. "Oh well, that will have to do. Honestly, if you did decide to prosecute I doubt it would come to trial in the time left to me on this Earth. I would just like my final days to be peaceful, not caught up in unpleasant legal entanglements. I suppose I shall have to leave that too in the Lord's hands."

He hesitated as if drawing on his resolve to continue; to Miriam he looked like a fading pit bull terrier steeling himself to admit, *Yes, I did eat your cat.*

"Well. As you know, a while back a few baubles were stolen from my apartment. What you do not know is that a few weeks after that some criminal gang sent me an untraceable message through my AI. Somehow they had discovered the contents of a safety deposit box I held, and they were demanding that I release those contents to them. They were extremely well informed. If I did not give them what they wanted, they would not only empty my bank accounts, they would reveal certain other information on my activities to people who would not be pleased to discover it. I am not a man who takes kindly to threats, and I admit I was less than submissive in my response. Such is the sin of hubris, I fear: for they chose to demonstrate their power by emptying a fifth of my funds, equally from each of my bank accounts—I suppose to show they could have taken it all. This was accompanied by another message to await further instructions."

Miriam asked, "You said 'untraceable'? You did not report this to the police. What steps did you take to trace these messages and to find out where your money had gone?"

"Oh, I have extensive resources, believe me, and I am not an amateur in these areas. But it is mystifying to me. My AI was good to start with and has been modified with all kinds of, shall we say, relevant software tools. But there was no trail, not even to a dead end. No trail at all. That should have been impossible. Whoever these people are, they are out of my class. I saw no alternative. I gave in. Of course I attempted to put a trace on the goods, but that too failed."

He spread his hands. "It failed because they knew. They were not happy with me. To punish me for my obstinacy and temerity, in their words, they took another quarter of my funds and released one piece of their blackmail. That is why I am now divorced from my wife of many years." He spread his hands. "Perhaps they were merely the Lord's tools in my humbling, as the Assyrians were to the Israelites. But I am talking to you in the hope that the Lord will punish them, just as he punished the Assyrians in their time."

"So what was in the safety deposit box? What was so important?" asked Miriam.

He sighed resignedly. "I suppose it can't cause any more harm if you know in general outline what these people now know in detail. Though they don't appear to have used their knowledge yet, so their true purpose remains a mystery to me. I have betrayed a great person, as well as my own principles, in order to cling to comforts which time has showed to be more ephemeral than I could imagine. I am ashamed, officers, ashamed."

He stopped talking, gazing into a distance only he could see. Finally he continued. "Years ago I was an ally of Lyn Felton in her campaign against the genetic engineers. You will remember how spectacularly successful she was, on a global scale. You don't get success like that in politics just through sheer brilliance and hard work, despite what the politicians say later in their memoirs. She made a lot of dirty deals in a lot of dirty countries so what had to be done, was done. And you are probably aware that GenInt, the child of her labors, has secret charters, charters that are secret for a reason. The common people would not understand. I speak of their power to summarily execute genetic monsters and clones, even babies."

Miriam was staring at him, open-mouthed. Stone had more control: he kept his mouth closed.

Tang misunderstood, and shook his head sadly. "Do not judge us too harshly. GenInt fight the Devil's work, officers, as you do in your own way. What they do is right and just, but in order to do it some things must remain hidden. The people as a mass do not think. They would see a baby and let it live, unable to see the monster that would rise up to slay them in years to come. Indeed, they would rise up against GenInt for trying to save their own lives at the baby's expense. Don't you see? The people must be protected from themselves. The art of government has always been thus. And Felton especially was doing the Lord's work, against great odds. Perhaps she sold pieces of her own soul in order to do it. But what greater, what more noble, sacrifice could a person make?"

"And... the material you gave the blackmailers?"

"I believed in Felton's work. I was one of her key operatives, and not for money but for principle. But I have always been what people call a sharp operator. Always playing the angles, always on the lookout for an advantage; always with backup plans and backups for the backups. There are some things I cannot help doing. I kept physical evidence of all the dirty dealings I was privy too. I had no thought of blackmail; if I had any specific thoughts at all they were for self-preservation: insurance if things went bad or I was in danger of being betrayed myself. And I kept details of GenInt's secret charters. Details of their activities in the early years. At the time I assumed I was not the only one, and probably I was right. Dangerous men gather around dangerous activities, after all, and to such men what I did was simple prudence, almost second nature. However it has become my eternal shame, because that is what I gave the blackmailers to save my own fleeting skin."

He lifted his eyes to look directly at them. "In my earlier days I worked to do a great thing, and I was proud, prouder than I have been of anything else I have ever done. I have made a great deal of money, but nothing compares to simply making something that is great. And then I betrayed it all, in a moment of weakness, cowardice and greed. And that is what now defines my life, officers. Perhaps God will forgive me even if I cannot forgive myself."

He looked away and added emptily, "I will find out soon enough. I hope to live long enough to see these villains brought to justice and their plans fallen to ruins. That is why I am telling you this. But what I dread above death is living long enough to see them succeed."

Miriam didn't think there was anything more to say, except for the one question burning in her mind in dread certainty of the answer. "Mr Tang, you mentioned that the blackmailers contacted you through your

AI. Could you ask it a question for me?"

He glanced at her, somewhat startled at the request. "Of course, if you think it would help. Though as I said, I have already done a thorough investigation of that side of things and found nothing."

"Could you ask it if it knows the phrase 'Kilroy was here' and if so, how it became aware of it?"

Tang stared at her with a puzzled frown. Miriam could practically read his thoughts in his expression: *What the hell kind of question is that?* But he shrugged and complied. Then his frown deepened. "Apparently that is an encryption hash salt it used a long time ago. Innocuous enough in itself—but... how could you know?"

Miriam stared back, heart thumping. *Oh dear God*, she thought. After a moment she said simply, "I didn't know, Mr Tang. It's just a strange lead we've been following."

He looked at her inquiringly, hoping she would elaborate, but now she was just looking off into the space beyond his shoulder, a worried frown on her face. *What deep waters are we wading in?* he wondered. But he stayed silent. *There are secrets here*, he thought, *dangerous secrets; this is larger than I knew. Larger than I want to know. Perhaps I was wrong to bare my soul and my shame. But if the waters are truly that deep—perhaps I was right to do it. Perhaps I have saved my soul after all.*

After a few moments Stone stood and said, "Well, thank you, Mr Tang. If there are any details that you think will help our investigation, please let us know. If we have any further questions or information, we'll contact you. Good day, sir."

Tang gestured in farewell, following them with his sad eyes as they took their leave.

On their way out, all Miriam said to Jack was, "At least this explains why so many of the victims don't want to talk to us."

"Yeah, blackmail has a way of keeping people's mouths shut. But we caught a break this time. Maybe enough of a break to get us that warrant for your DNA search."

Miriam nodded thoughtfully. They spent the rest of the trip back in silence, lost in their own private thoughts, all wanting to lead somewhere but leading nowhere.

CHAPTER 40: JENNY

It was getting late and long shadows stretched across the floor from the reddening sun beyond the windows of the offices beyond hers. Miriam was tired. She rubbed her eyes and thought, *time to go home*. Though it was not yet five she had come in early today and was already into overtime. She was reaching for her coat when a ping alerted her: the AI had decided it had something worthy of her attention even at this late hour.

It had found a match to the DNA from the fire. A blackmail scheme involving the President and GenInt had proved enough—just—to get a warrant for searches that preserved the privacy of any non-matching DNA sequences. But after a week had passed without anything, Miriam had stopped hoping; it had always been a long shot. Now she was energized anew.

"Bring it up," she commanded. She quickly scanned the data. Allowing for the ambiguities in the sequence it was a perfect match and the AI calculated a 94% chance that the DNA came from the same person. Her pulse quickened but she frowned with puzzlement when she saw that the record was from a scientific paper a quarter of a century old. Then Miriam saw the name.

"Grendel's Mother!" she swore. The person whose sequence matched was a Jenny Alderton, but the AI had used its initiative to ferret out a one-line bio ending with the notation: *Later Jenny Tagarin.* "Summarize all biographical information you can find on this Jenny Tagarin and why her genome is recorded!"

Miriam waited impatiently. After a few tense minutes, a couple of pages of summary appeared. Miriam swiftly scanned the document, taking in whole paragraphs in one mental gulp. *Sweet baby Jesus! Grendel's Mother indeed!* she thought. Her subconscious had made the connection immediately, she realized, bringing that particular curse to her lips. But not the mother of the ancient monster Grendel: the mother, of sorts, of the modern monster Katlyn. The DNA might indicate a 94% chance but Miriam was sure of it. She re-read the biography more closely.

Jennifer Alderton had been a bright, attractive woman with one flaw: a deadly genetic disease that had not made itself known until her late teens. It had soon become evident that her deterioration was accelerating and she would not survive her twenties. A young Dr Tagarin had been called in to investigate what the problem was and what could be done. The disease was rare and little was known about it; Tagarin had written a paper on her and her condition, and in the paper's confidential archival data was where her genome sequence had resided until the AI ferreted it out. But in the course of the study the two had fallen in love, and despite her condition had married. Tagarin thought he could save her. He hoped he could save her. But the technology was too young and her disease too deadly. He had failed.

"Can you find any photos of this woman?"

Another minute or so later her screen pinged and a photo of a smiling young woman appeared. Miriam stared at it. Katlyn: minus the eyes, a bit different in proportions, but Katlyn. *Oh God*, thought Miriam. *Oh God, Tagarin, what have you done?* But she knew what he had done. The sheer brilliant insanity of it made her head spin. Then another idea hit her. *Oh no*, she thought. *Oh no. It can't be. Not that as well.* The database would not be open to her fishing expedition; but it should open itself to an official targeted query. She did a quick search through her records, marked a case file number and instructed the AI to access and analyze.

After another few tense minutes, a file came through with the AI's analysis. Miriam stared at it. She did not know whether to feel elated or sick. She put her head in her hands. *No, no, no*, she thought. The enormity of it appalled her. Unbidden, the memory of Tagarin conducting his dance of life came back to her. But now the three of them were locked in a dance of death, and she was afraid to go forward but unable to turn back. She did not know if she would have the strength to do what she had to do; but she knew that she had to do it.

I joined the law to fight for what is right. But where is the right here? There is no right, and no path to find it.

Numbly, she connected to Stone. "Jack, I've got something. Something big. Meet me in the Chief's office." She disconnected without waiting for a reply then called Ramos to tell him they were coming.

~~~

"You look like you've seen a ghost," observed Stone when she came in.

"I think I have. Literally. Or as literal as a ghost can be. The AI got a match on the DNA fragments from the fire in a 23-year-old scientific paper. The DNA isn't good enough to be certain based on the sequence alone, but wait until you find out who it was. Jenny Tagarin! Our good doctor's dead wife! And look at this photo of her. Who does that look like?"

They both stared at it, then at her. Stone let out a low whistle. "Christ."

"And would you believe—there's more. I got the AI to access GenInt's records. The geneh infant GenInt killed in Tagarin's lab— she was a match too."

She paused, letting them digest it. Then she went on. "I don't think there's any doubt. Tagarin married this girl but he couldn't save her. And he couldn't forget her, or his failure. He kept a sample of her tissues and when he could, he fixed her DNA and brought her back to life. Well, not her, but you know what I mean. Then GenInt found her and killed her. And now he's done it again, only this time as a new, improved model. I don't know if what we're dealing with is *Phantom of the Opera* or *The Greatest Love Story Ever Told*, but Katlyn is the third incarnation of Jenny Tagarin!"

"Wait... wait," said Stone. "What about that other possibility you said earlier? Remember you thought that maybe Tagarin's first infant might not have been killed after all? That fits this new information just as well. Maybe better."

Miriam shook her head. "I thought of that too. But it doesn't make sense. You said several GenInt agents took the baby away. One having a fit of mercy I could imagine—barely—but four or five of them? So if our thief is that baby grown up, it means GenInt kept her deliberately. But if they'd done that there's no way in hell they'd have left her genome sequence in their records where I could find it with our modest little warrant and a case code. They'd have deleted it, or faked it, or hidden it under a blanket of top security."

Stone nodded. Then he turned to Ramos. "Well Chief, that leaves us with one prime suspect. If this isn't enough to get us a search warrant, if not an arrest warrant, nothing is."

Ramos nodded. "Good work, Hunter. I'll get on to it. It'll take an hour or so but you two get ready. Stone, arrange a team." He paused. "We're under no legal obligation to bring GenInt into this yet. They'll complain later if we don't, but that's all they can do: we still have jurisdiction for now. I am sure they would prefer being brought in on it now, which means they would like to take over, but they can prefer what they like. They'd just get in our way and we certainly don't want them getting there before we do. If either of you has a problem with that, now's the time to tell me."

Stone glanced at Miriam, who shook her head, then commented, "We're with you boss. As you say, all they can do is complain. Let's keep control of this. If GenInt take over who knows how many people will just disappear."

CHAPTER 41: PLANS

Daniel watched Katlyn attacking her dinner with her usual gusto. Tonight they were enjoying a superbly tender eye fillet steak on a potato-celeriac mash with crisply tender vegetables on the side, chased down with a well-aged shiraz. But he knew she would approach pizza and beer with just as much enthusiasm. He had given her a hard life, he knew, yet she had faced it with the same joy with which she attacked her food; and she had done so much with it, accomplished so much. He was so painfully proud of her that he didn't know whether what he felt was pride or love; perhaps there was no difference. *No*, he thought, *there is a difference: but they are two faces of the same thing.*

Katlyn noticed him watching her and smiled. "What are you thinking about, Mr Serious?" she asked.

"I was thinking I haven't given you much of a life, have I?"

Katlyn laughed, the tinkling musical bells so characteristic of her. That had not been designed; he occasionally wondered what unexpected genetic interaction had produced it. "Pfft! Who was it who told me, 'Fate deals us all a hand but what we do with it is up to us'?" she quoted. "Oh! It was you!"

She smiled, and he wasn't sure if it was a child's trusting smile at her father or a woman's smile to her equal. "And you were right. And I know you know it, when you're not feeling sorry for me. Life is a gift, the greatest gift there is. If Fate decides to deal you a really bad hand, then you might feel otherwise: but there's an easy solution to that, isn't there?"

She looked at him seriously. "You know there have been plenty of times when I've been sad or angry about things. But those are the fault of the people who made it so, not you. You gave me life, Daniel. And I'm happy that I'm alive. I'm happy I lived through the hard times. I hope I live for a long time yet. But If I were to die tonight, I would die without any regrets for the life I've lived." She reached across the table, gently took his hand, and kissed it.

He smiled and returned to his own food; there seemed to be something in his eye. He remembered when he was a boy and his parents had taken him on a trek in Nepal. Out in those high mountainous wilds he had met a couple of other young kids, dirty and dirt poor, living it tough with no anticipation of a better life. Despite that they had been happy, laughing and playing like kids anywhere. But so many people living with all the benefits of a technological civilization were miserable in their lives, when all they needed for happiness was at their call: all they had to do was get up and do something about it.

He frowned as that reminded him of an even worse sin, the cases of 'wrongful life' brought to the courts early in the century: people who reckoned their lives were so miserable that their parents, or society, or someone, should never have let them be born. He thought of the contrast with Katlyn, this happy spirit who had borne so much and done so much in her brief life. He looked up at her. *It will all be over soon, dearest Katlyn,* he thought; *one way or another, it will soon be over.*

"You're thinking again," she noted. "I hope you're not still feeling sorry for me."

He smiled. "I am thinking that all of this will soon be over. A few weeks, and we should be done. I think we've done enough already but the more the better. However you shouldn't go out any more for a while, for any reason: the risks are too high now. And we're too close."

"What's the latest status?"

Daniel leaned back and put his fingers to his chin. "Well, as you know the original strategy predictions gave us a good chance of getting through all this without anyone suspecting who was behind it. Then we could have just gone on with our lives with nobody the wiser. But the police got on to the case sooner than they should have. There's still a chance they'll give up when their leads dry up, but the latest simulations show that the most likely outcome is they'll cobble together enough clues for a warrant within a few weeks. If they do we'll have to cut and run."

"Will we be ready?"

"They've been so troublesome—for which I'm inclined to place most blame on the well-named Det. Hunter—that it's not safe to rely on even that much time. So I've already put what we need in place just in case. In other words, while I'm still hoping we can get away with Plan A, it's really looking like we're going to have to take the plunge into Plan C. And sooner rather than later."

Katlyn's eyes showed a mixture of fear and excitement. They could have simply fled to continue living much as they had been, hiding from the world, only with less resources and greater risk that the world would notice them. That was Plan B: short term safety at the price of long-term risk, paid for with nothing but hope. The alternative was far more dangerous and could quickly end with Katlyn dead and Daniel in prison or dead himself: but the potential reward was much greater. For all of Katlyn's life, safety had lain in hiding and concealment, whereas Plan C would reveal her to the world. The prospect filled her with instinctive dread, like an animal whose survival depended on camouflage that was suddenly thrust onto a sunlit plain. But if it worked she would no longer need to hide.

Daniel saw in her eyes that she was willing to risk death for a chance at that prize and they both knew she *was* risking death. For all that the chances looked good, they could not find out more certainly without the risk of tipping their hand, which in itself could be more quickly and certainly fatal. If anyone suspected their plan it literally would not get off the ground.

Soft chimes sounded in the air and a voice spoke, "Excuse me, sir?"

Daniel frowned. The AI would only interrupt private conversations if it decided it had to. "Yes?"

"I'm sorry sir, but police have arrived outside."

"At this time of the evening? How many?"

"Several, and they are armed. I cannot give a precise number because they are all wearing infiltration suits with signal disruptors. I deduce from this that they must have at least a search warrant and possibly even an arrest warrant: and they intend to vigorously pursue it."

Daniel thought quickly. "Analyze their warrant carefully and if it is valid and dangerous enough to trigger Plan C, initiate it immediately." He paused. "I expect it will be."

He looked at Katlyn. "Suddenly I'm glad things are already almost prepared. There are a few things in the front office I'd have liked to take but we'll have to forget about them, at least for now."

His eyes acquired the same mixture of fear and excitement that Katlyn's had moments before. "Let's get going. Things aren't quite ready yet so it will take us a few hours before we can go: but unless we get very unlucky we'll easily have that much time."

Chapter 42: Intruders

For the fourth time Miriam found herself in the driveway of Tagarin's estate looking towards the entrance. For the first time she had more than Stone for company: a van with ten heavily armed police pulled up behind them. They did not know what to expect and Ramos had decided that overkill was better than failure.

Stone got out and called two of the others to come with him. As they approached the front gate, the AI spoke. "Good evening, Detectives. I see you have a warrant this time. My owner regards this is rather inconvenient timing: could you perhaps return tomorrow? He promises to make himself available then."

Stone barked a short laugh. "Sure, it works that way. Open up or we'll have to rough you up a bit, Gate."

"It is always a pleasure to cooperate with the police, especially when they threaten me so nicely," answered the AI drily. Tagarin seemed to have successfully transplanted his personality into his AI, thought Stone. "Please wait."

Stone glanced cynically at his colleagues and waited. The wait began to stretch out and Stone shook his head impatiently. He was in two minds about whether to demand entry or just break the gate down when it spoke. No doubt if he had shown more patience it would have waited even longer.

"I have confirmed that your warrant is valid: I am opening the gate for you and have unlocked the door to the house; you may enter without violence. Be warned that any deviations from the terms of your warrant will have severe legal consequences."

"OK," said Stone. "Goodbye Gate, it's been a laugh. Jones, deactivate this outpost of the AI—I want to keep them guessing."

When Jones gave him the thumbs up they jammed the gate open with a rock, drew their weapons and walked cautiously up to the front door. Stone pushed it with his foot and it opened easily onto a dark corridor. "No welcoming committee with drinks, eh?" he commented. "I feel unloved. Jones, cover that camera and turn on your signal jammer." While he did so, he called the others to join them. "All right guys, show time. Jones, guard the door; Smith, go back and guard the gate. Don't let anyone in or out. Anyone who turns up, detain them; anyone who tries to leave, arrest them. The rest of you, let's go. Hopefully Tagarin will be as accommodating as his gate. If not, we'll just have to return the favor."

They went in and the two cops left behind stood at their posts, nervous and alert, weapons drawn.

Some minutes later one of the darker shadows under a stand of trees across the road detached itself and glided onto the road towards the entrance. Smith raised his weapon but the shadow kept coming, revealing itself as a man dressed in black with a high collar obscuring his face, holding his hands out and visible. Smith kept his gun trained on the man's chest and ordered him to halt, but the man simply smiled humorlessly and extended his identification. Smith grunted and lowered his gun. "What can I do for you, sir?" he asked with brittle politeness.

"You can stand aside, officer, I'm going in. I presume you have no objection?"

"Be my guest, sir," replied Smith. "Should I advise my team?"

"No, we don't want to warn any eavesdroppers." Smith waved to Jones to indicate to let the man past, and he moved quickly up the path and slipped through the door. Then he stole carefully and silently up the corridor. He turned suddenly at a metallic clang behind him: a steel door had descended, cutting off the way out. He hoped that was to keep the cops out, not that he had been detected and it was to lock him in. Grimly, he drew a slim gun from the folds of his clothes and crept cautiously into the gloom.

CHAPTER 43: TRAPPED

Stone's team had met no resistance. But nor did they meet any people. Just as the front door had opened but that was all, further inside the place appeared to be deserted and the lights refused to shine. "Funny guy, eh?" commented Stone. "Well if that's the way he wants to play it, we might just have to break down some doors."

Tagarin's visitors' annex was empty, as was the office where he met with his callers. They did not need to break down any doors; the doors simply opened at their touch. Yet the lights still did not shine: it was like a physical essay on passive resistance. Besides the door they had entered the office through, there was only one other door leading deeper into the complex. Stone nodded to one of his men, who stood beside it and pushed it gently. It opened as the others had, revealing a short straight corridor that split into two at the end.

"Why do I feel like we're being suckered?" murmured Stone. "OK, we're going to have to split up. This is the only way out and we already have guards out front, so we'll all keep going. You lot take the right branch, you others take the left one with me. Check every room. Split up if you have to as long as you can stay in pairs. I don't trust this place an inch."

He thought a moment then added, "First, search this room. Make sure there's nothing obvious like a place to hide or a hidden door. Once we've covered that angle we'll move in."

He whispered into Miriam's ear: "You stay put: when we start searching, duck under the desk. It's probably nothing and when this is all over you'll whine about missing all the fun, but I want you here. You know all the players and you're fast on your feet. You're my backup plan. I really like backup plans. And if this is a sucker play, you'll be our second chance—and maybe our lifeline. I don't think anyone watching will have been able to count heads, not the way we've been milling around shining lights everywhere: they won't notice if one of us vanishes. I hope."

Miriam nodded tensely.

They all began searching the room, looking into and under things and poking walls, while Miriam quietly slipped under the desk. Then Stone called out, "OK, looks like there's nothing here. Let's get going before they manage to come up with more tricks."

Their expressions tightened as they stalked down the corridor and split up. But Stone's suspicions were borne out: to explore everywhere at once his team had to split up again. It was like a fractal trap. It was a fractal trap.

Tagarin had been planning this for a long time. He knew that one day the surface of his plan might unravel and they might need to escape in the face of a police invasion. He wanted to avoid the necessity for battles and blood. He had remodeled his mansion accordingly.

Few people were granted access to Tagarin's domain. Had one of the few been a police spy, Stone would have been even more suspicious and things might have taken a different turn. It had taken mere seconds for the exit from Tagarin's office to be switched from the normal passageway, which led to his private rooms, to the bifurcating corridors, which did not. The change had been triggered the moment the police went through the gate.

Tagarin did not trust people in large groups. Fear fed on fear and they might panic. Or less likely but worse, thought might feed on thought and come up with a plan. He had always been a fan of jiu-jitsu, and his defenses were planned accordingly: let your opponent overextend himself and use his own thrust against him. So once the invaders had been split up into twos and threes, something else happened.

Stone and his two remaining companions were exploring a corridor, hoping that beyond the curve was not yet another bifurcation. For now, they stood outside a locked door, considering. For the first time, the door had not opened for them: but what did that mean? Progress or a trap? The question in their minds was answered when two doors slid shut ahead and behind.

Then Tagarin's voice came from somewhere. "Welcome to my uninvited guest quarters, noble officers of the law. The door you see in the wall is now unlocked and within are basic facilities to enable you to survive a day or two in modest comfort. Alas, I fear it will *be* a day or two. Personally I would be happy for all this to be done with as soon as possible, but I suspect your superiors will wish to haggle over my perfectly reasonable demands that are the price for your, and not coincidentally our, freedom.

"Rest assured I wish you no harm. You may even communicate with your colleagues outside. In fact, I encourage it: it might stop your more aggressive friends from bombing the place. I am sure you want that as little as I do. I suppose many of you have wives and children; if you want to spare them the grief of attending your funeral, you would be wise to reveal you are safe and counsel restraint.

"Now there are a few rules. Be aware that the walls and doors of your current home are steel and if anyone tries to blast their way in— or if you really came prepared, out—the shockwave will surely kill you. So please refrain from any such heroics, as they will achieve nothing but your own deaths. There are also more active defenses should you attempt some other form of escape: I encourage you not to find out what they are. Again I assure you that I wish you no harm; if you do not believe me, consider that I have merely imprisoned you when I could just as easily have shot you. So the only harm you will come to is what you bring on yourselves. As lawmen you must be aware of rules and the consequences of breaking them: act accordingly. You will be freed unharmed soon enough. In the meantime, take this interlude as a paid holiday. I regret that you will have to make your own entertainment, but you will be safe and comfortable enough."

The same scene played out elsewhere in the trap. Stone gave voice to the thought in all their heads.

"Shit."

CHAPTER 44: MIRIAM

"Miriam."

The whispered voice sounded in her ear.

"Yes? I'm here," she whispered.

"The bad news is, it was a trap. We don't appear to be in any danger but we've been neatly cut out of the picture. You need to know, but I don't know what you can do about it. Don't do anything stupid. We've already told the guys outside—who are now locked outside. An inner door slammed shut and Jones had to retreat to the gate when tear gas started spraying at him. Reinforcements are coming and they could try to break in, but we've been told in no uncertain terms that we're hostages and hostilities, including attempting to penetrate their perimeter, will invite retaliation. So we have a siege but are going to play it cool for now. Sorry kid, it looks like you might see some excitement after all. All I can tell you is that we were somehow diverted into a well set up trap: if you can find a way into his main facility you might be able to stop him, but I have no idea how you'd do it. I'll hang up now; the less chance we give them to discover you're still outside their trap the better. Good luck."

Christ, thought Miriam. *Only a few minutes in and it's already eleven down, one to go.* At least the others were alive, though it was easy to be merciful when you held the upper hand. Tagarin might play the gracious host when he felt safe, but if he found her prowling through his house with a gun his reaction could be deadly. Her fear and isolation told her that maybe she should just stay here cowering under the desk. It was unlikely anyone would fault her for it.

But she knew that would never happen: she couldn't stop trying any more than she could stop breathing. She had never been one to be a passive passenger of life, someone who just hoped that the world would deliver her wishes: to her, the essence of living was action. At least if you failed you died trying, she believed; you died as someone who had fought and so deserved to live.

But, she wondered as she identified that feeling in herself, wasn't that equally true of Katlyn and Tagarin? Wasn't that all they had been doing too, in their bizarre plot that had led to all this? She shook her head. No. Tagarin had not been forced into his life of crime; he had chosen to do it, knowing the consequences, knowing the risks. And however innocent Katlyn might have been, she in her turn had become a dangerous sociopath; the rights and wrongs of how her past had brought her there did not change what she was in the present.

Wonderful, Miriam thought, *you've rationalized your call to heroic action so well I can almost hear the trumpets: but what action are you going to* take? It wasn't at all obvious. If Tagarin had trapped the others somehow, how would she avoid the same fate? It was unlikely he had anything as obvious as a hidden button that opened up his true domain: everything would be computer controlled with no hope of access by an outsider.

Well, there's no point sitting here forever, she told herself. *If I start looking around and this room is under observation then I'm sprung, but if I do nothing I might as well be locked in with the others anyway.* Her best bet was to carefully explore the corridor the others had gone down, hope to find how they had been diverted and hope there was some way around it, or even better some way to release the others. It was either that or stay hidden here and wish for the unlikely event that one of the villains of the piece would come to her.

She was just standing up after crawling out of her hiding space when Katlyn stepped into the room.

CHAPTER 45: CAUGHT

So far things had gone according to plan, even if the plan had to be accelerated. With their sortie caught like crabs in a pot it would be a while before the police would try anything else. So Katlyn had gone to the front office to collect a few things they preferred not to leave behind: they would never return. She walked silently, more out of habit than caution. The light came on as she entered the room and she nearly jumped out of her skin when she saw a black-clad apparition rising up in front of Daniel's desk, face hidden by a dark visor; the apparition jumped too, so the feeling must have been mutual.

Miriam reached for her gun but Katlyn's reactions were much faster. Miriam was stunned by the speed and ferocity of the attack. Katlyn leapt at her and knocked her back onto the desk, slamming her forearm down so the gun shot from her hand and slid off the back of the desk, before whacking her head from side to side until her ears rang. Stunned, Miriam could only gasp as Katlyn tore off her helmet and hurled it away; there were two dull thuds as it hit the wall then fell to the floor. Katlyn looked back and stopped, startled. "You again! Will I ever be rid of you?" she hissed, then wrapped her hands around Miriam's neck and began to squeeze.

Miriam knew she had only seconds of consciousness left, but by the time her mind became aware of that fact her reflexes had taken over: her arms wheeled to break Katlyn's grip then grab and twist her arm, forcing her over sideways. Katlyn went with the move to escape Miriam's grasp but Miriam suddenly let go; her legs were already up and she kicked Katlyn hard in the stomach. Katlyn went one way and banged into the wall with an explosion of breath; Miriam went the other way, rolling back over the desk, and in a single fluid motion came to her feet with the gun in her hand, pointed straight at Katlyn.

"That's enough!" she ordered. "Stay where you are with your hands up or I'll shoot!"

Katlyn's eyes darted to Miriam, to the door and back. *No chance*, she thought. Miriam was too far to be jumped and the door too far for escape: not when, however fast she could run, all Miriam had to do was move her hand and pull the trigger. She exhaled and put her hands up slowly.

"You're making me regret saving your life," she said bitterly.

"Be thankful I didn't just shoot you where you stand! Now face the wall and kneel on the floor with your hands behind your head. This time I get to handcuff you."

Katlyn did not move. "Listen. I know you're mad at me. I know you're a cop and catching people like me is what you do. But if you don't let me go, I'm dead. Whatever else I've done, I did save your life. What did you say to me once? That you didn't deserve to die? Well I don't deserve it either. Let me go." She added roughly, as if it was a word she wasn't used to, "Please."

"You only had to save me because I was chasing you! Taking all our charming meetings into account, I think you're psychotic. Unpredictable and dangerous. Maybe it's not your fault. Maybe your genome has made you mentally unstable; maybe it was growing up the way you did. Or maybe it's just you. But that's not my call. My job is to uphold the law. You just tried to kill me and for all I know you've left a trail of dead bodies behind you! For all I know, you do deserve to die."

Katlyn sighed, and it was if the brash bravado left her body with the breath. Suddenly she looked more like a scared teenager than a hardened criminal. "No. I wasn't trying to kill you, just knock you out. I never killed anyone. I was never even going to hurt you, that first time, not seriously. Do you know why I treated you so badly then?"

"I don't care. On the floor. Now. Or I'll shoot you."

Katlyn continued as if she hadn't spoken. "'Know your enemy' is the first rule of war, and this is war, you know. Not much of a war, I admit; not much of an army. But war just the same. I needed to know your mettle and I wanted to scare you off if I could. I did what I had to, that's all. Well, maybe not all. I was angry: at the world, at you, at what you represented. But don't you see? If I'm what you say, do you think I'd have let you live?"

"How should I know? You're crazy! I wonder how many mice think the cat has let them go, when it releases them just to torment them?"

Katlyn looked at her sadly. "Back then, the first time we met, you talked about justice. Was that the truth? If it was—will you listen to me?"

"Save it for the courtroom. You'll have your chance then."

"There won't be a courtroom," she replied softly. "Not for me."

Miriam wondered if that was true. If she was sending this girl to her death, perhaps she owed it to her to understand, or at least to listen. From where she was standing she could cover the corridor as well as Katlyn: she could afford this small grant of time.

"You have a minute. No more."

"I will tell you the truth. If you'd shown you were what I first thought—my enemy, to your bones—then I might have killed you. That's what happens in war. Or I might have killed you in self-defense if I had to. But I found out who you really are: and I don't mean just that you're brave, or that you talked to me not as a monster but like you would to anyone else. It was the other way round: I saw that you're just a girl like me, just someone doing the best you can to live and do what you think is right. I laughed at you when you said you were innocent: but I think you are, down where it counts."

She paused, then went on. "Yes, I'm angry at the world. But no matter how much the world takes from you, you can't fight it by becoming the same evil yourself. Because then you lose yourself too; and if you lose yourself, you've lost everything. Whatever else I am, the innocent are safe from me."

"Yet you chose a life of crime."

"If the world makes you a criminal just for being, how can it complain if you accept the role? Would you have done any differently?"

Miriam studied Katlyn. Her breaths were rapid and shallow and her yellow eyes were wide with a fear she would not fully admit. *For once she looks like what she is,* Miriam thought: *for all her adult body and actions, for all that she's done, deep down she really is just a fifteen-year-old girl.* When she dropped her tough persona as the vicious criminal, her voice was soft and somewhat musical. But it didn't change anything.

"I'm sorry, Katlyn. I have to take you in. I have to uphold the law."

"You talk about justice," she replied bitterly. "But if you arrest me I'm dead. No appeal. No lawyers. No nothing. Some GenInt goon will put a bullet in my brain, before or after a bit of dissection to find out what makes me tick. Or makes me scream, more likely."

"No. We will have you, not GenInt. We can hold you, protect you. You will have your chance."

Katlyn laughed her incongruous laugh, though this time the bells were edged with a metallic bitterness. "You really are a young innocent, aren't you? No, I am afraid GenInt has legal jurisdiction. They'll take me whenever they want me, which will be sooner rather than later. Now listen. Your job is to prevent crime. Consider it prevented. My life of crime is over. I'm leaving, so I won't be bothering anyone here ever again, and I swear I won't be bothering anyone where I'm going either. Isn't that a good outcome? Without any further expense to our underfunded and overtaxed so-called justice system, Master Thief Katlyn has been reformed after a mere couple of conversations with you and is now a model citizen! All you have to do is stand aside and let me go. Nobody will even know."

"I will know."

"You will know that you've saved a life! I can't claim it is a perfectly innocent life. But I hope you believe me that I don't deserve to die any more than you did, that first time we met."

Miriam hesitated. This would be much simpler without that automatic death penalty. Like many cops who had learned what some people chose to do to others, Miriam had nothing against killing criminals if they were killers themselves. But it had to be during the execution of the crime or failing that, after due process of law, where the truth mattered. No truth mattered here except the plain fact of Katlyn's genes, and was that enough? How could it be enough? Still, the fact remained of Katlyn's treatment of her; talk was cheap when you were the one at the wrong end of the gun. And as a cop she had to trust the law to do what was right. Surely even GenInt couldn't just make someone disappear out of police custody. Not a grown woman talking and breathing like anyone else.

"I don't believe it is as bad as you say; we won't let them take you. Now on the floor."

"No. I'm not going to let you off the hook. You think you can serve justice and the law, but you can't. And the law isn't here. There's no big institution with marble columns and dignified judges applying abstract justice: it's just you and me, two people who have to make the decisions and bear the consequences. If you think you can avoid the responsibility by passing my fate on to someone else, I won't let you get away with it. You'll have to shoot me yourself: you, now, by your own hand."

She stood there for a moment, letting the silence underline the thought. Then she added softly, "Before you decide, there's one more thing you ought to know. You won't believe me, but that night on the roof wasn't the first time I saved your life."

Miriam stood still for a moment, then said slowly, "It was you in the park that day, wasn't it? I saw you but I thought I dreamed it. Tell me."

"I was waiting for you. I knew you were dangerous and I was thinking I should kill you myself, or at least hurt you so bad you'd be out of action," she admitted simply. "But I couldn't. It would have been so easy to let those guys finish you off for me. But I couldn't do that either. So I finished the fight for you."

She let that hang in the air. Miriam wondered whether it was true. Katlyn could have found out the details later; the way these people plotted and lied, she might even have planned the attack herself. But Miriam had seen it herself, just not believed what she had seen.

"Why would you do that for me?"

Katlyn replied softly, "I've heard you can be put in a situation that forces you to make a moral choice between two paths, a choice that defines the rest of your life. I guess that was mine." She looked toward the door then back to Miriam. "I guess it brought me here. More fool me, eh?"

Then she continued. "Now it's your turn. I'm going to walk out that door. You'll have to let me go or shoot me." She slowly started lowering her hands.

"Stop! I can't let you go!"

Katlyn shook her head gravely. "No. You will decide whether I deserve to die and if I don't, whether you will serve your laws or the justice you think gives them meaning. I've made my choice and threats can't stop me now: if you want to stop me you'll have to actually shoot me. So whatever you decide... goodbye Miriam," she finished softly.

Miriam felt her aim waver and opened her mouth to speak, but the only sound was the bang of three rapid gunshots.

Katlyn clutched her middle and looked down. "Oh no," she moaned softly. She looked up at Miriam, eyes dark and wide with shock. "Oh no." Then her eyes dulled and closed, her legs buckled under her and she slid down the wall. She fell onto her stomach, kicked a few times and then lay still.

Miriam looked on, horrified. It had happened so quickly her brain had had no chance to catch up, and she looked stupidly at her own gun, wondering how it had fired. Then she whirled at the sound of a familiar voice behind her, "Well, that wasn't so hard."

Miriam couldn't believe her eyes or her ears. "*Amaro?!* What are you doing here? *How* are you here? *What have you done?*"

Amaro looked at her, his usual playful expression replaced by something flat and hard. "I should think you would be grateful. A suspicious man might interpret what he just heard as one of the City Police being on the verge of letting a criminal escape justice. That would not be good for her career, nor perhaps her freedom. But fortunately Amaro is a carefree soul, always willing to believe the best of people. He is willing to concede he may have misheard or merely had less patience than you."

Then his voice hardened. "However my good mood is at risk from that gun you still have pointed at me. You might wish to lower it. You didn't appear to know how to use it a few seconds ago, so don't start remembering now."

Miriam had led with her gun when she spun around but in her surprise had forgotten she still had it pointed at him. Or perhaps she now thought of him as the enemy. She saw that Amaro had a gun himself, a relatively small .22, made more for concealment than firepower but deadly nonetheless. It was easy to tell it was a .22 because she was looking right down the barrel. She lowered her own gun. "Sorry, you startled me. But *what the hell is going on?*"

"Why, my dear, surely you have worked it out. I am doing my job. Superlatively, I might add. Amaranto Leandro Moreno, agent of the dreaded Department of Human Genetic Integrity, at your service," he replied, executing one of his signature bows.

"I appear to have missed the memo your department sent us about this raid, but when you told me you'd be late because something big had come up, it wasn't too hard to guess what and where. Your loyal guards let me in and I made my way to the little room outside here, where I was planning my next move. Then events intervened. You did well, by the way. An excellent interrogation, which I followed with great interest. Until the end anyway, when you were a trifle slow executing your clear duty when the subject became uncooperative."

Miriam stared at him in disbelief. She was suffering cognitive overload. Then her brain finally started to recover and make connections.

"You said you worked for the EPA, for God's sake!" she cried. Then she saw the full truth, and felt sick. She added softly, "You didn't meet me by accident. You've been spying on me this whole time, haven't you? You've been spying on us, the police, through me!" She looked at him, hopelessly, the enormity of the lie weighing upon her. "Please tell me it isn't true," she added softly.

Amaro just shrugged. "Oh, everything I told you is true. Well, nearly everything and nearly true. I am a scientist working for the EPA, but it is a cover. GenInt likes to have its finger on the pulse. What better place to keep tabs on illegal genetic engineering than in some other government department that analyses samples from all over, and pays for it out of its own budget to boot?

"But were we two lovers meeting by accident in a smoky room? Sorry. You're a job. We got your department's obscurely worded report on this—thing" he said contemptuously, waving towards Katlyn's body "—and got suspicious. It looked like you didn't want us to know but wanted to cover your asses—and a pretty ass it is too, I must add." He smirked. "You guys must think we're idiots. Anyway, we knew you were a key person. My job was to keep an eye on you and find out what I could. My natural charm did the rest."

"You *bastard!*"

"Come now, Miriam, grow up. Lots of cops go undercover. You might do it yourself one day. Get over it. We had fun, didn't we?"

"But I'm a cop! I'm not some low-life criminal you can happily lie to because he's a liar or worse himself! I loved you! Don't you know that? I loved you! How could you do that to me!?"

Amaro shrugged again. "What was I supposed to do? Anyway, don't blame me. I warned you from the start that getting too close to me might burn you, didn't I? You're the one who chose to do it anyway and who fooled yourself. I just told you what you wanted to hear. Sure, there had to be a few lies, but nothing major. I tweaked my resume and my background a bit to make myself sound more appealing, that's all. The rest you did to yourself. Most of it was even real."

"Except you never loved me. All that was a lie. Our whole relationship was a lie. Every touch, every kiss, every..." Her vision blurred, and she realized she was crying. *I won't give him the satisfaction,* she thought. *I won't.* She swallowed and glared at him, knowing her tears were there and would not be stopped, but refusing to acknowledge their existence or what they meant.

Amaro looked at her. Part of him was the agent of GenInt, unmoved. But he knew he had let her get under his skin. The agent felt he owed her nothing; but the man knew he owed her something. "If it makes any difference to you," he continued more gently, "it wasn't all an act. I did care for you, Miriam. But some things aren't meant to be. Think of us as Romeo and Juliet, except in our case"—he waved his gun at Katlyn—"somebody else did the dying. So a happy ending, of sorts. But I'm sorry I hurt you, for what that's worth. I suspect not much, but..." He shrugged.

The man's debt cleared, the agent felt free to take over again. "For the record, you were admirably if irritatingly discrete. That made my job harder, but more enjoyable at the same time: like a game of chess with a particularly talented opponent playing an unconventional game. But that's all history. Now we have to look to tomorrow, a much brighter vista. In honor of the good times we've had together, I'm letting you share the credit on this one. Really, I do appreciate how you backed me up, covering my back while I cornered this thing and dispatched it. Isn't that a much better story than what I might tell? You should be showering my feet with kisses, not tears."

"I understand, Amaro," she said tonelessly. "I understand you had a job to do. But I think your job stinks and you stink with it. You're just a liar and a killer. Go to hell."

His face hardened and he snapped, "That attitude can get you in trouble, girl! There are reasons for the geneh laws, very good reasons. That thing had to die. If you were willing to let it go then you should go to jail yourself!" His voice took on almost a pleading quality, though Miriam couldn't tell if it was a remnant desire to protect her or just one part of himself trying to convince another. "Listen. You know the law. We've even talked about it. Our opinions don't matter. She spoke to you about justice—but do you really think she had rights? That she deserved a trial? *Humans* have rights, and *humans* have decided that things like her aren't one of them."

His face hardened again. "If you don't like it, take it up with your fellow citizens. It is sweet, really, how you have such empathy for all God's and Satan's creatures. But get a grip. If I worked for Animal Control and had just shot a rabid dog, well, maybe you'd still feel sorry for the dog: but would you really condemn me for doing my job? For protecting people at the dog's expense? For deceiving you in order to track it down, when that's the only way I could because you were blind to how dangerous it was?"

Miriam stared at him. He really believed it, she realized. It wasn't just a job to him. None of that had been a lie. He really did see himself as a knight protecting the kingdom, defending the realm of man from the monsters of the night. She thought she hated him even more for it. Though for all she knew, he was right. She didn't know any more. All the fight left her. It didn't matter anyway now.

"All right, Amaro. I give up. Arrest me if you want to."

He smiled. "Oh, don't be like that. What happened to that tongue I so admired? I won't arrest you. You might feel like that now, but I suspect your tongue will wake up eventually and talk you out of it. No, much better if we share the credit, myself with the lion's share of course. If I try to ruin your career you will fight it, and your department will probably fight it too. Who knows how shabby you might make GenInt look? Going undercover and under the covers to spy on pretty rookie police girls can be made to sound so tawdry. No. Much better to make this a shining example of cooperation between noble GenInt and the loyal police force; between the global authorities and the local law. Our personal relationship, should it be revealed, was just the natural chemistry of two young people with shared goals. Why, the human interest angle would probably make the magazines."

Miriam felt sick.

"And you really should look on the bright side. I can understand that getting over me might take some time, but you will soon enough. It won't be that hard for a woman like you to find some other charming man to share your bed. Why, in a year you'll have forgotten me completely, except as the rocket that gave your career a boost most cops can only dream of. So dry your tears and get on with your job."

"So what do we do now?" she asked tiredly.

"Well, first let's make sure this thing is completely dead," he said, drawing his gun and stepping cautiously toward Katlyn's body.

"Actually, the first thing you two will do is drop your guns and raise your hands," growled a voice from the corridor. The voice belonged to Tagarin, as did the hefty automatic rifle that had preceded him into the room and was pointed in their direction. "And no sudden moves."

CHAPTER 46: JUDGMENT

They raised their hands and turned fully toward him, slowly. He frowned at them and jerked his rifle in their direction.

"I believe I mentioned dropping your guns?"

Amaro shrugged, laid his gun carefully on the ground and kicked it away. Miriam carefully removed hers from her holster and did likewise.

"OK James, take these two away. I'll take care of Katlyn. The last thing she'd have wanted is her body paraded before the cameras as a poster child for GenInt. You two murderers and I will have a little talk soon."

James came in, collected their guns then waved them toward the exit with his own gun. "This way, Sir, Madam," he said in his butler's voice. "But don't ask me to serve coffee," he added in a growl.

Miriam was almost through the door when she stopped. Like Lot's wife, she couldn't resist a last look behind. She caught a fleeting glimpse of Tagarin gently lifting Katlyn's limp body to his chest before James pushed her ungently into the corridor. Miriam noticed that it now ran straight to beyond where it had earlier divided into two, and realized how simply the others had been trapped; but the knowledge was no use to her now.

~~~

"The boss will be here soon, I imagine," James said after tying them to chairs and removing the phones from their wrists. "Make yourselves comfortable," he smirked. He added in a tone of idle conversation, "I hope he isn't too long. I get bored easily. I might feel like beating you two up a bit for something to do." He cracked his knuckles and smiled at them politely.

Neither of them had anything to say. Miriam was in no mood. Even Amaro, who normally couldn't resist wisecracks, knew when it was safest to just shut up.

A few minutes later Tagarin entered the room. He favored both of them with a look of disgust.

"I knew you'd be trouble," he said to Miriam, "just not this much this soon. And you," he said, turning to Amaro, "You were with her at the ball. So I presume it wasn't an accident you were both there after all." He glared at Miriam. "You're a better liar than I thought."

Miriam just shook her head dumbly. What was the point of arguing, she thought?

He turned back to Amaro. "I guess from your weapons that you're the one who actually shot her. What are you? GenInt?"

Amaro just glared at him.

"Not that it matters. You're both in it, both guilty. Now I have to decide what to do with you. I am most tempted to hang you both, and leave you to be found by your colleagues, when they eventually break in, swinging gently from the rafters. It would make a nice image for the less tasteful news feeds, don't you think? But I am sorry to say that killing you two is very likely to interfere with certain other plans of mine, which generally end in my leading a long and happy life in some tropical paradise. So I shall have to think of something else less satisfying but more strategic."

He glared at them a while longer. "My AI is currently negotiating with the police. If handsome here really is GenInt, his friends have either not yet made an appearance or are content to stay in the background for now. A pity, as I might have enjoyed a shootout with them. For all my flaws I am less inclined to shoot at the police, who at least fight real criminals part of the time. Such as myself, I suppose. But they know some of their own are in here and still alive. My AI's strategy programs estimate that it will be at least ten hours before your negotiators decide to either pretend to let me go or try to break in at the risk of killing you and all your colleagues, so we have time yet. And I have some important things to do during that time to ensure my future wealth and dissipated lifestyle."

He gave Miriam a hard glance. "But based on my experience of

Detective Hunter here, I don't trust you two not to find some way to interfere. Again. So I am afraid I shall have to knock you both out for a while.

"James."

Miriam steeled herself. She did not imagine this was going to be pleasant.

"Don't flinch, Detective. We are not going to be so crude as to hit you over the head with an iron bar, gratifying as that would be. A simple injection will suffice." James brought out a kit containing two syringes filled with clear liquid. "This will hurt no more than the usual injection and will ensure a restful sleep. Unfortunately it would be dangerous to give you a dose large enough to keep you out for very long, and even so there will be side effects. But you'll be out long enough to ensure you can't cause me further bother. First our detective here."

Miriam watched, helpless, as James injected the solution into her arm. She wondered if she would ever wake. "Now her friend here." Amaro snarled and his muscles bulged as if to break his bonds by pure strength, but to no avail. "Sweet dreams, children", said Tagarin. Miriam watched Amaro's eyes close as he slumped sideways. Then it occurred to her to wonder how she was still awake to see it.

CHAPTER 47: ANSWERS

"Now, Ms Hunter. You may be asking yourself why you are still with us. Think of it as a bit of misdirection. I wanted your GenInt friend out of this, but you I want to talk to you some more, without his knowledge or interference."

Miriam looked at him somewhat fearfully. "Aren't you better off doing something to get out of here?"

"Why, are you in a hurry to see me go? I would have thought luring me into conversation to give your friends time to find me would have been your own plan, if I hadn't offered it to you myself. But don't worry about me. For my escape certain things must be done that will take some time but do not need my personal involvement. We have hours."

He smiled at her reflexive quiver. "Ah, you fear a reprise of your first 'interview' with Katlyn? I am not interested in hurting you for hurt's sake and I am not after revenge, at least not on you. So don't worry, it doesn't involve hanging or even a beating. I just want to talk without your friend here hearing. I neither like nor trust GenInt, as you might have guessed."

"What makes you think I won't just tell him anyway?"

Tagarin shrugged. "Perhaps you will, though I would advise you not to trust him either." At Miriam's involuntary grimace he nodded. "Indeed. In any case I wish to tell you and my desire to exclude him is more policy than necessity. If you do tell him I don't expect it will make any difference."

Miriam looked at him curiously, but stayed silent. Tagarin smiled sharply. "You are still wondering why I should wish to tell you anything, but have finally realized that you should just keep your mouth shut and let me keep talking? But to answer why, think of it as a trade: I will answer your questions in return for finding out what you know. You must have learned far more than I thought you could or we wouldn't be in our current predicaments, I under siege and you at my mercy. You may also think of it as part validation—Katlyn's too brief existence needs to mean something, and perhaps my confession will give it meaning; and part strategy—we are enemies now, but I think that is a matter of circumstance not necessity. Perhaps if I tell you my story you will understand; and perhaps understanding, one day you will be my ally when I need one."

Miriam gazed at him intently. What could she say? She was not convinced she would be alive tomorrow, let alone that they would meet again. Even less that they could ever be allies. But he was offering her answers; she would be a fool not to take advantage of his desire to talk. She considered her first question.

"I guess events pretty much prove that Katlyn was a geneh and you are the one who made her. So how much of what you told us is true? How did you manage to create her, given the reasons you told us it was impossible?"

"Most of it was true," he replied. "I see no need for honesty when dealing with enemies, especially enemies with guns. But lies are risky, so I find it is best to follow the Jiu-Jitsu of deception: go with your enemy's flow and use it against him. In short, tell the truth rather than bend it, bend the truth rather than break it, lie only if you have to. Let the truth he already knows or can find out lend credence to the lies about what he cannot know.

"So it is true that none of us could have created Katlyn before the bans came in and that nobody could get the equipment afterwards or use existing facilities without detection. But in the years before, supply and disposal of those items weren't monitored with any rigor. Our lab was well funded and we were always upgrading to the latest machinery. As the climate for our kind of research worsened, I decided it would be prudent to have a backup, though I never dreamed the laws would go as far as they did. When nobody is looking very closely, it isn't too hard to dispose of older equipment so it vanishes without a trace: where for all the paper trail is concerned it has been scrapped. In fact, where it vanished to is a facility I built secretly here.

"That was all I needed. I did not need technicians as I was not attempting a full research program and the equipment is automated. I did not have the most advanced equipment but it was good enough. I had spare parts and if I needed more it would be much easier to get them than a whole machine.

"So I just continued my work in private and in secret. At the time, I thought the insanity couldn't last." He grimaced. "I was wrong.

"You know we had already successfully made a newborn, who was doing well until GenInt goons murdered her. With that proof of principle, I was interested in something more advanced: someone enhanced but not extreme; someone attractive, a bit fun, capable but in a non-threatening way. A showcase of what was possible, of what good was possible. Of course I had my failures, as you always do in science, but each one taught me something."

"Then fifteen years ago, Katlyn was born. She was the only survivor of a batch of five experiments. The others died before birth due to developmental problems. But I expected that. Getting the gene engineering precisely right is tricky."

"May I ask a technical question?" asked Miriam.

"Certainly."

"You said once that after you've engineered a stem cell, you let it recover then clone it. I thought cloning meant, you know, making copies. Why can't you, once you have a genetically stable stem cell, make as many copies as you want? Why aren't there a hundred Katlyns?"

He nodded. "You do ask incisive questions sometimes. The pluripotent stem cells used medically are easier to maintain and can be multiplied almost indefinitely. But to make an embryo you need totipotent cells, and totipotency is a tricky state to induce and maintain. It is easy to lose your chance if you go through more than a few generations: especially with engineered genomes, which we still don't have the ability to make exactly the same as natural ones. The same is true of nuclear transfer into eggs, which is the standard method of cloning from adults. To cut a long story short, it is a compromise. I did multiply my engineered stem cells, but only for a few generations. So I actually started with 32 identical cells, which resulted in only 5 viable embryos, of which only one survived to term. We expect such low survival rates. That is why we would do many more experiments with many more variations if we were free to do so. But it was enough for my purposes.

"The rest of the truth I also bent by omission. Katlyn is effectively a twenty-two year old woman: I inflated her apparent age a little to make your geneh theory seem even more implausible, but not so much that another expert could categorically dispute it. After all, with such limited data her age was a matter of judgement. It was indeed achieved by accelerated development both to puberty and to full maturity, as you guessed."

"But why didn't you make more, if you had the technology?"

"Before the geneh laws and with a bustling lab I might have. But I wanted to be cautious. Although I had a healthy baby, I wanted to follow her development a bit more to make sure nothing unexpected went awry. I didn't want to make ten babies just to see all of them die young of some ghastly developmental failure. Despite what GenInt say, I cared about the results of my experiments.

"Then by the time Katlyn was four I had decided to stop. The legal environment was getting worse, not better. I could see what kind of life Katlyn would have: at best hidden from the world, unable to show her face; at worst, hunted like an animal. You know, I read once about parents being jailed for keeping their child locked in a basement its entire life to protect it from the world. But that's what I was offering Katlyn, wasn't it? And there was still the chance that her accelerated development would kill her when she hit puberty, when humans change so radically. Or she would fall apart after it."

He looked at her. "Again, despite what GenInt might claim, the scientists who do this work aren't monsters, any more than their creations are. These are babies. Babies we made. You can't help but get attached to them even if you wanted not to." He looked into the distance. "By that time, I thought of Katlyn almost as a daughter. I was deathly afraid that puberty would kill her—because of what I had done. As I told you, accelerated development has risks. I couldn't bear the thought of risking the lives of other children until I knew.

"But, as you see, she survived. Oh, there were problems. Puberty was painful for her. It usually is, but she had some bad times of it. But not so bad they killed her, not so bad she ever wanted to die."

"How old was she?"

"She was through puberty by age twelve. Less than average for a woman, more than average for a chimp; and actually within the natural human range. By then she was effectively an adult. Even mentally she was more like a young adult than a child just entering her teens: she had gone through all the usual stages, just faster. She developed quickly, learned quickly, grew up quickly, matured quickly.

"But by then I didn't want more. I was not interested in cloning Katlyn herself: my interest was always scientific, in what could be done. I saw no point in just copying an existing success. And doing something new ran the same risks of failure as with her. But most importantly, for all that she was a success biologically, I didn't like the life I'd given her and didn't want to do that to another human being. Which," he added glaring at her, "is what she was."

He paused. "And while I ended up hatching plans that relied on Katlyn, I decided they would work with her or not at all. Don't get me wrong. I regard those plans as crucial for things I hold dear, including Katlyn and her kind. But if you do not understand hate, Ms Hunter, do you understand love? Sometimes it makes cowards of us. It can make a price we might gladly pay ourselves too high to contemplate when it might have to be paid by another. Katlyn was willing to risk her life for those plans. But I did not want to put anyone else into a position where such a choice must be made.

"In any event, it was probably too late. It would have taken several more years to do and what was the point? If Katlyn failed, I would almost certainly fail with her, leaving a helpless child at the mercy of the authorities."

He stopped, looking into the distance. Miriam watched, imagining him seeing all those years of labor, of falling in love with his creation, of fear and planning; hoping he would not stop to think of how it had ended tonight and Miriam's role in that end. If Katlyn had been driven mad by her life or her genes, she wondered, were Tagarin's own mood swings because he too had been driven mad by bitterness and isolation? She had better ask a question that might direct his mood back to the safe one of academic discourse.

"You have spoken of your hesitation in trying more times, your high failure rate, your fear that even a successful baby might not reach adulthood. Doesn't that support the intent of the Geneh Laws? Not GenInt's more extreme methods, but their bans?"

"I am a scientist not a philosopher, Ms Hunter. And I'm not sure the philosophers are much help: they don't even believe each other's theories, so why should we? And if we did, whose would we choose?

But if you want to look at it democratically, the ethical standards I followed are what most people actually believe: if you judge what they believe by what they do rather than what they profess. The fanatics in GenInt are no different from the old anti-abortion or anti-drink crusaders: they claim to speak for morality, decency and democracy, whereas in fact and in practice most people believe and do quite the opposite in private—whatever they may approve of in public.

"Most of my embryos die? Well, nearly everyone these days accepts the morality of abortion and *in vitro* fertilization, both of which involve the death of embryos—and not even accidental death. My creations might die as a result of their modifications? Many babies made by the standard method still have deformities or die; many will suffer severe problems as they grow up due to genetics, disease, accident or some chosen folly such as drug addiction. Many more are simply weak or dull. Do people therefore forego having children in order to prevent such disasters? No, and properly so. We do not, and should not, live our lives as if our purpose is to avoid the possibility of pain: we live in order to create life with all its hope of pleasure and happiness.

"Yes, the chance of problems in my research is higher: that is in the nature of research. But also in the nature of research is that the absolute numbers are far, far lower. Many more children have suffered and died through the natural course of events since I started my research than ever did because of it. In fact, far more children have avoided suffering or death and led full, happy lives because of my research than died from it!

"You must realize that this work wasn't just some academic game, it had a purpose: improving the human race. Our bodies are the result of the blind operation of evolution: what worked well enough for our ancestors and their ancestors, given the environments they lived in and the anatomy their ancestors left them. Compromise upon compromise. Then consider what people have valued throughout history, the people they have admired and the art they have created: their greatest athletes and warriors, their geniuses. The best that was possible to man, not the average. How can people admire greatness but choose mediocrity in their own selves? When we have the tools to make man better, how insane is it to refuse to use them?"

The look in his eyes seemed familiar. Then she remembered where she had seen it last: in the face of Amaro, when espousing exactly the opposite view. *Enemies with opposite ideals*, she thought; *sharing nothing but that look and the belief beneath it: that they stood for what was right.* How many battles had that caused? But how many less would it have caused if men had learned to stop forcing their beliefs upon others? She wondered which one of them was right; whether she could ever know. She wondered what difference it could possibly make.

"Earlier you mentioned you had plans for Katlyn. I presume you meant her career as a burglar?"

"Yes," Tagarin said. "And I think you already know most of it. I think it is your turn to talk."

Miriam wondered what to tell him. She wondered how it could matter now. She thought that her best chance of learning the full story was to give hers. "We know that the jewelry thefts were cover for taking over the victims' AIs, and we know that you used that power to steal substantial amounts of money and to gather material for blackmail. We also know that in at least one case you used this to gather material that could be used to blackmail yet further people, perhaps all the way to President Felton. But most of your victims were unwilling to tell us anything, so we don't know the full scope and we don't know why. You already have more than enough money. It all seems so small: too small to risk your own wealth, your own position and the life of Katlyn. What was it all *for?*"

He gave a grim smile. "Ms Hunter, I know you think you serve justice and you would tell me that breaking the law is no way to do it. And in happier days I would have agreed that taking the law into your own hands is not the way to go. But when the law does not serve life but the death of those you love, what should you do? Perhaps there is no good answer. Perhaps one day you will find your own answer and perhaps it will be a better one: but I have already given mine. My answer may have been wrong. Perhaps I should have stayed a law-abiding citizen, quietly working to overturn an unjust law. The calm voice of reason attempting to persuade the good citizens of the world, as they swigged their beers and voted on things they know nothing about. As they agreed, by intent or default, to kill what they fear, not out of knowledge but out of blind ignorance."

His voice hardened. "But I saw an innocent child shot according to your laws, and I say damn those laws, damn them to the hell they rose from: and damn the self-righteous citizens who cheer them on. And call it justice, or call it vengeance, if there is even a difference. But I will have it!"

"But... how?" she asked fearfully, afraid that what had seemed too small a moment ago might prove too monstrous. Afraid that if he told her, he would have to kill her after all.

He smiled, and Miriam thought it was the smile she would see on a wolf that had found her hiding in the snow. "I think you could work it out. You know our President's role in the Geneh Laws, but you might not know how near run a thing it was. Perhaps I am wrong to blame her entirely, but as she herself has taken the blame—the credit in her view—I take her at her word. As for the others, they are all supporters of the President: her friends, her donors, her colleagues from way back. I knew many of them would know things about the President and the deals she did to get the geneh laws through, things neither she nor GenInt would want the world to see. And many of them were very rich."

He paused. "Ms Hunter, while I am a criminal by your laws, that is not how I see myself—though I suppose you've heard that before. I have not killed or hurt anyone, and I have targeted nobody except the people I described. None of them are innocent. All of them, whether for power or money or simply hatred of the unknown, are in bed with the President and as guilty as she is."

He fixed his cobra stare on her. But she wasn't sure whether it was targeted at her as herself or as the avatar of his absent enemies. "But... you still haven't told me what it is all for," she said softly to that stare.

He smiled and the wolf returned. "As you have observed, I did not need their money. But they valued it, so I took it. And I used it to fight them. In this country and around the world there are think tanks and even philosophical institutes that champion human rights: those who are consistent enough to oppose the geneh laws have found themselves enriched by quite generous if anonymous benefactors. Similarly, certain influential bloggers and commentators who have made principled objections to such laws have found their freedom to do so enhanced by unsolicited material support. What sweeter justice can there be than to turn your enemies' own wealth against them to fight the evil they have brought into the world? To make them see their ideals, corrupt as they are, crumble into dust with their own money paying for it?"

"And the blackmail? Was that also simply punishment?" Miriam asked. She knew they had almost reached the full answer to the mystery; she could see the shape of it, just not clearly enough to name it.

"I would not pity my victims there either, Ms Hunter. The thing about blackmail is that in most cases the victim is trying to hide what they know deserves punishment, and the blackmailer is merely threatening to lift the lid. I have not blackmailed the innocent over peccadillos, foolish mistakes or lapses of judgement. I have blackmailed the guilty for their crimes. I expected that many of our targets would have evidence of dirty dealings by GenInt and our illustrious President, either in anticipation of blackmail of their own or for protection. I was not disappointed. You will be entertained over the coming months by all kinds of revelations—with proof, or at least with enough detail for those who care to ferret out proof to do so— about the President and GenInt. It will not be pretty. With any luck, it will be enough to destroy them all. I doubt it will get that far: but it will go a long way toward finally eliminating them from the world."

Miriam looked at him wide-eyed, stunned at the ambition and enormity of the plot. Stunned that he might have achieved it. Her earlier vision of Tagarin orchestrating a giant dance came back to her: but she had not known the half of it, she realized. "Why are you telling me this?" she whispered. "When telling me could ruin it all?"

"Don't worry, Ms Hunter. The knowledge is not your death warrant. I actually think you will not report this conversation at all. I strongly advise you not to: shooting the messenger is a time-dishonored response of politicians throughout the ages. And the guiltier they are the more inclined they are to do it. Even if you do, all you can achieve is your own martyrdom: nobody can stop it now. And why would you? It is after all nothing more or worse than revealing the truth to the world. You would wish to stop that—merely to protect the guilty?"

He stared into her eyes, as if he could divine the soul within and see if she would be so corrupt or foolish. Or perhaps to see if she deserved his next words.

"Now, I had another reason for telling you. I know you are torn between your duty and the sense of justice that made you choose it— which means you do actually care for justice. So I told you these things for your benefit, that you would truly understand the issues. I would prefer that you do not reveal them to others. Unless you really trust this young man"—Miriam snorted—"I certainly wouldn't tell him. The fact I knocked him out and not you, for such a long time, would surely look suspicious to him no matter what you say. You cannot gain anything by revealing what I told you, except a cloud of suspicion smelling of collaboration over your own head."

"Now," he continued. "Two pieces of advice. The drug I gave him is rapidly metabolized and will be undetectable by the time you can be tested. But it has a side effect of severe thirst. If you wait for him to wake then say you are very thirsty, it will help convince him that you too were drugged—should you wish to hide our conversation from him.

"Second is the same advice I gave your colleagues. Consider the rest of your time here a paid holiday. You are in no danger from me and in no danger at all so long as the people outside refrain from monumental stupidity. By the time your friend wakes up we will be gone, and it will not be long after that until you are released.

"Now it is time for me to leave you. I have said this before but one day it might become true: I do not expect to see you again. Goodbye, Detective Hunter."

With that, he left the room, leaving Miriam alone with her thoughts. They did not make good company.

CHAPTER 48: SIEGE

Outside, sirens wailed, searchlights played and heavily armed police began to position themselves. It was like a carnival on adrenalin. As is traditional, power to the building was cut. This had no effect whatever, as Tagarin had his own fuel cell power plant with enough reserves for a week's siege. Nobody was going to let this continue that long.

The mansion was set in extensive natural countryside. The fence was alarmed and armed but Tagarin did not attempt to defend such a large area; he knew the perimeter was too long and the area inside too large with too much shelter. He made an exciting show of it: alarms rang, searchlights searched and tracer bullets flew without fatalities and so on. This slowed the police down, while giving them hope for ultimate victory once they proved their mettle by finally breaching the outer defenses and beginning their careful approach to the center.

The house itself was like a cross between an ancient Roman villa and a medieval keep. Like the villa the house was built around a central atrium, which was home to private gardens. Like the keep it was cylindrical, and once closed up very difficult to breach. It was not truly cylindrical, being twice as long as it was wide. It had no moat but did have an extensive cleared area around it which, given the technology at Tagarin's disposal, was rather better than water, even water infested with crocodiles.

The police gathered in the shelter of trees around the house or at the front gate. Any attempts to get closer were repulsed by force, which, while not deadly, made it clear this was a courtesy that could become deadly to anyone who came closer. The police would brave that firestorm if they had to, but that time had not yet come.

The gardens within the house were beautiful. Near one end of the long axis was a sparkling glasshouse, home to a collection of exotic orchids that had even made the magazines whose readership admired such things. The circling helicopters were not allowed to admire this view: any attempt to fly overhead or even penetrate beyond the positions of the police on the ground was met with laser defenses that would certainly down any craft that continued on its course.

The commanders outside were aware that there were several police and one GenInt agent trapped inside as hostages. They had not heard from the GenInt agent but were comforted by the fact that communications with most of the police officers were open and indicated no imminent threat. They were also aware that any attempt to use a higher level of force would have unwanted consequences. It was a standoff. It would not last forever. But the police were patient: they had the place surrounded on land and blockaded by air. Tagarin and his henchmen had nowhere to go.

CHAPTER 49: SPY

Miriam wondered how long it would be before Amaro woke up, and she thought about Tagarin's advice. *Oh screw it*, she decided. She wasn't going to sit here tied up for hours just so she could put on an act for Amaro. She wouldn't tell him everything, but she couldn't see any real harm in Amaro knowing what Tagarin had done: it had been his choice not hers.

That decision made, she began working on her bonds. She soon discovered that James had tied her securely enough for when they were guarded but lightly enough that she could work herself loose when free to struggle. In only a few minutes she had released her hands, then she untied her legs and was free.

She stood there rubbing her wrists. Tagarin would not be so foolish as to trust her, so the fact that he had left her awake and able to free herself certainly meant there was no way out. She tried the door anyway, but there was nowhere to get a good grip on the smooth metal and the lock plate ignored her. *Still, better than being tied to a chair.* She pondered Amaro sourly, then shrugged and untied him as well. Whatever he was or had done they were allies for now. And a kernel of her outraged affection for him still remained, albeit terminally ill.

She spent a few minutes exploring the room but found nothing that offered a chance of escape. Her captors had left them a silver jug full of iced water with some floating slices of lime, a pair of sparkling glasses resting on little paper mats next to it. She had to smile. Tagarin, still playing the gracious host even to his kidnap victims. She poured herself a glass of water, pulled her chair over to the table and sat down to think.

Much sooner than she had imagined she heard Amaro groan, then a minute later he lifted his head and said groggily, "Oh... God. Miriam? Miriam? Ugh. God I'm thirsty!"

Miriam gestured at the jug. "Fortunately, it appears our host has been reading *Sociopath Weekly*'s home entertainment section." She brought him a glass of water, extending her arm as if for once she was the knight riding to someone's aid. He noticed and smiled at her ironically. She said, "That didn't take long. You've been out less than an hour. I thought our host would have been more cautious, to make sure he was long gone by the time you came to."

Amaro smiled like a cat that had fooled a mouse. "Our host has merely miscalculated—for once. Apparently while he has guessed I am a GenInt agent, he does not realize that it is 'agent' in the sense of 'spy'. I have been given defenses against many common chemical agents; apparently his was one of them, or at least similar enough for me to make a rapid recovery."

He regarded her speculatively. "But enough about me. I saw you injected just before me, yet here you are wide awake, already free and waiting for me. You aren't going to tell me that my jests about the high circles you move in are actually true?"

"Hah. After tonight's debacle that's never going to happen. No, Tagarin just wanted to talk to me alone: a trade of information, you might say. He hates GenInt and didn't want you to be part of it. He even suggested to me that I feign being under so you wouldn't know."

"That seems a bit odd, wouldn't you say?"

Miriam just shrugged. "That man has so many plots, counter-plots and plans within plans that I think he does it out of habit. I'm not even convinced he's sane."

Amaro gazed at her as if trying to read her mind. Then he too shrugged. "Oh, no matter. No doubt I will learn all about it later, but first things first. May I assume that despite our differences, the fact that I find myself untied means we're still on the same side? I can trust you? Even though Katlyn saved your life?"

"We're on the same side in this," she replied grimly. "I don't even know why Katlyn saved me. Besides, whatever should have been done with her doesn't matter any more now she's dead. Even if I had compunctions about her they don't apply to Tagarin. He's a plain criminal and, unlike Katlyn, if he thinks he has good reasons he'll have his chance to argue them in court. That's all I owe him. All I owe anyone."

Amaro looked at her for a few more seconds, weighing her words, then nodded curtly, apparently satisfied. "Well, whatever you now think of me, this is not the best date we've been on, has it?" he said. "Personally I would be happy to call it a night, how about you?"

Miriam raised her palms. "I am assured we are perfectly safe and will be released after our host makes his daring escape, whatever it is. But I've checked as best I can and can't find a way out. I think we're stuck here until it's all over, like the rest of my team."

"Perhaps, perhaps not. I have a few more tricks up my sleeve, you might say," replied Amaro with another cat's smile.

He examined the doorplate and made some manipulations on his forearm with his other hand. Miriam could see some faint lights now shining through his skin. He put his palm on the plate and waited. After a minute or so the indicator on the plate changed to green and the door slid open.

"We spies find locked doors tedious, and fortunately my superiors wished to spare me such vexations. After you, My Lady", he said, bowing her through the door ahead of him.

Miriam wondered whether it was his habitual gallantry or he was simply worried there might be an armed guard waiting outside.

CHAPTER 50: JAMES

Fortunately there was no guard.

Miriam and Amaro crept silently down the corridor, ears alert for any sound. They had been relieved of their guns as well as their phones; they just had to hope for the element of surprise. Assuming there was anyone still around to surprise.

They had passed a few open and closed doors. The open ones were empty, the closed ones they listened at, heard nothing and decided to leave for now. They did not know how long it would take Tagarin and his crew to finish whatever had kept them here, if indeed they hadn't left already; they did not want to waste time breaking into rooms that were probably empty and might alert their quarry if they tried.

They approached another open door and stopped to listen. Amaro put his finger to his lips: he'd heard a faint sound. There was no good solution to this: the act of looking might give them away, but they had to look. Amaro took a quick peek but luck wasn't with him: Miriam heard a growled "What the hell?"

Despite her soured opinion of him, Miriam had to admit Amaro's courage matched his reflexes: he launched himself into the room without a moment's hesitation. James had been walking toward the door carrying a box when he saw Amaro, and after a brief moment of surprise dropped the box and reached for his gun. Miriam heard the sound of a collision and ran in after Amaro: he had reached James before he could point his gun and was tussling for it.

"*Son-of-a-BITCH!*" she yelled as the sound of a gunshot was accompanied by the searing pain of a bullet ripping a furrow across her forearm.

She crouched, holding her arm and wondering which way to jump next as the gun jerked around; trying not to think how few inches lay between a wounded arm and lying dead on the floor. Then Amaro did something with his arm and the gun skittered across the floor into the corner, and Miriam skittered across the floor after it. By the time she had retrieved it and spun around, James had overpowered Amaro and was holding him as a shield, arm around his throat.

Miriam pointed the gun at them, ignoring the blood running down her arm. "OK James, it's over. Let him go," she commanded.

James gave her a calculating look. "I don't think you'll dare to fire, Ms Hunter," he said. "Not when you're likely to shoot your pal here instead. And," he added, squeezing tighter for emphasis, "I can easily break his neck if you don't put that gun down. Now would be a good time."

As if to confirm his first point, Miriam saw a red laser cross focused on Amaro's chest. She realized that the gun felt unusual and something about that red cross rang a dim bell in her memory. Her eyes flicked to the weapon in her hand. Then she remembered. She had read about these recently: it was a Beretta Duallo, so new they weren't yet commercially available. The Duallo had a twin-loader grip that could be switched in a moment between normal bullets and fast-knockout darts. It had come to her attention because it had been designed for police work, specifically for those occasions where a choice between lethal and non-lethal force had to be made quickly and on the spot. She wondered how Tagarin got hold of so many advanced gadgets: it was like fighting Batman.

She flipped the toggle and saw the light on Amaro's chest change to a blue spot. "Now I think I can dare, James," she said. "Give it up."

"I don't think I can do that, Ms Hunter."

"James, do you have a family?" His eyes flickered to hers, but he said nothing.

"Your loyalty to your boss is admirable, but it's over. Tagarin will get his day in court if he thinks he can justify what he has done. It's him I'm interested in, not you. If you surrender now I can forget about the resisting arrest, I can forget about a lot of things. You'll get off lightly. But if you don't you might be put away for a long time. Do you want to do that to your family? Maybe you should think about where your loyalties truly lie."

She did not know how, but she had miscalculated her appeal to his loyalties. At her words, James just gave an inarticulate growl and started to dance forward, randomly jerking Amaro this way and that like a rag doll; whenever Miriam thought she had a shot, before she could take it she'd lost it. Finally she could risk no further delay and took her chance, but James had anticipated well and she hit Amaro instead. "Uurrgh," he noted. But he was certainly quick, she thought. In his few seconds left, using James as a support he lifted his knees to his chest and Miriam took the opportunity to shoot James in the leg. He roared, dropped Amaro like a sack of wheat and headed toward her. But it was too late. She skipped out of the way and watched him fall. Then she switched the gun back to bullets and ran from the room.

CHAPTER 51: CHOICES

Miriam walked as quickly but quietly as she could down the corridor. She heard a soft voice coming from a room just ahead, and silently crept toward it. She took a deep breath then stepped into the doorway, gun held in front of her.

Tagarin had laid Katlyn's body on a bed and covered her, and he was leaning over to place a tender kiss on her forehead. He had told her the truth, she thought; he had loved her, and the sorrow of the tableau before her made tears prick her eyes again, though whether for his loss or for hers she did not know. His gun was leaning against the wall, out of his immediate reach. She swallowed and stepped inside, pointing her gun at him.

"You will have to come with me now, Dr Tagarin. I am sorry for your loss, truly sorry, but it is my duty to arrest you for..." she began: then stopped in shock as Katlyn opened her eyes and turned to raise herself onto one elbow, staring at Miriam.

"But, you're dead! I thought she was dead! She's alive?"

"I guess you can't kill me that easily," Katlyn said softly, with a solemn smile. Her usual bravado, which had been slipping in the office, seemed to have been knocked out of her completely for now; she had the simple manner of a young girl, with no trace of the hardened adult.

"But how? I saw you shot! She was shot! Don't tell me she's bulletproof as well!?"

Tagarin shook his head. "Sadly no. But when you are a famous scientist with many contacts and even more money, it is remarkable how much you can learn about what's going on in advanced research and development labs. Take this material, for example," he said, pointing to Katlyn's skintight outfit. "She doesn't wear this just to look sexy, though I think it serves that purpose admirably well," he smiled. "It is thin and supple yet warm, while allowing the evaporation of sweat. But its main virtue is it is made of narrow fluid-filled channels with Kevlar reinforcing spiraling through their walls. The fluid is a gel full of suspended multicore carbon nanotubes modified to have an affinity for the gel. Have you heard of non-Newtonian fluids, Detective Hunter?"

Miriam shook her head. Keeping track of Tagarin's conversations was sometimes a trial.

"They are fluids whose viscosity changes with the force applied to them. There are several kinds and in one, most infamously quicksand, viscosity increases rapidly with stress. You can see the same thing if you mix cornstarch with water. To put it simply, the fluid stiffens the more you push against it but becomes runny when you ease up. Because of the exceptional strength and length of carbon nanotubes and how they interact with the gel, the fluid in this material is highly dilatant above a certain threshold of stress. In layman's terms the material remains soft and pliable under the forces applied by normal human movement, even Katlyn's, but if you apply extreme force the material stiffens dramatically. Owing to the strength of Kevlar and carbon nanotubes it is enormously strong for its thickness as well."

"So all that collapsing on the floor was just an act!?"

"Unfortunately not. If you have ever seen a high-speed photo of a bullet hitting a bulletproof vest, you'd see how far the bullet actually penetrates before stopping. The bullet may not put a hole in the vest or your skin, but it still packs quite a punch. If you are ever shot while wearing one yourself you'll see what I mean." He looked at her darkly, as if wishing that fate upon her sooner rather than later.

"Remarkable as this material is, for Katlyn's needs we had to keep it thin, and while it provides protection it is not as effective as a normal bulletproof vest. She is lucky she was shot with a .22. If you had shot her at such close range, suit or not she'd have probably ended up with a ruptured liver or spleen and died regardless. As it was she collapsed due to the shock."

"Will she be all right?"

He gave her a bitter glance. "Oh, you care? She is in pain and has serious external and internal bruising, but nothing life-threatening. Except for you and your gun of course. Now what are your intentions?"

Miriam ignored the question. "So let me get this straight. This material, and I suppose all your other little tricks, are things you acquired from labs working on advanced materials and processes? How did you get them?"

"Oh, as I said, I have contacts, friends and money. Sometimes I am given samples. Sometimes it requires, shall we say, off the books gratuities to staff seeking an improved standard of living. If something interesting comes out of a research lab but is just an idea, I may fund the development myself: either by a grant to the scientists or perhaps within my own companies—though you would find it hard to discover that they are mine. On rare occasions I confess, officer, we have resorted to plain theft. Another charge for you to add to my sheet."

"Now," he added, voice hardening, "What are your intentions?"

"My first intention is that I have some unfinished business with Katlyn from our first meeting," she replied coldly, moving towards Katlyn with her gun aimed at her head. Katlyn blinked and simply looked at her, attempting no defense.

As Miriam approached Katlyn, she saw Tagarin tense and focus on her trigger finger like a bird of prey watching a snake approach its chick. She got the distinct feeling that the moment he saw that finger twitch, he would launch himself at her whatever the risk to himself. She stopped but kept her gun leveled.

She stood there regarding Katlyn, then said in the tone of idle conversation, "You know, there's something that really bugs me about my job."

"If you're going to give me another speech about how sorry you are that your duty forces you to kill me against your better instincts, I might have to hit you again, bitch," said Katlyn, in a soft self-mocking echo of her tough persona.

"Believe me, that question still preys on my mind," said Miriam seriously. "However, that is not what I was thinking of," she continued lightly. "I work long hours. And what do I get? I get insulted"—she looked at Tagarin—"beaten up"—she looked pointedly at Katlyn—"and people keep offering to shoot me. Sometimes they succeed," she added, waving her injured arm. "But do you think they pay me enough to compensate for all that?"

Katlyn's smile faded to a look of puzzlement. Tagarin had a look of puzzlement that hardened halfway into contempt then stopped, unsure of whether to complete the transformation. He said harshly, "If this is your way of suggesting that a bribe will persuade you to let us go, then of course I will comply. Name your price. Though I have to admit I am surprised: I did not suspect it of you. If I had known it was that easy I'd have done it earlier and avoided all this."

Miriam replied, still in a tone of idle conversation. "Oh, don't blame yourself. This has been a night of education for me too. Not only have I learned all about non-Newtonian fluids, but I have discovered that I am an utter fool who fondly imagines that a life in the service of justice is somehow good for me, while all around me people deceive me, betray me and advance their careers at my expense. I think it is time I said 'screw them all' and did something for myself—don't you think so?"

"Name your price," he said thinly.

"Frankly, it isn't even the pay scale," she continued lightly. "It's the overtime that really bugs me. Take tonight for instance. I know those skinflints. They won't care what I've had to go through. They won't pay me any more than if I'd been sitting in the office doing filing."

"So..." she said, with a look of calculation. "Taking into account my sterling efforts, especially compared to my colleagues who are all either locked up or unconscious; what the department will actually pay me; and various quality of life considerations: I calculate, let me see.... Yes. I calculate that I went off duty five minutes ago."

With that she holstered her gun, stepped forward and reached out her hand to Katlyn. Katlyn looked surprised, then hesitantly reached out and shook Miriam's hand. Her handshake was surprisingly gentle. Miriam smiled at her. "I think that finishes our business."

Katlyn gave her a surprised but delighted smile. "But why? What about you?"

Miriam looked from one to the other. "I once read that while the Secret Service devote their lives to protecting the President, they are actually sworn to defend the Constitution: if the President goes bad their duty is not to him but to the country. I serve the law not because some people wanted it or some politicians voted for it but because the law upholds justice. I still believe that: only not this time. Like you said, Dr Tagarin, it may be a dangerously slippery slope to make an exception, to allow myself the indulgence of taking the law into my own hands. But I can't live with the alternative. If the law says to kill you for what you are, Katlyn, not what you have done—then that law be damned. I won't do it. If I lose my job: well, I can't do it and keep doing my job anyway.

"Now to quote you, Dr Tagarin: get out. The two of you, get out and don't come back. Before I change my mind."

Then they heard feet rushing up the corridor. Miriam drew her gun, unsure of what she'd actually do with it if the feet belonged to Amaro, but it was James. James panted and looked around wildly, then pointed his own gun at Miriam. He looked the worse for wear but had obviously come to earlier or overcome his opponent again. Miriam spread her arms then slowly put her gun away.

Tagarin said roughly, "James, please keep your gun pointed at Ms Hunter. Ms Hunter, stay where you are and don't move."

Miriam looked at him, confused. *Oh God* she thought, *not again, not again, is there anyone left who hasn't betrayed me?* "But, what...?" Tagarin smiled sharply at her as he retrieved his own weapon and covered her with it. "No more questions. James, please disarm Ms Hunter."

"Kindly be seated over there," he said, waving his gun towards a chair. She complied. "Now James, tie her to the chair. Arms and legs: she's slippery."

Miriam looked at him. She wasn't sure whether to be furious or afraid and if furious, at him or herself. "What are you doing?" she asked dully. As for Katlyn before, it was too much. All of the fight had left her. Katlyn herself was watching the proceedings wide-eyed and uncertain.

"James, kindly strike Ms Hunter."

"No!" cried Katlyn softly. Both Miriam and James looked at her in surprise. But James shrugged and lifted his hand.

The blow knocked her head sideways. James must have been feeling uncertain himself, for the blow could have been much harder.

"Good. Again, other side, slightly harder this time."

Miriam looked up at him through hooded eyes, breathing heavily, feeling her cheeks swell and tasting blood in her mouth. "But why? Why?" she breathed. "I was letting you go."

Tagarin ignored her, lifting her chin to examine her face, glancing at her wounded arm and her other injuries. "Yes, that will do nicely," he commented to himself. Then he looked at her and smiled wolfishly. "As for why, you are not the only person who believes in justice, Ms

Hunter. I really think I need to repay you for what you've done."

Miriam just looked at him, not knowing what to say. She felt as if the world had gone insane and nothing she thought she knew was real, and it made her unable to think or move.

Tagarin smiled and turned to address James. "It's lucky you showed up when you did, James. To fill you in, stricken with grief I was determined not to let Katlyn's body fall into the hands of her enemies. Unfortunately, carrying her slowed me down enough for Det. Hunter here to catch up with me before I could escape. Taken by surprise and encumbered by Katlyn as I was, she had little trouble arresting me. But as she was escorting me out to become more closely acquainted with our admirable legal system, you surprised her and freed me. Of course, as Katlyn was still unconscious Det. Hunter has no idea she actually survived."

He smiled at Miriam, who was now looking at him wide-eyed. "Ms Hunter, I think you are too honest for your own good. Honest people tend to get themselves hurt when those around them are less so."

He stood in front of her, looking down on her with a faint smile. "I'm sorry for that little show and the minor beating. But," he paused, glancing toward Katlyn, "I know you have survived worse. I meant what I said. I wish to repay your—I was going to say kindness, but I think I mean justice. Perhaps they are the same thing in this case.

"You now have a plausible story for how we escaped and your role in it. Like all good lies it is mainly true. I suggest you use it. You can tell the truth and nothing but the truth, exactly as it happened, without danger to yourself: just neglect to tell the whole truth. You do not deserve to lose your career or your own freedom for what you have done. For that matter, I believe you are one representative of the law who tries to protect innocent people. They do not deserve to lose you either."

He looked away into the air, as if hearing something transmitted privately to him, then turned back to her. "Well, goodbye Ms Hunter—Miriam, if I may call you that now. Katlyn? I don't think you should walk too far yet. James, will you carry her?"

"Wait," said Katlyn. She got carefully to her feet and hobbled over to Miriam. To Miriam's surprise, she sat on her lap and wrapped her arms around her. "Goodbye Miriam. You might have noticed I'm not good with apologies, but what I did to you on our first meeting—I know you didn't deserve it. I think I knew it even then. Will you forgive me?"

"Of course, Katlyn," she said. "I especially forgive you for not choosing to kill me," she added.

"And don't you forget I could have, bitch!" replied Katlyn with a grin. She leaned over and kissed Miriam on the cheek. "Goodbye then, Miriam. Perhaps we will meet again some day." She rose shakily to her feet.

"Katlyn?"

She looked at her enquiringly.

"Is it true? That you saved me in the park? Or was that another of your lies? I won't hold the truth against you: I just need to know."

"It's true. All of it. Don't forget that 'all', including why I was there in the first place. I know I'm not blameless."

Miriam looked into her golden eyes. "Thank you," she said softly.

James picked Katlyn up as if she was a bag of feathers and they turned to leave.

"Wait," said Miriam. "Where are you going? This place is surely surrounded by now."

Tagarin smiled. "It is not a secret that I have a Gulfstream executive jump jet. What is a secret is that it is currently parked fully fueled in a hangar outside that looks like a glasshouse. In fact, it *is* a glasshouse. My collection of rare and exotic orchids has even featured in magazines, revealing my softer side to a cynical world. Alas, those flowers are about to become casualties of war. In a short while any helicopters your colleagues may have circling this place will find it prudent to get out of the sky. We shall then make our daring escape, to everyone's shock and amazement."

"But what will you do? Where will you go?"

He smiled again. "Capital."

CHAPTER 52: FLIGHT

Miriam was amazed. "Capital? You're going to Capital? The anarchy? Are you crazy? Even if you survive, the first bounty hunter to come along will shoot you or bring you straight back here! Katlyn will end up dead or chained up in a freak show!"

Tagarin shook his head slowly. "Capital is only an anarchy in comparison to our own over-regulated state. And it is a convenient slur bureaucrats encourage to protect their own power from any shade of a viable alternative. Capital is actually what used to be called a free country, the freest country on Earth. In any event, it is the only real hope we have. It is possible I am wrong about its nature and we are walking to our deaths. It is possible that I am wrong about it in the other direction, and they will turn us straight over to our enemies: whether for their own protection or because their prejudices— whatever their publicity—are no better than anywhere else. But if I am wrong about it, well, we won't be any deader than if we stay here.

"Now Miriam, there is no danger to us if you manage to release yourself once we are gone. Indeed, your colleagues will be freed then, so nobody will find it remarkable if I leave you the means to free yourself too. So I have left you a knife on the table over there. Please ensure you can hop yourself over there, acquire the knife and begin cutting your bonds."

Miriam complied. She couldn't avoid a few cuts on her own skin but knew she would be able to free herself within a few minutes. Tagarin held up is hand for her to stop.

"That will do. The physical evidence here and on your wrists will now match your story. James, finish the job for her, will you?"

Miriam stood massaging her wrists for the second time this day.

"OK Ms Hunter, I guess this is goodbye. Give us a few minutes. When you hear our jet lift off you can escape without risk to us. You are a good person, Miriam. You could almost change my opinion of the law. I wish you good fortune and a long life." He bowed to her formally.

Miriam noticed that his habitual air of bitterness was gone. For the first time it was replaced by a relaxed eagerness even though he was flying off into unknown danger. He looked years younger. He looked happy. She smiled at the transformation as much as at him.

Katlyn had James put her down and ran over to Miriam to give her a final hug. "Goodbye Miriam. I second the motion. All happiness to you." Miriam hugged her back. "You too, my friend."

Katlyn blinked at her. Then James picked her up and they walked quickly down the corridor as Miriam watched them go. As they turned the corner, Katlyn looked back at her and waved a final goodbye. They both silently wondered if they would ever meet again.

~~~

They trotted along the corridor, occasionally exchanging glances, half afraid at what might still go wrong even now. Nobody felt like talking. In a minute they emerged into the hangar and saw the gleaming jet waiting, breathing vapor like a steed anxious to run. They looked at each other again and walked up the waiting steps, then the door sealed behind them to lock out the rest of the world.

James deposited Katlyn in a seat and fastened her belt. There were a few other people on board but they were in the rear section of the aircraft. James and the pilot had both opted to bring their families along: they didn't know what kind of revenge GenInt or their own government might inflict on them if they had to come back, or on their families if they left them behind. That had caused no difficulties: James' family lived on site anyway, his wife helping with various tasks around the estate; and the pilot with his family had already been brought in as Tagarin's guests as part of his preparations for escape. The adults were all a bit nervous about the prospect of Capital, but they respected their boss enough to help him in his mad scheme and to cast their lot in with him. The kids just thought it was an adventure.

"OK, time to go," Tagarin said to the pilot. Outside lit up as remote controlled weaponry opened up on the circling helicopters and the encircling police. Or appeared to. The rounds were for show rather than effect, but the pilots got the message and got out. Anyone on the ground brave enough to keep watch would be unable to see much among the pattern of bright flashes or hear anything among the loud booms.

The doors of the hangar opened and most of the glasshouse panels blew out as the plane rose on its jets; then the pilot swiveled them to give some forward thrust and the plane slowly floated out, accelerating as it went. As soon as it was clear, the pilot shifted to maximum power and increased the angle of the jets. In seconds the plane had reached enough airspeed to fly using its wings alone, and the pilot swung the jets to horizontal at an attitude of 35 degrees. The plane rocketed away into the sky. Nothing the police or GenInt could throw at it now could stop it.

~~~

Miriam stood still, looking down the corridor. After a few minutes she heard the roar of the VTOL takeoff jets, followed shortly after by a rapidly diminishing note as it accelerated into the sky. Then that too was gone. "Goodbye people," she whispered to the ether. "I hope you find what you're looking for."

CHAPTER 53: CAPITAL

The country of Capital had an unlikely birth.

It started life as an oil company. The father of the company's current president had founded it decades ago in South America when his country was still a democracy, and by a combination of good luck and even better judgment had built it into a rich and powerful corporation.

Then like many countries before it, the democracy had succumbed to the blandishments of a strong and charismatic leader, who had moved quickly to discredit or eliminate his competitors and then consolidated his power into a dictatorship. The particular brand of dictatorship he inflicted on his country was the kind that approved of private enterprise, so long as an enterprise proved it deserved its privacy by contributing handsomely to the public good. In the dictator's view this was the best of all possible worlds. The enterprise took all the risks and the country benefited whether it failed—in which case it was taken over and gutted for what value remained—or it succeeded, in which case the country took its fair share of the profits. A cynical observer may have noted how much of the country's benefit was manifested in grand public buildings to the glory of the dictator or in large country estates for the pleasure of him and his clique. But cynical observers were discouraged in his country, often permanently.

The company founder had grown up in a democracy and did not approve of this turn of events. But he realized that the dictator was likely to reward criticism in the same way he rewarded cynical observation and other exercises of free speech. So he always gave the dictator the respect and obeisance that was manifestly his due, and worked hard to leave a legacy for the dynasty he had always wanted to found. In his view no dictatorship would last forever and his country would eventually return to sanity. If he could do anything to hasten that process he would, but his efforts were limited to some rather creative accounting of his international holdings. There may also have been anonymous gifts, through untraceable donors, to some extremely private enterprises in his country: enterprises whose members the dictator would have dearly liked to have gotten to know much better, if for a very brief but painful time.

The founder had three children, whom he had educated in far lands. He did not want them used as bargaining chips by either the dictator or his enemies. He was a traditional man, who wished his firstborn son to succeed him as president of the company: he was sent to school in the United States of America, which the father thought of as a shining if flawed example of a moral republic. But if the father was traditional he was also wise: his other son and daughter were educated in a similar manner, in the hope that at least one of the three would have the talent and inclination to take over the reins when the time came.

If the father chafed under the rule of a dictator, the son seethed. Unlike his father but like many of the young, his idealism exceeded his practicality. And he was not merely a democrat like his father. He had come under the influence of the more libertarian wing of US politics and had read avidly the works of the free enterprise economists and the pro-freedom philosophers. His father, wisely, kept him away from his home country until he could learn to temper his fiery idealism with a more patient wisdom and restrained tongue. It was not that the father disapproved of the son's beliefs. He just believed that a man could only do so much, and reasonable goals in a reasonable timeframe were the route to contentment and, in his home country, life itself.

The son, if anything, was even more astute than his father. He waited, and thought, and planned. He did his apprenticeship for his future position by working in numerous positions in various international subsidiaries of the parent company. This, his father had decreed, would give him the operational understanding he needed to run the company when his time came. His father did not approve of the dynasties he had seen in which heirs were plucked straight out of school and placed in a high office, served by a bevy of assistants and protectors, and far removed from what the company actually did. No, he thought, any heir worth the name must be worthy of the name. The son, it seemed, turned his considerable energies from political idealism to the intellectual and physical challenges his father had set him. He performed superlatively. His father was extremely proud.

Peak oil was coming, as it had been coming for decades. But peak oil or no, father and son agreed that prudence demanded diversity. If their company was to last for generations it needed flexibility as much as it needed strength. They agreed that the father would continue to do what he did best, running the company; and what only he could do, dealing with the dictator without attempting regicide—or insecticide, as the son would put it. Meanwhile the son applied his youthful creativity and energy toward diversifying the company into new forms of energy.

While investigating geothermal energy, the son learned of a cluster of seamounts just within the territorial waters claimed by his country. Had they remained for a few more millennia over the geological hotspot that had formed them, they might have grown into another group of islands like Hawaii, inhabited by proud descendants of Polynesian seafarers. As it was their crests remained under the waves, and though they were close enough to the surface to cause ships grief at low tide they were of little interest to anyone: except to mark on the charts and avoid, or for the more adventurous species of diver to visit.

Though the seamounts had moved on from their nursery, their hearts remained a furnace of magma and incandescent rock. Such things took a long time to cool once cocooned in solid rock. To the son this looked interesting. The geologists assured him there was no chance of volcanic eruptions, as the magma plume that had driven their formation was now distant in time and space. But the amount and level of heat trapped in their cores was enough, potentially, to drive immense geothermal electricity generation for centuries. And while they were far too distant from shore to be an economical source of power for now, the son knew that technology had a habit of turning yesterday's impossible into tomorrow's commonplace.

The father and son talked. The son anchored pillars on the highest point of the highest seamount and added a platform above the waves, upon which he built the nucleus of a geothermal research facility. The father bought the seamounts and the ocean around them to a distance of 100 kilometers, under private title free and clear. The dictator looked at this deal somewhat suspiciously, as he looked at all deals where somebody else got something. But like many of his kind the long term meant little to him and the price paid was generous. And the father had pointed out the many advantages to the dictator beyond mere cash. It was a shining example of the forward-thinking nature of his regime, in a world where alternative energy had been an underperforming ideal for decades: his country could become a world leader in this field. And while the seamounts were worth nothing at present, if this succeeded it would be worth a fortune to the country. Even if it didn't, the investment would bring many jobs and many technical experts to the country. And besides, the dictator was in an expansive mood. He was enjoying his new estate high in the hills above the bay, a generous donation by this very oil company: proving yet again his farsighted wisdom in supporting private enterprise.

But the dictator, like most of his species, was rarely content. He looked upon the resources of his neighbors with an avaricious eye, encouraged by a somewhat inaccurate view of the history of who had discovered what when, and whose territory properly ended where. He began to cause trouble for his neighbors.

His neighbors, who bordered his land to the east, north and south, had their own view of history. Indeed, in their eyes their respective proper territories met at a point that left no room for his country at all. An objective historian may have objected that the ebb and flow of migration and invasion could prove anything, so the fairest division of countries was generally the current one. Not because it was necessarily fairest, but because the previous ones were no fairer and the present one had the advantage of currency. However an objective historian would not have said this to the dictator, because an objective historian would have learned from history. And there would have been no point telling it to his neighbors. They had been perfectly happy to leave well enough alone: like most countries, their people were too busy making a living to want to get mired in war. But they were getting very tired of this dictator and had been dusting off their own history books.

Some diseases are sufficiently rare that there is no cure. In some cases, if someone found a cure they might decide to leave well enough alone. The disease of dictators, especially those who had risen to spectacular success early; had surrounded themselves with advisors whose advice was always remarkably similar to their own opinions; and had managed to hit on a formula which did not totally destroy their country from under them: is thinking they are better than they are. He must be a genius, for who else could have done so well?

This dictator had a relatively well off country, though if asked with immunity much of the population might have expressed a lower opinion. And to be fair, he had done one function of government with gusto. He had a large standing army, with a core of loyal supporters fired with the loyalty only money could buy. A much larger body of troops served him because it was the easiest way to keep themselves and their families alive: whether through their slightly higher than average pay, or their slightly lower than average chance of nocturnal visits by the secret police. These men gave their noble leader the respect traditional among the lower ranks of armies everywhere when their leader was, in their unexpressed opinion, an ass.

But his people loved him. Or at least, they earnestly desired to please him. So he saw only the crisp ranks and crisper salutes of his elite troops. He saw the gleaming rows of their rifles. He multiplied that by the total size of his army. He was invincible.

There were gold mines in the recently disputed territory to the north, close to the border. By coincidence his northerly neighbor was the weakest. The dictator pondered these two facts. He closeted with this advisors and strategists. One pointed out that the mines were in a mountainous region, hard to attack and hard to supply. Another noted that a much easier approach was to skirt the border mountains and sweep back up from deeper in enemy territory; and while this would certainly provoke the neighbor even more than liberating the mining region, their army was obviously far superior and could do it. His political advisor opined that their neighbor to the north was not very popular with the other neighbors. It too was ruled by a dictator, though a more liberal, that is a weaker, man than His Excellency; while the others were democracies. A second military adviser pointed out on a map, purely for his Excellency's information, their army's best route for reattaching the mountains to the country where they belonged. That route came quite close to the capital city of the country that had stolen them.

His Excellency was not a man to hesitate to accept the blessing of Destiny. Why take just mines, rugged mountains with no other value, when rich agricultural lands also beckoned? Why merely restore the ancient borders, when given the chance to expand his country to unprecedented greatness? Was that not the course taken by all the great men of history, men whose names were still spoken with awe thousands of years after their time?

The plan was set. They would liberate their northern neighbor while assuring the others of his peaceful intentions towards them; then consider what further glory might be possible to a man, to a country, of Vision. A prudent advisor might have named some other facts and counseled caution; but a prudent advisor would have known when to keep his mouth shut.

The country went quiet. Its neighbors looked on with some trepidation, not trusting this new peaceable nature. The dictator sent emissaries with offers of treaties of eternal peace and cooperation. The troop movements were just exercises. It was whispered by agents that this was a lie: they were an implied threat to encourage concessions in the negotiations.

Suddenly his armies swept north. As predicted, the defenders were overmatched and within days their beleaguered capital faced a ring of steel to their front and the sea to their rear. The dictator was ecstatic.

But his neighbors were treacherous. They had signed a secret agreement of mutual defense, almost as if they did not trust him. Armies attacked from two directions and drove deep into his country. Divisions had to be pulled back to meet this new threat. The northern country's army rallied and began driving the remaining army back. Many of his troops then decided that on sober reflection, their beloved leader did not deserve their help, let alone their lives: and whole platoons began to desert.

The dictator cursed the perfidy of his neighbors and the cowardice of his troops, had a few advisors shot, and railed in general against the injustice of reality, which unlike the advisors didn't care. He launched all he had against the invaders.

Over the years, the son of the oil magnate had, at an expense out of all proportion to the apparent benefit, built up one of his seamounts with rock so his facility now stood, not on a platform above the sea, but on newly created dry land. He chose this moment to send a notice to the dictator, formally seceding from the country, citing its political instability and that it was led by "a complete prat". The dictator was furious. Only a fool would have thought he would allow such an outrage. The son was not a fool.

The dictator could do little, being now in the middle of a war for his own survival, but being the man he was could not do nothing. He consulted with his remaining advisors on how much of his dwindling forces he could spare to punish the upstarts, and one gunship and two precious attack helicopters were dispatched to retake the island or raze it. One helicopter fell in flaming debris into the sea and the ship sank into the depths, both victims of guided missiles not part of the usual inventory of a research station. The second helicopter landed but its commandos soon realized they were outnumbered, surrounded and doomed unless they surrendered. That they quickly did, thus beginning brief second careers as prisoners of war along with the survivors from the boat.

The dictator was even more furious but could spare no more materiel, and he wisely decreed that vengeance would await his victory in the more pressing war at home. It was a short wait but not for victory. Within days the dictator no longer cared. Nor did his country. It had ceased to exist along with its leader: the ancestral borders of his neighbors, at least as understood by them, had been restored.

They were happy. It was like when a nagging splinter has at last been removed from one's foot. There was even talk of a united federation of states. And part of their victory, or at least its speed and thus the saving of many lives, was due to their possession of a certain quantity of superior arms. Those arms, it was discovered loudly by the press, had been supplied by a certain oil company, in secret deals that would have rather stretched the dictator's imagined friendship with the founder had they been revealed in time for him to hear of them.

The legal standing of the new country was in doubt. Nothing like this had ever happened before. But the son's attention to detail matched the grandeur of his vision: he had done his homework. He had new but real land that was his legal property, and when it had still been property under the jurisdiction of a recognized nation had formally seceded from that nation. It had even won a war of independence, such as it was, after which the new country had been left alone. In addition, there was nothing to tempt anyone else: nobody really cared about some rocks in the sea and nobody thought it would last. Also a certain rich oil company, now nominally stateless, was publicly wondering about what new home it might move to if the new political climate of its old home proved too "unfriendly". At the same time it privately noted, to the former neighbor whose territory now included the site of its current headquarters, just how rich it was. Nothing concentrates the mind of even the most liberal country than the promise of lucrative tax revenues. Some additional private communications from the island further suggested that if its statehood were not recognized it "would blow the whole thing back into the sea anyway."

In addition, while the son had not known when or if his crazy plan would bear fruit, he had been cultivating it for years like some secret garden hidden in the hills. He had simply grasped the opportunity when it arrived: he had suspected that the late unlamented dictator might offer one to him sometime. So before the dust had settled in the war his new country had a flag, an anthem, a Constitution and a government. It even had an air force, in the shape of one slightly used military helicopter and some guided missiles. There were a few people who noted the irony that while the dictator's dreams of eternal glory were dust, they had perhaps given birth to glory in a different form.

It was enough. The existence of the new country was formally recognized by most countries in the world and ratified by the United Nations. The world waited with curiosity to see what this new thing would become.

The father who had founded an oil company was proud of the son who had founded a country, if stunned. His dynasty already assured, he retired, retaining a role as advisor to his company and advisor to his son. He was happy, and fascinated by what his son had done. He faced the future with new vigor.

The new country was named Capital because, the son said, "Well, I am a capitalist, am I not? And I believe that capitalism is not only the most productive but, not coincidentally, the most moral political and economic system on Earth. It is the system of freedom, trade and justice. The name is in honor of that."

The world was unimpressed. Political philosophers snorted at his view of capitalism from their taxpayer-funded ivory towers. Political scientists examined its surprisingly short Constitution and scoffed at its naivety: it was as if nothing had been learned in the centuries since the birth of the USA. Indeed it was even more repressive, in terms of what the government was allowed to do, than that earlier document on which it was modeled. Lawyers shook their heads at its simplistic legal system, speechless. Intellectuals alternated between being aghast at its principles when speaking in public and riotously amused at its folly when drinking with friends. Pundits predicted the imminent demise of the experiment in a blaze of man-eat-man anarchy; privately relishing the delightfully ironic prospect that the only way to save it would be the rise of a strongman dictator much like the one whose ambitions had midwifed it. Everyone who wanted to be thought intelligent agreed. It was doomed.

That was a quarter of a century ago. There had been mistakes, there had been problems, there had been the need for reform and overhaul. But in what country had that ever not been true, from the oldest to the youngest? At first it survived. Then it thrived. It attracted all kinds of rebels, nonconformists and refugees. Other governments hated its principles but liked its existence. It was the trashcan of the world. Even the most repressive dictatorships, which scorned any kind of human freedom, recognized that their worst internal dissidents, too prominent to kill and too dangerous to let loose, could be safely dumped there. More liberal governments had a similar attitude to their own more outspoken rebels. Capital became something like the United States had been in an earlier time.

There are rebels of many kinds. Those who came to Capital for the wrong reasons did not stay long. Those who came for the right ones thrived, and Capital thrived with them. The most creative people, the ones most sympathetic to ideals of human achievement unchained by mindless rules, were the most attracted to it. Many moved there to start new careers. Many companies, whose owners admired its principles and whose operations were not geographically constrained, moved there too. It gained industry, wealth and population. As a nation it was still small. But it would not be stopped.

CHAPTER 54: LIVE FREE

Katlyn woke from an exhausted sleep. She had changed out of her work costume into something softer. It made her feel good. Like she was a normal person greeting a normal day, not a criminal or freak who needed to wear armor just to survive another night.

She rubbed her stomach; she was still sore, but she was getting better quickly. She remained nervous about what they were doing, but if it worked she would never be shot again. Nobody would want to shoot her. She rolled that phrase slowly around in her mind. *Nobody would want to shoot me.* In one sense it was an enormity, hard to grasp, hard to fit into the reality of her existence. In another, it was the way life was meant to be. Was this what it was like, to be normal? She hoped it wasn't just an illusion, to be shattered on landing in their hoped-for refuge.

Through the windows of the Gulfstream she could see the expanse of the Pacific Ocean, sparkling away into the distance until it was lost in haze and the curvature of the Earth. She thought of the first men who had travelled that expanse in fragile ships of wood and canvas; of how easy this was for her compared to them. What took them weeks or months would take her hours. Yet how farther a gulf was she travelling? Perhaps her gulf was too far, as theirs had been for so many of them. But she had to try, just as they had. It was part of being human.

Tagarin was still asleep. But she smelled coffee brewing and her stomach growled with something other than pain. James was up, cooking a light breakfast.

"Good morning, Katlyn," he said. He stood formally and intoned, "Breakfast is served, madam." Then he smiled. "I wonder how many jobs there are for butlers in Capital," he wondered.

"How long until we get there?" asked Katlyn.

"We must be pretty close. Not long."

The conversation and aromas had finally woken Tagarin. He came to join them. After they'd eaten he said, "We'll be there soon. Let's go to the cockpit."

The pilot had set the jet on auto and was also sleeping. He stretched and said, "Morning boss. Nearly there?"

"Yes. Mind if I sit in?"

"Be my guest."

Tagarin sat in the copilot's chair. Katlyn stood behind him, her hands resting lightly on his shoulders. She looked ahead. "There it is! Is that it?" she cried excitedly.

"It's the only thing out here," said the pilot. "Showtime."

In less than a minute a light came on in the communicator and an AI voice spoke. "Calling executive jet Gulfstream AX1002-B. This is Capital air traffic control. Please state your business."

"We wish to land at Capital."

"Landing course has been uploaded to your flight computer. You may land."

"Wait," said Tagarin.

"Yes?"

"Can we take a look around first? Do a bit of a tour? We have never been here before."

The request must not have been all that uncommon, as the AI did not shunt them to a higher level or a human but after a few seconds simply stated, "That is permissible. Acceptable altitude and distance parameters now uploading. Please do not encroach within the proscribed limits as that may be viewed as a security threat by automated defense systems. You will be warned but if you do not comply you may be shot down. Do you understand? Do you still wish to sightsee or would you prefer to come straight in?"

They looked at each other. This was a funny anarchy, Katlyn thought. "We understand and that is acceptable. We will fly around a bit."

"Confirmed. When you wish to land, simply accept the earlier flight plan provided. If there is a problem, you will be advised then. Over and out."

The jet banked to the left and began a long slow circle around Capital. Tagarin pointed out the features.

"See that smaller island, with all the high buildings? That's the original location of the first settlement, and is still the home of what government there is and much of the industry and commerce of the country; they call it Capital City. The larger island half surrounding it also has industry but is mainly residential and recreational. And you see that curved body of water between the two? The one shaped like a big letter 'C'?" he asked. "They call that 'The Capital Sea'". He grinned. "The founders had a bit of a sense of humor. Anyway, as you can see the Capital Sea isn't very wide and there are several bridges. But it is very deep: there is quite an abyss between the two seamounts. Or what were seamounts."

Katlyn took in the sight. The water was a sparkling aqua and looked very clear; she could see dark ledges fading into the depths of the Capital Sea. "What are those ledges under the water?" she asked.

"Those are coral reefs. Waste heat is released into the sea and the water there is a bit warmer. Apparently the reefs are glorious. It is a very popular spot for divers."

"Waste heat? So where do they get the power for all that industry and housing?"

"The seamounts are still mostly magma inside. This place actually started as a geothermal energy research station, would you believe. The research was successful and Capital has an abundance of cheap electricity."

"What is that grey-brown mass stretching away from the houses into the sea?" asked James.

"That's new land in the process of being formed. They use an army of small solar powered and self-refueling robots to extract minerals from the ocean and build floating honeycomb blocks. The company that does it takes the more valuable metals and the waste gases like chlorine that the robots collect, and sells them here or as exports. The building side is almost a charity: it about breaks even with land and development sales, I hear. But they do it because they figure the more people who live on Capital the bigger a local market they have, and the richer they'll get in the long term."

James said, "I can see how that could be economical, and even I could probably afford to buy a house here as much as at home. But that's now. How the hell—excuse me, my butlery is slipping—how could anyone have afforded to move here in the early days? Building up the initial infrastructure must have been fantastically expensive."

"That was the founder's decision. He was scion of a big oil company, and the big oil company had a lot of money. This put a bit of a dent even in its bottom line. But the founder basically donated the capital cost, as it were, to Capital. People asked why—at heart he was a shrewd businessman, not a philanthropist. From memory his answer was: 'My father wished to create an oil dynasty that would serve his family for generations. I wished to create a legacy to support my family for generations in a different way: by creating a place for them to live. And my family includes everyone with the same ideals.'

"He thought that once it got started, things would rapidly get cheap enough for almost anyone to move here, whereas if he priced things by the usual formulae it would never get started. It appears even capitalists can believe there are some things worth more than money."

They were silent for a while, pondering the reality of what the man had created, now spreading its wings across the sparkling sea below. Then Katlyn said, "Wow. A whole floating city. But what about storms and that kind of thing?"

"The blocks ride fairly high and are all linked together with cables, so not only is each block heavy, the total mass is enormous. And they have cables connecting them to the seamounts to hold them in place. The structure also makes an effective wave break. People don't live on the outer rings. They are all for future development when they themselves are protected, or for special purposes where a bit of rocking isn't a problem. Mainly recreational facilities, diving platforms, fishing boat moorings, oyster and clam farms, that sort of stuff.

"The only real danger is tsunamis. But a tsunami is only a problem when it hits land: they pass right under ships at sea without being noticed. The small island is still land, but I believe they have some underwater structures intended to divert much of the tsunami energy, and all the buildings on it are as tsunami-proof as they can be. Because the rest is floating with good clearance underneath, any tsunami will pass right under them."

They flew around for a while longer, taking in the sights. It didn't look like the traditional view of an anarchy: no burning buildings, for one thing. It looked—peaceful. Buildings glittered in the sun, green parks dotted the landscape, sailing boats flew before the wind. Tagarin lifted his hand to hold Katlyn's. "OK, let's go in, people."

~~~

Capital had the reputation of letting anybody in, but the anybody couldn't just rock up on an outer reef. Well they could, but it was frowned upon by the inhabitants. And there was little point anyway unless you were a spy or violent criminal, which was even more frowned upon.

The Gulfstream landed on its assigned pad outside the main entry point to Capital. After landing Katlyn put on dark sunglasses and tucked her tail under her shirt; it would do for casual inspection. Then they all disembarked and walked up the path to an imposing entrance. Above was written in large gold letters, "Live Free".

James looked at it quizzically. "What's that? It looks like half the motto of New Hampshire."

Tagarin replied, "It's the official motto of Capital. I guess they figured that here, the second half is unnecessary."

Beyond the entrance the options for further progress split into three, one labeled "Visitors", one "Citizens" and one "Immigrants." The others elected to enter as visitors. They weren't entirely sure about this, and after discussing it among themselves had decided to check the place out. If they hated it they'd take their chances back in the States. They could always claim coercion. That their families were on the jet could be explained as extortion rather than aiding and abetting, and who could prove otherwise? If they took one look and even that was too much they could leave immediately.

Tagarin and Katlyn had no such choice. Their roulette wheel was already spun and there was no chance for another bet. "Oh well, this is what we came for. Let's go," said Tagarin.

They walked along the pathway. It was still early morning and the place wasn't busy right now. Only one official was present but there was an automated prescreening point to get through first. As they approached it an AI spoke. "This entrance is for people seeking immigration into Capital. Weapons are not allowed inside Capital except for citizens. If you have weapons you must leave them secured outside: storage is available for a fee if needed. Capital has no entrance requirements except for respecting the rights of others. Violent criminals are not allowed. Most other things are allowed. Respecting the rights of others includes taking responsibility for your own livelihood. You must have a job or your own resources. You may enter without a prearranged job but if you cannot find one before your money runs out, you will almost certainly have to leave: while Capital has private charities in case of genuine need, there are enough opportunities that failing to support yourself is not normally accepted as need. Most citizens do not accept foreign currency but most banks will exchange it for local credit. Many places will also buy valuables from you. If you understand and agree to these conditions, please place your palm on the plate. If not you may leave without penalty."

They looked at each other. Each placed their hand on the plate and the door opened. "Please proceed to the officer you see ahead of you."

They walked up to the immigration officer, who asked, "Do you understand what you just agreed to?"

They nodded. "Yes."

"Do you have identification?"

Tagarin held out his arm so his phone was near the scanner. "Please confirm by placing your hand on this plate and looking into the device I am holding."

"Thank you, Dr Tagarin. There is an outstanding warrant for your arrest in the United States of America. The charges are theft, fraud, blackmail, consorting with known criminals, resisting arrest, assault on police officers and violation of the human genetic integrity laws. These are serious charges, and if your government traces you here they may choose to request your extradition. If they do you may surrender yourself or choose to appeal. If you appeal, you will be required to show in a Capital court why the charges are invalid or a violation of your rights. If you fail to satisfy the court you may be expelled, and some or all of your property may be confiscated to pay for the costs of your appeal. Do you understand?"

Tagarin nodded. It was better than it might have been. He didn't know what his chances would be if GenInt or the government tried to get him, which they probably would. On the one hand he had done everything he was accused of. On the other he had done them for reasons he thought justified; he had done them for justice, not against it. Whether a court would agree was the question. He hoped Capital had some good lawyers for hire.

Katlyn marveled at the officer's dispassionate, almost machinelike manner and wondered for a moment whether he was actually a machine. Then she noticed that he wore a strange device, a combination of earpiece and glasses; and that a faint flickering glow could be discerned in the glass. It must be some kind of computer link, she thought, feeding him information. How much of his mechanical manner was due to his interaction with the AI or was just his own personality, she could not tell.

The officer continued. "The laws of Capital are simple. You may not commit physical force or fraud against another person: citizen or visitor. To clarify differences many visitors ask about: public nudity, drug taking and all forms of voluntary sex between adults are legal but private establishments may forbid them. The principle is that anything that imposes an involuntary physical cost on another person is not allowed, while anything that merely offends another person is allowed except on their property. Property rights in Capital are absolute.

"Penalties. Until you are a citizen, clear use of physical force or fraud will result in immediate expulsion from Capital and possibly confiscation of your property. Once you are a citizen you may be held in confinement at your expense until your trial; if judged guilty, depending on the seriousness of the crime you may be stripped of your citizenship and expelled, or given the choice between expulsion and bonded labor for a period determined by the court. Other breaches bring lesser penalties. There is a one-week waiver of penalties for minor crimes but not for restitution to victims. The laws are simple and available online, and it is recommended that you study them in that first week. After that ignorance is not an excuse. Do you understand?"

"Yes."

"After one week's continuous presence you may choose to remain in Capital as a visitor or apply for citizenship. The only differences besides the criminal penalties are that citizens have the right to vote in elections and referenda, the right to petition the government regarding laws or repeal of laws and the right to bear personal arms for their own defense. Visitors are under the same protection of their rights as citizens, may take jobs, buy property, and come and go as they choose. However if they commit a crime they will be expelled if a magistrate deems the evidence sufficient. They may appeal at their own expense, but while their appeal is pending they will be held under guard, again at their own expense. Do you understand?"

"Yes."

"Do you still wish to apply for citizenship at this time? If you choose not to, you may choose to at a later time without penalty. In your case, Dr Tagarin, I am obliged to tell you that if you remain as a visitor we are bound by treaty to deliver you to your government if they formally request it, subject to any appeal you may lodge."

"I understand. I wish to apply for citizenship."

"Thank you. Now, your companion. Please identify yourself."

"I am sorry, she has no official identification."

The officer looked at her. "Intriguing. Please state your name."

"Katlyn." She looked at Tagarin. "Katlyn Tagarin." It was true however you looked at it, as guardian and surrogate father or as husband.

"Please place your hand on this plate and look into this device."

She took a deep breath and removed her sunglasses; she hesitated then freed her tail as well. *No point in half measures now*, she thought; this was the point of do or die. For once there was a break in the man's machinelike manner: he stood stock still for a few seconds, lips parted. "Please place your hand on the plate and look into this," he repeated at last, and she obeyed.

He waited for a minute, silent. "That is correct. You are not registered in any database we have access to, including criminal databases."

He stepped away from his station to look her up and down slowly. "Please hold your arms out and spin around slowly." Katlyn complied.

"You are a geneh."

"Yes."

"Genehs are illegal and the penalty is death. The Department of Human Genetic Integrity is authorized by the United Nations to execute genehs on sight."

He paused. "Capital does not recognize the authority of the United Nations or GenInt. The Constitution of Capital forbids the death penalty for anything short of murder and extreme assault. As you are under automatic sentence of death by a foreign power under an invalid law, you may be eligible for refugee status. Refugee status means you will not be released to a foreign government for any cause other than murder or other very serious real crimes. Do you wish to apply for refugee status?"

Katlyn looked at Tagarin. He nodded to her. "Yes."

The man paused again. "Your case is unprecedented and has attracted the attention of higher level nodes of the system AI." He paused for a minute then looked at Katlyn.

"It wishes to know your relationship with Dr Tagarin. You are strongly advised not to lie. A lie may result in expulsion from Capital for fraud in a matter of State, or at a minimum, loss of your refugee status."

They looked at each other. It was a question with two answers, both true: one looking toward the past, the other toward the future. Katlyn made a decision. "I am his wife."

"You have no registered identity. Therefore there is no legal record of such a marriage. However Capital does not recognize the sole authority of the State to grant or refuse marriages. Rather it recognizes the rights of citizens to voluntary and private arrangements. Can you produce a contract of marriage that can be authenticated, dated more than one week ago?"

"No."

"I see. Are you two living together in a sexual relationship that has been ongoing for more than one month?"

"Yes," she said softly.

"Is it your intention that this relationship continue while you are resident in Capital?"

"Yes."

"In that case Capital recognizes you as a married couple. By law and treaty, this allows Capital to make a second determination at its discretion. Due to the unusual nature of your circumstances, it is so determined. Your protection as a refugee is extended to your husband."

He turned to address both of them.

"Be advised that your biometric data will be stored until you achieve full citizenship. At that point it will be erased from government records: the government of Capital only holds biometric data on visitors and criminals. It may be stored by private entities with which you have agreements to do so, such as some banks. Citizens are all entitled to a gold citizenship ring, which records your citizenship status and biometric data. Its use is required only for restricted activities such as voting and purchasing weapons. However most citizens regard it as a badge of honor and wear it always."

The man paused.

"Welcome to Capital."

His official role over, the man stepped away from his station to examine Katlyn more closely. His face broke into a broad grin. "Well, this will be something to tell the family," he said. "And speaking from me personally this time—welcome to Capital, folks." With that, he moved his arm in an arc as if welcoming them into his home, and they thanked him and walked away towards the exit.

They stopped before it. Katlyn put on her glasses and began to hide her tail again, then stopped. She looked at the sky beyond the entrance then back to Tagarin. Slowly, she removed her glasses and freed her tail again. Then she nervously took Tagarin's hand. He looked at her gently. "Not every standard human hates you on sight, Katlyn, as you've seen. And the kinds of people who want to move to Capital are the kinds most likely to accept or even celebrate difference. If there's anywhere on Earth that we can live in the sunshine not the shadows, this is it."

She looked up at him and smiled gently, then said softly, "Live Free—or Die."

They straightened their shoulders and walked through the gateway out into a plaza. It was neatly maintained, more a park than a plaza, with rows of shady trees. It was surrounded by attractively decorated shops, a mixture of food, fashion and souvenirs, all hoping for the business of people entering or leaving Capital. In the center of the park stood a large stainless steel sculpture of a man and a woman reaching towards the sun. The real sun flashed off its complex surfaces, spraying rays over the figures. Katlyn thought it was beautiful.

People stopped to stare at Katlyn. But nobody ran for cover, nobody called the police, nobody pulled a gun. They just stared then, belatedly remembering they should respect their privacy, turned away. Though many could not resist a second peek. Or a third. A couple of people did scream, but they were a pair of young children who ran to her not away from her. Less civilized than their parents, they wanted to stare up close. For the first time, Katlyn felt at home.

CHAPTER 55: TEARS

Miriam pushed open the door to her home and went inside. She was exhausted. There had been explanations, debriefings, all the usual debris from a major operation, especially one that had gone sour. If anyone had died she would still be there.

Miriam's story of what had happened was accepted, at least for now; there was no reason to doubt it. Amaro's story supported hers, at least for the times they were together, and her injuries bore silent witness to her ordeal. Amaro had been spirited away by his own people, while Miriam and Jack talked with theirs and wrote up their preliminary reports. Finally they saw her wilting, and let her go. There would be more in the days to come, but for now she was wrung dry.

The place felt oddly empty. She looked around and realized that Amaro was gone in body as well as spirit. He must have let himself in and taken his things; the few possessions he habitually left in the lounge room and kitchen were gone. On the table was a single long-stemmed red rose laid on top of the keys he had left behind. *Typical Amaro*, she thought, *even after all this*. She sniffed the rose. It had no perfume. Like their relationship, she thought. Pretty on the outside but not fully real. She threw it in the bin.

She went and lay down on her bed. It still smelt of Amaro. Anger boiled out of her, and she practically ripped the sheets and bedclothes off the bed and threw them into the washer. She added a double dose of detergent and viciously put it on its heaviest duty cycle. Then she put her elbows on the machine and lowered her head into her hands.

You're being irrational, she thought. *What do you want to do, burn down the house to be rid of every trace of him?* But she knew the intimacy of the sense of smell. She wouldn't have been able to bear it.

Mechanically, she put new sheets on the bed and sought refuge under the covers. She stretched out, feeling the crisp new sheets. *Crisp new sheets for my crisp new life,* she thought. She was spent. There was a limit, she thought, to what anyone can bear in one day.

But she could not sleep. She sat up cross-legged on the bed. Beneath the roller coaster ride of the evening was her anger and grief over Amaro. She remembered how in the past she had held on to the happiness of a relationship rather than wallow in the sadness of its end. But this was different. While there had been plenty of fun and pleasure during her time with Amaro, the underlying relationship that had given it meaning had never really existed. It was like a betrayal of the happiness she thought she had, and all that pleasure had turned to pain because of it.

Then under the anger and grief was shame, shame that she had been so thoroughly taken in by him. In the past she had seen, with the clear eyes of the dispassionate observer, the folly of women who had fallen for rogues. Was her own judgement any better? But if that was the lesson, what was the solution? Refuse to trust her own mind? Then spurn the man who would bring her real love, not because he wasn't there but because she refused to see him? Were the only alternatives to be a sucker for charming pretenders or an embittered cynic, someone who locked the door to happiness to avoid opening it onto pain?

She shook her head, remembering Tagarin's bitterness, his wasted years. Yet while his bitterness was real, it had been not an end but a spur, possibly to something great. No. She would not let one mistake engender a greater one. Amaro was an exception, not the full reality. He was a caution, not proof that happiness was beyond her reach.

She lay down again. She knew there was more, but only the future would condemn or acquit her. For below even the shame lurked fear. If Amaro had fooled her, what if Tagarin and Katlyn had too? She had let them go. She had thought it was right, the only thing that could be right, the only way to give Katlyn her first real chance at life: a chance she deserved if she was truly what she seemed to be. But what if all Miriam's dereliction of duty had done was unleash two deadly criminals on an innocent world? They had duped her before. What if, like Amaro, the good she saw in them was wishful thinking, serving a dark plot she knew nothing of? *Any evil they now commit*, she thought, *it is on my head.* In her mind she saw Katlyn's golden eyes as they had been, no longer merciless and cruel but open and innocent, and she could not believe it. But the girders of her self-confidence had buckled, and the fear and guilt would not be banished.

Then she curled up, and the dams that had held back her emotions for so many hours broke. She cried herself to sleep.

Chapter 56: Tempest

Miriam went back to work and found that Amaro was right: she could forget him. It was easier to get over him when she knew that their whole relationship was a lie, that none of it was real. Who would waste their life pining after a lover they had only known in a dream? It was like Pygmalion with a bad ending, she thought. She had created Amaro out of her imagination and finally peeled back his finery to discover nothing but cold, uncaring stone.

But to lose him this way had its own pain, different from the pain of loss due to death, different again from the pain of the more mundane betrayals that had ended relationships since people first fell in and out of love. She still cried occasionally. But that was more in token of the loss of a dream than loss of the man.

She had little time for pain anyway, except in the loneliness of her nights. There were hearings, debriefings, interrogations. A diplomatic storm had gathered around the country of Capital and Miriam was a minor second epicenter.

GenInt and a good part of the world were appalled that Capital would shelter a geneh. Its reputation as a lawless anarchy grew. But their enemies discovered it was difficult to criticize a country for lawlessness if you did not respect the law yourself: and Capital was acting within the letter of its treaties with other nations and the UN itself. It had the right to shelter refugees: it is what made it such a convenient dumping ground. If anyone had ever attempted to impose the Geneh Laws on Capital, the attempt had been rejected out of hand

and nobody had thought the issue worth pressing.

And the world's attention was distracted by another storm brewing around President Felton and GenInt themselves. Substantial evidence of dirty dealings and corruption in the days leading up to the enactment of the Geneh Laws and GenInt's charter had been leaked to the world. It was what happened in politics all the time, but the good citizens of the world never liked having their noses rubbed in it, especially when they had approved of it and thus felt themselves tainted by uncomfortable feelings of guilt. The President and GenInt found themselves in the difficult position of railing against the perfidy of Capital while being railed against for their own perfidies.

In any event, Capital was safe. Other than some automated defense systems it relied on treaties with other nations for its defense. It could defend itself physically against casual attacks but not against a sustained large-scale one. But so many world businesses were based there, so many eminent statesmen had retired there and so many famous human rights activists now lived there, that not even the most powerful of countries would dare move against it, and no vote could pass in the UN to do more than issue sharply worded rebukes.

So while Capital was besieged, it was besieged by forces who found their own feet sinking in sands of their own creation. It did not even bother to send diplomats. On the legal side it simply published its treaties and charters and invited the world to see for itself. On the moral side its President issued a simple one-sentence statement: "Capital defends the right to life, liberty and the pursuit of happiness of all human beings: whatever their sex, race, religion—or genome." And a number of previously obscure think tanks and commentators had somehow acquired the resources to vigorously and loudly champion its right to do so, and did so with passion and conviction.

Photos and videos rippled out from Capital. The most popular video showed a man and a woman sitting on a sunlit park bench, arms loosely around each other's waists, looking into the distance with a contented happiness; like survivors of a war now taking their rest. The man was older with chestnut hair. The woman was younger with large golden eyes. A little boy and girl were playing and laughing around her feet, chasing her tail as it twitched one way then the other. The boy then climbed on to her lap and looked fascinated at her eyes. The woman simply looked down, smiled and patted his cheek. Then she turned back to her contemplation of the distance, as if contemplating a future known to no one, not even herself.

Many people began to wonder why the world wanted to kill this exotic but harmless young woman. Some began agitating against the geneh laws. The world was not yet ready for their repeal. But it was now ready to think about it.

Miriam smiled at the video when she saw it, touching her fingers to the face on the screen. She smiled again when listening to President Felton's resignation speech a month later. The President denied any wrongdoing, but in order to protect the honor and reputation of the Presidency had decided to step down and retire to private life. She regretted any disappointment to her friends and supporters. She hoped everyone would now put this behind them—probably meaning, Miriam suspected, that she hoped nobody had enough on her to prosecute her—and wished the nation well.

Then Miriam's smile faded at the thought that she might well follow her.

Chapter 57: David

David sat at his desk going over his notes. He was just an intern here, not paid to think deep thoughts about the issues he was involved in. He did that thinking free of charge. His true passion was philosophy, and he had taken this job not only to earn money but also to earn experience of how things worked in the real world. It was perhaps a rare attitude for a student on the verge of a doctorate in such a field, but he was a rare student.

It had turned out more interesting than he could have hoped, with the current brouhaha about the geneh Katlyn and the fallout from her escape from the law. His department was engaged in a politely, and sometimes impolitely, raging debate over the fate of Trainee Detective Miriam Hunter, and both the issue and the debate were fascinating in their own ways.

In their desire for a disposable scapegoat GenInt had applied pressure to have her fired, but that may have done her more good than harm: her department was furious that GenInt would spy on one of its own and in such a manner. Had GenInt been its usual self that would not have saved her. But GenInt was having its own problems with the revelations that had brought down the President. Having had one of their own present and equally unable to prevent the fiasco did not help: if they wanted Miriam to be a sacrificial lamb, then Amaro would have to join her on the block.

To the surprise of many, GenInt showed admirable loyalty to their agent, choosing not to press matters against either of them. Cynics opined that they couldn't afford yet more embarrassment. They may have changed their minds, though not their cynicism, had they heard certain remarks Amaro idly made to his superiors. These concerned the contents of his memoirs, should they ever be published; he had then ruminated on the difficulty of finding the time to write books while one remained gainfully employed.

But that did not end the debate within her own department, a debate which David watched as an entomologist might watch the frantic life under a log. In his view there was no question. Perhaps, as some argued, Miriam was not as innocent as she made out. There were inconsistencies in her story. There always were, her supporters countered: such were the twin fogs of war and memory. The latter view was particularly popular among those who had spent part of their career in the field themselves rather than entirely behind a desk reading and writing reports. In his own mind, David dispelled the fog with a simple binary logic. If Miriam had done exactly as she said, upholding her duty to the end but failing, there could be no grounds for censure when she had done better than everyone else involved. But if for some reason she had been complicit in Katlyn's escape, then in David's view she had done what was moral, or as moral as anyone could be in the circumstances they had been thrust among.

These views he kept to himself. He had worked here long enough to know they would not be understood, and if they were understood they would not be welcome. He might have told anyone who asked but he knew that nobody would. The people around him did not seem concerned with the issues or even with the truth of the matter. They seemed concerned only with navigating the safest course between the battling flames of public opinion. And even that was by the indirect means of divining which way their political overlords would jump in reaction to those flames, rather than watching the actual fire.

David did not blame them for this: not much, anyway. It was the inescapable nature of a bureaucracy that it would devolve into a web of competing pressures, set by the fears and ambitions of men more than reality or the morality needed to survive in it.

He rested his chin on steepled fingers and stared into the depths of his tea. *The moral issue is the key*, he thought. He felt he might admire this Miriam Hunter if the truth was what he suspected, but he did not envy her. What could a cop on the street do with a moral contradiction between the law and what she thought was right? For all the times in history when "just following orders" was rejected as an excuse after the fact, following one's own ethics instead was rarely accepted as justification at the time. In liberal times you were likely to lose your job; in harsher times your life.

He could see why the police had to obey the law, but he could also see why an unjust law set up an intolerable moral dilemma. What was an honest cop to do? Enforce the law at the price of her own ethics? Resign, depriving the law of its best people? Or betray her own oath? If this Miriam Hunter had somehow sought him out to ask his advice, what would he have told her? He did not know.

The only solution was that the law must always be just. But how to do that was the question: the central question of the philosophy of law, he thought.

So what of the politicians who made the laws? They too were more dancers to the tune of public opinion than its conductors. No free country had been born and no dictator voted into power in the absence of fertile soil in the minds of the citizens. True, a great leader could push the people in one direction or another, could even inspire them: but only by kneading or sharpening the ideological clay he was given, not by changing their minds in any fundamental way. Genghis Khan had not made the Mongol hordes out of peaceful farmers any more than Washington had made the United States out of compliant serfs.

Genghis Khan had done what he did because that is what people did. But Washington and his friends had made something new, because they believed something new and enough other people believed it too. And sometimes one man might be enough to light the fire. He thought of the man who had had the courage and vision to make the country of Capital a reality, which had grown into a haven for a desperate creature for whom no other haven existed; which had led to all of this.

No, David thought, politics itself is not the answer. If you want to change the world you first have to change minds, and that was a process beyond the purview of bureaucracies or the timeframe of elected leaders.

He sat still, pinned by the thought. His love of philosophy had started with a love of existence, the burning desire to understand it, and the unshakable belief that it could be understood. That love had taken something of a battering when faced with the reality of much of the field as it was: the tortured arguments and flights from reality that he had seen too much of. He had begun wondering whether a career in philosophy was really what he wanted; whether he should just take his shiny new doctorate when it was granted and use it as a ticket to other pastures, perhaps science. But it was what he wanted, and now he knew the want was both real and necessary. He was idealistic enough to care about changing the world; young enough to think he could.

He was also old enough to know he might not. He wondered whether his work would be remembered by the world, or remembered only by the students he might one day teach. Or perhaps not even by them. He decided it didn't matter. You could only change the world one mind at a time. Perhaps he would change the right one, or perhaps he would merely lighten one corner of the world for a brief instant and then be forgotten. But it was enough. And who knew how far in space or time the ripples might then reach. He did not know the captain of the yacht *Seabitz*, or even that he existed; yet the far faint ripples of that man's life had touched him in a way he would never know.

He looked up to see a man gazing at him with a look of mild amusement. "You look done in, Samuels. Do you have much more to do? Time to go, I reckon."

David smiled back at him. "Oh, I have a lot more to do. But yes, time to go."

~~~

In the end they couldn't decide whether Miriam should be punished for what she had failed to achieve or rewarded for what she had. They saw dangers in both courses, which was an uncomfortable position for those whose aim was to avoid danger entirely. So in the manner of bureaucrats in any place or age they followed their principles: they passed the decision to her own boss.

Ramos had looked at this non-decision with cynicism honed by years of never having it disappointed. He knew they didn't really care about Hunter; they didn't care whether they threw away the career of a good cop or saved that of a bad one. They would be happy with whatever decision he made and happy if they had to fire him for it in turn.

Of course they did not put it that way. No, as her supervisor he was in the best position to understand the nuances of the case, and he had the experience to do what was fair while giving due weight to the views of the public. The same thing, in other words.

But Ramos was an honest man who had come up through the ranks, and while he knew how to play the game he thought the game had to be kept in its place. He had made many compromises in his life, but no more than he had to, and there was one principle he held dear: when there was no safe course, the safest course was to just do what was right. *Screw the lot of them*, he thought. When boldness and justice gave the same advice, he would grasp the double-edged blade and see who had the courage to try to turn it on him.

He made the decision that would make everyone better off in the long run, from the citizens he was sworn to serve and protect to his superiors, whom he merely had to. Citing her diligence, courage, creativity and perceptiveness, he promoted Miriam Hunter to full detective.

Chapter 58: Friends

So Miriam again found herself at a party hosted by her uncle. It was much the same as the last one, with quality food and champagne flowing freely, and sundry relatives close and distant come along to offer their congratulations and just catch up with each other.

But this time it was more than family: she had acquired new friends as well. She spent a riotous time with Rianna, Darian and Kimberley, toasting each other's achievements and careers, with occasional digressions into the follies and perfidies of the male of their species. If a point of pain remained within Miriam on the subject, it kept itself quiet.

Stone had arrived and Miriam saw him out of the corner of her eye, having a long chat with Seth. He then came over and said laconically, "Well, I guess we're not going to be rid of you anytime soon, kid: I just hope your next partner has good medical insurance. But try to learn some caution. For all your many flaws, I really don't want to see you killed." He smiled and shook her hand, then moved off to relate tales of Miriam's exploits to her eager relatives. The tales sprouted embellishments proportionally to how well watered they were with champagne. Miriam overheard a few and rolled her eyes.

Even Ramos made an appearance and took her aside. "Congratulations, Detective Hunter. I have some more good news for you too. With all you've been through you've earned a couple of week's vacation time. When you come back we'll assign you a permanent partner."

"Can I make a request?"

"Sure."

"I'd like to keep working with Jack Stone if I can. I know our partnership was just a convenience and not meant to last. I also know all those beatings and bullets might have persuaded him that a desk job might be a good idea after all. But we work well together and he can teach me a lot. So I have to ask."

"I'll talk to him, see what I can do. In the meantime enjoy your vacation: you deserve it." He toasted her with a smile then moved off into the crowd.

As usual, Miriam eventually found herself at the window. There was a fog, and the buildings appeared to rise out of a faintly glowing sea, the lights of vehicles like fish in its depths. Seth joined her and they looked out over the city together in silence. Then he said, "So, I hear you'll be taking some time off. About time too, I think. Have you made any plans?"

Miriam stayed looking over the city rising from its sea and replied, "You know, I've always liked snorkeling. That feeling of utter peace and stillness, just drifting through all that beauty. The opposite of my work," she added with a crooked smile. "Isn't it funny, how you can love two opposite things for two opposite reasons?"

Seth nodded slowly. "I know what you mean. Do you want some advice? With your time and bonus you can afford to treat yourself: do something exotic. I've dived in Vanuatu and it's magnificent; I hear the Maldives are still good too."

Miriam smiled. "Maybe. Or maybe I'll do something even more exotic. I think I might visit that weird country, Capital. I have friends there."

ABOUT THE AUTHOR

Dr Robin Craig has a PhD in molecular biology and a keen interest in science and philosophy. He believes that novels, like all art, should be one in thought, theme and style: to nourish the mind as much as the soul. His books specialize in blending fact and speculation in dramatic and engaging stories, driven by strong characters and intriguing philosophical themes.

In addition to near future science fiction exploring contemporary issues such as artificial intelligence (*Frankensteel*), genetic engineering (*The Geneh War* and *Leonardo's Child*) and cyborg technology (*Time Enough for Killing*), his books include time travel (*The Time Surgeons* and *Hannibal's Witch*), alternative history (*The Passion of Judas* and *Hannibal's Witch*) and a collection of short stories (*Past, Present, Future*).

He also writes non-fiction. In addition to 14 scientific papers and a long-running philosophical series in *TableAus* (the journal of Australian Mensa), he has published numerous philosophical essays on Amazon.com and was a contributor to *The Australian Book of Atheism* with his chapter *Good Without God*, an essay on the importance and validity of secular ethics. He also answers philosophical and scientific questions on quora.com, and is a presenter on cruise ships across the globe, on science and philosophy including AI, time travel, space travel and numerous other futurist and historical topics.

Dr Craig is an independent author. If you like this book please spread the word with reviews and recommendations to your friends or library... and enjoy more of his books!

To keep up to date on new and upcoming works and events, like his Facebook page: fb.me/authorcraig

www.ingramcontent.com/pod-product-compliance
Lightning Source LLC
Chambersburg PA
CBHW020354120726
47904CB00002B/562